Streaker

was the slang term among pilots for a ship so badly
ged that it was sent hurtling clear of battlespace on a
r that would take it into the cold and empty Beyond.
or knew there would be no SAR vessels, no search
escue to track her course and come to pick her up.
Slan, her telemetry told her, were breaking through
where. Huge vessels that most likely were Slan troop
transports were entering the atmosphere and closing with
the Silverwheel colony.

Her AI did suggest that at least some repairs were possible.
She directed the damage control systems to focus on
pa ing the quantum tap array, with a view to bringing her
m in power systems back on-line. With enough power,
anything was possible.

hout power, she was dead . . .

By Ian Douglas

Star Carrier
EARTH STRIKE
CENTER OF GRAVITY
SINGULARITY

And the Galactic Marines Series

The Inheritance Trilogy
STAR STRIKE
GALACTIC CORPS
SEMPER HUMAN

The Legacy Trilogy
STAR CORPS
BATTLESPACE
STAR MARINES

The Heritage Trilogy
SEMPER MARS
LUNA MARINE
EUROPA STRIKE

DEEP SPACE
STAR CARRIER

BOOK FOUR

IAN DOUGLAS

HARPER
Voyager

Harper*Voyager*
An imprint of HarperCollins*Publishers*
77–85 Fulham Palace Road,
Hammersmith, London W6 8JB

www.harpervoyagerbooks.co.uk

This Paperback Original 2013

Cover art by Gregory Bridges

A catalogue record for this book is
available from the British Library

ISBN: 978-00-0748375-4

Printed and bound in Great Britain by Clays Ltd, St Ives plc

FSC
www.fsc.org

MIX
Paper from
responsible sources
FSC™ C007454

GIFT

For Brea, who made it all possible

DEEP SPACE

Prologue

Agletsch Data Download 783478
Extant Galactic Civilizations
Classification: Red-Alfa

Civilization Classification Code: A548B7C

Polity Name: Sh'daar

OTHER NAMES: Sh'daar Empire, Sh'daar Network, N'gai Cloud Civilization

HOMEWORLD: Unknown, but assumed to be a number of planets located within the core of Omega Centauri T$_{-0.876gy}$, a small, irregular galaxy located roughly ten thousand light years above the plane of the Milky Way's spiral arms and 876 million years in the past. This dwarf galaxy was absorbed by the Milky Way approximately 700 million years ago, and exists now, in vastly reduced form, as the Omega Centauri globular star cluster, some sixteen thousand light years from Sol.

HISTORY: In the remote past, the N'gai Star Cloud was dominated by the ur-Sh'daar, a collective of advanced, star-faring civilizations. At a time estimated to be between 876 million and 900 million years in the past, the ur-Sh'daar went through the so-called Vinge Singularity, when accelerating technology effected a still poorly understood transformation that brought about the collapse of the ur-Sh'daar culture. While a majority of the sentients comprising the ur-Sh'daar seem to have vanished—translated, perhaps, to a parallel universe, an otherwise inaccessible higher dimension, or even a virtual reality of their own making—many beings were unable or unwilling to make the transition. Known as Refusers, these remnant groups and cultures rebuilt their civilization after the galactic catastrophe that became known as the *Schjaa Hok*—the "Transcending." These Refusers ultimately became the Sh'daar.

GALACTIC CONTACT: The ur-Sh'daar created a number of artificial wormhole pathways between their galaxy and the Milky Way, variously known as gateways, as Sh'daar Nodes, or as TRGA cylinders—for the Texaghu Resch gravitational anomaly, the first such device discovered by Humankind. Since these pathways traversed spacetime, meaning space *and* time, some gave the ancient Sh'daar access to their remote future—our present. There is evidence of Sh'daar activity within our own epoch around twelve thousand years ago, with the extermination of a race called the Chelk, somewhere in the vicinity of the Texaghu Resch star system and the TRGA cylinder.

Over the next twelve thousand years, numerous other technic species within Sol's galaxy were either destroyed or forced to abandon or curtail certain lines of scientific research or technological development—notably the so-called GRIN technologies: genetics, robotics, information systems and processing technologies, and nanotechnology. Among these are Sh'daar client races with which Humankind has been at war since 2367, including the Turusch, the H'rulka, the Nungiirtok and their Kobold symbiotes, and the Slan. One other Sh'daar client species within our own galaxy with which Humankind has been in contact since

2312 is the Agletsch, a mercantile race that has provided Humankind with much of what it knows about the Sh'daar.

SH'DAAR POLITY COMPOSITION: As noted previously, the Sh'daar properly is a grouping of numerous technic civilizations, none even remotely human in appearance or psychology. Some, including the Sh'daar Refuser remnant, appear to exist now solely in electronic form, occupying computer networks or artificial bodies mimicking their ancient existence as ur-Sh'daar. Other Refuser species still exist in corporeal form—including the Sjhlurrr, the F'haaz-F'heen swarm symbiotes, the Adjugredudhra, the Groth Hoj, the Zhalleg, the Baondyedd, and numerous others. The total number of distinct species within the Sh'daar Network numbers in the thousands.

TECHNOLOGY: Though the Sh'daar seem determined to limit the technology of other species in certain key areas, their overall level of advancement is somewhat beyond that of Humankind *circa* 2400. This seeming paradox is best explained by their desire to prevent Transcendence in other technic species, a process that appears to be linked to GRIN technologies but not to gravitics and drive technologies, military weaponry, or energy. The Sh'daar seem to fear those technologies that bring about radical change in body or mental processes within both artificial and organic intelligences.

According to Agletsch sources, the Sh'daar possess the technology necessary to detonate stars and obliterate entire star systems.

Whether the Sh'daar xenotechnic paranoia is religious or philosophical in nature, or based on the Sh'daar equivalent of hardheaded practicality, is at this point completely unknown. . . .

> Partial extract from Agletsch data transmission
> 14 March 2420

Chapter One

TC/USNA RSV Endeavor
The Black Rosette,
Omega Centauri
16,000 light years from Earth
1330 hours, TFT

Nothing like it had been seen ever before, even in a galaxy as strange and as wonder-filled as the Milky Way. The USNA deep-space research survey vessel *Endeavor* edged as close to this particular wonder as her captain dared, as clouds of drones and AI reconnaissance vessels probed the outermost fringes of the Rosette's twisted central vortex.

They called it the Black Rosette—six black holes balanced in a tight, gravitational embrace and whirling about a common center. Each was slightly larger than Earth; each possessed a mass of some forty times Earth's sun and was moving at almost 26,000 kilometers per second . . . better than 0.08 *c*. A total mass 240 times that of Earth's sun, rotating that quickly, twisted the fabric of the spacetime within which it was embedded and did unexpected things to the geometry of local space. From the perspective of the crew on board the *Endeavor*, organic and otherwise, it appeared that the central void between the whirling black holes was filled with soft white starlight.

As the *Endeavor* drifted past the open face of the Rosette, however, details of that light shifted and changed, revealing, it seemed, a succession of starscapes, densely packed alien starclouds and constellations flickering from one to another . . . a gateway into myriad alternate panoramas of thick-strewn stars.

At certain angles, *Endeavor*'s sensors detected fierce storms of radiation emerging from the gateway; at others, the emerging radiation was at normal background levels, though a certain amount of hard gamma continued to flood through local space from the six mutually orbiting black holes. The whirling sextet appeared to be enmeshed in a thin, hot cloud of gas drawn from surrounding space, and the planet-sized black holes were made somewhat visible as the resultant blue-violet plasma was greedily devoured in shrieks of gamma and X-ray radiation.

Endeavor's commanding officer, Captain Sheri Hodgkins, checked the ambient radiation levels on the research vessel's skin and decided that they were quite close enough. In fact . . .

"Pull us back a few hundred kilometers, Mr. Colger."

"Aye, aye, Captain. Maneuvering . . ."

Hodgkins was linked through her cerebral implants to the ship's AI, and in the window open within her mind she could see the *Endeavor* pulling back slightly from the massive whirlpool ahead. Like most large star-faring vessels of Earth, *Endeavor* was mushroom-shaped, her labs and drives within her axial stem, her hab and command modules rotating about the stem, and both tucked away within the shadow of an immense mushroom cap. The water within the shield cap both provided fuel for her fusion drives and protection from sleeting radiation at near-c velocities. The shield was serving now to deflect or absorb most of the radiation from the Rosette ahead; her magnetic hull shields provided some protection, but she didn't want to take chances with the radiation storm outside the ship's hull.

Endeavor's two escorts, the destroyers *Miller* and *Herrera*, maintained their formation on the survey vessel. No one was quite certain what the Sh'daar response would be to a survey probe this deep inside their cluster. For sixteen years the Omega Treaty had held. And yet . . .

"Captain, we're detecting movement inside the vortex."

"What kind of movement?"

"Multiple targets at very high speed! Closing vector! . . ."

"Helm! Pull us back! Comm! Alert our escorts!"

But the *Miller* was already breaking in two, its central spine and portions of its mushroom cap dissolving in a smear of white hot plasma. *Herrera* had time to lock on and trigger her main particle beam weapons, but within seconds her grav shields had overloaded and she was being pounded into fragments by a storm of relativistic particles snapping up out of the vortex.

Endeavor was hit, her shield cap ripping open and disgorging a vast and glittering cloud of gleaming crystals as her water reserves hit hard vacuum and froze. Hodgkins grabbed the arms of her command chair as the bridge shuddered, then tore free, tumbling wildly into space.

"Comm! Emergency broadcast! . . ."

. . . and then the bridge was engulfed by the expanding white flare of a small detonating sun as her fusion core ruptured.

Five seconds later, the AI of a robotic HVK-724 high-velocity scout-courier on station 1.5 million kilometers away noted the destruction of the expedition's three capital ships and immediately engaged its primary program.

Earth lay sixteen thousand light years away. At its maximum Alcubierre warp effect, the courier would arrive in another forty-four days.

7 November 2424

Confederation Naval Base Dylan
Arianrhod, 36 Ophiuchi AIII
0618 hours, TFT

"Bay doors are open," the voice said in her head. "VFA-140, you are clear for launch."

Lieutenant Megan Connor felt her fighter shake and tremble, the shock of a nearby explosion propagating through rock, the ferrocrete of the fighter bay dock, and the structure of her fighter. "Copy, Arianrhod Control," she said. "On my command, Dracos, in five . . . four . . . three . . . two . . . one . . . *launch*!"

Acceleration slammed her back against the embrace of her fighter's cockpit as she hurtled down the magrail toward a distant point of light. The point expanded with startling swiftness, then exploded around her, a burst of brilliant, golden daylight as she emerged into the open air.

She thoughtclicked a control, and the intermittent singularity off her fighter's bow flared into a dazzling arc-bright glare, the microscopic black hole gulping down atmosphere in flaring blue-white light. Behind her, a pair of incoming missiles slammed against the mountain housing the Confederation base but she held her Stardragon level, forming up with the other fighters matching her vector to left and right. The Silverwheel Sea, vast and straw-yellow, surged beneath her fighter's keel.

More missiles incoming. "Going vertical!" she called to the others, "in three . . . two . . . one . . . *break*!"

Together, the flight of nine SG-112 Stardragons swung to an ascending vector, streaking up into a brilliant golden sky stacked high with billowing clouds. Falling skyward at five hundred gravities, the fighters swiftly punched through the clouds and fast-thinning atmosphere and into open space.

"Combat mode," she snapped. "Formation break!" The Dragons' adaptive nanomatrix hulls shifted and flowed, changing from sleek, black deltas to Y shapes, the weapons pods extended at the ends of the three forward-canted wings. Those two incoming missiles had curved upward, following the flight of Draco squadron Stardragons all the way up from the deck. Lieutenants Allende and Larson, bringing up the rear of the formation, loosed bursts of KAM pellets—kinetic-kill anti-missile projectiles that slammed into the Slan warheads and detonated them 10 kilometers astern.

Within Connor's in-head display, a Slan destroyer changed vector to intercept them, the image magnified to show the flat blade of a hull and eight projecting shark fins, the vessel painted a flat white with bold red slashes and blotches. Little was known about the Slan save that they were another Sh'daar client race. The characteristic color scheme of their warship hulls, Intelligence thought, might represent some predator from the Slan homeworld, but even that much was pure guesswork.

She selected the destroyer with her inner eyes, selected a weapon—a VG-44c Fer-de-lance antiship missile—and clicked the blinking launch icon in her mind. "Ferdie armed!" she cried. "Fox One!"

A nuclear-tipped missile slipped from her low-keel fin and streaked toward the destroyer. The other fighters were peeling off in every direction, engaging a sky filled with targets. . . .

The star 36 Ophiuchi was a triple-star system just 19.5 light years from Earth, and 10 light years from the enemy-occupied system of 70 Ophiuchi, and the world Osiris. The A and B components, both K2-class orange stars, circled each other in an extremely elliptical mutual orbit lasting 570 years, the two coming as close to each other as 7 astronomical units and receding out to as far as 169 AUs. Currently, they were 30 AUs apart, and 36 Oph B appeared as a tiny orange spark in the blackness well beyond the nearer disk of 36 Oph A. A third, smaller red-orange star, 36 Ophiuchi C, orbited the two main stars at a comfortable distance of 5,000 AUs, or some eight hundredths of a light year, a spark so wan and dim it could not be picked out by the naked eye.

The system was still young—less than a billion years old—and filled with asteroidal debris and comets. A dozen comets blazed with icy light, their tails smeared across the heavens away from the orange sun. The planet dubbed Arianrhod by its colonizers was properly 36 Ophiuchi AIII, the third of four small and rocky planets. Located a little more than half an AU from its sun, it lay near the center of the system's habitable zone. Mostly covered by liquid water, the world was twice the mass of Earth. The major land-mass was the Caer Arianrhod Archipelago in the southern hemisphere, and was the location of the research colony of Silverwheel.

Arianrhod offered Confederation xenoplanet specialists the splendid opportunity to study an Earthlike planet still in the final stages of formation. Earth itself must have looked much the same 3.5 to 4 billion years ago. The atmosphere was a poisonous brew of carbon dioxide, methane, nitrogen, and sulfur dioxide. Volcanoes dotted the vast and rolling oceans, and asteroids and comets continued to slam into the young world, generating apocalyptic tidal waves. Silver-wheel, most of it, was underground, as was the large USNA naval base protecting it. The land, when it was above water, was rocky, barren, and lifeless.

Yet, despite this, life bloomed in the oceans, raising questions about the nature, variety, and extensiveness of early life in Earth's seas. It was known that life had appeared in Earth's seas within a scant few hundred million years of the formation of a solid crust . . . but that life had remained single-celled and relatively simple for the next 2.5 billion years or so, and hadn't learned how to manage the multi-cellular trick until about a billion years ago. Multicellular life forms, some of them as complex as things like colonial jellyfish and free-swimming tunicate worms, had already evolved in Arianrhod's seas.

Theorists had suggested that life might have evolved not once, but many times on Earth; others suggested that radiation from the planet's sun had given evolution a swift kick in the ass. Arianrhod offered xenobiologists the unparalleled opportunity to watch the process in action. The planet had been named deliberately for an ancient Celtic goddess of fertility, rebirth, and the weaving of cosmic fate. Someday, in a billion years or so, this world might be another Earth; in the meantime, it offered Humankind an unparalleled chance to study planetary evolution. Silverwheel's twenty thousand inhabitants were almost all scientists and their families.

The Slan attack had not been entirely unexpected.

Osiris, 70 Ophiuchi AII, had been hit and overrun twenty years ago by a combined Turusch-Nungiirtok assault force. Osiris, though, was one of a handful of so-called garden worlds, planets with oxygen-nitrogen atmospheres and extensive biospheres where humans could live and work without cumbersome biosuits or nanoskins. The government council at Silverwheel had been hoping that the enemy wanted to take over pleasant, Earthlike worlds, not poisonous biomes-in-the-making like Arianrhod. And as year followed year, they'd begun to relax. Arianrhod did not appear to be on the enemy's target list.

Until now. Unlike the civilian government at Silverwheel, the Navy had long suspected that one or another of the Sh'daar client species would make a grab for 36 Ophiuchi, and deployed three fighter squadrons to defend the system. Two, the Dracos and the Reapers, had been stationed at the naval base protecting Silverwheel, with a third, the Blood Knights, operating out of an orbital base called Caer Gwydion. Picket drones in the outer system had noted the approach of a sizeable naval force two days ago, apparently coming from the general direction of 70 Ophiuchi.

The fleet, which had turned out to be Slan, was a mix of the lance-blade destroyers and a large number of planetary bombardment vessels, code-named Trebuchets by Confederation Military Intelligence. The three squadrons had been flying almost nonstop, with brief returns to base for rearming and repairs between missions. Caer Gwydion had been struck by a trio of two-hundred-megaton warheads ten hours ago and turned into an expanding cloud of hot gas.

But the surviving fighters continued to hurl themselves at the enemy force, as their numbers dwindled and casualties mounted.

Lieutenant Sheridan's Stardragon took a direct hit from a Slan beam weapon, her fighter vaporized in an instant, like a moth in an open flame.

"All Dracos!" Connor called. "Vector on the Trebs on planetary approach! Let's see if we can break up that attack!"

The alien Trebuchets were ungainly, boxy affairs utterly unlike the sleek destroyers. Each was a little more than 200 meters in length, painted black with random, bright green slashes, and carried piggyback a single massive nuclear missile with a five-hundred-megaton fusion warhead. They approached in waves, lining up on the target planet and loosing the missiles as they streaked inbound. Even from 15,000 kilometers out, Connor could see the periodic twinkles of detonations concentrated on the northern coast of the Sumatra-sized landmass where Silverwheel lay buried, and more planetbusters were inbound. Even the deeply buried research colony wouldn't be able to hold out for much longer against that savage planetary bombardment.

Dropping into a trajectory that put her on the stern of one of the inbound Trebs, she selected the target with a thought, then thoughtclicked the mind's-eye icon for a VG-10 Krait, armed it, and loosed it, sending the smart missile streaking in toward the falling enemy bomber. Before the missile could cross the intervening gulf, however, the enormous missile strapped to the Treb's dorsal hull released, drifted clear, and then began accelerating toward the planet. Connor targeted the missile as well, sending a second VG-10 streaking after it.

She couldn't take the time to watch the results of her shots, but spun her Stardragon end for end, decelerating sharply, then spun through 90 degrees to acquire another target. She marked a second Trebuchet and sent another Krait smart missile flashing toward it.

Surrounding space was filled with pulsing flashes of silent light, the brilliant detonations of nuclear warheads in space, and with softly glowing clouds of expanding debris, chunks of shredded spacecraft, and occasional disabled fighters tumbling end for end, streaming atmosphere. Through her communications link, Connor could hear the calls and warnings of the other pilots in her squadron:

"Draco Three, Draco Seven! You've got a Stiletto on your six. . . ."

"I see him, Seven! I can't shake him!"

"I'm on him! On my mark, break high and right . . . three . . . two . . . one . . . *break*!"

"Draco Ten! Draco Ten, this is Four! Close and assist!"

"Copy, ten! Arming Kraits! . . ."

"Stilettos! I've got six Stilettos, bearing one-seven-niner . . ."

"Fox One! Fox One! Missiles away!"

"Let's nail those Trebs at zero-one-eight!"

"Hit! I got one! I got one!"

"Draco One! Watch it, Skipper! Three Stilettos high and on your six! Coming out of the sun! . . ."

With a thought, Connor spun her fighter around, flying backward now, as she searched the sky through her Stardragon's enhanced senses. *Stiletto* was the Confederation name for the Slan equivalent of the space fighter, a slender, three-winged delta like an arrowhead, built around a powerful spinal-mounted fusion weapon that could chew through even a Stardragon's nanomatrix hull with a direct hit. The modern space fighter was designed to repair battle damage even while the craft was still in combat, but a beam of mag-bottled fusing hydrogen coming in at a substantial percentage of c could overwhelm the best defenses and leave very little behind but expanding hot gas.

"Copy!" Connor yelled, and she fired another Fer-de-lance, targeting the middle of three enemy fighters bearing down on her. VG-44c shipkillers were intended for use against *large* enemy vessels . . . a hundred thousand tons and up . . . but a big enough plasma ball might take out all three of the deadly Slan fighters. *If* it could get through . . .

No joy. A fusion beam snapped out from one of the Stilettos and vaporized the missile a thousand kilometers short. A second Slan beam lanced across the intervening gulf and narrowly missed her Stardragon as her fighter's AI, anticipating the shot with reactions far faster than any human's, jinked to starboard.

Connor launched a cloud of spoofers—pencil-sized projectiles that continually broadcast the image, mass, and RF noise of a Stardragon, creating a cloud of images where an instant before there'd been one. Enemy sensors and computer targeting would be good enough to maintain a target lock despite the decoys, but a burst of gravitic pulses scrambled the Slan targeting picture. A second fusion beam swiped through the decoys, vaporizing dozens of them but missing her. She fired another Fer-de-lance . . . then a third and a fourth, hoping to overwhelm the Slan fighters' defenses.

At her back, her first Krait detonated astern of the Slan Trebuchet, a blossoming white fireball that consumed the enemy vessel in a searing, hellish instant. Connor's fighter continued to twist and dodge, accelerating hard into a new vector that should take her past the fast-approaching limb of the planet. The first Fer-de-lance aimed at her pursuers was vaporized by an enemy fusion beam. *Damn . . .*

Something slammed into her fighter, a savage shock that put her into an uncontrollable tumble. She scanned the data scrolling through her mind, lists of damage, of system failure, of power-plant shutdown. "Dracos, Draco One!" she called. "I'm hit!"

The second Fer-de-lance was wiped from the sky. The Slan fighters were closing fast. . . .

"Draco Two!" she added. "Do you copy?"

"One, Six," another voice replied. Draco Six was Lieutenant Yamaguchi. "Two's bought it. Can I assist?"

"Controls and power unresponsive," she said. "You've got the squadron."

"I copy, One. Vectoring for—"

Yamaguchi's voice was chopped off by a burst of fusion-beam static.

An instant later, her third Fer-de-lance swung through a broad curve and swept into the midst of the Stiletto fighters now just 3,000 kilometers distant. The explosion lit up the sky, and as the light faded, nothing but fist-sized debris tumbled out of the thinning plasma cloud.

Connor began assessing the situation. Her power plant was off-line; the pair of microsingularities that pulled unimaginable power from hard vacuum had evaporated. Her magnetic shields were down too, as well as her fighter's gravitic drive. Weapons were dead. So was maneuvering. Life support was still going, thank the gods, sustained by her reserve fusion generators, and so were her flight sensors, her instrumentation, and her AI, but precious little else was working.

She asked the AI to plot her course toward Arianrhod, watching the curved green line come up on her in-head, skimming past the vast bulk of the world. She was falling at nearly 20 kilometers per second, her speed when she was hit. That was a good 5 kps or better than the planet's escape velocity, and it looked like she was going to skim the atmosphere, then whip around, clean and clear, and continue falling out into deep space.

Connor wasn't entirely sure how she felt about that. It meant she wasn't going to burn up in the atmosphere in another few hundred seconds . . . and that meant that she had some time to let the ship regrow some of the damage.

But a quick, fiery death during re-entry might be better than freezing or asphyxiating as her life support gave out . . . or starving to death when the onboard nanoprocessors failed.

She didn't have a lot of options.

Five minutes later, she hit atmosphere, her crippled Stardragon shaking and trembling as it shrieked through the tenuous outer layers and skimmed across gold-yellow oceans and swirling cloud banks just 80 kilometers up. Arianrhod's atmosphere, under higher-than-Earth-normal gravity, was compacted more than the gas at this altitude over Earth. Near the surface, the atmospheric pressure was something like five times the pressure at Earth's surface. Here, it was tenuous to the point of near vacuum . . . but Connor was traveling fast enough that hitting it jolted her with savage ferocity, and the black outer layers of her nanomatrix hull began to heat from friction. The temperature inside the close embrace of the cockpit climbed. Her pilot's skin suit struggled to dump excess heat. She might still plunge deeply enough into thick air to burn up, a blazing shooting star streaking from the day side of the planet across the terminator and into night.

And then, miraculously, the trembling stopped, and she was outbound once more.

Blessedly, the brief passage through atmosphere had arrested her craft's tumble as well. The sky no longer pirouetted around her head. She'd lost some velocity in the near passage, but she was still falling outbound at 16 kps . . . more than enough to escape from Arianrhod forever.

Streaker. That was the slang term among pilots for a ship so badly damaged that it was sent hurtling clear of battlespace on a vector that would take it into the cold and empty Beyond. Connor knew there would be no SAR vessels, no search and rescue to track her course and come to pick her up. The Slan, her telemetry told her, were breaking through everywhere. Huge vessels that most likely were Slan troop transports were entering the atmosphere and closing with the Silverwheel colony.

Her AI did suggest that at least some repairs were possible. She directed the damage control systems to focus on repairing the quantum tap array, with a view to bringing her main power systems back on-line. With enough power, anything was possible.

Without power, she was dead. . . .

Almost five and a half hours later, a robotic HVK-724 scout-courier in a cold, distant orbit 40 AUs from Arianrhod caught an emergency transmission sent from Silverwheel. The transmission included an update on the battle for the 36 Ophiuchi system . . . news of the orbital Caer Gwydion station plus three fighter squadrons destroyed, of serious damage to the main colony facility on the surface, of reports of landings by heavily armored assault forces and the destruction of the Dylan underground naval base.

The scout-courier engaged its primary program, dropping into Alcubierre space and vanishing from the sane and normal matrix of spacetime. It had taken the signal 5.3 light minutes to crawl out from the planet, but at its maximum Alcubierre warp effect, the courier would cross the 19.5 light years between 35 Ophiuchi and Sol in just one hour, eighteen minutes.

It was pure coincidence that news of *two* Confederation naval disasters would arrive at Earth within a day of each other.

Freedom Concourse
Columbus, District of Columbia,
North American Union
0749 hours, TFT

"Captain Gray, Comm. Important message coming through, priority urgent."

Trevor "Sandy" Gray, commanding officer of the star carrier *America*, paused in mid-stride as the AI voice spoke in his head. Around him, the Freedom Concourse was thronged with people, part of the brawling, noisy celebration following the president's re-election. "Go ahead," he thought.

"Voice only, full immersion, or text?"

"Text, please."

A window opened in his mind and the words scrolled down.

PRIORITY: Urgent
FROM: Confederation Naval HQ
TO: All CN Commands

Courier packet reports Confederation research colony Silverwheel on Arianrhod, 36 Ophiuchi AII, has just fallen to Slan assault forces....

The message, terse and to the point, went on to say that at least twelve Saber-class destroyers, fifty Trebuchet-class bombardment vessels, and a large number of Stiletto fighters had taken part in the attack, and that both the colony and the underground naval base were now presumed lost. The final attack had gone down less than two hours ago.

The message was signed Ronald Kinkaid, Admiral, CO CNHQ, Mars.

The words faded, and Gray's awareness returned fully to his surroundings. A man, fashionably nude except for animated tattoos and an anonymously opaque sensory helmet bumped into him from behind. "Sorry, Captain."

"S'okay." The man's tattoo display included the word FREEDOM stretching from collar bone to groin, flashing across the entire spectrum of colors and highlighted by the strobe and flash of fireworks writhing across his skin.

Gray shook his head and started walking again. The crowd was thick enough that stopping in midstream could be hazardous. Ahead, the government building towered above the plaza in a series of curves and ornamental buttresses, and the mob appeared to be centered on the building's base.

Koenig's victory, he thought, appeared to have opened the Freedom party floodgates, an anti-Confederation mandate for USNA freedom.

Or possibly, the cynic within Gray's mind suggested, it was just that Americans enjoyed the popular sport known as politics. Give them something to cheer about, to demonstrate about, to vote about, and they were there.

It was, he thought, exactly the right sentiment at exactly the wrong time. If 36 Ophiuchi had fallen to the Slan fleet, it meant that the Sh'daar were on the move once more, and it meant that North American independence simply was not going to happen. Humankind, a *united* Humankind, would have to face that threat, and all the popular demonstrations, all the fireworks, all the noise on the planet wasn't going to change that.

Gray had come down on a shuttle early that morning specifically to offer his personal congratulations to the president . . . but this, he decided, would not be the best moment for personal visits and reminiscences.

He hesitated a moment, bracing himself against the

crowd, then turned and began to retrace his steps toward Starport Columbus.

Gray needed to get back to Synchorbit, back to the ship, and quickly.

He was almost all the way back to the Star Carrier *America*, on board the shuttle, when the *second* message of disaster arrived.

Chapter Two

Approaching USNA Naval Base
Quito Synchorbital
1435 hours, TFT

Lieutenant Donald Gregory eased back the acceleration of his SG-92 Starhawk as the seagirt dome of NAS Oceana dropped away behind him and was swiftly obscured by clouds. Sunlight exploded around him as he pierced the cloud deck and the sky almost immediately deepened from blue to ultramarine to black.

In close formation with him, the eleven other Starhawks of VFA-96, the Black Demons, arrowed skyward, boosting in high-velocity mode. Nanosensors embedded within his fighter's fluid outer coat fed data directly to his brain, allowing him to see with crystalline clarity in every direction, and to see the blacker-than-black long-tailed teardrops of the other fighters of the squadron formation, forms that would have been invisible to the unaugmented eye or brain.

"Keep it tight, chicks," urged the taclink voice of their squadron leader, Commander Luther Mackey. "Hold formation. Show the braid we're as sharp as any hotshot Vee-crappers."

"Yeah, Boss, but how do you *really* feel about 'em?"

Lieutenant Nathan Esperanza cut in. Several of the others in the squadron chuckled.

"Hell, I think he just wants a crack at the Sh'daar," Lieutenant Caryl Mason said, "assuming the scuttlebutt is true, of course."

"Oh, it's true," Esperanza said. "I got a buddy in Base Commo who saw the intercepts. One of our survey vessels got nailed out at Omegod Cent, and the Slan overran Arianrhod. That's why the recall."

"It don't rain but it pours," Lieutenant Jason Del Rey observed.

"Why bother with grapevine shit?" Lieutenant Joseph "Happy" Kemper said. "Just ask ol' Nungie. Get the straight shit hot from the source."

"Fuck you, Kemper," Gregory said with a quiet calm he didn't quite feel. *Nungie* had not been his choice as a squadron handle, and he despised the implication.

"Keep it down, people," Mackey said. "Engage squadron taclink."

Gregory gave the mental command that synched his fighter's AI to the rest of the squadron. The twelve Starhawks were now, in essence, a single organism hurtling up and out of Earth's embrace.

"On my mark, acceleration at two thousand gravities," Mackey added. "And three . . . and two . . . and one . . . *mark!*"

Gregory couldn't feel the savage, gravitationally induced acceleration. His fighter fell toward the tightly projected artificial singularity pulsing at a billion times per second out beyond the blunt prow of his Starhawk, its gravity acting on every atom of his body simultaneously. He was in free fall, his vector matched perfectly with those of the other ships in his squadron. Earth, filling the sky aft with white swirls and mottled banks of white cloud, began dwindling rapidly into the distance astern. Starhawks were capable of boosting at fifty thousand Gs, which could accelerate them up to close to the speed of light in under ten minutes. Within the relatively close confines of Earth orbit, however, it was necessary to keep to a more sedate pace. It would take forty-two seconds to reach the midpoint of their journey, at which point they would flip end for end and decelerate the rest of the way in to their docking with the carrier.

Ten more seconds.

Seething, Gregory tried to put aside Kemper's gibe. It wasn't worth saying anything. Protests would just elicit more of the same; he knew that much from long experience.

For years, Gregory had wanted to be a fighter pilot, wanted to be a member of that elite fraternity so bad he could taste it. Star carrier pilots were the aristocracy of the Earth Confederation's military, but that wasn't what had led him to volunteer . . . or to endure the years of training and heavy-duty AI downloads that had made him one. Born on the colony world of Osiris—70 Ophiuchi AII—he'd been eight when his world had been subjected to a savage bombardment by a Turusch battle fleet, followed by Nungiirtok assault forces landing in wave upon relentless wave. That had been early in 2405, just less than twenty years earlier.

Gregory still had acid-sharp memories of that time . . . especially of the moment when his father had put him aboard a freighter packed with refugee children at Nuit Starport days before the final collapse. He still remembered shrieking that he didn't want to go . . . remembered his father's calm assurances that they would be together again soon. . . .

It hadn't happened. When the Sh'daar Treaty was announced seven months later, Osiris remained under Nungiirtok control. The Earth Confederation government had attempted to open negotiations with the martial beings, but no progress had been made in all that time.

Year had followed year, and Gregory had grown progressively more bitter. It seemed clear to him that the Confederation wasn't going to force a confrontation. Even now, there was no formal contact with the Nungiirtok, no way of even determining if his mother and father were still alive.

Three years ago he'd joined the North American Star Navy, applying for a training slot as a combat pilot. The star system of 70 Ophiuchi was strategically important, quite apart from its value to Gregory personally. Just sixteen light years away from Sol, it formed the deadly tip of a salient driven deep, deep into the Confederation sphere, and gave the Sh'daar client races a base within easy striking distance of Earth. Surely, it was only a matter of time before the Earth Confederation moved to get Osiris back . . . and Gregory intended to be there when it happened.

The other members of his squadron, though, had given him the handle Nungie, and joked that he was working for the Sh'daar. Gregory could have ignored that much. The problem was that there was an undercurrent of hostility, even paranoia there. They kept asking him if he was carrying a Sh'daar Seed inside his head. . . .

Midpoint. Surrounding space slewed wildly across 180 degrees, and now a vastly shrunken Earth lay directly ahead, but still dwindling in apparent size. Forty-two and a half seconds after boost, the Black Demons were now traveling at over 850 kilometers per second. Still pulling two thousand gravities, they were decelerating now, backing down toward their destination.

The Sh'daar War had lasted for thirty-eight years, from the time the Agletsch had delivered the Sh'daar Ultimatum until Admiral Koenig's brilliant and unexpected victories at Texaghu Resch and Omega Centauri. Most civilians thought of the war now as history, while most military personnel were content to wait and see. By any reasonable assessment, the Sh'daar represented a technology some thousands of years in advance of Humankind, and yet they had just stopped.

Smart money said that they weren't yet done with the upstart Earth Confederation.

Slowing rapidly, the Black Demons drifted tail-first past the collection of spheres, struts, holding tanks, domes, and rotating hab modules that comprised the synchorbital part of the Quito space elevator. Anchored deep in the solid rock of Mt. Cayambe, on Earth's equator 36,000 kilometers below, the elevator had offered cheap, easy, and high-volume access to space since the early twenty-second century.

The synchorbital naval base was located a dozen kilometers from the upside terminus of the elevator, a vast structure including hundreds of docking spaces and gantries for military vessels. A joint project of the Confederation and the United States of North America, it housed some thousands of military personnel, as well as home port facilities for those warships, the bigger ones, unable to enter planetary atmospheres.

Largest of these was the TC/USNA star carrier *America*. Mushroom-shaped—1,150 meters long—CVS *America* was docked at a special gantry offering multiple mag-tube access for personnel and supplies. The forward cap, 500 meters across and 150 deep, served as both radiation shielding and as a holding tank for 27 billion liters of water, reaction mass for the ship's maneuvering thrusters. The slender, kilometer-long spine held quantum-field power plants, maneuvering thrusters, and stores, while two hab rings, counter-rotating and tucked in close behind the shield cap, carried the ship's human complement of 4,840. Around her, like swarming midges, a cloud of drones and remote vehicles kept watch, or serviced her external hull.

"VFA-96," a new voice said. "You are cleared for two-by-two trap in Landing Bay One. Please alter your hull shape to facilitate capture."

It was a woman's voice, but with the precise diction and phrasing that likely indicated an AI, an artificial intelligence.

"Copy. Black Demons on docking approach," Mackey's voice said. "Morphing from sperm mode to turkey. Okay, people. Switch to AI approach."

Maneuvering to approach over the immense vessel's stern, the Black Demons shifted their hull structure from their high-boost configuration—popularly known among the pilots as "sperm mode"—to flight mode. The nanomatrix hull of an SG-92 allowed the craft to mold itself into a variety of shapes during flight. In atmospheric or flight mode—"turkey mode" in the pilot lexicon—growing wings that better allowed the landing bay magnetics to trap inbound fighters. Massing just twenty-two tons—her usual weapons loadout massed more than that by a considerable margin—the bulk of Gregory's Starhawk flowed like water at his thought command, extending delta wings, negatively charged to give the flight deck something to grab.

The first two fighters, Lieutenants Anderson and Rivera, dropped into their final approach side by side, sweeping up along *America*'s spine from tail toward the base of the mushroom cap. The next pair followed twenty-eight seconds later—Esperanza and Nichols—followed by Mason and Del Rey.

Next up on the list were Gregory and his wingman— Lieutenant Jodi Vaughn. Fighters didn't use their gravitational drives for maneuvering close aboard a carrier, not when the microscopic knot of a twisted spacetime comprising the craft's drive singularity could shred the fabric of a capital ship's hull like a particle cannon. Cutting their drives, Vaughn and Gregory opened aft venturis and fired their maneuvering thrusters. Jets of plasma, using superheated water as reaction mass, bumped them into their final vector at three Gs—a kick unlike the free-fall acceleration of a gravitational drive.

Dropping into a landing approach, Gregory's AI adjusted his ship's velocity as *America*'s long spine blurred overhead. The landing-bay entrance yawned wide ahead, rotating around to meet him, his onboard AI microadjusting his velocity and attitude to meet it. The landing bay was rotating at 2.11 turns per minute, providing the module's out-is-down spin gravity. The bay's entrance swung around every twenty-eight seconds, just as each incoming fighter pair was there to meet it.

Traveling at 100 meters per second, they flashed into the shadow beneath the carrier's spine, the domes, blisters, and sponsons housing the ship's drive projectors blurring past, seemingly just above his head. It took them almost ten seconds to traverse the length of *America*'s spine. At the last instant, his AI tapped his starboard-side thrusters to find the moving sweet spot that matched perfectly the

7-meters-per-second lateral movement of the rotating landing bay. The moving opening ahead suddenly appeared to freeze motionless in space, as Vaughn and Gregory flashed across lines of approach-acquisition lights.

When the fighters hit the flight deck's magnetic tanglefield, he felt again a sudden shock of deceleration, and the side-by-side fighters came to rest. Magnetic grapples embraced his fighter and moved it forward to a nanosealed patch on the deck. A moment later, he was dropping through the seal to the pressurized deck one level below.

His neural feeds cut out, and abruptly Gregory was enfolded in a tight, close, suffocating darkness. He thought-clicked the cockpit open, and the hull melted away around him as he emerged into the bustling noise and glare and movement of the pressurized hangar bay. A robot, all arms and spindly plasteel framework, met him on the access scaffolding, its optics adjusting independently as it scanned him and his fighter. "Welcome aboard, Lieutenant," the machine said.

"Move your metal ass, damn it," a human flight chief said nearby. As the robot shifted to one side, a crew chief appeared. "Hey, Lieutenant. Welcome aboard the *America*."

Gregory removed his flight helmet, blinking under the harsh lighting filling the cavernous space, and nodded. "Thanks, Chief."

He wasn't home, but maybe, *maybe*, someday, if he was lucky, the star carrier *America* would get him there.

TC/USNA CVS America
USNA Naval Base
Quito Synchorbital
1440 hours, TFT

"VFA-96 is recovered, Captain," *America*'s CAG reported.

"I see it, Connie. Thank you."

Back on board his ship, now, after the shuttle flight up

from Columbus, Captain Gray relaxed in the embrace of his command seat on the carrier's bridge, allowing incoming streams of data to flood through his consciousness. With his cerebral implants hardlinked to the carrier's artificial intelligence, he could follow all of the preparations for getting the immense vessel ready for debarkation directly, as though he himself was the central awareness of *America*'s AI network. Through the AI's electronic eyes, he'd watched the Starhawks of VFA-96 hurtling in, two by two, and trapping on *America*'s Bravo flight deck. A shift in perception, and he was watching now as the Starhawks peeled open and the pilots emerged.

Gray had a special fondness for the old SG-92 Starhawks. As a raw, newbie lieutenant twenty years earlier, he'd flown a Starhawk as part of the long-disbanded VF-44 Dragonfires. Those fighters were considered relics nowadays, compared to the much newer and more powerful SG-101 Velociraptors, the SG-112 Stardragons, and other modern space fighters. There was talk of retiring the Starhawks permanently . . . but the Navy had been dithering on the issue for several years, now, and if the scuttlebutt was true, if the Sh'daar were coming back, that procrastination was a damned good thing. Earth would need a lot of fighters in the coming months, if *Endeavor* had been burned out of the sky by Sh'daar clients . . . and if the Sh'daar were planning on moving in from the Ophiuchan colonies.

Hell, even if the Sh'daar had nothing to do with the *Endeavor* attack, the Slan capture of 36 Ophiuchi meant that Earth was going to need every fighter available, and *now*. There wouldn't be time to grow new Velociraptors or Stardragons, not when every moment counted in intercepting the aliens before they reached Solar space. *America* and her battlegroup had been on full alert since the news of Arianrhod's capture and of *Endeavor*'s destruction had come through from Mars. Supplies for an extended deployment were coming up through the space elevator now, or arriving down-tether from Anchorage, the small asteroid 36,000 kilometers farther out that kept the elevator structure taut and in place. Crews on liberty and leave on Earth and on the moon were being recalled, and two fresh squadrons—VFA-96 and VFA-115—had just arrived.

Similar preparations were under way on board all of the ships in CBG-40, the designation for *America*'s current battlegroup. The expectation was that they would be getting the affirm-go from Geneva at almost any moment.

The only real question was where the battlegroup would be deployed . . . Omega Centauri, as originally planned? Or to a much closer objective, to 36 Ophiuchi?

Gray pulled back from the interior view, shifting instead to *America*'s logistical displays. Supplies of raw material—carbon, nitrogen, and the other elements necessary to nanufacture food and most other consumables used by the nearly five thousand personnel on board—were stored in sponsons along America's kilometer-long spine. Hydrogen, oxygen, and water itself were tapped from the 27 billion liters of water stored in *America*'s shield cap. While the carrier could resupply from convenient asteroids in almost any star system, Gray wanted to have every stores module full-up before they departed Solar space. Faced with a hostile unknown, there was no telling how long it would be before they would have the luxury of resupply.

"Connie?" he asked. "What's the logistics status for the Wing?"

Captain Connie Fletcher was *America*'s CAG—an anachronistic three-letter acronym for commander air group, even though the squadrons on board the carrier comprised a wing, not a group, and rarely operated within a planetary atmosphere. The Navy was nothing if not wedded to tradition, and some of the terminology had stuck through four centuries from the days of ocean-going navies and pre-spaceflight aircraft carriers.

"We're at ninety-four percent," she told him. "We're still waiting on the plutonium and the depleted U."

"Expedite that."

"We are, Skipper."

Plutonium was necessary for the nuclear-tipped mis-

siles carried by *America*'s fighters, Kraits, and the newer
Boomslangs, Taipans, and Lanceheads. Depleted uranium
was used in the cores of kinetic-kill rounds for the fighters'
Gatling weapons and for larger mass-driver weapons.

"And your crews?"

"We currently have four hundred ninety-six personnel
still ashore, Captain. But the alert is out and they're all on
the way back . . . all except for five hospital cases and thirty-
nine in one slammer or another."

"Very well. Let me see." Five medical no-shows and
thirty-one under legal detention out of over 2,500 fighter-
wing personnel wasn't too bad at all. Extended liberty
always meant a few people getting into fights or getting so
brain-buzzed they ended up AWOL. Some ninety of *America*'s non-aviation personnel had reported sick or under arrest
as well.

The data from Wing Personnel joined to the streams
moving through Gray's consciousness, and he filed it with
the rest. He would need it all in order to compose readiness
reports for Mars, for Columbus, and for Geneva.

There were times—lots of them—when Gray seriously
wished he was still a Starhawk driver, with no more administrative responsibilities than his own evaluations and flight
status uploads. Point him at an enemy-held star system and
boost him in at 99.7 percent of *c*, and he knew exactly what
was expected of him.

No more. He'd left the old VF-44 in 2406, deployed to
Mars HQ for three years, then served on board the light carrier *Republic*, first as assistant CAG, and later as CAG. In
2414, he'd been given command of a Marine light carrier,
the *Nassau*, but five years later he'd taken a career side-step
to serve as executive officer of his old ship, *America*.

And now, with the rank of captain, he was *America*'s
commanding officer, and flag captain to the battlegroup
commander, Rear Admiral Jason R. Steiger.

Not bad at all for a monogie from the Periphery, the Manhattan Ruins.

Best, perhaps, not to think about that. . . .

He focused instead on the matter of *America*'s Alcubierre Drive, and Engineering's concerns that the ship would have trouble matching the emergence ZOP—the zone of probability—of the rest of the fleet.

Executive Office, USNA
Columbus, District of Columbia
United States of North America
2050 hours, TFT

The fireworks were spectacular.

Hands clasped behind his back, the newly elected president of the United States of North America stood before the viewall in his office. Its luminous surface was currently set to display in real time the scene in the Freedom Concourse outside. The Concourse, some eighty stories below, was still packed with cheering people as the dark skies overhead pulsed and rippled and flared with celebratory pyrotechnics. It was odd, Koenig thought, that in an age when most entertainment was downloaded directly into people's brains through nanochelated implants, audiences still seemed to have that primal, almost atavistic need to come together in massed crowds, packed in shoulder to shoulder and shrieking at the tops of their lungs.

"It's quite a show, Mr. President," his aide, Marcus Whitney, observed.

"Eh?" Alexander Koenig said. "Oh, yes. Yes, I suppose it is."

"The crowd's enthusiasm seems a splendid validation of your policies, sir. Two nights, now, and still going strong!"

"Ha. Makes me wonder what I'm supposed to do for an encore."

Those crowds, he thought, might not be so enthusiastic if the Sh'daar Treaty unraveled within the next few days, as it showed every sign of doing. He'd downloaded a fresh report from Mars only hours ago: *Endeavor* and two Confederation destroyers had been lost out at Omega Tee-prime. Intelligence suspected that the Sh'daar were behind the attack. This news, coming so close on the heels of the disaster at Arianrhod, seemed to promise the final collapse of the Sh'daar Treaty.

"They re-elected you because they know how you feel about the Confederation, Mr. President. You promised to give North America more sovereignty within the world government."

Koenig grunted at that. The *Pax Confeoderata* had been formed in 2133, a union popularly known interchangeably as either the Earth or Terran Confederation. The creation of a single polity embracing most world governments had been a necessity arising from the chaos of the First and Second Sino-Western Wars, the Blood Death plague, and the widespread devastation caused by the Chinese asteroid strike into the Atlantic Ocean. The Pax had held now for almost three centuries and had followed Humankind to the stars.

But with the apparent defeat of the Sh'daar twenty years before, there'd been a resurgence of spirit, of independent thought and goals—and a new wave of calls for American independence from Geneva. *North American sovereignty.* It was an intriguing dream and one that Koenig himself very much wanted to see realized.

If the Sh'daar were renewing the old conflict, though, this was exactly the wrong time in which to do it. If ever Earth needed to stand united, this was the time.

Koenig had retired from the USNA Navy in 2408, four years after his startling victory over the Sh'daar. Elements within the American party had pointed out that his popularity would all but guarantee his election as president of the USNA.

His refusal to follow Confederation government orders in the face of Geneva's blunt stupidity had had a lot to do with that. He'd ordered his battlegroup to leave the Sol System deliberately before orders to the contrary could arrive, won a surprising victory at Alphekka, skirmished with a French squadron at HD157950, and eventually beaten Sh'daar client forces at Texaghu Resch. Ultimately, Koenig had taken

CBG-18 through a Sh'daar transit node into the remote past to confront the Sh'daar puppet masters within their home galaxy and epoch . . . though that hadn't been clear at the time. The Sh'daar threat had collapsed with astonishing suddenness, resulting in the treaty guaranteeing Earth's interstellar borders.

When CBG-18 had returned to Earth, Geneva had had little choice but to forgive Koenig's de facto mutiny and declare him a hero.

He'd resisted getting into politics, but the ongoing battle with Geneva over Periphery Reconstruction had drawn him in, and he'd been elected to the USNA Senate in 2410. As North America began rebuilding the shattered, half-submerged cities along its drowned coastal areas, Geneva insisted that these regions, formally abandoned by the USNA centuries before, now properly belonged to the Pax world community. Once again, the former admiral had aligned himself against the Terran Confederation government, this time in the senate halls in both Columbus and in Geneva. In 2418, Koenig had left the Senate to run for president, and been elected to a six-year term.

And now, just two days ago, he'd won a second term.

The big question was what Geneva would decide to do in light of the news of the twin naval disasters . . . and whether President Koenig would be able to support their decision, whatever that might be.

And would the American public, caught up in their new enthusiasm for independence, support *him* if he decided that he must first support a united Earth?

Much depended on the alien Sh'daar, and at the moment they were a complete unknown in the equation.

The Confederation maintained at best only a tenuous connection with the Sh'daar. The so-called Sh'daar Empire, the remnants, apparently, of an ancient extragalactic federation of mutually alien civilizations, maintained a far-flung polity of mutually alien species, both now and in the remote past. That they feared the Terran Confederation, despite their considerable technological advantage, was indisputable. But Humankind understood them so poorly, even down to exactly what it was about humans that the Sh'daar feared.

Attempts to open new negotiations with the aliens through their usual representatives, a species called the Agletsch, had repeatedly failed. The Sh'daar had ignored Geneva's call for a dialogue over the Osiris question, refused to put human diplomats in touch with the alien Nungiirtok still occupying the 70 Ophiuchi system, and rejected point-blank Confederation requests to revisit Omega Tee-sub, as the Sh'daar home cluster in the remote past was commonly known.

And now, according to the packet that had just arrived at Fleet HQ in Mars orbit, the Navy survey vessel *Endeavor* and her escorts had been destroyed by unknown attackers at the central core of Omega Tee-prime.

"Tee-sub" was a manageable shorthand for "$T_{-0.876gy}$," an unwieldy mouthful pronounced "Tee-sub-minus zero point eight seven six gigayear," a physics notation referring to an epoch 876 million years in the past. Tee-prime, on the other hand, was Time Now, November of the year 2424 in common usage. Time travel, Koenig reflected, not for the first time, made things almost unendurably complicated. And conducting a *war* across a span of almost a billion years made everything infinitely worse.

Sixteen thousand light years from Sol lay the largest globular star cluster in the galaxy, Omega Centauri, a swarming beehive of 10 million suns packed into a sphere just 230 light years across. Close inspection, however, had proven that Omega Centauri was not, strictly speaking, a proper member of the cloud of regular, smaller globular star clusters orbiting the center of the Milky Way galaxy, but the stripped-down core of a separate dwarf galaxy devoured by the Milky Way hundreds of millions of years in the past.

Some 876 million years ago, Omega Centauri had been an irregular galaxy much like the Greater Magellanic Cloud of the present day, hanging just above the far larger galactic spiral. *That* Omega Centauri, existing almost a billion years ago and known to its inhabitants as the N'gai Cloud, was the home of some thousands of mutually alien civilizations called the collective name *Sh'daar*.

The central core of Omega $T_{-0.876gy}$ and Omega Centauri Tee-prime were in fact one and the same, the same starswarm in two epochs, separated by just less than a billion years. The ancient version teemed with life, with inhabited worlds and with the incomprehensibly vast structures of a highly advanced and utterly alien technology; the modern version was uninhabited, its worlds silent and empty, the polyspecific civilization it once had held long vanished.

Why? What had happened to them?

The Sh'daar weren't discussing it, obviously. In fact, they'd long seemed distinctly nervous about the entire topic, and lately all communication with the Sh'daar had ceased.

It was distinctly possible that the Sh'daar were on the point of renewing the war, and that, Koenig thought, could be very, very bad news indeed for all of Humankind.

He turned from the viewall display. "Marcus?"

"Sir?"

"Get me time with Konstantin. The sooner the better."

"Yes, sir."

The problem, Koenig thought, demanded more-than-human consideration.

Chapter Three

Sh'daar Node
Texaghu Resch System,
210 Light Years from Sol
0105 hours, TFT

Red Mike fell through emptiness, accelerating gently toward the blurred haze of distorted light now only 10,000 kilometers ahead. At his current velocity, he would reach the maw in another fifteen minutes.

"Deep Peek, *Peleliu*," a voice whispered within his awareness. "You are on course and clear for departure."

"Copy," Red Mike replied, using a tightly packaged, low-powered, and coded burst transmission. "Further communications suspended until mission return. Deep Peek out."

His ship was a black lump of nanomatrix artfully shaped to look like a meteoroid, a small chunk of nickel-iron massing just thirty kilograms. Red Mike was an artificial intelligence, a complex set of interlocking software downloaded from the far larger AI on board the Marine assault ship *Peleliu*. His name was taken from U.S. Marine history, from Lt. Colonel Merritt A. "Red Mike" Edson, the commander of the 1st Raider Battalion in World War II. A patch of the rock's outer surface a few centimeters square provided his sole data feed from the universe outside. He was tumbling slowly, so he could see his objective only intermittently for a few seconds at a time.

The maw was growing larger, more defined. Red Mike was not capable of emotion as humans understood the word, but he was as focused, as aware as any human combat pilot entering a dangerous flight zone under enemy observation. Just how good *were* the Sh'daar servants watching the gate, and could they see him from the other side?

Properly known as the Sh'daar Node or as the TRGA, for the Texaghu Resch gravitational anomaly, the maw was the product of an unimaginably advanced technic civilization, an artificial construct located just 210 light years from Sol at a star called Texaghu Resch. A mass equivalent to that of Earth's sun had somehow been crushed down into a cylinder twelve kilometers long and one wide, rotating about its long axis at close to the speed of light.

Centuries earlier, the mathematical physicist Frank Tipler had described theoretical devices—black holes stretched into spaghetti-thin strands and set spinning at billions of rotations per second—that became known as Tipler machines. Their rotation, Tipler postulated, would open closed, timelike curves through spacetime, allowing access across vast distances of space . . . and through time as well.

Ultimately, a flaw was discovered in the concept; a Tipler machine would have to have *infinite* length to function as a shortcut across space or time. The Sh'daar, however, appeared to have found a slightly different approach. The movement of that much mass dragging on the fabric of spacetime opened paths *inside* the rotating cylinder. Twenty years ago, Admiral Koenig had taken Carrier Battlegroup 18 through the Sh'daar Node at Texaghu Resch and emerged . . . somewhere—some*when*—else.

At first, Koenig's tactical group had assumed they'd jumped some sixteen thousand light years, to the heart of a globular star cluster called Omega Centauri. Only later did they discover the truth: that they'd jumped to that cluster in the remote past, when it was still the core of a small galaxy just outside the spiral arms of the Milky Way.

The TRGA/Sh'daar Node was much more than a kind of super-high-tech galactic transport system.

It was also a time machine.

For Red Mike, the thought of traveling across tens of thousands of light years and hundreds of millions of years of time in a single swift leap was not at all daunting. Both distances were mere sets of spacetime coordinates reflecting the knowledge that the universe was both far larger and far more complex than cosmologists had thought before the Einstein revolution. Tipler machines and the TRGA cylinder both were derived ultimately from the Van Stockum-Lanczos solutions to the equations of General Relativity, and therefore could claim Einstein as their father.

But Red Mike was concerned, in a coldly calculating AI sort of way, about whether or not Sh'daar technology would be able to pick him out from among the molecules of nano-embedded nickel-iron encasing him. The microcircuitry within which his consciousness resided took up less volume than a human brain and resided among the shielding atoms, woven through and among them within the nanomatrix, rather than inside a hollow within the core. Both ends of the TRGA cylinder attracted matter—dust, gas, and small bits of meteoric rubble—and drew them in and through constantly, sending them through the lumen of the cylinder in gravitational currents running both ways, in and out. The planners of Operation Deep Peek were counting on the Sh'daar watchers on the far side of the gate to assume that Red Mike was just another chunk of interstellar rubble.

To pull it off, Red Mike would have to power down to almost nothing, cutting back to the point where he was radiating heat at just a few degrees above absolute zero. He could accomplish this by dropping into power-saving mode, his conscious awareness slowed to a rate so sluggish by human standards that, for him, the minutes flickered past like seconds.

An instant before entering the maw, the encircling sphere of stars warped and puckered, the infalling light wildly distorted by the sharply bending fabric of space. His passage through the rotating cylinder was a blurred instant . . . and then he emerged far indeed from Texaghu Resch, a place where stars blazed around him as if from a solid wall, where only scattered and isolated patches of black, empty space peeped through the dazzling mass of closely packed suns.

Red Mike's inbound trajectory had been carefully adjusted to match that of CBG-18 twenty years before . . . which *should* mean that he'd emerged deep within the central core of the Omega Centauri galaxy, and at $T_{-0.876gy}$, almost 900 million years in the past. However, according to the Van Stockum-Lanczos solutions, different paths through the distorted spacetime vortex within the rotating cylinder would translate to different paths through both space and time; it was distinctly possible that Red Mike had emerged off-target, somewhere and some*when* else.

Confirming his exact spacetime coordinates was vital.

It would also be extremely difficult.

Executive Office, USNA
Columbus, District of Columbia
United States of North America
1124 hours, TFT

It was the next morning before President Koenig's request could be processed and time secured on the Tsiolkovsky Array. Konstantin worked on a twenty-four-hour schedule, but there was always a backlog of high-priority requests. Geneva had been attempting, in fact, to designate Konstantin as a Confederation asset, but so far the USNA had managed to block the move, and individual governments within the Confederation could still consult the technological oracle on a first-come-first-served basis.

At the designated time, Koenig settled into his office chair, placed the neuronet contacts exposed on the palm of his hand against the chair's contact plate, and thought-clicked a connection through to Tsiolkovsky.

Located on the far side of the moon from Earth, the crater Tsiolkovsky was a somewhat irregular 180-kilometer depression with an off-center central peak. Named for the Russian physicist Konstantin Tsiolkovsky, the feature was one of the very few dark-floored maria features visible on the moon's far side, its central peak looking like an island within a circular, black lake.

Buried deep within the central peak was a man-made cavern housing the Tsiolkovsky Array, originally the control center for a farside lunar radio telescope, but now the site of a long-running experiment in artificial hyperintelligence.

Konstantin was a fifth-generation digitally programmed and enhanced artificial intelligence, a machine mind running within a vast network of Digital Sentience DS-8940 computers. What made Konstantin unique was that humans had not programmed him; he was an AIP.

During the first half of the twenty-first century—possibly as early as 2020, though definitions were fuzzy and the records from four centuries earlier were frustratingly inexact—computers with human levels of intelligence had made their first appearance, machines with the equivalent of around 10^{14} neural connections. According to the records, those early human-equivalent systems and networks weren't *conscious*—at least the software engineers involved were fairly certain that they weren't—but under the relentless, driving whip of Moore's Law, computer power had continued to double and redouble, until by the middle of the century such markers as numbers of neural connections or raw processor speed simply were no longer relevant. By 2084, a computer had written a complete operating system for a new generation of information processors—the first AIPs, or artificial-intelligence-programmed machines. One early AIP—an IBM-Lenovo Mk. 1 Brilliant e-Mind—had been instrumental in designing the first Earth-to-Synchorbit space elevator, in the early 2100s.

Within another century, computer programs and operating systems were routinely written by computers, which were designing ever more brilliant and innovative systems.

Nowadays, most computers possessed something on the order of 10^{17} neural connections; a typical ship network might boast 10^{19}, while Konstantin was rumored to possess about 10^{24}.

But . . . just exactly what did it mean to say that a computer was 10 billion—10^{10}—times more powerful than the human brain? It wasn't a matter of *speed*; computers had been faster than humans at basic arithmetic since ENIAC in the late 1940s, and had been more complex, at least in terms of the numbers of interneural connections, since the 2020s.

And even now, experts engaged in acrimonious debate over whether Konstantin or any of his electronic kin were even *conscious* in the same way as were humans. They *acted* as if they were . . . and when asked directly they claimed to be so. But if modern AIs had been programmed to *act* as if they were self-aware, how would humans even know?

It didn't help, Koenig thought as he felt the return-flow of data flooding into his brain, that computer intelligence was of a vastly different type than most known organic minds— humans and the Agletsch, for instance. It was difficult to pinpoint exactly *how* it was different . . . but the machine network's thoughts, quick, all-encompassing, and fluid, were unlike those of humans both in their precision and in their scope. It seemed as though Konstantin was considering *everything* about each question, every angle, every possibility, before it spoke.

A window opened in Koenig's mind, and he saw Konstantin's avatar.

White-haired, balding, with a small, square beard at his chin and antique pince-nez, the image of Konstantin Tsiolkovsky was anachronistically seated within a data-feed donut, a circular workstation ringed with large viewscreens, ghostly virtual control panels, and floating display monitors. The real Tsiolkovsky, Koenig knew, had been a hermit who'd spent most of his life in a log cabin on the outskirts of Kaluga, in Russia, when he wasn't teaching high school mathematics in a nearby school.

He'd also been one of the twentieth century's foremost

technophilosophers, an advocate of space colonization who'd believed that Humankind one day would spread throughout the galaxy, perfecting itself as humans became immortal. Eventually, Tsiolkovsky had become known as the father of spaceflight, and had been the first person to describe how a space elevator might work.

The image turned in its seat, peering querulously at Koenig over the top of its pince-nez. "So, the president of North America," it said, speaking English. "Until you Americans learn to take a truly *global* view, there is little I can do for you."

"I am not here on behalf of just Americans, Konstantin," Koenig replied. "The decisions I must make have . . . a more-than-global significance. They will affect all of Humankind."

As always, there was a hesitation, a two-and-a-half second pause as the signal crawled from Earth to the moon, and the response crawled back.

"Indeed." Was that a twinkle in the old man's eye? It was there and gone so swiftly Koenig couldn't be certain he'd really seen it. The illusion of life, he had to admit, was perfect.

Koenig became aware of a low-voiced susurration in the background, a sea of many voices, none distinct enough to make out. The display monitors surrounding Tsiolkovsky, he saw, showed a dozen different scenes from around the world and out in space. He recognized a Senate debate in progress on the floor of the Neocapitol Tower in Columbus, and the face of Ilse Roettgen, the president of the Confederation Senate, delivering a speech in the Legislators' Grand Hall of the Ad Astra Government Complex in Geneva. There was an external view of a large, rotating nanufactory in synchorbit, and another of a freighter landing at Crisium Starport. Papess Maria II spoke to an enthusiastic crowd packed into St. Peter's from her apartment balcony, while under a cold, white moon, armored Chinese troops and hunter-killer robots hunted insurgents in a Philippine jungle. The Washington Monument rose from flooded swamps interrupted here and there by the white and gray of vine-shrouded granite buildings, but in the distance, hovercranes floated above the mangrove forest, where the domed Capitol Building, after more than three hundred years, once again stood on dry land.

The monitor images were flickering from one to another in rapid succession, thousands, perhaps, each appearing for a few seconds before being replaced by something else. The whisper in the background was a blend of countless voices emerging from the virtual sea.

"Kazakhstan is approaching a crisis point," Konstantin said in a far-off voice, seemingly distracted. One monitor briefly showed the rusted hulk of a robotic harvester half submerged in blowing sand. "They still rely primarily on organic crops rather than agronanufactories, but increasing desertification, especially in the West, has sharply reduced the area of grain-growing regions and make famine likely. I estimate an eighty percent probability that something in excess of fifteen million humans will die of starvation and disease within the next five years.

"The Chinese Hegemony, on the other hand, has surplus agronanufactory capabilities, but, seeking a buffer against Russia, will demand political concessions from Astana in the East—in particular the arcologies at Almaty, the largest Kazakh population center.

"A serious confrontation is developing between your United States of North America and the Earth Confederation government . . . particularly with members of the European Union. The Verrazano Seacrete project is nearing completion, making possible the full-scale renovation of the Manhattan Ruins. The Potomac Dam has made possible the draining of the Washington, D.C., ruins, where approximately forty percent of the submerged land has already been reclaimed.

"Geneva, however, is arguing that since the North American government renounced all claim and control over the Periphery centuries ago, control and ownership now legally reverts to the planetary government, under laws designed to allow the annexation of failed states as legal wards of Geneva. More worrying still, there is currently a bill within the Geneva Senate calling for an invocation of the Confederation's Military First Right, which would put the USNA Navy under the direct control of Geneva. I estimate a thirty percent chance of armed conflict breaking out between the United States of North America and the Earth Confederation. If such a conflict escalates beyond regional clashes, and if neither party backs down, the exchange could become a full-blown civil war fought in space as well as on Earth, leading to the deaths of hundreds of millions of people."

"And why are you telling me all of this, Konstantin?"

Again, that hesitation. It made the old-man avatar seem more human. "To be certain that you understand the complexity of the global balance at this point in time. Humans are not rational creatures when it comes to either politics or to claims of national sovereignty. They are not rational in terms of perceived external threat. The destruction of the *Endeavor* can only further complicate matters, and could easily lead to a full break between the USNA and Geneva, with consequences that would threaten human civilization."

"I understand that. I also understand that there are no easy solutions." He wondered, though, if Konstantin grasped that fact.

"If the Chinese hegemony were to donate nanufactured food to Kazakhstan as a humanitarian gesture, without demanding recompense in land and population centers, famine would be averted without forcing a political crisis. If, rather, Kazakhstan cedes control of her eastern provinces to the hegemony, including the city of Almaty, famine will again be averted, since the feeding of the citizens of Almaty would then be the responsibility of the Hegemony government. Unfortunately, neither outcome is likely." Konstantin paused, a distinctly human affectation. "I despair, sometimes, of you humans. Your passions may well destroy you."

"My concern right now is that we might be destroyed by the Sh'daar."

"A valid concern."

"The Sh'daar seemed worried about the possibility that humans could defeat or destroy them by somehow accessing the past. *Their* past. I'd like you to tell me if this is possible, and how we might bring it to pass."

"Ah," Konstantin said. "The time-travel option."

"Is it possible?"

"Time travel is possible, yes, at least within certain constraints. The Sh'daar Node, certainly, clearly allows access to both past and future, within certain limits."

Koenig started to give a sharp reply, but bit it off. "I know," he said instead, with a mild shrug. "I was there, remember?"

Twenty years earlier, Koenig had led Carrier Battlegroup 18 through the Sh'daar Node and emerged within the central core of Omega Centauri $T_{-0.876gy}$, almost a billion years in the past. The fact that the Confederation military had been able to reach so far back into time appeared to have caught the Sh'daar utterly off-balance, to the point that they'd requested what amounted to a truce rather than risking a temporal war.

And that was what had led Koenig to link with Konstantin. If the Sh'daar were afraid of something, that implied that it could be used as a weapon.

Time travel as a weapon. The obvious possibility, there, was that humans might travel back to some point *before* $T_{-0.876gy}$ and somehow edit the Sh'daar out of existence. That course, however, carried considerable risks for both sides. The Sh'daar had first interacted with Humankind almost sixty years earlier, in 2367. If that bit of history changed, *all* recent human history would be rewritten as well—the Battles of Beta Pictoris and Rasalhague, of Hecate and 9 Ceti, the loss of Sturgis's World, Mufrid, and Osiris, and even relations with other star-faring species—the Agletsch, the H'rulka, the Turusch, and others. How much else might be edited into nonexistence?

With a different history, people alive now—like Koenig—might be dead. But people who'd died during the war with the Sh'daar would be alive, and people never born in Koenig's universe would also be alive.

Koenig felt an icy, inner shock. Karyn—Karyn Mendelson—would not have died in the high-velocity impactor attack at Mars.

Yes . . . so *very* much would be different.

But the change would also run full-boost into that hoary puzzle central to all discussions of time travel: the grandfather paradox.

A man uses time travel to go back and kill his father's father—or otherwise divert him—so that the man's father is never born. The man himself is never born . . . and so cannot go back in time to change the flow of history. But then . . . granddad lives, the man travels back into time, and on and on, around and around, a paradox without end.

Only in this case, entire civilizations were on the wheel. If CBG-18 succeeded in editing out the Sh'daar, the Sh'daar War would never be fought, CBG-18 would never have found the Sh'daar Node and used it to change the past, so the Sh'daar would live . . . on and on and . . .

Karyn Mendelson would be alive. . . .

But Konstantin was speaking to him, dry words within his mind. "The possibility of a serious paradox, of a so-called grandfather paradox, would not be an issue, at least not to human civilization at large."

"Eh?" Had Konstantin somehow been eavesdropping on his inner thoughts? "Why not?"

"Quantum theory predicts that any change to the flow of time as we experience it would simply result in a branching through to another parallel universe, one of what may be an infinite array of universes where every possible determination and outcome not only may occur, but *must* occur."

Koenig was startled. He'd heard that theory, but so far as he knew it was *only* theory. "Is that proven?"

"Proving it would require experimentation that would eliminate access to the original universe and strand the experimenters in the product of a different causal outcome."

In other words, the man who went back and killed his grandfather would find himself in a universe where he'd never been born. The universe from which he'd originally come would be forever closed to him, since further attempts at time travel would carry him back and forth only along this *new* time stream.

And if CBG-18 managed to eliminate the Sh'daar in the remote past, the fleet's personnel might take comfort in existing in a universe cleansed of that enemy, but they could never go *home* to the universe and time line from which they'd come. If they were somehow able to return to 2424—and that in itself would be a real problem without the Sh'daar Node time machine—it would be to find a completely different world. Karyn would be alive . . . and in a relationship with *another* Alex Koenig, assuming the two had gotten together in a universe without the looming threat of the Sh'daar.

Even so, it was tempting. *Karyn . . . alive . . .*

"You're saying that it's all futile," Koenig said after a moment's unhappy thought. "If we managed to stop the Sh'daar in the far past, we, the squadron, would find ourselves in a different universe . . . but *this* universe, the one we left, would not have been changed at all."

"Obviously," Konstantin said, "since it would be necessary to travel through a Sh'daar Node to effect the requisite changes."

"So far as this universe was concerned, CBG-18 would have just disappeared . . . and the Sh'daar would still be here."

"Precisely."

"So what would be the point?"

"None, really. According to the many-universe hypothesis of quantum physics, all possibilities, all possible outcomes exist, each within its own universe. This would be the case whether you traveled through time or not, and the only witnesses to such change would be you and those traveling with you."

"It's not my intent to be some damned time-traveling *tourist*," Koenig said, angry. "The point is to stop the Sh'daar . . . in *this* universe."

"Indeed."

"So my question for you is . . . is there any way to use time travel—or the *threat* of time travel—to influence Sh'daar intentions? To make them back off . . . or to defeat them on a strategic level?"

"That will depend, President Koenig, more on the Sh'daar than on us. We don't know exactly what it is that the Sh'daar fear . . . or why they asked for a truce twenty years ago. And if the *Endeavor* and her escorts were destroyed by Sh'daar action—and I should point out that we do not as yet know that it was the Sh'daar who attacked our survey squadron—we do not know what their current motivations might be."

That gave Koenig pause. He'd not thought of this new possibility. "You're saying the *Endeavor* might not have been destroyed by the Sh'daar?"

"We know only that there was an attacker," Konstantin told him, "not who or what that attacker was."

"But the Sh'daar . . . damn it, Konstantin. Who else could it be?"

"President Koenig, you humans *must* learn to take the longer and larger view, and not assume that all of the cosmos centers on your small experience. There are something on the order of 50 million species in this galaxy alone that humans would probably recognize as intelligent. We know of two that are so highly advanced that humans would be justified in thinking of them as quite literally godlike—the ur-Sh'daar and the Starborn."

Koenig considered this. Little was known about either culture. What little information they *did* have had been acquired by a fighter pilot twenty years ago—"Sandy" Gray—during a mind-to-mind encounter with the Sh'daar.

The ur-Sh'daar—the prefix *ur* was from the German, and carried the meaning of "original," "primitive," or "proto." According to Gray, during his intelligence debriefing, the ur-Sh'daar had been a multispecies interstellar culture occupying a small galaxy—Gray's Sh'daar source had called it the N'gai Cloud—that possibly had been ejected from the Andromedan galaxy during a collision billions of years before. That cloud eventually had been captured and devoured by the Milky Way, and all that was left of it now was the star cluster known as Omega Centauri.

At some point close to a billion years ago, before Omega Centauri was absorbed by the far larger spiral of the Milky Way galaxy, the ur-Sh'daar had entered something known as the Technological Singularity. In brief, their technological prowess had advanced so far, so fast, that they had become—to use Konstantin's word—godlike. Though the details were still poorly understood, the ur-Sh'daar had all but vanished . . . into another dimension, into higher planes, into the remote future . . . no one knew for sure. What was known was that the Sh'daar were the residue, the lower-tech cripples, the ones left behind when the gods blinked out of the here and now.

As for the Starborn, even less was known about them. One of the Sh'daar client races, a very powerful, technically advanced civilization of huge gas bags that had evolved in the atmosphere of a planet much like Jupiter in Earth's solar system, was known as the H'rulka. The question was how a species resembling titanic Portuguese men-of-war adrift in the upper atmosphere of a gas giant could possibly have developed mining, smelting, and advanced spaceflight when they had neither free oxygen in their atmosphere to support fire, nor a solid planetary surface from which to mine metals.

The H'rulka themselves spoke of the "Starborn," an advanced species that had come to them before they'd joined with the Sh'daar, taught them how to filter metal from the atmosphere, and given them the technology to reach, first, their world's system of moons, and then the worlds of other stars. Confederation Intelligence assumed that the Starborn were the Sh'daar . . . but Koenig had never bought that. The Sh'daar, apparently in terror of the technic singularity that had taken the ur-Sh'daar beyond their ken and left them behind, seemed driven to *prevent* the development of high technology, not foster it. Koenig was pretty sure that whoever or whatever the Starborn were, they were not Sh'daar, and most xenosophontologists seemed to agree with him.

Nor did it seem likely that they were related to the ur-Sh'daar, evolved in a different galaxy some billions of years in the past. The H'rulka, though the xenosophs weren't sure of the details, had been given their technological boost something like twelve to fifteen thousand years ago, after which they were contacted—and subsumed—by the modern Sh'daar, who'd found a means of reaching from the N'gai Cloud of 900 million years ago to the Milky Way galaxy in the recent past.

"You're saying we need more data," Koenig said after a long moment.

"That would certainly help, Mr. President. We have no way of evaluating the threat with little or no hard information. I would recommend deploying a carrier battlegroup to Omega Centauri to confront whatever it was that destroyed the *Endeavor*. Once we know whether we are facing Sh'daar, ur-Sh'daar, Starborn, or something else entirely, we may be able to formulate a more comprehensive plan of action."

It made sense. A modern starcarrier battlegroup was the most flexible, most powerful means of confronting an unknown nonhuman threat.

"That would make sense, Konstantin," Koenig said. "The *America* battlegroup is already preparing for a deployment out to Omega Centauri. However . . . the decision will be Admiral Steiger's, and the Confederation Naval Command. The Slan capture of 36 Ophiuchi may . . . complicate matters. A *lot*."

"Indeed. However, if the Sh'daar clients follow past tendencies, they will pause to digest what they have swallowed. The need for information about the identity of the destroyers of the *Endeavor* is critical."

"Will you make that recommendation to Geneva?"

"In so far as my recommendation carries any weight there, yes, of course. Keep in mind, however, that I am technically the . . . *property* of the United States of North America, and that my input would be considered politically suspect by Geneva. At least until they succeed in assuming control of this facility by mandating that I am an asset for all of Humankind, not just for North Americans."

"Politics . . ."

"As you say. It is a political issue, certainly."

"I will do what I can, Konstantin," Koenig said. "I can't make any promises."

"Keep me informed," Konstantin told him. "I have a keen interest in how this will play out."

So do I, Koenig thought. *Karyn . . . alive . . .*

Chapter Four

Omega Centauri
$T_{-0.876gy}$
1546 hours, TFT

It had taken hours, but Red Mike at last was able to confirm his location both in space and in time.

The encircling panorama of stars was nearly solid, but individual stellar spectra could be identified like fingerprints, and the patterns of stars, distinguished by color, age, and luminosity, matched perfectly the photographs taken by the CVS *America* twenty years ago when she'd passed through the TRGA cylinder and entered this space and time. A careful search across that glowing backdrop had revealed the Six Suns, a circlet of brilliant blue stars half a light year away, each forty times the mass of Sol, all orbiting a common center of gravity.

That was Red Mike's final confirmation. He had stepped across from Omega Centauri Tee-prime to Omega $T_{-0.876gy}$, the dwarf galaxy falling in toward the spiral arms of the Milky Way more than 800 million years in the past.

Omega $T_{-0.876gy}$, the N'gai Cloud of the Sh'daar, pulsed and throbbed with electronic life.

A quartet of deep space fortresses guarded this end of the TRGA cylinder, small asteroids bristling with weaponry and sensory gear. They'd ignored him as he drifted out of the cylinder, apparently unable to detect him when his internal energy currents were channeled down to such a low, slow level.

Deeper into the central core of the tiny galaxy, toward the blue-hot mystery of the Six Suns, radio and laser communications wove a complex and tangled network of technic civilization. Numerous planets were in high-velocity transit in the distance, their wakes of distorted space visible across several light years. The Sh'daar, it had been discovered twenty years ago, were able to move entire planets by warping a bubble of space around them—the faster-than-light Alcubierre Drive on an unimaginably huge scale.

Red Mike noted the fact of the moving planets, but remained incurious as to where they were being taken, or why. He detected the movement of starships as well. Many would be piloted by the Sh'daar equivalent of AIs, electronic life forms more akin to Red Mike than to their organic predecessors. Others, he knew, were piloted by organics. By *Refusers* . . .

The tiny probe spent several more hours recording and mapping, all the while using local magnetic fields to very slowly decelerate until its velocity was zero relative to the surrounding space. Then, equally slowly, it began accelerating once more, moving back in the direction from which it had come.

There appeared to be no response from the fortresses, no indication that he'd been noticed.

With luck, the Sh'daar instrumentation on those guardian fortresses had not picked up the tiny surge of electromagnetic energy from a thirty-kilogram lump of nickel-iron when it unobtrusively reversed its course.

Squadron Common Room
TC/USNA CVS America
Quito Synchorbital
1820 hours, TFT

"Look, I know how you feel, Nungie," Lieutenant Willis Cross said with a careless shrug as he entered the common room.

"I told you, Nape. Don't call me that."

"Okay, okay . . . but you gotta take the big picture, y'know? The universe doesn't revolve around you and your personal problems!"

Cross and Gregory had just had chow at the Hab Two mess hall, and were contemplating a free evening. Gregory glanced at the viewall display covering two bulkheads—a real-time view of Earth and the synchorbital base outside—then slumped into one of the low, deeply cushioned seats that had been grown out of the deck. Vincent Ramey had told him at chow that, yes, the scuttlebutt was true. *America* was being deployed to Omega Centauri.

Gregory had been in the Navy long enough that he put little credence in scuttlebutt—an ancient naval term for shipboard rumor. Such rumor routinely took on a life of its own, no matter how outrageous or unlikely it might be. But when you heard the same story again and again from a number of different sources, no matter how outrageous it might be, it seemed more and more possible with each hearing. The word circulating through America's hab decks now was that a survey vessel, the *Endeavor*, had been attacked and destroyed by the Sh'daar at Omega Centauri, that Sh'daar forces were emerging in force from the Black Rosette, that *America* and her battlegroup were to be deployed there immediately. Cross and several others had been talking about the rumors at chow. Gregory had been resisting buying into the tales. Almost a month earlier, he'd heard stories circulating through the junior officers' quarters to the effect that the battlegroup was bound for Osiris, for home, and he didn't want to surrender that hope just yet.

"Having the Nungies parked just sixteen light years from Sol is not my 'personal problem,' okay?"

Gregory slapped his left palm down on the table next to his chair, allowing the exposed circuitry woven into the skin across the heel of his hand to come into contact with the table's linkpad. *Coffee*, he thought, and added his personal code. A couple of seconds later, the coffee materialized on the receiver plate next to the pad, built up atom by atom so quickly it seemed to flash into solidity out of nothing in an instant. He picked up the mug—cool to the touch, with an animated image of *America* dropping out of Alcubierre Drive in a dazzling pulse of light—and sipped the coffee—hot enough to scald, with his preference of cream and sugar automatically added.

Cross dropped into the seat next to Gregory's and ordered a glass of scotch on the rocks. Alcohol would have been unthinkable on board a USNA ship a couple of centuries ago . . . but the swarms of nano circulating through his body would block damage to his organs, and permit a pleasant buzz without allowing him to get drunk.

"Maybe 'King' Koenig doesn't agree with you," he suggested after taking a sip.

"The way I heard it, the Confederation bigwigs were in a panic over just how close the Nungies and their friends were. They were pushing for an Osiris relief expedition."

"Some of them, maybe," Cross admitted. "And the Chinese want Everdawn back, and the Islamics want Mufrid back and . . . fuck it. It's all just politics anyway."

Gregory nodded in glum agreement. The Confederation seemed glacial in its resolve to win back worlds and systems taken from Sol decades before. There was plenty of *talk*, sure . . . talk about Humankind claiming its place among the stars, about systems belonging to humans but now ruled by beings so alien that a meeting of minds with them was virtually impossible. But, somehow, nothing was ever actually done after all of the promises and resolve. The Islamic colony at Mufrid—Eta Boötis IV—was the perfect example. Evacuated when the Turusch had invaded in 2404, Mufrid had been briefly freed a few months later when *America* and a small fleet returned and raided the system.

But the battlegroup had moved on and Eta Boötis had been abandoned. The evacuees rescued from the planet's inhospitable surface, some thousands of them, had been shipped back to Sol and ultimately transferred to refugee camps on Luna and within the Islamic Theocracy on Earth, where they remained to this day—still waiting.

It was all so . . . *stupid*.

Despite the clamor in some quarters of the Confederation itself, the Directorate in Geneva appeared to be in no hurry to reclaim Osiris or any of the other worlds taken from Confederation control during the past half century. As Cross had pointed out, it was all about politics. Neither the Theocracy nor the Chinese Hegemony were members of the Earth Confederation. Both, in fact, had been enemies of the Confederation at various times over the past few centuries, and Geneva certainly was not going to take care of their territorial issues with aliens before their own problems were addressed.

Confederation, Theocracy, Hegemony, and the Independents—none seemed able to confront the Sh'daar clients as a united front, as Humankind rather than a ragged confusion of separate nation-states.

"So," Gregory said, "you coming in with me?"

Cross downed the last of his drink and made a face. "Might as well. They're not letting us off the damned ship, that's for sure."

"All liberty cancelled," Gregory said. "I know."

"I can see calling back the guys who might've gone Earthside or out to Luna. But why do they have to lock us up like we were prisoners, or something?"

Gregory shrugged. "You played the sexinteractives at Angelo's lately?"

"Yeah, man. Hot. You're not only *there*, smack in the middle of the fantasy of your choice, but it feels like your nerves are 'cubing on double capacity."

"Yup. Direct nanostimulation of the midbrain to stimulate a dopamine dump. Instantly addictive. Maybe they just don't trust us to come back to the ship."

"Aw, it's harmless as long as you're pumped full of anti-a," Cross said. "Battlegroup Command is just on a power trip, is all."

"Or," Gregory said, settling back in the chair and closing his eyes, "maybe they just want to make sure we review this stuff." He brought his palm down on the contact plate and relaxed.

He had to deliver a mental code group, to get clearance. The information he was downloading came from the Agletsch, by way of Naval Intelligence, and was not for public access.

After a moment, the data began scrolling past his mind's eye.

Executive Office, USNA
Columbus, District of Columbia
United States of North America
2034 hours, EST

"What the hell do your . . . *masters* think they're doing?" Koenig demanded.

He was in a virtual conference, standing in a . . . *place*, a world with towering mountains of ice on the horizon, and a night sky ablaze with the shifting green and red hues of a spectacular aurora. Stars gleamed, myriad pinpoints peeking through the auroral haze, and the intricate clots and twists and curlings of the Milky Way stretched across the zenith.

It was a real place, Koenig knew, a Confederation colony established in 2294 by settlers from North America and Russia. Themis was the human name for the cluster of cities on the great southern continent of Zeta Doradus V, some thirty-eight light years from Sol. The place was surprisingly Earthlike in a galaxy of hundreds of billions of planetary bodies, most of which were quite different, quite *alien* from Earth. A living, vibrant world of vast oceans, violet forests, and brilliant sunlight, Zeta Doradus was best known as the place of First Contact—Humankind's first meeting with an extrasolar species.

Two of them—Gru'mulkisch and Dra'ethde—stood before Koenig now, looking up at him with almost comical twists to their stalked eyes—four apiece, rising from the spidery, flattened, sixteen-legged bodies covered in a velvety-brown leather patterned with gold and blue reticulations. Humans called them "bugs" or "spiders," but in fact they were not much like either, with unsegmented bodies, an unpleasant mode of eating through their bellies, and sixteen limbs—short at the back and quite long at the front. Both were female; their male companions, like the mates of female Angler fish on Earth, were small parasites attached to their bodies. Properly, the beings were known as *Agletsch*.

"The masters have told us nothing, President Koenig," Gru'mulkisch said, speaking through the small translation device affixed to what might approximate its chest. "It is not in their nature to do so, yes-no?"

"Are you certain that the attackers at Omega Centauri were Sh'daar?" Dra'ethde added. "Others might use the ancient transport systems. Others occupy the Great Deeps of the stars."

Koenig glared at the two small aliens. He'd known these two particular individuals for a long time, ever since he'd commanded CBG-18. When the fleet had departed for Operation Crown Arrow, striking deep into Sh'daar space in order to buy time for a desperate Earth, he'd taken them along as native guides.

It was still difficult sometimes to follow how they thought. Their social conventions were strange—their need for privacy when they ate, for example. These two seemed to have been around forever, and had aged, outwardly at least, not at all. He didn't know how their life span compared with that of humans. Were they still young? Old? Did age even make a difference for entities so alien, so different physically and emotionally from Humankind?

Generally, the Agletsch seemed friendly, unassuming, and at times eager to help . . . though they were not always forthcoming with important information. The Agletsch were interstellar traders. What they traded was information, exchanging data about star systems and life forms and interstellar civilizations for information about Earth and humanity, occasionally leavened with the stores of heavy elements that appeared to be a common medium of trade throughout the known galaxy, in particular platinum, iridium, rhenium, as well as some of the longer-half-lived artificials—neptunium-237, and californium-251.

And they gave *nothing* away for free.

"There are times," Koenig told them, "when we do not ask you to sell us information because we do not know what to ask. If there is a threat to my species—whether it's the Sh'daar or some other predatory race out there, I want to know about it."

"This we understand, Mr. President Koenig," Dra'ethde told him. "And if we had something definite to trade to you on the matter, we would be certain you were aware of the fact, yes-no? But in this instance we are . . . *bleep*!"

Koenig smiled. Agletsch translators sometimes encountered concepts they couldn't handle in English, and the result was a brief, shrill, electronic tone. In twenty years, the Agletsch had gotten a lot better with English, but they still occasionally bleeped out.

"We are as ignorant as are you," Gru'mulkisch supplied.

"I see." Agletsch translations could also sometimes come across as blunt to the point of rudeness.

"The destruction of your *Endeavor*," Dra'ethde continued, "may well have been caused by Sh'daar forces . . . possibly by elements of the Sh'daar Network in disagreement with current policies."

"The Sh'daar don't speak with one voice?" Koenig said, feigning surprise. "How very . . . human! I never would have thought it of them!"

"The Sh'daar Network is unimaginably vast," Gru'mulkisch told him, missing the irony in Koenig's voice, "extending, as it does, across a large part of this galaxy, and across an immense gulf of time. There can be, there often is . . . dissonance among disparate parts of the system."

"They have my sympathies," Koenig said with dry amusement.

Who speaks for Earth? That had been the cry of Carl Sagan, a late-twentieth-century cosmologist and philosopher. After four centuries, it was still an open question. It was interesting that the galaxy-spanning Sh'daar, unimaginably more advanced than Humankind, had the same problem.

"What you call the Black Rosette, however," Dra'ethde said, "remains a mystery to us. Over hundreds of millions of years, it has evolved into something quite beyond its builders' original intent . . . beyond even their imaginings, yesno?"

"Evolved how?"

The two Agletsch went into a momentary huddle, conversing with each other in a rapid-fire burst of eructations. Native Agletsch speech was produced by a kind of controlled belching impossible for humans to imitate. Their translation devices handled English fairly well . . . and also translated burps to *Drukrhu*, an artificial trade pidgin that had established the Agletsch as the galaxy's premier data traders, diplomats, and interspecies liaisons.

The two faced Koenig again. "Since there is no certainty," Gru'mulkisch said, "since the information is largely supposition, we expect only first-level compensation."

Koenig opened a window in his mind and entered a thoughtclicked notation. Trade with the Agletsch was based on a well-established scale of prices for specific types of information. Some things—a complete description of a previously unknown alien star-faring civilization, for instance, including their location within the galaxy and a description of their world, were classified as Level Eight, and had a base price of some tens of tons of rhenium, or slightly less of artificial heavy elements. If Geneva could add new information to the exchange, the price in metals came down . . . but in fact there was surprisingly little that Humankind knew that the Agletsch did not. Earth depended on heavy metals as the medium of exchange with the interstellar trading network.

And as head of the USNA, Koenig had to check large transfers of metal with the government in Geneva.

This time, though, he could make the decision by himself. Level One information could be obtained for only a few hundred kilograms of rhenium or iridium, an amount easily within the reserve capabilities of North America.

"Done," he said. "Is half platinum, half iridium okay?"

"Satisfactory," Gru'mulkisch said. "As you put it . . . done."

"You are aware, of course," Dra'ethde told him, "of the Six Suns located within the N'gai Cloud of nine hundred million years ago. . . ."

The virtual panorama around Koenig shifted, showing now a view recorded by the *America* twenty years earlier, within the core of Omega Centauri $T_{-0.876gy}$. The planetary surface was gone, and Koenig now drifted in open space, a space completely filled by brilliant stars. Ahead, six particular stars blazed in a hexagon flattened by an off-center viewing perspective, each blue-hued and intensely brilliant. They burned so brightly that the near-solid wall of millions of bright background stars faded into the haze of light, lost in the glare.

Looking away, Koenig saw silhouettes against the encircling haze—several small worlds visible as perfectly black disks, along with a number of smaller, more complicated structures—deep-space factories or bases, perhaps— along with several immense starships. Two minute knots of gold and blue-white fuzz marked a pair of artificial singularities—Sh'daar Nodes leading to other, distant locations in space and time.

"Of course," Koenig said. The image, he realized, was being stopped down to tolerable levels by the software running this digital illusion. Had he been seeing those brilliant stars as they really appeared from that distance—roughly 300 million kilometers, two thousand times the distance between Earth and Sol—he would have been immediately, searingly blinded.

"These stars," Dra'ethde continued, "were artificially created by merging lesser, older suns together, yes-no? Each of those stars masses some forty times the mass of your Sol. They were positioned roughly fifty astronomical units from one another, and set into motion about their common center of gravity."

Koenig nodded understanding. Human astronomers had

known of the phenomenon within globular clusters called "blue stragglers" for centuries. Stars were so close-packed within the heart of such clusters that collisions were fairly common at the core. When two ancient red giants merged, they formed a single new star, a blue-hot stellar resurrection, young and hot, an anomaly among millions of ancient red suns.

"The ur-Sh'daar," Gru'mulkisch said, "engineered the merging of old stars to create more massive, younger stars. Our supposition is that they created the stellar hexagram you see here to create multiple gateways through space and time."

"The rapid rotation of these super-massive stars would distort the region of space between them," Dra'ethde added, "opening a myriad of what you call wormholes, and allowing rapid passage from one region of spacetime to another."

"We'd already figured that much out twenty years ago," Koenig told them. There was even a term for the process now: *stellarchetecture*, using entire stars to build artificial structures or devices on a literally astronomical scale. "But the TRGA cylinders—the Sh'daar Nodes—those already do that. How are the Six Suns different?"

"A Sh'daar Node is only about one of your kilometers wide," Dra'ethde told him, "and involves the mass of one star the size of your sun. The hexagon of six stars is nearly one hundred of your astronomical units across . . . roughly fifteen billion times larger than a TRGA cylinder, and with a total system mass of two hundred forty of your suns. The number of distinct and separate spacetime paths through the volume defined by the Six Suns is not infinite, but may be a number so large as to be indistinguishable from infinity in any practical sense."

"We estimate ten to the twenty-six distinct spacetime pathways," Gru'mulkisch said.

Koenig gave a low whistle. One octillion paths. That was more than any survey could possibly map, a number that might as well be infinite. "Why would they *want* so many?" He asked.

"In part," Dra'ethde said, "the Six Suns were designed as a cultural center, a kind of monument to the greatness of ur-Sh'daar technology and power. There is also evidence that they were . . . experimenting with the structure space."

"Experimenting how?" Koenig asked.

"We believe that the Six Suns served as a portal to other destinations than ordinary spacetime," Gru'mulkisch told him. "They may have been trying to reach another universe, another *brane* altogether."

The shock of the cold statement was like a blow. They'd been trying to reach not just a remote region of space and time, but another *universe*?

For centuries, now, cosmologists had hypothesized a large number of universes—possibly an infinite number—existing side by side within a kind of higher dimension or hyperspace physicists called *the bulk*. Each universe in this series was called a *brane*, from *membrane*, and appeared flat—two-dimensional, like a sheet—from the perspective of the bulk, but three-dimensional and coexistent with the other universes when viewed from within. Such a "universe of universes" was called the *multiverse*.

By definition, those other universes were forever unreachable, completely unconnected with the familiar universe of Sol and Earth and all that Humankind knew. Each existed as a self-contained and isolated sphere of existence with its own set of physical laws, its own nested set of time lines, its own reality. This was something quite different from the more familiar *branching* of reality invoked in discussions of time travel in order to exorcise the dreaded grandfather paradox. Such branching universes—the so-called many-worlds solution to the Copenhagen Interpretation of quantum physics—*were* accessible if time travel into the past was possible. Koenig himself had proven that accessibility by reaching Omega Centauri $T_{-0.876gy}$.

Whether unreachable branes or the accessible temporal branches of a quantum tree properly described the multiverse—or whether reality somehow incorporated *both* types of parallel universes—was still a matter of heated discussion. Physicists had proven the existence of alternate universes in the mid twenty-first century by showing that some types of subatomic particles that seemed to vanish from this universes in fact had moved . . . someplace else, but they still argued about what might be on the other side.

By definition, there was no way to reach another brane, and yet Gru'mulkisch was telling him that the ur-Sh'daar had managed to do so . . . or at least that they'd tried. The mere fact that they'd attempted it said something profound about the level of that civilization's technology . . . and about their understanding, their mastery of the cosmos.

"So . . . I was asking you about the evolution of the Six Suns," Koenig said after digesting this information. "We've already figured out that the Black Rosette is what the Six Suns turned into . . . *evolved* into. Stars with forty times the mass of Sol would be ephemeral . . . a lifetime of only a few million years."

The more massive a star, the greater the pressures within its core, and the faster it burns through its supply of hydrogen before detonating as a supernova or, for the most massive stars, as an even more powerful hypernova. What's left after the explosion is most of the star's mass compacted down to a black hole, a singularity with gravity so powerful that not even light could escape.

"Yes," Gru'mulkisch said. Her four stalked eyes twisted in a dizzying and untranslatable pattern. "We're not sure how long the Six Suns existed in their original configuration. The ur-Sh'daar built them, merging sun with sun over the course of millions of years to keep them burning. The Sh'daar, however, apparently lost this technology and, eventually, all six of the stars aged, exploded, and collapsed. Over many more hundreds of millions of years, the black holes descended into tighter and faster orbits, until they became what you call the Black Rosette."

"The Black Rosette," Dra'ethde added, "covers a much smaller area of space, of course. However, the gravitational vortices it generates are, we calculate, much more numerous, much more far reaching than the ur-Sh'daar originally planned."

"More than an octillion spacetime pathways?"

"Considerably more. It may reach across a large portion of the multiverse, and involve both the creation and the destruction of this universe."

Koenig was silent for a long moment. When he didn't respond immediately, Gru'mulkisch added, "We told you that much of this is supposition on our part."

"I know," Koenig said. "I was just realizing what it was like to be a small child getting his first glimpse of a quantum power tap."

"I do not understand," Gru'mulkisch said.

"It looks *so* pretty," Koenig said, "with that blue glow surrounding a couple of orbiting microsingularities . . . but I'm a kid and I have no idea at all what it does, how it works . . . and I don't realize that if I'm not *very* careful, it could swallow me whole."

Chapter Five

Sh'daar Node
Texaghu Resch System
210 Light Years from Sol
1024 hours, TFT

Red Mike fell clear of the TRGA cylinder's entry, once again back in Time Now. Ahead, the Marine light carrier *Nassau* waited with her escorts. Mike sent the coded, tightly compacted message declaring his arrival and accelerated for home.

"Welcome back, Red Mike," a voice said within the probe's consciousness. "Happy birthday!"

It took Red Mike several seconds to decide what the officer on board the carrier was talking about. AI reconnaissance probes are not in the habit, after all, of thinking about *birthdays*.

But he could reason, within certain parameters, and he did possess a simple outline of history within his files, designed to give him both context and a framework for his conversations with humans. The date—November 10—was the 694th anniversary of the creation of the original Continental Marines, at Tun Tavern, Philadelphia in 1775. The later United States Marines and, now, the USNA Marines, continued the tradition of observing this date with what amounted to a religious fervor, celebrating it with parades, speeches, cake cuttings, and formal balls wherever possible. The *Nassau*, a tiny microcosm of the Corps with several thousand Marines embarked on board, was no exception.

Red Mike was as incurious about human traditions and customs as he was about anything else not specifically within his purview, but the birthday greeting did raise one question. If the Marines were busy cutting cakes and making speeches . . . were they ready for what appeared to be gathering just on the other side of the Sh'daar Node?

TC/USNA CVS America
USNA Naval Base
Quito Synchorbital
0840 hours, TFT

Gray was in his office going through the daily briefings when Rear Admiral Steiger's avatar entered Gray's inward awareness. "Excuse me. Sandy?"

"Yes, sir?"

"I've been directed to link with Geneva for a strategic conference. I'd like my flag captain there with me."

"Yes, Admiral. That sounds promising. You think we're getting our flight orders?"

"I do. The question is, what's our destination?"

Gray gave a mental shrug. "Seems fairly obvious to me, sir. All of those simulations of a deployment to Omega Cent we've been running . . . and then we get word of the *Endeavor*."

"Maybe . . . maybe. Unless the Confed Senate decides we need to block the Slan at 36 Oph. But the real question may be *when* is our destination?"

"Through the TRGA? Maybe so. But we're going to need more than a carrier battlegroup to take on the Tee-sub minus Sh'daar. When is the linkup?"

"Twenty minutes."

Gray checked his inner clock. Nine hundred, then. Barely time to download the latest intel feeds. "I'll be there, Admiral."

There was a lot to go through. Nano reconnaissance probes returning from the 70 Ophiuchi star system suggested that the Turusch and Nungiirtok were preparing for something, bringing in more forces from elsewhere. Probes from 36 Ophiuchi seemed to show the Slan working on consolidating their conquest. More ships were arriving in-system, *big* ships. Likely they were digging in, preparing for a possibly human counterattack . . . but it was also possible that they were preparing a new assault of their own, one aimed, quite probably, at Earth.

And there was more. Signals Intelligence satellites in the Kuiper Belt had picked up the whisper of high-velocity microprobes churning through the fabric of space on outbound vectors, and the likeliest explanation was that Sh'daar clients were already scouting the solar system in preparation for an attack.

Gray was put rather forcibly in mind of the situation President Koenig—then *Admiral* Koenig, commander of CBG-18, had faced twenty years ago. Convinced that the only way to stop the expected Sh'daar assault on the Sol System was to take the war into Sh'daar space, Koenig had arranged to miss expected Confederation Naval Command orders to stay in Solar space by leaving before they arrived. Later, he'd fought a French squadron sent to bring the "rogue" battlegroup in.

The decision, as it turned out, had been the right one. A renewed Sh'daar assault on Earth had not materialized, and Koenig had gone on to discover their spacetime and force a truce. Biographers had pointed out, however, that had he been wrong Koenig would have been reviled as the man who'd abandoned Earth to the Sh'daar forces.

The Confederation might well want the battlegroup to stick close to the Sol System, just in case the Sh'daar struck out from Ophiuchus.

It was time. Gray alerted his personal AI that he was not

to be disturbed, then opened a channel through to Admiral Steiger. The Admiral's AI routed the connection to Geneva, and Gray found himself in a virtual conference.

The European Unionists tended to be conservative in their virtual backgrounds. The venue was a large conference room, with two walls and the ceiling set as windows, the other two walls showing gently shifting abstracts of pastel light. Twelve men and women were seated around the conference table—it had the appearance of mahogany—half in EU military uniforms, the others in civilian dress. Through the windows, Gray could see the labyrinth of the Plaza of Light outside, a hundred stories down . . . and beyond it, the glitter of late-afternoon sunlight on Lake Geneva.

"Admiral Steiger," a bearded EU admiral named Longuet said. "Captain Gray. Thank you for linking in. We need to discuss a change to your upcoming mission."

"We feel that a deployment to Omega Centauri is not . . . *critical* at this time," one of the civilians added. Her name was Ilse Roettgen, and she was the president of the Confederation Senate.

"Indeed, ma'am?" Steiger said. "Our operational plan has been set for some weeks, now. In light of the new reconnaissance information from Omega Centauri, it seems to me that the mission is, if anything, more critical than ever."

"*Not* in light of the information from 36 Ophiuchi," Admiral Longuet said.

"We are in the process of assembling a strike force," another civilian said. Gilberto Lupi was the Brazilian imperial minister of Defense. "We intend to take back 36 Ophiuchi, before the enemy entrenches himself, before he becomes too strong for us to oust him."

"I see," Steiger said. "And I take it you've consulted with my government on this?"

"There is no need," Longuet replied. "We are invoking Military First Right."

Gray felt an inner jolt at that, a kind of psychic shock. Military First Right? After almost three centuries, it was possible that the *Pax Confeoderata* was about to fail.

And when it did, the USNA Star Navy would be smack at the heart of the storm.

First Right had not been invoked before, not since it had been passed by the Confederation Senate twelve years earlier. The law was assumed to be unenforceable in America. It looked like that assumption was about to be tested.

The Confederation had arisen from the ashes of the Second Sino-Western War, a sharp and brutal conflict fought in the first half of the twenty-second century. The Battle of Wormwood and the subsequent fall of a small asteroid into the Atlantic Ocean had seriously weakened the old United States politically, forcing the union, first, of several North American nations into the USNA, followed by the merging of the USNA with the newly founded Earth Confederation. Under the original terms of the amalgamation, each member state kept control of its own military—especially its spaceborne forces. For a state's military to be put under the direct control of the Geneva government required, literally, an act of that state's congress . . . in the case of the USNA by a two-thirds' majority vote in both the Senate and the House.

But in 2412, Geneva had passed the Military First Right Act over two dissenting votes, Great Britain and the USNA. The star navies of Earth's Confederation were the property, the military arm, and the responsibility of the Earth Confederation, not of any lone member state. North America, of course, and Great Britain had disagreed. For the two of them, ancient allies, the Earth Confederation had always been a loose alignment of independent nation-states, a planetary government more in name than in fact.

That this belief put the USNA at odds with every other Confederation member state save one seemed to have mattered little. Not until the Sh'daar Ultimatum in 2367 had there been a serious need for a united Earth military . . . and even then, the union had been an awkward and incomplete cooperation rather than a single-fleet command. Military First Right had been intended to change that . . . and, obviously, to prevent a repeat of the so-called Koenig's Mutiny, which had led to his defeat of a combined French-British fleet at HD157950 in 2405.

That Koenig's decision had been *right* was immaterial. He'd decided to face the Sh'daar forces in their own space, rather than assuming a purely defensive posture within Earth's solar system, but, in so doing, left Earth open to a possible attack . . . an attack that, thank God, had never materialized. Geneva had acted to prevent such a situation from ever happening again—or, at least, so they'd planned it. That the Military First Right Act might backfire on them and lead to a civil war and the collapse of the Confederation seemed never to have entered their minds.

"This," Longuet said, indicating another Confederation officer at the virtual table, "is Admiral Christian Delattre. He and his squadron are en route now to join the *America* battlegroup at Synchorbit. He will be assuming command of the battlegroup, at which point he will transfer his flag to the *America*, which shall become his flagship. Admiral Steiger, you will remain in command of the USNA battlegroup, but you will take your orders directly from Admiral Delattre. Is this understood?"

"I will need confirming orders from Columbus, sir," Steiger said.

"No, Admiral, you will not," Mykhaylo Serheyev said. Gray had to check a mental sidebar to see who the man was—the prime minister of the Ukrainian Union. "The Act of Military First Right is specific on this point. There was a final vote on this in Geneva just this morning, one that passed with a comfortable majority. Carrier Battlegroup Eighteen is now under direct Confederation control."

"Nevertheless," Steiger said, "it is my duty as a USNA officer to confirm these orders through my own government."

"Of course, feel free to consult with your government," Roettgen said. "But you *are* now working for us."

"And if you resist, gentlemen," Longuet added, "you will be replaced by officers who see political reason, by *Confederation* officers without your, ah, conflict of interest."

And with a jolt, Gray was back in his office, alone with the monitors and virtual screens at his workstation. He and Steiger, it seemed, had just been summarily dismissed.

Not good, he thought. *Not good at all. . . .*

Executive Office, USNA
Columbus, District of Columbia
United States of North America
1215 hours, EST

"Ms. Valcourt would like a moment for consultation, Mr. President," his secretarial AI told him. "She says it is *most* urgent."

Koenig looked up from a report displayed on his desktop—the Confederation robotic freighter *Dione* was landing at Giordano Bruno Base on the moon with an un-usually large shipment of supplies—and sighed. He'd been expecting this. "Very well. Link me in."

Julie Valcourt, a Canadian, was Speaker of the North American House, and one of Koenig's more powerful op-ponents in the government. A member of the Global Union party, she was an outspoken advocate for the Global Union platform—that the USNA must fully integrate into the Con-federation government.

"Good afternoon, Mr. President," she said. "I haven't yet had the opportunity to congratulate you on your victory."

"Thank you, Madam Speaker," Koenig replied. He knew, however, that congratulations were not the primary thought on Valcourt's mind. The woman never did *anything* without a frank political motive behind it. "That's very kind of you."

"Not at all. The people, as they say, have spoken."

"Well, some of them have."

The news downloads were calling Koenig's election vic-tory a landslide and a popular mandate, but Koenig knew better. The population of North America currently stood at nearly three quarters of a billion people. Of those, perhaps half had bothered to link in and vote, and the only reason that the Freedom party had won was the stark fact that the Global Unionists and the Progressives hadn't been able to agree on a common anti-Freedomist platform. The Progressives, like Koenig's own Freedomists, wanted to extend the franchise to AIs; the Unionists feared the loss of human sovereignty and the possibility of second-class status for organic citizens somewhere down the line. But the Progressives felt that the military needed to be run by the Confederation, which of course was where they parted company with the Freedomists.

As a result the Progressives and the Unionists had knocked each other out of the running . . . but Koenig remained painfully aware that he'd been re-elected with just 44 percent of the vote. Despite the fireworks displays and enthusiastic mobs in the concourse, less than a quarter of North America's population had actually voted for him.

"I thought," Valcourt continued, "that you should know that the Europeans are going to be trouble."

"Tell me something I don't know."

"They approached me yesterday with a question."

"Yes?"

"Is the USNA population going to accept a Confederation take-over of our military?"

"Military First Right," Koenig said, nodding. "I know."

"You *know*?"

"I was informed a few hours ago. Geneva has assumed command of one of our carrier battlegroups."

"I . . . didn't think they would move this quickly. Have you agreed to this?"

"Apparently, it doesn't matter whether we agree or not. The battlegroup commander was simply told how it would be. We need to decide how we're going to respond, however. We could refuse. . . ."

"Civil war? A complete break with the Confederation?"

"It could come to that." He thought for a moment. "Tell me, Madam Speaker, how did they approach you? In person?"

"No. It was a direct e-link."

"Did you record it?"

"Apparently, Mr. President, the link was one-view specific."

"Ah."

E-links allowed data to be downloaded directly into the hardware nanotechnically grown within most people's brains. Neural connections allowed what amounted to telepathy, mind-to-mind, as well as the downloading of information from the Global Net, direct interfaces with AIs or with machines—anything from a spacecraft to a door. And anything that was downloaded, from a conversation to an encyclopedia reference, could be stored . . . usually. Private messages could be embedded with code that erased the data as it was being transferred to memory. The recipient retained his or her organic memory of the message—though this was often fuzzy and indistinct, like the fast-evaporating memory of a dream—but there was nothing on record, nothing that could be uploaded to a database as, say, evidence for criminal proceedings.

"That message could be interpreted as an attempt by a foreign government to manipulate the election," Koenig said.

" 'Foreign government'? Sir, this is the *Confederation* we're talking about! *Earth's* government!"

"The relationship of the USNA to the Confederation is still . . . let's just say it's still being tested. What I'm saying is that interfering with a nation's choice of its own government violates the provisions of the Confederation Charter."

"We've been part of the Confederation for three hundred years! We were one of the founding states of the Pax!"

"Yes, and the original constitution stated that each nation within the Pax was sovereign, that it would determine its own form of government and that it would retain control of its own military forces. This First Right thing is something new . . . an abridgement, an *erosion* of our rights under that charter."

"Sometimes, rights must be surrendered for the good of the whole," Valcourt said. "An individual doesn't have the right to kill another person, where a national government can wage war and kill millions."

Koenig gave a mental shrug. "I know we don't agree on this, Madam Speaker. Just how did you reply to the question?"

"About how our citizens would respond to Geneva taking control of our military? I told them to take a look at the celebrations going on outside in the Freedom Concourse," she said. "It would appear that the citizenry approves of less interference from Geneva, not more."

"And their response?"

"They said that things change, situations change . . . and that the people can be led. That, after all, is the whole purpose of government."

"I would say that government is supposed to express the will of the people, and to secure and protect that people's rights. 'Life, liberty, and the pursuit of happiness,' remember?"

"I would suggest, Mr. President, that you are a few centuries out of date. Those words were destroyed when the Chinese dropped Wormwood into the Atlantic Ocean."

Koenig sighed. Sometimes he *did* feel out of date. "Shall we agree to disagree, Madam Speaker? Once again?"

"My apologies, sir. I didn't intend that to sound impertinent."

"Not at all." He hesitated. "I'm curious, though. What were these . . . Europeans, you say? What did they want from you? Why did they approach you?"

"I think they genuinely wanted to know how we Americans would react to the invoking of the Military Rights Act. They approached me because I am the Speaker of the House . . . which means, technically at least, that I speak for the American people." Her image gave a wan smile. "After this past election, I doubt that that will be so for much longer."

Koenig nodded. Valcourt represented an uneasy alliance within the House—Unionists, Progressives, and a half dozen smaller parties, including the Reclamationists, the

New Order Socialists, and the Popular Neodemocrats—and as such she'd been the face and the voice of the loyal opposition throughout most of his first term as president.

The term *loyal opposition* had just taken on a new, stronger meaning for Koenig. Valcourt had come to him with the warning, rather than seeking political advantage for herself or her party through some kind of alliance with Geneva. He was impressed. He'd not known Julie Valcourt was capable of passing up a political opportunity.

"I don't know about that, Madam Speaker," he told her. "There's nothing like a threat from outside to pull a people together, and let them know they're all working for the same goal."

"We'll have to see about that, Mr. President. For now, though . . . I must ask you. What are you going to do about this . . . this power grab? Will you risk a civil war?"

"I don't know, Madam Speaker. Like I said, I only heard about it a few hours ago."

"A delicate situation, sir."

"Delicate doesn't tell the half of it. If I give in, I set a precedent, and it'll be all but impossible to reverse it. If I refuse, even if we don't end up in a civil war, Earth will end up divided and scattered, unable to agree on a common front against the Sh'daar."

" 'Who speaks for Earth?' " Valcourt quoted.

"You mentioned the Europeans. Do you think there's a faction within the Confederation? A split we could use?"

"I'm not sure. I think Brazil has sided with the EU. Russia may be undecided. Ukraine is with the Europeans. I think North India and the EAS are sitting on the fence, waiting to see how it all shakes out."

"Pretty much business as usual," Koenig said. "China and the Theocracy will be watching closely too, but I suspect they'll be siding with us."

Neither China nor the Islamist Theocracy were members of the Confederation . . . the gulfs left by several world wars continued to exclude them from a world government.

Which, of course, meant that the Confederation wasn't

truly a world government, did not, in fact, represent a united Earth.

"I'm terrified, Mr. President, that this is going to end in world war. Humankind may not survive. If it does, it will not be able to resist the Sh'daar when they finally come."

"On that, Madam Speaker, you and I are in complete agreement," Koenig told her. "I just wish I could see a third alternative. . . ."

TC/USNA CVS America
USNA Naval Base
Quito Synchorbital
1315 hours, TFT

"Here they come, Captain," Connie Fletcher told him. "They're making the most of it, aren't they?"

"You think that display is just to impress us?" Gray replied.

"Maybe they just want to impress themselves," Admiral Steiger observed. "Kind of like team spirit, y'know?"

The Confederation flotilla was decelerating into synchronous orbit, inbound from Mars after a two-hour passage. Those warships, Gray knew, had been assembled from all across the Sol System, and several had arrived over the past few days from the nearer extrasolar colonies—Chiron, Hel, New Earth, Bifrost Orbital, Santo Iago, and Thoth.

In the van were four star carriers—the British *Illustrious*, the North Indian *Kali*, the European Union's *Klemens von Metternich*, and the EAS *Simon Bolivar*—light carriers measuring from 600 to 850 meters from their mushroom caps to the ends of their drive stems.

In a loose swarm of vessels moving astern and on the flanks were fifty-one additional Confederation warships, from fleet gunboats and light bombardment vessels to Admiral Delattre's flagship, the massive railgun cruiser *Napoleon*. With tightly controlled bursts from their plasma maneuvering thrusters, the Confederation fleet began edging toward the open gantries of the synchorbital military docking complex.

"Fifty-five warships," Gray observed. "That's a hell of a lot of team spirit. They outnumber us, that's for sure."

The *America* battlegroup currently numbered just twenty-four vessels, though eight more USNA warships were docked at the Quito Synchorbital, undergoing repairs or refits. The Confederation fleet was trying deliberately to overawe the North-American squadron, of that Gray was certain. He wondered if Steiger was going to roll over and play dead on this one. Steiger had commanded a number of vessels before his appointment as CO CBG-40, but it had been a long time since he'd seen combat. Word was he'd been a lieutenant commander in the CAG office on board *America* during Crown Arrow twenty years ago. He might be pretty rusty.

But then, it had been twenty years since Gray had seen combat, and he was rusty as well. The Sh'daar Truce had been two decades of quiet . . . no raids, no planetary assaults, and even potential human enemies—the Islamists and the Chinese Hegemony, for instance—had been keeping a non-confrontational profile.

Training sims helped maintain basic skills, but they were no substitute for the real thing.

The big question about Steiger was how aggressive he might be. Where Gray had been wearing a Starhawk at Alphekka and Omega Cent, Steiger had been driving a console in PriFly—not at all the same thing.

Gray frowned at the thought as soon as it arose and pushed it aside. Steiger was the CO, and that meant he required the loyalty and the full support of every officer in the battlegroup. His normally laid-back attitude didn't mean he wasn't a fighter; look at Koenig, the CO of CBG-18. The man certainly wasn't a coward, not with something like twenty-five years in the service.

But would the man be able to stand up to what amounted to a naked Confederation power play?

Gray didn't know. He wasn't sure *he* would be able to

refuse direct orders from Geneva, not when doing so might well result in civil war.

What he *did* know was that the parade of Confederation warships sidling up to the docking gantries out there was nothing less than a cold-blooded threat.

Chapter Six

Intermundi
Civilian Sector Green 7,
Quito Synchorbital
1915 hours, TFT

Lieutenant Donald Gregory leaned back in his seat, taking another deep inhale of firedust from the golden sphere in his left hand. The nanometer-sized particles were absorbed directly through his sinus cavities and into his bloodstream, triggering a release of dopamine in his brain and a sharp, rippling wave of pleasure surging through his body. He gasped, then went rigid for a moment as the wave peaked, then ebbed. "Oh, yeah . . ."

His right hand was clasped tight around the bare waist of Lieutenant Jodi Vaughn, who giggled as he started to come down from the hit. "Good stuff, huh?"

"Babe, right now I'm *flying*! Wrapped up in metaspace and 'cubing at max!"

They were in the Intermundi, a club located just outside the synchorbital naval base catering mostly to military personnel. Gregory had had the duty tonight, but Teddy Nichols had been willing to swap with him, allowing him to keep his date with Jodi. Located within a huge, rotating wheel, the club featured numerous small rooms heavily draped and cushioned, providing privacy and comfort, and with hidden arrays of netlink connections to cater to every pleasure need.

Firesmoke was not addictive . . . not *physically*, at least, though Gregory had heard of pilots who'd developed emotional dependencies and needed partial memory wipes to shake them. Smoke worked through cerebral implants, which meant you could fine-tune the effect and clear the neural pathways afterward. The registered forms, served in joints like the Intermundi, were completely legal, though shipboard regulation frowned on using the stuff. They came down hard on you if you let it knock you off the duty roster.

But it felt *good* . . . BETS, as the slang put it, Better Than Sex. And you could hit it again and again and . . .

"You want some more?" he asked her.

She accepted the sphere, held the sweet spot up to her face, and breathed in, her eyes closed. Firesmoke actually consisted of artificially manufactured receptor-key molecules tucked away inside C_{64} buckyballs . . . carbon spheres so tiny they formed a nearly invisible mist. They were absorbed straight through the mucus lining of the sinus cavities, hitched a ride on blood vessels leading into the brain, and then unfolded inside the pleasure centers for a quick, hard jolt of pure ecstasy.

Gregory watched Vaughn inhale the nanodust, watched the bright red flush spread down her throat and shoulders and across her breasts. They'd been sex partners now for more than four months, ever since just after she'd joined the squadron. What had started as a casual recreational fling had been . . . changing lately, growing into something deeper.

He still wasn't sure how he felt about that.

Gregory liked Jodi Vaughn, liked her a *lot*. In a service that tended to attract aristocratic hotshots and fast burners, she was an attractive brunette from the Chicago megalopolis with neither money nor political connections. Rumor had it she'd started off as a Prim, an inhabitant of the half-submerged badlands of the Periphery in what once had been the city of Baltimore.

Rising sea levels had flooded the city in the late twenty-first century; Wormwood Fall in 2132 had sent a tidal wave up the Chesapeake that had largely destroyed Baltimore's remains, along with Washington, New York, Miami, and other low-lying East Coast metropoli.

Over the next few decades, the old United States had abandoned the drowned and wrecked cities, vast coastal swamplands, for the most part, that became known as the Periphery. People continued to live there, and more had arrived from the more civilized reaches of the interior . . . criminals, scavengers, religious zealots escaping the laws of the White Covenant, and antitech *Prims*, primitives who didn't care for the ways that modern technology was transforming the very definition of the word *human*.

Most people didn't care for the Prims. To be antitechnology alone meant you weren't going to fit in with most people. It meant you were different. An outsider.

And maybe that was why the Prim Jodi Vaughn had accepted Gregory when she'd been assigned to be his wingman. He was an Osirian colonial, perhaps the ultimate outsider, at least as far as the North Americans were concerned. She'd become his friend, and, before long, his lover. The two shared a lot in common. They'd not gone out of their way to flaunt their relationship, but some of the others in the squadron knew. Nichols, for instance. And probably that bastard Kemper as well.

With considerable affection, he watched her take another hit from the sphere.

"Full thrust engaged!" she said, then handed the sphere back, gasping a little.

"How you feeling, Wing?"

"Like I could spit in a Slan's eye."

"The Slan don't *have* eyes." He frowned. "At least we don't think they do."

"Okay . . . a Nungie's eye, then."

"Nope. They have sensor clusters that process light— well, red and orange light, anyway, and short infrared— but they're not really eyes. Squishy-looking tentacles and spongy tissue, more like."

"Okay! Okay!" She laughed. "What are those three-legged octopus things?"

He had to pull down a list of known alien species inside his head and scan through an array of photographs. There it was.

"Jivad Rallam? Okay. *They* have eyes a lot like ours, agreed. Just more of them."

"Fine. I could spit in *its* eyes. *All* of them!"

"Outstanding!"

Gregory stood up, stretching. The nanodust had left him feeling a bit light-headed and weak, almost trembling. He stepped to the entrance of their privacy area and looked up at the swimming sphere, internally lit with shifting, colored lights and hanging 20 meters above his head. Nude couples, threesomes, and a few larger groups cavorted within the shimmering globe of water.

The Intermundi Pleasure Club was an enormous structure, 100 meters across, rotating to provide about a half G of spin gravity at the outer deck, less on the elevated levels and walkways closer to the center. Outside the labyrinth of smaller privacy areas, the club's interior opened up into a vast cavern. Transparencies in the floor looked out on the slow-wheeling stars of space punctuated occasionally by a blast of light from Earth or sun; multiple decks, verandas, and soaring arches gave a multilevel fairyland effect to the architecture, and at the exact center of the space a 10-meter bubble of water hung motionless as the club rotated around it. Gregory and Vaughn had chosen an open deck well above the main floor; spin gravity here was only about a quarter G, more than the moon but less than the surface of Mars, and the water was an easy climb overhead.

"Want to go for a swim?"

"No, I want something to *eat*. I'm hungry!"

"Whatcha want?"

"I'm feeling carnivorous. Surprise me."

"One surprise, coming up." He palmed a contact on the entrance to their cube, scrolled through the menu that opened in his mind, and selected Steak Imperial for two.

What arrived in the receiver a moment later, hissing and moist, had never been within 36,000 kilometers of the Brazilian Empire, but the program that had assembled the component atoms and heated them to palatability had been designed by world-class chefs—probably AI chefs—and could not be distinguished from tissue that once had been alive and roaming the pampas south of the Amazon Sea.

"How do you think it's going to end?" she asked him later, as they ate.

"What?"

"I was just thinking . . . so many alien species out there, and most of them seem to be on board with the Sh'daar and out to get us. We can't face them *all*."

Gregory shrugged. "Yeah, well, they seem pretty disjointed, don't they? The Turusch attack us here . . . the H'rulka attack there . . . then the Nungies show up someplace else with their little Kobold buddies. They're all as different from one another as any of them are from humans. Coordination, planning, even basic communication must be a real bear for them."

The thought was not original with Gregory, but had been circulating through the squadrons as a series of morale downloads from the Personnel Department. It was propaganda . . . but it was propaganda based on fact and that actually made sense.

The Turusch were things like partially armored slugs that worked in tightly bound pairs and communicated by heterodyning meaning into two streams of blended, humming tones. The H'rulka were gas bags a couple of hundred meters across; they had parasites living in their tentacle forests that were larger than individual humans. The Nungiirtok were 3 meters tall and very vaguely humanoid . . . except that what was inside that power armor they wore was not even remotely human. The Jivad were like land-dwelling octopi that swarmed along on three tightly coiled tentacles, and used both speech and color changes in their skin patterns to communicate. The Slan used sonar as their primary sense, rather than a single weak, light-sensing organ, and apparently could focus multiple sound beams so tightly that they could "see" as well as a human; they couldn't perceive color, of course, but according to the xenosoph people they could tell what you'd had for breakfast and watch your heart beating and your blood flowing when they "looked" at you. Communication for them appeared to be in ultrasound frequencies, patterns of rapid-fire clicks at wavelengths well beyond the limits of human hearing.

"That shouldn't matter that much, should it?" Vaughn said. "I mean . . . those translators the Agletsch wear seem to work pretty well. Communications wouldn't be that much of a problem for them."

"No, it *is* a problem," Gregory replied, "and a big one. Alien biology means an alien way of looking at the universe. Like the dolphins, y'know?"

Centuries ago, attempts to communicate with the dolphins and whales of Earth's seas had demonstrated that differences in biology dictated how a species might communicate—dolphins, for instance, simply could not form the sounds required for human speech. And different modes of speech shaped how their brains worked, how they thought of themselves and the world around them. There were, Gregory knew, AIs residing within implants in dolphin brains now designed to bridge the linguistic barriers between the species, but those translations had only proven that dolphin brains were as alien to humans as the group minds of the abyssal electrovores inhabiting the under-ice ocean of Enceladus.

"Anyway," Gregory went on, "the theory is that the different va-Sh'daar species have trouble cooperating militarily because of the biological differences among them. They're so different from one another that the damned war has dragged on for fifty-seven years, now, and they *still* haven't been able to get their act together enough to move in and swat us. And since we have the same trouble communicating with any of them, we can't really negotiate an end to it."

"But there are so many of them. Sooner or later they *will* swat us. Nice image. And we can't fight them all."

"Maybe not. But maybe we can keep fending them off one at a time. If they can't work together, we can defeat them separately."

"Do you think we can?"

He shrugged. "Beats me. But fighting the bastards is better than becoming their slaves, right? *Humanity va Sh'daar.*"

No one knew how many species the Sh'daar controlled within the galaxy, not even the Agletsch. Estimates ranged from the thirty or so mentioned by various Agletsch data purchases—their so-called living *Encyclopedia Galactica*—to several thousands of civilizations scattered across half of the galaxy.

Sh'daar client species, in the Agletsch lingua franca known to humans, were properly referred to with the suffix *va Sh'daar* tacked on to the ends of their names—"Turusch va Sh'daar," for instance—a term that seemed literally to denote ownership. The fact that Sh'daar clients had tiny implants of some sort, called Seeds, might be a means of unifying the otherwise disparate species and cultures, but Confederation Intelligence had not yet been able to determine what these Seeds were capable of, or how they worked. Apparently, they gathered information and periodically uploaded it to Sh'daar communications nets, but how they might control Turusch and H'rulka and Slan forces or individuals was still unknown.

So many, many unknowns . . .

"We know they don't want us to explore certain technologies," Vaughn said after a time.

"GRIN," Gregory said, nodding. "Genetics, Robotics, Information systems, and Nanotechnology. They're afraid we're about to hit the Technological Singularity and really take off."

"Become stargods," Vaughn said, repeating a popular theme from various entertainment downloads.

Gregory was impressed. Lots of Prims didn't know much about high-tech issues—the Sh'daar Ultimatum and the Technological Singularity. But then, he'd never asked her about her Prim background. Some Prims knew a lot about modern tech; they just chose to ignore it, especially the ones who opted out of having electronic implants nanochelated inside their brains for whatever reason. Some Prims joined the military—"came in from the wet," as the old saying had it—and their training downloads required that they have the same implants as everyone else. Not for the first time, he wondered what her childhood history was . . . how she'd grown up, why she'd been a Prim, and what had led her out of that life to join the Navy.

"Problem is," Gregory said after a thoughtful moment, "we don't know exactly what it is the Sh'daar really want, or why. They want to block us from the Singularity, yeah . . . but why should what happens to us affect them? It's a damned big galaxy. . . ."

"We're not going to go along with those demands, are we?"

"Doesn't look like it. The Confederation might be willing to negotiate with the bastards . . . but I can't see President Koenig giving in by one millimeter. He'll fight before he agrees to lose our tech."

"Yeah. But can we win?"

"Maybe the best we can hope for is a standoff. Hold them at bay until . . ."

"Until what?"

"I don't know. Until we become stargods? After that, all bets are off."

For a time, they ate in silence, finishing their meals and dropping the plates and utensils into a recycler in the wall.

"That was good," Vaughn said. "I'm glad they allowed liberty again."

"Sandy Gray might have had a mutiny on his hands if he didn't," Gregory laughed. "With the Marines, especially, it being their birthday and everything. What I'm wondering, though, is if those Confed warships that pulled in this afternoon are the reason our departure was delayed."

"Scuttlebutt says that Geneva scrubbed the mission to Omega Cent." Playfully, she punched his shoulder. "Hey! Maybe you're headed for Osiris after all."

"About freakin' time if we are."

It was, Gregory thought, the uncertainty that was the

worst part of military service. You were always waiting, it seemed. Someone higher up in the hierarchy was always making the decisions, calling the shots . . . and more often than not the decisions were changed at the last moment, with the result that flight officers and enlisted personnel never knew where or when they were deploying next.

A return to Osiris. An *invasion* of Osiris, to liberate his homeworld.

He scarcely dared hope . . .

A familiar tone sounded inside his head. "Aw, shit . . ."

"Not *now*!" Vaughn cried. "*Damn* them!"

"Attention, all *America* personnel," he heard. "Liberty is cancelled. Repeat, liberty is cancelled. Return to the ship immediately. I say again . . ."

The two of them had had plans for a long and lingering evening at the pleasure club, but, once again, the Navy had intervened.

"Speaking of all BETS being off," he said with a wry smile. He rummaged inside the small hip bag he'd brought on liberty, pulled out a uniform pellet and slapped it against his chest. The contents spread out from under his hand, activated by the pressure, spreading swiftly to cover him head to toe in skin-tight Navy black, complete with rank tabs and a gold sunburst on his left chest. He picked up another pellet and tossed it to Vaughn. "Get dressed, love," he told her. "Duty calls."

It would take them perhaps fifteen minutes to get back on board the *America*.

Bridge
TC/USNA CVS America
USNA Naval Base
Quito Synchorbital
2028 hours, TFT

America was coming alive.

Sandy Gray relaxed into the virtual reality projected into his mind by the ship's AI network. He'd put in a request to link with President Koenig, and at the moment he was within the Executive Office waiting area, a virtual room equipped with chairs, a table, and floor-to-ceiling viewall imagery of space and distant worlds. One wall was particularly spectacular, showing a view taken from one of *America*'s high-velocity mail packets twenty years ago from a vantage point just outside of the dwarf galaxy that was home to the ancient Sh'daar. Visible was the sweeping expanse of the Milky Way galaxy imaged from about ten thousand light years above one outer spiral arm, looking in toward the red-orange beehive swarm of the galactic core.

America's packet was, so far, the only vessel of humanity that had looked back at the home galaxy from the outside. The vista was spectacular—billions of stars swept up together in the curves of spiral arms, interlaced with the sinuous twists of dark nebulae and the scattered blue-white gleam of rarer, brighter suns.

Gray wondered if Koenig had posted that image here to overawe visitors, to remind them of the America battle-group's visit to the remote past . . . or simply because he loved the panorama's beauty and wanted to share.

An adjoining wall displayed a live view of *America*, still tethered to her docking gantry. Another reminder, perhaps . . .

What Gray was doing—trying to get a direct mind-to-mind link with the president of the United States of North America, was technically illegal, a blatant and straightforward attempt to bypass the usual chain of command entirely. Admiral Steiger was his commanding officer . . . and normally the hierarchy went up through CO to USNA Naval Command, to the Joint Chiefs, and finally to the USNA secretary of Space Defense. The arrival of Admiral Delattre at Quito Synchorbital had dropped even more buffering layers between him and the president, including the Confederation Bureau of Extraplanetary Affairs in Geneva, but Gray was ignoring all of that and going straight to the top.

He had the *right*. Not one recognized by Geneva or USNANC, perhaps, but the right of warrior to commanding officer. They'd both been at Arcturus and Eta Boötis, at Alphekka and Texaghu Resch . . . both had been through the TRGA to another galaxy 900 million years in the past to face the Sh'daar in their home space and time. Both of them had commanded the CVS *America*, and that alone counted for a hell of a lot.

Even so, his decision had surprised him a little. Gray was still a Prim, an outsider from the Manhat Ruins, even if his decision to join the USNA Navy twenty-three years ago had conferred upon him full citizenship. And with the universal access afforded by modern neural-link communications, the barriers afforded both by differences in rank and by social status simply no longer existed. The president could refuse his link request, of course . . . but Gray didn't think that was going to happen.

They'd both been in the figurative trenches all those years ago. He looked again at the view of Earth's galaxy seen from outside and almost a billion years ago. They'd both been out *there*, so distant in time and space that you were to all intents and purposes alone, beyond the reach of orders from Earth, beyond anything save your own personal concept of duty.

"Captain Gray!" a remembered voice said, as the electronic avatar of President Koenig snapped into view. "It's good to see you again!"

"Thank you for seeing me, Mr. President."

"Not a problem. You're here because of the Confederation orders, aren't you?"

"Yes, sir. Admiral Steiger appears . . . committed to following those orders. The *new* orders. But I'm not convinced that those orders are in the best interest of the United States."

"Obviously." Koenig gave a wry grin. "You're stepping way outside of the proper chain of command here. You must think it's pretty serious."

"Yes, sir."

"Serious enough to commit an act of mutiny?"

"I . . . no, sir." Gray felt . . . flustered. Off balance. He wasn't sure what he'd expected Koenig to say, but he hadn't expected *that*. "Not mutiny. Sir, I'm here to ask your advice, not go against my oath."

"What do you think we need to do?"

"Well, for a start, something damned big and scary came out of the Black Rosette. We need to know what it is."

"Right now, I think Geneva doesn't *want* to know," Koenig said. "And whatever it is, it's a long way away."

"If our drive technology can 'cube a capital ship cross sixteen thousand light years in less than six months, I expect that Sh'daar technology can as well. Whatever destroyed the *Endeavor* could be here sometime in March. Maybe sooner. *We don't know*."

"*If* it's the Sh'daar who destroyed the *Endeavor*," Koenig reminded him. "And if it *wasn't* the Sh'daar . . . and there are reasons for doubting that it is . . . then it's somebody else, and we have no reason to assume they know where Sol is."

"What reasons, sir?"

"That we doubt the Sh'daar came out of the Black Rosette?" Koenig shrugged. "Mostly the fact that we haven't been able to ID the ships."

One of the viewalls cut to a recorded image, one taken, the block of text in one corner reported, from one of the scout vessels off of the destroyer *Herrera* and transmitted to the HVK-724 high-velocity courier that had returned to Sol with the news of the attack.

Blue-white beams snapped out from the center of the Rosette, riddling the *Endeavor*, the *Herrera*, and the *Miller*, shredding their forward water-storage tanks in expanding clouds of ice crystals, puncturing sponsons and hab modules and drive blisters. An instant later, all three vessels were enveloped in expanding plumes of plasma as hot as the core of a star. The plumes grew and merged, forming what looked like a miniature and grossly misshapen sun surrounded by minute and outward-tumbling bits of debris.

And then the ships began emerging from the soft-glowing orifice of the Black Rosette . . . tens of them—no, *hundreds*—a cloud of highly polished ovoid shapes visible only because they were reflecting the glare from the destroyed ships in their mirror-perfect reflective hulls.

And the silver objects continued to swarm as something larger, something *much* larger, slowly emerged from the Rosette. The shape looked organic—egg shapes partially overlapping one another or partially merged together—its hull mirror-smooth like the tiny spheres traveling in its shadow.

And then the vid broke off as the ship recording and transmitting the images went off-line, presumably destroyed.

"Those ships," Gray said, "what were they? I've never seen anything like them."

"Exactly. They're not Turusch, H'rulka, or any other technology with which we're familiar. And the weapon they used . . ."

"Yeah, what *was* that?"

"Antiprotons accelerated to near-light speed. They do damage by both kinetic impact and by matter-antimatter reaction."

"An AM explosion would also cause damage from the X-ray and gamma radiation it released," Gray said, thoughtful.

"Exactly. We've not run into this kind of weapons technology before. If the Sh'daar had it, they never used it on us."

"Maybe the Sh'daar have been busy inventing stuff for the last twenty years."

"Maybe . . . but not likely. Remember, the Sh'daar are *extremely* conservative, not given to tinkering with established designs or technologies. Intelligence thinks these . . . these mirror ships are something new. A new species . . . a new civilization we haven't encountered before."

"All the more reason to find out who they are, what they want . . . and why the hell they destroyed three of our ships without warning."

"I agree with you."

"Okay . . . so what would you advise, Mr. President?"

"Are you asking because I am president of the USNA?"

"No, sir. I'm asking because you were once CO CBG-18. And before that, you were Captain of the *America*. You made command decisions that were not exactly approved by Geneva."

Koenig seemed thoughtful for a moment. Was he thinking? Or remembering? "I am not going to undercut the authority of Admiral Steiger, son."

"I would not expect you to, sir."

"All I will say . . . all I *can* say, is that you will need to use your best judgment. You're going out where Geneva can't keep a tight leash on Admiral Steiger or you . . . and neither can Columbus. You'll have to use your discretion, do what *you* think is right. That's what I did."

Twenty years before, Koenig had been declared a rogue by the Confederation government when he'd violated operational orders and taken the carrier battlegroup off to face the Sh'daar on his own. They'd sent a pan-European squadron out to bring him home. Had his gamble not worked, he would likely still be in a Confederation correctional institution on Mars or Triton.

Assuming, of course, that Earth and the human species still survived.

"Admiral Steiger is a good man," Koenig added after a moment. "He knows what he's doing. Follow his lead, support his decisions, and watch his back. That's what a good flag captain does."

"Yes, sir."

"Beyond that, all I will tell you is that when you get out there, your duty is to your conscience . . . and to the human species. Not to Geneva, not to Columbus, and not to me . . . because you're going to be well beyond the reach of any human government."

"Yes, sir." Gray hesitated. "It occurred to me, though . . ."

"What?"

"These new orders put over a quarter of the USNA fleet under the direct command of the Confederation, and most of the rest of our ships are scattered the hell and gone across seven star systems. If Geneva was going to try some sort of a power grab, the time to do it would be when CBG-40 is nineteen light years away. At 36 Ophiuchi."

"Believe me, Captain, that's occurred to us as well." He didn't add *but that is* my *responsibility*. He didn't need to.

The unspoken words hung within the virtual meeting room as President Koenig's image began to fade out.

"Good luck, Sandy," Koenig said.

The use of his nickname startled him. "Thank you, sir."

And then he was back on the bridge of the star carrier *America*.

Chapter Seven

11 November 2424

TC/USNA CVS America
USNA Naval Base
Quito Synchorbital
0715 hours, TFT

America was leaving port.

Grav tugs with magnetic grapples extended gently eased the huge ship clear of the docking gantries, working her well clear of the delicate traceries of the synchorbital port facilities. Her own maneuvering drives were powerful enough that a careless drift left or right, high or low, could collapse beams or support structures and cause as much damage as a kinetic-kill warhead.

Gray, immersed in the navigational virtual feed, noted four of the largest Confederation ships standing off a few thousand kilometers in the distance—an unspoken threat, perhaps. If *America* made some untoward or unexpected move, she might well find herself under the guns and missiles of her nominal allies.

"Tugs releasing," helm officer Alicia Byrnes reported. "We are drifting free at twenty-eight meters per second and clear of the gantry."

"Very well," Gray replied. "Bring us about to the proper heading."

"Aye, aye, sir."

As *America* pivoted slowly in space, swinging about to face just to one side of Earth's sun, Gray opened another feed, downloading the available data on their destination.

Planetary Data Download
Arianrhod

PLANET: 36 Ophiuchi AIII

NAME: Arianrhod, Silverwheel

COORDINATES: RA 17h 15m 21.7s, Dec -26° 34' 16.32", distance 19.5 ly

TYPE: Terrestrial/rocky superEarth; reducing atmosphere

MEAN ORBITAL RADIUS: 0.766 AU; Orbital period: 265d 9h 40m

INCLINATION: 15.1° 23' 12.2"; **ROTATIONAL PERIOD:** 12h 28m 08s

MASS: 5.084 Earth; **EQUATORIAL DIAMETER:** 21448.4 km = 1.7 Earth

MEAN PLANETARY DENSITY: 5.62 g/cc = 1.02 Earth

SURFACE GRAVITY: 1.8 G; **ESCAPE VELOCITY:** 19.4 km/sec

HYDROSPHERE PERCENTAGE: 95.7%; **CLOUD COVER:** 50%; **ALBEDO:** 0.35

SURFACE TEMPERATURE RANGE:~ -15°C – 45°C.

SURFACE ATMOSPHERIC PRESSURE: ~5095 millibars = 5.028 atmospheres

PERCENTAGE COMPOSITION: CO_2 48.1; O_2 14.1; SO_2 9.6; NH_4 8.63; $H2S$ 7.1; N_2 5.95; SO_3 4.15; $CH3$ 2.1; Ar 0.2; others <700 ppm

AGE: 0.9 billion years

BIOLOGY: C, N, H, S_8, O, Se, H_2O, CS_2; Free-floating and motile photoautotrophs, chemoautotrophs, and chemoorganoheterotrophs in liquid water. Anomalous biology may be due either to periodic flares from parent star drastically accelerating the local biosphere's evolution, or to biological contamination by unknown alien visitation within the past few million years....

COLONIAL HISTORY: Silverwheel research colony established in 2278 under auspices of the Confederation Xenoplanetological Directorate to study local biology and causes of anomalously rapid evolution ...

The reasoning behind changing the mission objective to Arianrhod was, frankly, bewildering as far as Gray was concerned. The colony of Osiris—70 Ophiuchi—was closer to Earth and, therefore, more of a threat. Presumably, the invaders at 36 Oph wouldn't have had time to fortify their conquest—they'd had twenty years to do so at Osiris—but in terms of the system's usefulness it didn't make sense. Osiris was a *far* more habitable world than Arianrhod and, twenty years ago, had had a much larger population. Arianrhod's surface gravity of 1.8 Gs was no joke unless you were a gen-altered transhuman, and even then the problems of creating an enhanced subspecies able to endure that environment for more than a very short time were daunting enough that there had to be a *significant* reason to make the effort . . . something more than research that could have been conducted from orbit.

And there was still the matter of the arrival of unknowns at the Black Rosette.

But all of that, Gray knew, was now decidedly SEP—

someone else's problem. The USNA military had a long, long tradition, one going all the way back to the original United States, of encouraging independent thought up and down within the hierarchy of the command structure. Both enlisted personnel and junior officers were actually encouraged to ask questions . . . and to question orders. *Why* must we take that hill? *Why* are we retreating? *Why* are we fighting this war? *Why?*

That kind of democratization of the battle force could cause a hell of a lot of headaches for the high command and the nation's political leadership, but it made for a stronger, healthier, and more self-reliant war-fighting force. It was also an approach almost unknown in the military traditions of other Confederation member-states—the European Unions, the Brazilian Empire, the various squabbling republics of los Estados de las Americas del Sur, the North India Federation. And with the Confeds preempting the USNA battle group and strong-arming it into their operation, questions by mere ship commanders would no longer be tolerated. Gray had been taking a rather large risk by going to Koenig, but if Confederation Security had been tracking his link communications, there'd been no sign. He was still the captain of the *America*.

"Captain," Steiger's voice said in his command link, "Admiral Delattre has given the command. We are clear to accelerate."

"Very well, Admiral. Helm initiate Acceleration Program One."

"Initiating Program One, aye, aye, Captain."

America began to move forward, falling toward the stuttering, on-again, off-again knot of intense gravitational warping projected ahead of her titanic mass. *Bootstrapping*, the technique was called, a seeming violation of the common-sense of basic physics, but the ship's velocity continued to increase as an intense singularity was repeatedly projected and switched off just beyond the vast, round shield of her forward cap at a rate of some hundreds of times per second. The fabric of spacetime around the ship began to reshape itself as *America* slid forward, leaving a fast dwindling Earth astern.

Gray decided that what he most objected to was Delattre's high-handed commandeering of the *America* as his flagship. Yes, *America* was a Confederation warship first, a USNA vessel second but that had always been little more than a technicality of intraconfederation law. Twenty years ago, Admiral Koenig had had Confed political officers looking over his shoulder on the flag bridge but when he'd sent one packing nothing had been done about it, nothing overt, at any rate.

Geneva might have decided that Steiger wouldn't dare do the same to a Confederation naval service *admiral*. . . .

But the system was clumsy and inefficient, adding another layer to the battlegroup's chain of command. It was also humiliating, as if Geneva's military hierarchy just didn't trust the Americans.

Gray was forced to admit, though, that they might have just cause on that point. Anti-Confederation sentiment was at a fever's pitch back home; he remembered the crowds celebrating Koenig's re-election.

But in Gray's book Jason Steiger was *not* Alexander Koenig. He was a good officer, a good CO, but Gray couldn't see him kicking against the command structure. He would follow orders, so long as they were legal.

Following the software instructions of Program One, *America*'s acceleration gradually but steadily increased. Earth all but vanished astern, a tiny blue star, now, with the moon a minute attendant. The sun appeared at first to lie almost directly ahead, but as minute followed minute it began drifting off to the right, swelled huge for an instant, and then flashed past on *America*'s starboard beam.

At this time of the year, Sol appeared to be in the constellation Scorpio, right next door to the constellation Ophiuchus; in another two weeks it would actually track through Ophiuchus—the so-called thirteenth constellation of the Zodiac—much to the embarrassment of traditional astrologers, and in the first week of December would pass quite close to 36 Ophiuchi, at least as viewed from Earth.

The Earth was now drowned out by the sun's glare astern, and the familiar stars of Scorpius, Ophiuchus, and the teapot of Sagittarius now hung directly ahead. Giant Antares hung a little to starboard, its ruby hue now beginning to blue-shift toward orange as *America*'s velocity began creeping up on *c*. The navigational tank showed the rest of the battlegroup— the entire Confederation battlegroup of sixty-nine other warships spread out in a rough cone formation around, behind, and ahead of the *America*.

Hours later, they reached the orbit of Neptune and the so-called "flat metric," where the gravitational effects of the sun were slight enough that the fleet could switch over to Alcubierre Drive. The gravitational drive projectors extended their effect, curving local space around each individual ship until it existed within a tiny, walled-off bubble of space apart from normal spacetime. Within metaspace, as the bubbles' interiors were called, each ship remained at legal, sublight velocities relative to the space within which they were embedded . . . but there were no such restrictions on bubbles of space. Indeed, during the first instants of the big bang, space itself had expanded at what amounted to many, *many* trillions of times the speed of light, carrying matter and energy along with it.

America and the other ships of the battlegroup couldn't manage velocities like that, not with the vacuum energy available to them. Drive technology had improved considerably in the past twenty years, however, and they could now manage the equivalent of about four hundred light years per day. At that rate, they would have been able to reach 36 Ophiuchi in about an hour and ten minutes.

The energy requirements for that fast of a metaspace transition, however, were literally astronomical. Battlegroup *America* would make the passage in twenty-five hours, a pseudovelocity of "only" about 18.7 light years per day.

It wouldn't be long enough. Gray had been going over the Confederation plan for entering the 36 Ophiuchi system, and he didn't like what he saw one bit.

Slan Protector Vigilant
Low Orbit, 36 Ophiuchi AIII
1535 hours, TFT

Its name was a high-pitched chatter of clicks and chirps, but an Agletsch translation of the sound-symbol would have been something close to "Clear Chiming Bell." The Slan— that name, too, was the product of Agletsch translation, a shortened version of the phrase "Dwellers in Night"—could see visible light after a fashion, but poorly, in infrared frequencies only, and without depth or detail. They relied instead on high-frequency sound to image their surroundings clearly. Clear Chiming Bell was listening to the view of the alien planet below.

Vigilant had been orbiting the ocean world since their arrival nearly sixty *ch'k'!tt'cht* earlier. Clear Chiming Bell spread its heads farther apart to better appreciate the globe's delicate, cloud-wreathed beauty.

The Slan had been a long time in reaching space . . . sixties upon sixties upon sixties upon slow-marching sixties of *!cht'k'k'k'!cht*, their homeworld's years. It had been sixties of thirty-six hundreds of their years more before they were even *aware* of the stars in their endless night skies, and sixties of sixties years beyond that before they learned what stars were. The single light-sensing organ each Slan possessed high on its torso between the rubbery stalks that held its *!k'ch't't* organs could sense differences in light intensity, could tell the difference between light and dark, but could make out only the very brightest of stars in their night skies.

Fortunately, their home sun was located close to an open cluster, some hundreds of stars in a loose grouping the Slan had called The Mystery. Those vague and blurred blobs of light had drawn them on, leading them to develop technologies that could convert even weak electromagnetic wavelengths to clearly visible patterns of sound.

The discovery of the galaxy, of the far vaster universe around them, had transformed the species forever.

"Lord!" Clear Chiming Bell's second-in-command, Sighing Wind, called over the bridge comm. "We have found a living alien and captured it!"

"Indeed?" Clear Chiming Bell replied. This was excellent news. "On the planet's surface?"

"No, Lord. It appears to be a pilot of one of their fighters, damaged during the battle. One of our scouts discovered it on an outbound trajectory, and took it under tow. It is being brought on board now."

Numerous members of the alien species—designated as *Nah-voh-grah-nu-greh Trafhyedrefschladreh* by the Sh'daar—had been recovered, both in past engagements and on the poisonous surface of the world below, but always they'd been torn and lifeless. Clear Chiming Bell wanted a living specimen.

Knowing one's enemy always was the key to victory. There were puzzling aspects of these creatures. For one thing, they did not appear to have *!k'ch't't* organs for beaming sound at objects in their vicinity. This would represent a serious handicap for the creatures, not being able to form detailed sonic images of their surroundings.

"Once you are certain it is not distressed by our environment, bring it to the command compartment. Protect it! We want it unharmed."

"Yes, Lord."

Trafhyedrefschladreh: the Agletsch sound patterns created as a common language among those Sh'daar client species that could use them meant roughly "carbon-oxygen-water," the basis of the alien biology. Slan, too, were carbon-based, breathed oxygen, and used water as a biological solvent and transport mechanism. The aliens might not be so different from the Dwellers in Night after all. It was odd, however. The planet below possessed far too little oxygen and far too much carbon dioxide to support oxygen breathers. The sulfur dioxide was probably a poison to this type of life as well, as it was for the Slan. What were they doing here if they could not breathe the atmosphere?

"Lord," another subordinate said. "There is news. The enemy fleet is in motion. Its flight path suggests that it may be coming here."

The Sh'daar masters had identified the home system of the aliens, and Clear Chiming Bell had dispatched a cloud of sensor drones to its outskirts, each smaller than one of its projection heads. The drones were programmed to listen and wait, and to dispatch one of their number back to the fleet at high velocity if any significant movement of the enemy was detected.

"As we hoped," Clear Chiming Bell replied. "The trap is set?"

"It is, Lord. Half a sixty of ships, in five positions, powered down and silent. They will appear to be background debris."

"Alert them all, then maintain communications silence. You expect the enemy when?"

"Within less than a *k'k'k'cht't*, Lord."

"Then we will be ready for their arrival."

TC/USNA CVS America
In transit
1725 hours, TFT

America was ten hours out on her programmed flight, which put her just under nine light years from Earth. There was nothing to be seen by the ship's sensors, however, no view of slow-passing stars, no impossible starbow of velocity-distorted light, as appeared ahead of ships pushing close to *c*. Wrapped tightly in its Alcubierre bubble of meta-space, *America* effectively was outside of the familiar universe of stars and matter and light. Even the other vessels of the fleet, the nearest technically only a few kilometers distant, were completely beyond the star carrier's sensor arrays.

They might as well have been on the far side of the galaxy, impossibly distant, utterly beyond reach.

No matter. The ship's AI was counting down the nanoseconds until emergence, the precise timing necessary to ensure that all of the vessels in the Confederation fleet came out of Alcubierre Drive within very roughly the same volume of space. There was always *some* scattering on emergence, of course, but it was important that the fleet lose as little time as possible forming up on the other side.

"What do *you* think, Dean?" Gray asked. He was staring into the tank, a 3-D holofield projection based on the ops orders transmitted by Delattre moments after he'd come on board.

Commander Dean Mallory was *America*'s chief tactical officer, the head of the Tactics Department, which planned operations with an eye to maximizing the battlegroup's efficiency and getting the CBG's individual ships to work together.

"Precise and by the book, Captain," Mallory replied. "Maybe a bit *too* by the book."

"What do you mean?"

"Emergence at forty AU," Mallory said. "Fighter launch at E plus sixty seconds, deployment in standard wedge formation . . ."

"Like you say, by the book."

"Yes, sir. And what if the Slan have read the book?"

"That hardly seems likely."

"No, sir. But we don't yet know their capabilities. And the ghost signals have me worried."

Ghost signals was the term used for the whispers and stray radio-frequency signals Naval Intelligence had been picking up on the outskirts of Earth's solar system for the past few months. There'd been speculation that the Slan were deploying drones in Sol's Kuiper Belt that would help them track ship movements in and out of the system.

"So what do you recommend?"

"I'm not sure, sir. I'd like to have some tactical flexibility worked into the deployment, though."

"I understand." And he did. Gray had been thinking about this problem for some time, now, ever since they'd departed Quito Synchorbital, in fact. There was only one way to address the problem that he could see, and the decision would put his head on the chopping block if anything went wrong. "If we hold back . . . say . . . two squadrons of fighters . . . would that help?"

"Maybe." Mallory didn't sound enthusiastic, however. "Two squadrons may not be enough to protect the ship . . . and four squadrons might not be enough for the main effort."

CVS *America* carried six squadrons of strike fighters—three of SG-101 Velociraptors, one of SG-112 Stardragons, and two of the older SG-92 Starhawks. The battle plan, as presented by Admiral Delattre, called for sending all six of those squadrons in ahead of the main fleet, accelerating to near-*c* and flashing through the targeted battlespace around 36 Ophiuchi AIII, smashing everything possible during the brief instants of their passage. Again, this was standard tactical doctrine with star carrier strike fighters; the high-speed pass would cause enough damage and confusion that the main fleet, arriving at a somewhat more sedate velocity hours later, would be in a position to mop up a shattered enemy while taking little in the way of return fire.

That was the idea, at any rate. Generally, battlegroup commanders held back one or two fighter squadrons to provide close space support for the capital ships, just in case there was an unpleasant surprise. The limitations set by the speed of light meant that maneuvers by enemy ships at a distance wouldn't be noticed right way. Forty astronomical units was five and a third light hours, a distance dictated by the need to enter or leave normal space in a reasonably "flat metric," far enough from the local star that there was a minimum of gravitational interference. Any defending Slan ships close to Arianrhod wouldn't notice that the Confederation fleet had arrived for some five hours and eighteen minutes after they'd actually emerged from metaspace. By the same token, though, there would be a speed-of-light delay before the incoming ships would be able to see what the defenders were doing in reply.

Modern naval tactics all were predicated on these elements—emergence from Alcubierre Drive at least 40 AUs from the target system's star, a high-velocity fighter strike, and a follow-up attack by the main fleet. Gray knew that this wasn't the *only* way to do things, but current Confederation technology sharply limited the options.

The biggest question always was about the enemy's technological levels . . . about how far advanced the technology of any new and unknown species would be beyond that of Earth.

Perhaps, Gray thought, Humankind owed the Sh'daar a debt of gratitude. They were why the various alien civilizations Earth had been fighting since 2367 were within a century or so of human technology, and not thousands of years ahead . . . or millions. Their fear of the Technological Singularity seemed to be behind the limits they put on the technologies developed by their client species. The ultimatum they'd delivered fifty-seven years earlier had required Humankind to curtail all the so-called "GRIN" technologies—genetics, robotics, information systems, and nanotechnology. For centuries, now, these had been seen as the driving force behind the coming Singularity. Confederation Intelligence assumed that the Sh'daar were attempting to stop other technic species from entering their respective Singularities and evolving into . . . something else.

Stargods . . .

As a result, Sh'daar client species tended to be somewhat in advance of human technology—especially military technology—but not so far ahead that they possessed an impossible advantage in combat. Their weapons systems were similar to human weapons—with an emphasis on particle beams and kinetic-kill projectiles. Human forces at least had a chance against the Turusch, the Slan, and all the rest, even if they were usually badly outnumbered.

Sometimes, Gray thought, it felt like Humankind stood completely alone against a hostile galaxy.

Slan warship
Low Orbit, 36 Ophiuchi AIII
2015 hours, TFT

Lieutenant Megan Connor stumbled as the monster dragged her away from the broken shell of her fighter. She had a blurred impression of something large holding her, but at first her brain wasn't able to assemble a coherent picture. *Brown*, *purple*, and *wet* were all she could see. Her surroundings were . . . *dark*. Utterly and completely dark.

She was completely disoriented, exhausted, and weak, so weak she could scarcely stand in what her suit told her was a 1.9 G gravity field. She'd been trapped inside her dead Stardragon for four days, at least according to her in-head timekeeper. Her suit's nanorecyclers had kept her fed and hydrated, but her e-links to the ship's sensors and onboard AI carried nothing but static. She'd been unable to move or see as hour followed empty, dragging hour.

She'd maintained a wavering grip on her sanity by running docuinteractives stored in her cerebral implant memory. There were several propaganda pieces of the "Why We Fight" variety; she'd saved them in her CIM because they included quite a bit of information on various Sh'daar client species, especially the Turusch, the Nungies, and the weird, drifting H'rulka. Unfortunately, there was nothing on the Slan, a species that she'd heard of, but never seen in person.

There was also a rather simplistic role-playing game, a fantasy with an epic quest to complete, hideous monsters to slay, and a kingdom's throne to win. She hadn't liked the hideous monster part, because there was every possibility that she was going to encounter real monsters if the Slan detected her disabled fighter.

They had. She'd felt the bumps and slight acceleration as something big had grappled with her ship. A probe with a nano-D tip had penetrated her cockpit, evidently sampling the internal atmosphere and environmental conditions. There'd been a long wait after that . . . several hours. With the ship's nanomatrix hull no longer responding to her thoughts, she couldn't get at the fighter's emergency survival pack behind her seat, which included a small hand-laser weapon.

And if she had gotten her hand on the laser . . . what then? She wouldn't be able to fight them off.

Maybe she could take her own life.

She wasn't ready—quite—to consider that option.

And then the Dragon's cockpit had ripped open fore and aft at the touch of a brilliant light, and she thought at first that her bubble helmet had turned opaque in response. It took a moment for her to realize that the darkness wasn't in her helmet's polarizing circuitry, but in the room itself. Something dragged her through the opening; her feet found the deck, but her legs gave way and she crumpled. She could feel heavy ropes encircling her arms and legs, lifting her.

Her skin suit utilities had a powerful lightpanel at her throat, just below her helmet. She triggered it with a thought-click.

Somehow, she managed not to scream. . . .

That was when she got her confused impression of brown and purple, and it took a moment more for the thing's actual shape to begin making sense. *A two-headed monster* . . .

The body was squat and round with a hump in the center, with skin like wrinkled rubber. It appeared to slide along the deck on its belly, and was surrounded by a writhing mass of tentacles ranging from hair-thin to as thick as a man's leg. Whether it was gliding on its stomach, moving along on a layer of tentacles, or in fact had very short legs hidden by the squat body, she couldn't tell. The heads were large, blunt, and cone-shaped, attached to the base of the central hump by a pair of 2-meter necks, rubbery and bonelessly flexible. She *assumed* they were heads and necks. She didn't see any eyes or mouths or anything else she recognized as a sense organ. No . . . wait. On either side of the body were thin, membranous flaps of tissue that could open, twist, or lie flat. At first, she thought they might be involved in the creature's breathing, but the more she watched them, the more she thought that they might be external ears, capturing and focusing faint sounds.

Connor tried to concentrate on her environment. She would need to know about it if she was to survive for very long. Her skin suit was feeding readouts to her in-head display. The outside temperature was hot—55 degrees Celsius—and the humidity was 100 percent. The air, in fact, appeared to be filled with a mist that captured the light from her suit and turned her surroundings into a thick, white haze. Her transparent helmet was by now covered with droplets of water, as were the glistening bodies of the massive beings around her.

The atmosphere, she noted, was high in oxygen compared to the air of Earth—28 percent—and the carbon dioxide was high—over 5 percent—with enough ammonia, methane, and hydrogen sulfide that she didn't want to have to try the air without a respirator. The pressure was high, too, about five times that of sea level on Earth, a thick, hot, and poisonous soup.

Interesting. The pressure was close to that of Arianrhod at the surface, the gas mix was roughly similar, if different in its component percentages, the gravity felt similar, and even the temperature was only a bit higher than Arianrhod's upper extremes at the equator. The Slan environment was a lot closer to Arianrhod's than it was to Earth's. Was that why they were here? A land grab?

The Slan, she thought, were likely as curious about her as she was about them.

She just hoped that they didn't plan to peel her out of her skin suit just to see if she could breathe the air.

Chapter Eight

11 November 2424

Slan Protector Vigilant
Low Orbit, 36 Ophiuchi AIII
2029 hours, TFT

Clear Chiming Bell didn't quite know what to make of the alien. How could it possibly *see*?

Held upright by a Slan soldier, it tottered into the control chamber on two stumpy, awkwardly stiff tentacles, and gave the impression of being constantly about to fall over. It had two more tentacles on the upper end of its body which branched at the ends; curiously, these protrusions appeared to be stiff and jointed as well. The creature must be nearly crippled in its lack of dexterity.

The upper end of the being was a perfectly round, smooth, and sonically opaque ball perhaps two *k'k't!!* across which was almost certainly artificial, though it might have been some sort of natural shell. Clear Chiming Bell increased the frequency of its sonar scans, and managed to get a vague image of an interior air space, within which a smaller, roughly spherical organ rested. At first, Clear Chiming Bell thought that this might be the creature's sound projector, its *!k'ch't't* organ, but there was no sound coming from it—nothing coherent and focused, at any rate—and with only a single projector it would be unable to see in three dimensions. Unless, perhaps, it could judge distances through minute time delays in its echolocation? That was possible but seemed far-fetched, and it would really work only for fairly distant objects.

Clear Chiming Bell turned its sonar to focus on and into the rest of the creature's body. It appeared to be wearing some sort of fabric, apparently nanotechnically grown, with various devices wired into it, all clearly artificial. Beneath that, the creature had a smooth integument . . . though even here there were signs of some sort of bioengineering . . . minute wires and patches of circuitry grown in or beneath that extraordinarily thin and smooth skin. Deeper still, Clear Chiming Bell could see internal organs and cavities—a rapidly pulsing muscle that might circulate bodily fluids; two spongy masses to either side that appeared to be porous and full of air; a kind of twisting, close-folded tube that was probably associated with digestion; and lots of other organs of unknown purpose. The brain was probably *that* . . . a large and massive organ tucked into the right side of the body halfway down, partially enfolding and covering the muscular organ that most likely was a stomach.

After a long inspection, Clear Chiming Bell finally decided that the sound-producing organs were the twin globes of fatty tissue protruding somewhat from the creature's upper body, just to either side of the pulsing circulation pump inside. They were roughly spherical, somewhat flattened, but cone-shaped enough to be analogous to Slan *!k'ch't't,* and tipped by small, rough-skinned patches with central protuberances that might serve to focus sound beams. They did not appear to be as mobile as Slan projectors, however, attached as they were to the creature's torso instead of being mounted on slender, twisting necks. Indeed, Clear Chiming Bell didn't see how the creature could aim them with any accuracy at all. In fact, if the roughened patches of skin at the tips were any indication, the creature wasn't even aiming them in the same direction.

And while Clear Chiming Bell could hear the thump of

the creature's fluid pump, and a periodic rasp that might be respiration, it heard neither the squealing and rapidly pulsing chirps of scanning sonar, or the squeaks, buzzes, and clicks that might be speech. How did the creature communicate?

And above all, *how did it see its surroundings?*

"Have you tried to communicate with it?" Clear Chiming Bell asked the soldier holding it by its upper tentacles. The creature writhed and twisted in the Slan's grasp, and appeared to be in discomfort.

"It does not respond to speech at all, Lord," the soldier replied. "We *have* picked up radio frequency transmissions, however, though these appear to be generated by artificial means, not by the creature's organic substance. The transmissions do not appear to convey information, however."

"We may simply not understand the code." Clear Chiming Bell considered the creature a moment longer. "That covering it wears is clearly artificial, probably grown as a nanotechnic matrix. Likely it is an environmental suit, and therefore self-sealing. Take it to the medical labs and get a sample. We need to know the thing's environmental and metabolic needs." Clear Chiming Bell reached out with a pair of medium tentacles and touched what it suspected were the strange being's sound projectors, eliciting a sharp, violent struggle as the thing tried to pull away. Interesting. "I suspect that these swellings are its *!k'ch't't,*" it said. "They consist of fatty tissue much like our own sonic projectors. Monitor them closely, for signs that it is trying to image its environment."

"Yes, Lord."

"Tell the lab-Dwellers in Night that we *must* understand this being's biological makeup and environmental needs if we are to learn anything about this alien species."

"Yes, Lord."

Knowing that the aliens were *Trafhyedrefschladreh* was not enough. Not by far. A species could use oxygen to metabolize foods and water as a transport medium and solvent, and still be impossibly alien both in their biochemistry and in the way they perceived the universe. The Slan *must* learn how these aliens thought, what drove them, what brought them into deep space to colonize worlds to which they clearly were not adapted.

Clear Chiming Bell dismissed the soldier, which glided out of the chamber, its struggling captive in tow.

Another oddity, it noted. Slan were radially symmetrical, while the alien appeared to be bilaterally symmetrical, a right side mirrored by a left side. If those two prominent swellings were what Clear Chiming Bell thought they were, the creature must have a preferred front end, a side toward which it always moved, and its paired *!k'ch't't* would indicate that directionality.

It didn't appear to *like* being dragged backward.

A *very* strange concept. *Alien* . . .

Clear Chiming Bell gave the equivalent of a shrug—a deliberate rippling of the finer tentacles all the way around its circumference—and returned to the more pressing issues at hand. The alien fleet, it knew, would be here soon . . . possibly within just a few more *t'k'k'k'cht't*, and it intended to be ready for their arrival.

12 November 2424

TC/USNA CVS America
In transit
36 Ophiuchi A System
0725 hours, TFT

Emergence . . .
The tightly-wrapped bubble of spacetime surrounding *America* opened in an intense burst of photons. Gray watched from his command chair as the stars flashed back on, after more than twenty-five hours of unyielding, impenetrable darkness. In the navigational tank below and in front of him, other ships in the battlegroup, one by one, began dropping into existence, the nearest vessels first—the USNA destroyers *Bradley* and *Henderson* . . . the *Simon Bolivar* . . . *Napoleon*—then more distant ships as the light bearing

their images crawled across intervening space and reached *America*'s sensors—*Kali, von Metternich, Normandy, Ariel, Caesar Augustus, Illustrious.*

After a transition of less than twenty light years, most of the constellations ahead remained recognizable—Scorpius, the teapot of Sagittarius, the backward question mark of Leo well off to starboard. To port, the familiar summer triangle was missing one star; Altair, only sixteen light years from Earth, now lay astern.

Astern, too, a faint yellow star had winked into being between the outstretched horns of Taurus, just north of the familiar constellation of Orion—Earth's sun, now shrunken to a fourth-magnitude star.

From forty astronomical units out, the star system of 36 Ophiuchi showed as three orange suns, with two, A and B, appearing perhaps 20 degrees apart from this angle, and with C a dimmer companion much farther off to one side. Star A was a type K0 orange star, its close companion a K1, while 36 Ophiuchi C was a K5 that didn't even orbit the other two, but simply shared their proper motion through the galaxy. Stars A and B circled each other in an extremely eccentric orbit, coming as close together as 7 AUs and moving as far apart as 169 AUs, the two taking about 570 years to make a complete orbit. Currently, the two were 30 AUs apart, about the distance between Sol and Neptune.

Gray studied in-head downloads of the triple system. The twice-per-millennium close passage of B around A sharply limited the size of A's family of planets. There were four. Planet III, Arianrhod, was 0.766 AUs out from its star, a hair farther from its primary than was Venus from Sol. Planets I and II both were hot Jupiters, gas giants in the process of evaporating in the heat of their star like enormous comets, though both were closer in size and mass to Sol VII than to Sol V. Planet IV was the size of Neptune's moon Triton, ice-clad and frigid at 1.5 AUs out, while beyond that was a ring of planetoids, left-over bits and pieces from the system's formation, which could not form planets because of the periodic gravitational interference of 36 Ophiuchi B.

Both 36 Ophiuchi B and C had planetary systems of their own, but surveys made during the late 2200s, while Arianrhod was being set up as a base, had established that none of those other planets even came close to the idea of habitability for human visitors. Ice giants, ice-cloaked moons, heat-baked and barren rocks, hot Jupiters, planetoid belts—worlds of interest to planetologists, perhaps, but not to xenobiologists.

At least, not *yet*. There was life beneath the ice of several of the gas-giant moons in Sol's planetary system, as well as the recently discovered alien growths at the radiation-warmed deep boundary beneath Pluto's icy surface and its still-hot interior. If life could exist *there*, under such extreme conditions, it might well have evolved here as well . . . but for the time being, humanity's focus on the 36 Ophiuchi system was centered entirely on planet AIII, the oceanic and poisonous super-Earth named Arianrhod.

Gray still wondered if the place was worth it. . . .

"We're starting to pick up the opposition," Commander Mallory reported. "Fifteen targets, clustered in close orbit over Arianrhod."

"Very well."

"Captain Gray?" Connie Fletcher's voice said. "All strike squadrons are ready for launch."

"Thank you, CAG. Stand by."

Gray turned in his seat, glancing up and back at the closed bulkhead behind him. *America* possessed two primary bridges, one immediately behind and "above" the other, though both resided in the command tower rising from *America*'s spine and therefore were in zero-G, where concepts such as "above" or "below" were meaningless. The bulkhead between them could be opened, but during combat operations it was generally sealed shut to avoid losing both in the event of catastrophic depressurization. Gray's was the ship command bridge, from which he ran the ship. Aft was the flag bridge, formerly Admiral Steiger's domain, but now ruled by the Confederation's Admiral Delattre. Steiger was wired in next to Delattre, and Gray didn't envy him one bit.

According to long-fixed tradition, the admiral commanded the entire fleet, while the captain commanded the ship. As *flag captain*—the commanding officer of the admiral's flagship—Gray was also expected to serve as the admiral's chief of staff, offering both strategic advice and coordinating the admiral's tactical planning staff.

Delattre's arrival had risked scrambling the USNA battlegroup's command structure, however. Rather than demoting Steiger to the post of *America*'s CO, or putting him ashore at SupraQuito, both moves that would have seriously affected shipboard morale, Steiger had been shunted off to one side. In theory, he still commanded the 23-ship USNA battlegroup, but only under Delattre's direct supervision. Technically, he was on Delattre's staff and served as a senior advisor, but everyone in the fleet knew this was a polite fiction masking the fact that the Confederation didn't trust the USNA CO, or the forces under his command.

So morale had plummeted anyway.

Gray was aware of shipboard morale as a graph created by *America*'s AIs. Electronic monitors throughout the ship recorded overall levels of efficiency, and also picked up certain key words in overheard conversation. Those sound bite recordings were supposed to be anonymous—a human could listen in on them only with a court order or a direct and unanimous request from a court-martial board—but certain words and phrases, taken *en masse*, could provide a snapshot of the emotions of the entire crew. *Bastards, gold braid, mutiny, stupidity, idiots, damned Confed, REMFs* . . . there were actually several hundred key words and word groups in the database the AIs used to assess crew morale.

The words themselves were not the problem . . . even potentially nasty ones like *mutiny* or *take over the ship* or *disobey orders*. Naval personnel *always* griped, bitched, and complained. It was considered a time-honored tradition, and "a griping sailor is a happy sailor" had been a cliché in the Navy's lexicon for at least five hundred years, perhaps more. But when the frequency of those words picked up in overheard conversations shot up nearly 300 percent literally overnight, something was seriously wrong. Efficiency was down by 8 percent, too, with more mistakes and slower reaction times from sensor suite, engineering, and flight-deck personnel. Not good. Not good at *all . . .*

America's fighting trim might well be compromised in the coming battle, and Gray didn't know how he could change that.

It would help, he thought, *if the bastard would give the damned order. . . .*

Standard naval tactical doctrine required that the strike fighters be launched as soon as the carrier emerged from Alcubierre Drive. Each second, the light emitted by the fleet's arrival out of folded metaspace traveled another light second toward the waiting enemy sensors. Five hours and eighteen or so minutes after the fleet's emergence, Slan sensors would record its arrival. If the first wave of fighters arrived within a few minutes of the light wave announcing the fleet's emergence, the enemy wouldn't have time enough to deploy and meet the threat.

What the hell were the Confed idiots playing at?

"Captain," Fletcher said, gently prodding. "Do we have a launch command yet?"

"Negative, CAG," he said. "Wait one."

He checked his internal timekeeper. Almost four minutes had passed. Incoming vessels out to a range of four light minutes were now visible in the tank, representing perhaps half of the entire fleet. Was he waiting until every ship was logged in?

"Captain Gray," Delattre's voice said. "You may execute the launch order."

"Aye, aye, Admiral," Gray replied. He opened the CAG channel. "CAG, you may launch the fighters."

"Yes, *sir*," Fletcher said, and he heard the emotion, the *relief* in her reply. "Launching fighters!"

An instant later, the first pair of SG-101 Velociraptors from VFA-210 flashed in hard-vacuum silence from the side-by-side launch ports centered in *America*'s broad forward shield cap. There was a pause, and then two more SG-101s followed the first two . . . and then two more . . . and two more. . . .

At the same time, the fighters from other squadrons began spilling into space from the three rotating hab modules aft of *America*'s shield cap, flung into space at 5 meters per second by a half-G of spin gravity.

Other carriers in the battlegroup were launching as well, and, minute by minute, the fighters began forming up for the assault. At 0758 hours, they initiated boost: twenty squadrons in all—240 fighters—accelerating at fifty thousand gravities toward 36 Oph's inner system in a single wave.

It would take 339 minutes Objective for them to get there.

The main body of the fleet, however, continued to drift in the emptiness at the remote fringes of the star system. A few of the Confederation ships were still unaccounted for as the light bearing news of their arrival continued its agonizingly slow crawl toward *America*'s position.

Gray assumed that Delattre was waiting until all of the ships of the combined fleet were accounted for, but the delay chaffed at him. The longer they waited, the more time the enemy would have to prepare.

Gray wondered at Delattre's delay in getting the rest of the fleet under way.

Lieutenant Donald Gregory
VFA-96, Black Demons
36 Ophiuchi A System
0759 hours, TFT

Gregory felt the jolt as magnetic grapples released and his Starhawk plummeted through the launch tube. For an instant, gravity vanished and he was in free fall; stars burst into view ahead and around him, as the vast, flat surface of the forward shield slid past his keel.

Once clear of the underside of the shield cap, Gregory nudged his fighter's controls with his thoughts, accelerating just enough to get well clear of the carrier and drop into formation with Commander Mackey, Lieutenants Esperanza, Nichols, and Kemper, and Jodi Vaughn, his wing. One minute before, fighters from other squadrons had begun boosting hard, vectoring toward the nearer of the two stars 40 AUs ahead. VFA-96, however, had another mission. They were flying CAP—Combat Air Patrol—around *America* . . . an ancient term from the time of atmospheric fighters and navies cruising Earth's oceans.

The remaining six fighters of VFA-96 dropped from the hab module flight decks and took up station with the others.

"*America* CIC, this is CAP One," Commander Mackey said. "Handing off from PriFly. All Demons clear of the ship and formed up."

"Copy, CAP One," a voice replied from *America*'s Combat Information Center. "Primary Flight Control confirms handoff to CIC. You are clear for maneuver. Take up station at Delta-one-five starboard."

Primary Flight Control—PriFly—was in charge for fighters during launch or trapping aboard the carrier at the end of a mission. The Combat Information Center, or CIC, a cavernous chamber located immediately below *America*'s command and flag bridges, ran the actual missions.

"Okay, Demons," Commander Mackey called. "Assume station. Eyes sharp, *brains* sharp. We don't know what surprises the Slan have waiting for us."

Delta-one-five starboard was the code designation for the Demons' station, 15 kilometers to starboard of *America* and slightly behind. The idea was that if Slan ships tried to close with *America*, the CAP squadron was in a position to move up and engage them.

"So why the hell are we on nursemaid duty?" Esperanza asked.

"Shit, Espie, the velocicrappers don't want to be seen with the likes of *us*," Caryl Mason told him.

"That's right," Del Rey added. "We're flyin' antiques. *I* don't want to be seen with us!"

"Can the chatter, people," Mackey told them over the

taclink. "Focus on your sensor feeds. If one of those bastards so much as twitches, we want to know about it."

Gregory was already immersed in the scan data being fed to him by his fighter's AI. He wasn't much bothered by "nursemaid duty," as Esperanza had put it. The older SG-92 Starhawks were better suited to close defense than to mixing it up with the enemy planetary defenses.

He was far more upset that the brass had elected to attack 36 Ophiuchi rather than stage a liberation of his home, just ten light years away. He'd been sitting on his anger ever since learning that the fleet's destination would *not* be 70 Ophiuchi.

To say that the inner system of 36 Ophiuchi A was a mess was understating things by far. The system was young, a fifth the age of the Sol System, and still populated by clouds of asteroids. Repeated close passages by 36 Oph B kept things churning, and there were numerous strays outside of the established belts. Comets stretched ghostly fingers out away from the star by the dozens. The picture was much as it would have been in the solar system three and a half billion years before, with migrating gas giants stirring the orbits of worlds, moons, and planetoids, and the resultant late heavy bombardment slamming the newly formed planets.

The fighter CAP wasn't interested in stray rocks at the moment, however, but in the blips representing Slan spacecraft within the inner system. The trouble was that those myriad rocks strewn across the inner system, ranging in size from gravel to dwarf planets hundreds of kilometers across, provided ideal hiding places for alien warships. AIs on board *America* were busily separating the wheat from the chaff, identifying Slan ships and orbital facilities from rock by their infrared and microwave emissions. The enemy ships were warmer than bare rock, but only fractionally. Either the Slan environmental systems operated at fairly low temperatures, or their ships' waste radiation outputs were well screened. Enemy ships that had been positively identified so far were tagged red; unknowns were yellow. Right now, there were entirely too many yellow blips scattered across the sky.

One cluster of red targets was entirely too close . . . just ten astronomical units away from the fleet's position. They weren't moving toward the battlegroup yet; it would be eighty minutes from the time of the battlegroup's emergence before they were aware that the fleet had emerged from metaspace, and eighty minutes more for the light revealing the enemy's response to make the return trip.

"Hey, Commander," Ted Nichols called. "We have a cluster of Slan ships designated Tango One, at zero-one-nine slash one-zero. They're right off the flank of our inbound course. Should we hit them?"

"Negative," Mackey replied after a silent moment. "CIC says to maintain our position at Delta-one-five starboard. The battlegroup should be accelerating in another few mikes."

A few minutes? That could be an eternity in space combat ops. What was the brass waiting for?

"I thought the idea was to hit the bastards before they could hit us," Gregory said. If the fighter squadron was to accelerate at maximum boost, they would be pushing *c* in less than ten minutes, and slam into those enemy warships scant minutes behind the light bearing the news of the battlegroup's arrival. Ignoring them raised the specter of an intact enemy strike force on the battlegroup's flank during boost toward the inner system.

This, Gregory told himself, was *not* the way to do things.

TC/USNA CVS America
Emergence Point
36 Ophiuchi A, Outer System
0801 hours, TFT

"I suggest, sir," Gray said, "that we deploy part of the CAP to go hit them. *Now*."

"Your suggestion," Steiger said, "has been taken under advisement."

Gray's hands clenched at his side. He was floating on the

flag bridge, speaking in person to Admiral Steiger rather than using virtual presence through a neural link. Admiral Delattre was strapped down in the main command seat, obviously listening in from above and behind Steiger, though such terms were purely relational in zero gravity. A dozen of *America*'s flag bridge personnel plus members of Delattre's personal staff were scattered about the large, roughly circular compartment manning their own workstations and pretending not to eavesdrop.

"Sir—" Gray began.

"I *understand*, Sandy," Steiger told him. "But our orders are to concentrate on the Slan vessels orbiting Arianrhod. We will redirect the CAP should the ships of Tango One take an interest in us."

Tango One numbered about twelve Slan vessels, though the exact number was difficult to determine because they were mixed in with a small cloud of planetoids. They were located roughly 8 AUs off of the fleet's inbound flight path, and about 5 AUs closer to Arianrhod, with a straight-line distance from *America*'s current position, a hypotenuse, of 10 AUs.

"Basic fleet tactics, Captain," Delattre put in. "We must not allow ourselves to be distracted by what may be a diversion. I want the group to stay together."

Delattre's words startled Gray. The Confederation admiral had not spoken until now. He allowed himself to rotate slightly in space, facing the man directly.

"It can't be a diversion, Admiral," Gray said. "They wouldn't know we were going to emerge here. But they *are* in a good position to hit us in our flank while we're accelerating toward the planet." Almost as an afterthought, he added a bitter, *"sir."*

The predominant tactical problem in defending an entire star system was the sheer ungodly size of the thing. Incoming ships emerged from metaspace at 40 AUs out or more because of the need for a flat spacial metric for the Alcubierre Drive. Even a single AU was an unimaginably vast stretch of territory—the distance between Earth and the sun, almost 150 million kilometers, or eight light minutes. A sphere with a diameter eighty times larger enclosed an immense volume of space. The surface area alone of that sphere was something just under 450 quintillion square kilometers, a staggeringly huge number. In terms of tactics, there was simply no way to patrol such an aching expanse of emptiness—much less protect it with orbital forts or fleets—and have a chance in hell of having your assets by sheer chance be close enough to an emerging fleet to be able to engage it. The problem became inconceivably worse when you realized an incoming fleet could pop into normal space anywhere out to a hundred AUs or more from the target star . . . within a volume of some 1.3×10^{31} cubic kilometers. While emergence generally took place along the Alcubierre line of flight between one star and the next, the fact remained that the emergence point of a fleet was more or less random among all of that emptiness.

In other words, the Slan could not possibly have deliberately positioned Tango One ten astronomical units away from *America*'s emergence point, *knowing* that that was where the Confederation force would re-enter normal space. Chance alone had placed the enemy squadron there, but any opponent worthy of the name would certainly take advantage of such a chance if it was offered. By sending in the CAP fighters at high velocity, Tango One might be broken up before it could organize an opportunistic attack against the carrier battlegroup.

"You Americans have an expression, I believe," Delattre said with a dangerous mildness, "*by the book*. Yes? This operation will be conducted 'by the book.' In this case, that means we conserve our resources, and not go haring off after targets of opportunity."

"Tango One consists of at least twelve Slan vessels," Gray said, "positioned within an easy striking distance of our projected path, sir—"

"And this fleet numbers *seventy-nine* capital ships, Captain. More than enough to brush off any threat such as this one. Besides, by the time the light announcing our deployment reaches them, we shall already be passing them at eighty percent of the speed of light, and still accelerating. They will be struggling to catch up with us. A stern chase, as they say, is a *long* chase."

"Sir—"

Delattre cut him off. "I have already been through all of this with Admiral Steiger, *Captain*. Your proper sphere of responsibility is this vessel, *not* the strategic overview or operational deployment of my entire fleet."

By stressing his rank, Delattre was putting him in his place, or trying to. Gray was already angry, but now he came close to losing all semblance of professional detachment. "*Sir!* As Admiral Steiger's flag captain, it is my responsibility to point out both strategic and tactical options, and to raise issues that have a bearing on the entire battlegroup."

"And you have done so, Captain, thank you. And I suggest now that you return to your bridge and see to the handling of the *America*. We will begin acceleration as soon as the remaining ships of the fleet have checked in."

Gray glanced at Steiger, but the admiral was staring into the flag bridge navigational tank, as though lost in thought.

"Sir!"

Gray turned in midair, grasped a nearby cable guideline, and hand-over-handed himself back toward the carrier's command center. *The idiot!* The self-absorbed, condescending, blind-to-reality, couldn't-find-his-ass-with-both-hands *idiot . . .*

By the book? Well, yeah, the book stressed having your entire fleet linked in after emergence . . . but it *also* stressed moving quickly—even beginning acceleration before all of your ships had checked in, in order to win as much of a tactical advantage over the opposition as possible. Such decisions were judgment calls, pure and simple. Delattre seemed convinced that twelve enemy ships could not pose enough of a threat to the battlegroup to justify accelerating immediately, before the more far-flung stragglers of the fleet even showed up in *America*'s navigational tanks. The delays imposed by the speed of light meant that as much as half an hour or even more might pass before all of the vessels were accounted for.

With Tango One just eighty light minutes away, it was sheer stupidity to just sit there adrift for thirty minutes, doing nothing, and stupidity again to assume that twelve ships posed no threat to the battlegroup. By all accounts, the Slan had made short work of the squadron defending Arianrhod.

Angry, Gray hauled his way through the hatchway between the flag bridge and the ship command bridge, the door hissing shut and sealing as he floated over to his chair, hauled himself into its embrace, and felt it close around his legs. He fumed for a moment, fingers drumming on one arm of the chair, then opened a neural link to Connie Fletcher. "CAG?"

"Yeah, boss."

"Have our CAP squadrons move out ahead of the ship . . . make it one AU. And in the direction of Tango One."

"Aye, aye, sir."

"And do it gradually. I don't want anyone to notice."

He didn't specify who "anyone" was—the Slan or Admiral Delattre—but he knew Connie got the message.

"We'll do it on the sly, Captain. Don't worry."

"Thanks, Connie."

It was a hell of a note when you had to keep your maneuvers secret not only from the enemy, but from your own side as well. . . .

Chapter Nine

12 November 2424

Executive Office, USNA
Columbus, District of Columbia
United States of North America
0835 hours, EST

President Koenig, once again, was linked in with Konstantin, the hyperintelligent AI located within Tsiolkovsky Crater on the lunar farside. His body was relaxing in his office recliner in Columbus; his mind's eye was within a virtual reality created by Konstantin, an old-fashioned study, this time, with the elderly avatar of Konstantin Tsiolkovsky seated in front of a log fire. Through a window in one massively timbered wall, heavy snow was blowing in a windy night.

Koenig was concerned. Normally, he, as president of the USNA, would request time on the Konstantin array. The trouble was that Konstantin was autonomous. While technically he was the property of the USNA government and the research organizations that had overseen his development, Konstantin, as a self-aware individual, *belonged* to no one. Each time Koenig requested time on the Tsiolkovsky Array, he wondered if the hyperintelligent AI would even deign to receive a mere USNA president.

This time, however, Konstantin had requested to speak

with him. Having the USNA president summoned by the AIP was, if not unprecedented, at least a rare occurrence. The last time Koenig remembered it happening was . . . when? Not during his tenure as president, certainly. He remembered reading that USNA President MacIntyre had been summoned by Konstantin during the H'rulka Incursion, late in 2404. It might have happened during the Avalon Crisis eight years later. AIPs were not in the habit of going to humans for advice. . . .

"President Koenig," the Konstantin avatar said, nodding. "Thank you for linking in. We have a . . . problem."

Koenig's mind flashed back across several potential crises, wondering what a being as powerful as Konstantin would perceive as a *problem*. The Confederation fleet should have emerged at 36 Ophiuchi by now . . . might already be engaged with the Slan warships occupying the system, but it would be more than another day before the outcome of that strike could be known back here in the Sol System, across 19.5 light years.

The Confederation Senate in Geneva had recently issued what amounted to an ultimatum. Under certain terms of the Confederation Treaty, the Periphery regions of the United States of North America were to be turned over to Confederation control. That was a likelier source of trouble. Columbus had a month to respond to the directive, though, so any threat of USNA-Confederation hostilities was less than immediate.

"How can we help, Konstantin?" Koenig asked.

For answer, a transparent display materialized to one side, and an image winked on. The view appeared to be from the forward scanner of some type of spacecraft, but traveling at an extremely low altitude across a dark and crater-pocked surface. Electronic view overlays showed range and navigational data—altitude 20 meters, velocity 1330 meters per second, mission elapsed time 9.3 minutes . . .

The scene could have matched any of a thousand airless bodies in the solar system alone. "Where is this?" Koenig asked. He looked more closely at the display. The transmission was coming from something identified as Bruno One. "Where's it coming from?"

"A Confederation/EU Type 770 VA gunboat seven hundred forty-two kilometers south-southeast of Giordano Bruno Base on the lunar farside. Approximately sixty kilometers from the northern rim of Lobachevski Crater."

The scene jolted a bit as the craft accelerated, rising 50 meters to clear a low rise ahead.

"Giordano Bruno? What the hell are they doing with a Type 770 there?"

"Judging from their current course, I believe they mean to capture me. *Possibly* to destroy me, but more likely they intend merely to take control of me in order to deny this facility to the United States of North America."

The information hit Koenig squarely in the gut. If it was true, he was witnessing the opening round in a civil war between the USNA and the Earth Confederation. . . .

Giordano Bruno was a particularly bright and young crater on the lunar farside, a crater so young that many selenologists believed it to be the impact crater caused by a celestial spectacle witnessed by five monks at Canterbury in the year 1178. Bruno Base was a Confederation facility located at the bottom of the crater's twenty-two-kilometer-wide basin. Established in the early 2200s, the outpost had begun as a selenological research station, but eventually had become little more than a surface communications relay on the moon's northeastern limb. Lunar libration—the moon's slow nodding back and forth as it circled Earth, periodically brought the region into view from Earth. It was one of a dozen Confederation bases and outposts on Earth's moon, and the only one on the lunar farside.

But it wasn't a military base. Although . . .

He remembered seeing a report to the effect that a Confederation freighter, the *Dione*, had landed at Bruno Base two days earlier. Perhaps the freighter had not been carrying routine supplies after all.

He pulled up some calculations from his in-head connections with the Net. Bruno Base was 1853 kilometers from the Tsiolkovsky Array . . . a twenty-two-minute trip for a military force skimming the lunar surface at close to orbital velocity. And they were almost ten minutes into their flight.

"A flight of fifteen Type 770s was noted on radar by the L-2 Station eight minutes ago," Konstantin said, apparently anticipating Koenig's next question, "though they have not yet formally reported it. I used the L-2 communications array to hack the craft's navigational AI and retrieve these images."

Koenig nodded his understanding. Against an AI as powerful as Konstantin, normal encryption methods were useless. L-2 referred to the Earth-Moon LaGrangian Point, above the lunar farside, the gravitationally stable point at which the farside's communications net station and some orbital logistical depots were located.

"According to standing orders," the AI went on, "your release order is required to defend this base. Failing that, your order to the base personnel to surrender might save more than two hundred lives."

"Surrender? Fuck that. Where are the nearest Marines?"

Tsiolkovsky Array
Tsiolkovsky, Lunar Farside
0838 hours, EST

Captain Barry Wizewski was getting old, was *feeling* old, and he didn't like it. He was still in excellent health due to the effects of modern nanomedicine, but his religion prevented him from using anagathics—especially for cosmetic purposes—and as a result he *looked* every one of his eighty years.

It might be, he decided, finally be time for him to retire.

The Purist sect of the Rapturist Church of Humankind believed that they were expected by their Creator to be fully human when He returned for His people. Some of the more extreme members of his congregation refused even the most basic implants that might tinker with their humanity—

cerebral and neural implants that let them control automated home systems, pull data down off the Net, communicate mind-to-mind, or receive in-head entertainment.

Wizewski had never gone that far in his own beliefs. He'd joined the USNA Navy almost forty years ago, and that meant either receiving a whole suite of neural implants, or getting a technological deferment that would have put him into dead-end career track. Wizewski had taken the implants, eventually becoming a captain, and the *America*'s CAG.

For the past twenty years, however, his religion had— be honest, here—begun holding him back. For almost 350 years, now, the White Covenant had made it illegal to try to spread religion—*any* religion—to others, and, while it wasn't illegal to hold religious beliefs, it often seemed like people with religious preferences recorded in their personnel files tended to be passed by for promotion or for important commands.

Wizewski now found himself in command of the tiny naval-Marine garrison at Tsiolkovsky—a hole if ever there was one. He was still a captain and had no hope of ever commanding anything larger than a desk. Antireligious prejudice, pure and simple, and there wasn't a damned thing he could do about it.

Emigration had been much on his mind of late. There were extrasolar colonies founded by various churches and religious groups . . . if only to get away from the secular intolerance on Earth. Muslims, fundamentalist Christians, Gardnerian Wiccans, Mormons . . . even the Ancient Alienists all had founded colonies off-world where they could practice their own beliefs and not worry about the White Covenant laws.

The trouble was, colonies tended to look for younger men and women, not sour and wrinkled seniors ready to retire. Even the orbital colonies wanted youngsters; the O'Neil cylinders had been built with custom-created biospheres, but they still wanted men and women who could work the hydroponic arrays, tend the fish farms, and otherwise pay their keep with hard work. A kid nowadays might look forward to two or three centuries of active life, thanks to nanoanagathic life extension. Wizewski—unless he violated one of the prime tenets of his faith, *might* manage another twenty or thirty years.

And . . . would it be so bad to accept some of the life-extension options offered by modern medicine? That was the worst part of where Wizewski found himself wondering if his lifetime of faith in a Father-God Who demanded that His children be fully human when he called for them had been . . . a mistake. Lately, God had seemed increasingly petty; surely it was the *soul* that counted, and not the details of body shape or genetic prosthesis or electronic enhancement. . . .

His in-head comm chirped him out of a depressive cycle that had been gnawing at him for months, now. And the ID on the incoming call startled him to full awareness.

"Barry? This is President Koenig."

ID verification codes dropped into place in Wizewski's mind. This was the real deal. "Sir!"

Twenty years ago, Koenig had been the commanding officer of the star carrier *America*, when he'd been commander air group. The skipper had come a long way. . . .

"This is a formal and direct order, Barry. You have at least fifteen weapons carriers coming toward you from the north. Their intentions are believed to be hostile. You have full weapons release. Do what you feel is necessary to defend your base."

"Yes, sir. Uh . . . is this the Sh'daar? Who's attacking, Mr. President?"

"The Confederation, Barry. Konstantin can fill you in . . . but he needed my decision on whether to fight or not. What kind of defense can you put up?"

Wizewski chewed at his lip. He never had liked giving the Old Man bad news. He'd already opened a side window that showed a graphic of the approaching threat. They had less than ten minutes now before the hostiles reached Tsiolkovsky.

"In ten minutes? Mr. President, I have one Marine weapons platoon and about twenty naval personnel, plus two hundred civilians."

"We're looking for Marine or naval assets that can reach you in time. You're going to need to buy us that time."

"Yes, sir. How much time do you need?"

"Not sure yet, Barry. As much as you can manage."

"Aye, aye, sir."

As the connection with Columbus switched off, Wizewski was already giving orders over the base Net channels. Forty-two Marines—a platoon of three squads and an HQ element—plus twenty Navy people, most of them his own staff. And they had to buy time from fifteen . . . oh, God. Type 770s?

He shook his head as data came avalanching in from Konstantin. This was not going to be pretty.

Executive Office, USNA
Columbus, District of Columbia
United States of North America
0839 hours, EST

"Please hold, Mr. President . . ." the in-head voice of an AI told him.

Koenig scowled. Geneva, evidently, wasn't taking his call. That wasn't entirely unexpected, but he'd thought they would have *something* to say to him. *Surrender or be destroyed*, perhaps.

The timing of the attack at Tsiolkovsky, obviously, had been carefully calculated to coincide with the Confederation fleet action at 36 Ophiuchi. Geneva, obviously, had been planning this for some time—use the Military First Right law to dragoon the majority of USNA warships within the Sol System and get them out of the way, then lay claim to the Tsiolkovsky Array.

And what else might they try to grab while the USNA fleet was absent?

After thirty more seconds, Koenig thoughtclicked the disconnect in his mind. Marcus Whitney stood before his desk, a quizzical look on his long face. "No go, sir?"

"Seems like they don't want to talk to us, Marcus. You've got the alert out to all commands?"

"Yes, sir. General Mancuso at the Hexagon says that all USNA military forces are going on full alert, but it'll be a few minutes before all commands check back in."

The Hexagon was the iconic building north of Columbus that had housed the USNA's command center ever since the drowning of Washington, D.C., and the earlier Pentagon.

"Fighters?"

"Two Starhawk squadrons at Oceana, sir."

"Get them in the air." He hesitated. He wanted to send one to Tsiolkovsky, but didn't dare. If the Confederation was making a grab for Konstantin, it might also take advantage of the moment to grab the Periphery, those stretches of flooded USNA coastline abandoned by Columbus . . . and only now being reclaimed. "One to the Manhat Ruins, one to Washington, D.C."

"Yes, sir."

"Tell them if Confed forces show up, don't shoot until I give the order. We want to keep open the possibility of a peaceful resolution if we can."

A communications request chime sounded in his head. It was Ilse Roettgen.

"Excuse me, Marcus." Within his mind, he opened the link. "President Koenig."

"Yes, Alex," she said, smiling sweetly. "Were you just trying to call me?"

Ilse Roettgen, as president of the Confederation Senate, was as close to a supreme leader of the Earth Confederation as the World Constitution permitted. She was also president of the European Union.

"What the hell are fifteen Type 770 gunrafts doing attacking Tsiolkovsky?" Koenig demanded. He was stretching things a little, hoping to get more information. The 770s hadn't actually attacked Tsiolkovsky yet . . . and it was possible that Roettgen would call them back if she realized the assault had been detected before they were in place.

He saw a flicker of surprise in her eyes, quickly concealed. "Attacking? Mr. President, I am sure I have no idea what you are talking about."

Koenig had been expecting that ploy. "Then permit me to bring you up to date, Madam President." He thoughtclicked a mental icon, dropping the forward scanner data feed recorded by Konstantin into the link.

"How did you . . . ?" She shut down the emotional response.

"Kind of hard to sneak up on us when we can peek over the shoulders of your pilots."

She changed tactics. "The Tsiolkovsky Array has been declared a strategic asset of the Confederation, Mr. President. The Confederation will control access to Konstantin from now on. Those gunrafts have merely been deployed to . . . to facilitate the peaceful transition of control."

"I must protest, Madam President," Koenig said. "Konstantin was created by USNA facilities, with USNA funding. His programming was carried out primarily by USNA AIs. In any case, if you feel you have a claim, I suggest that you take it up with the World Court, and not try to sneak in and steal it while the majority of our fleet is out-system."

Koenig could feel the woman's fury as she severed the link.

"Well," he told Whitney, "that went well, I think."

His eyebrows arched higher. "She's calling them off?"

"Oh, no. She thinks she has the high hand . . . and that very well might be true. But she's also angry, now, and angry people make mistakes."

"I . . . see, sir."

"You don't agree?"

"It seems to me, sir, that if you're trying to keep open the possibility of a peaceful resolution—your words, I believe, sir—making the other person mad is the *last* thing you'd want to do."

"The other guy just threw the first punch, Marcus,"

Koenig replied. "But we might still be able to make her miss and fall on her face. Now . . . what Marine assets do we have at Mars?"

Tsiolkovsky Array
Tsiolkovsky, Lunar Farside
0846 hours, EST

"Move it, move it, *move it*!" Gunnery Sergeant Christopher Ames bellowed as Marines thundered past him into the ready room. "I want to see nothing but amphibious green blurs, *do you read me*?"

The members of First Platoon, Bravo Company, 3rd Battalion of the 2/3 Marines pounded past Ames with a thunder of bare feet, banging equipment lockers, and massive gear being slung into place. They were clambering into the shells of their Mark 1 battlesuits, and helping one another with the heavy backpacks of He_{64} meta. The moon's gravity, just one-sixth of a G, meant they could hoist loads onto their backs that would have required powered exoskeletons on Earth, but the rocket packs each still had a mass of nearly two hundred kilos, and a careless movement could send the wearer stumbling out of control.

First Lieutenant Jennifer Burnham watched the evolution, as Marines loaded one another up, squeezing into the shells that hissed shut around them, then checking one another for loose buckles, snaps, or straps. As each Marine checked ready, he or she then toed the line, falling in along three parallel green stripes painted on the steel deck.

As the last Marines took their positions, Ames pivoted to face Burnham, and snapped off a crisp salute. "*First* Platoon ready for *ex*ovehicular deployment, *sir*!"

Tradition—the deep-down bones of the Corps. Burnham was *sir*, not ma'am, at least for formal evolutions . . . and they were about to go "exovehicular" even though they were inside a sealed and pressurized underground cave within Tsiolkovsky Crater's central mountain. Within the Marine lexicon, a shore base was always treated like a ship, with bulkheads, not walls, and decks, not floors.

"Thank you, Gunnery Sergeant," she said. "No time for speeches, Marines. Hostiles are closing on the base from the north. We're going to stop them. We will accomplish this by meta-vaulting sixty-two kilometers to the crater north rim, spreading out in a defensive partial perimeter, and holding the high ground. Questions?"

"Yes, ma'am," Lance Corporal Rodriguez said, raising a heavily armored hand.

"Rodriguez? Make it quick!"

"Uh . . . scuttlebutt says we're up against humans, not Shads. Is that true, ma'am?"

Scuttlebutt, Burnham thought. *The only form of communication faster than light.* "True. We appear to be under attack by Confederation forces, and we have been ordered to intercept them. Other questions?"

"But that means this is a fuckin' civil war," Sergeant Daystrom said.

"About fucking time," Corporal Thomas growled. "Freedom!"

"*All* that will concern you, Marines, are my orders. We're not here to debate politics. We're here to defend USNA property and personnel. Do I make myself clear?"

"*Sir, yes, sir!*" the three ranks of Marines chorused, a bellow ringing back from the steel bulkheads.

"Gunnery Sergeant Ames!"

"Sir!"

"Move 'em out!"

"Aye, aye, sir! Okay, Marines! You *heard* the LT! Lef' *face*! Forrar *harch*!"

Thirty-six Marines, massive, hulking figures in their battle armor, and with meta tanks each half again as large as a complete battlesuit precariously balanced on their shoulders, shuffled toward the main lock.

And Burnham decided that she'd lied, that this really was a political debate. The Marines were called in when the talking failed . . . but who was it who'd said that war was simply a continuation of politics by other means? She pulled down an answer off the Tsiolkovsky Base Net. Von Clausewitz, of course.

She wondered what the famous Prussian military theorist would think of flying Marines.

Burnham followed the Marines out into the vast emptiness of the hangar airlock, moving toward what appeared to be a taut, black sheet stretched against the far bulkhead. In two columns, the Marines marched straight into the sheet, which stretched, bulged, and filled in around them as they walked through and vanished.

Nanoseal technology allowed movement between pressurized compartments and the hard vacuum of space without the need for pumping out atmosphere and cycling through locks. The material molded itself to Burnham's battlesuit as she stepped into it, offering a tug of resistance, as though she were stepping through something like a sheet of molasses.

And then she was outside the base cavern, walking north down a barren, powder-covered slope, a desolate panorama of bare rock, intense sunlight, and midnight-black shadow. The reactive nanocoating of the Marines armor did its best to match the surrounding colors and intensity of light, creating patchworks of harsh white and black.

"First Squad! Assume launch positions!" Ames called over the tactical net, as the Marines fell in to extended squad formations, each man or woman well clear of those to either side. "Link in with tac-AI. One bounce! In three . . . two . . . one . . . launch!"

In utter silence, the regolith beneath the first twelve Marines exploded in a swirl of heavy white dust, and the battlesuits turned into tiny, one-man spacecraft.

Meta was a so-called exotic rocket fuel that had been in use since the late twenty-first century. High-energy lasers were used to pack helium gas into a meta-stable configuration—He_{64}—that remained inert at temperatures close to absolute zero, but which released that stored energy when it leaked into a reaction chamber and was heated. A three-second burst was sufficient to kick an armored Marine and his equipment and fuel load into a low, soaring trajectory calculated to bring him down just over 60 kilometers from the base.

Burnham watched the last of the Marines fire their meta boosters, then linked in with the tactical AI, allowing it to calculate the exact thrust and vector. She felt a hard, noiseless jolt, and then she was flying . . . drifting at high speed across the black maria on the floor of Tsiolkovsky . . . a dark regolith that swiftly gave way to bright, harsh, and rapidly rising bare rock.

Tsiolkovsky Crater was about 180 kilometers across, but the central mountain was offset toward the north. Sixty-some kilometers from the base, the crater's ring scarp rose over 1400 meters—very nearly a mile—in a near-vertical cliff like a white wall of rock. Burnham's trajectory was just high enough to clear the rock wall . . . and then her suit's jets automatically fired, bringing her down on the regolith with a hard thump.

The tac-AI had dispersed the three squads, as per plan . . . spreading them across nearly 25 kilometers of bare rock. The timing, she noted, could not possibly have been any tighter.

The enemy 770s were already in sight.

Lieutenant Donald Gregory
VFA-96, Black Demons
36 Ophiuchi A System
0847 hours, TFT

At long last they were moving, accelerating in-system.

At 0805 hours, the last of the emerging ships of the fleet had checked in, and the fleet admiral had given the order to begin accelerating at ten thousand gravities toward the heart of the 36 Ophiuchi A star system. During that time, the twelve Black Demon fighters had been edging farther and farther away from *America*, circling around to port, moving ahead, and increasing the separation from the carrier. They masked the move as a series of course corrections and station-keeping maneuvers. No one had said anything, but he was pretty sure that someone on board the carrier—CAG Fletcher or possibly even the skipper himself—had given the order for CAP One to maneuver away from the ship in such a way that the Confederation officers wouldn't be aware of it unless they were paying close attention. Delattre and his people wouldn't be watching CAP deployments, but would be more interested in the capital ships.

Gregory had to admit that it actually felt good to do something of which Delattre wouldn't approve—a way of striking back in a very small way against Confed officiousness. It had been Geneva and Delattre's people who'd made the final determination that the fleet would liberate Arianrhod instead of Osiris.

America was nearly a hundred kilometers distant, now, invisible to the unaided eye, but showing as a bright green blip on Gregory's AI-enhanced navigational feed. Forty minutes ago, the long-awaited order had come through, and the carrier battlegroup had begun accelerating toward the star's inner system. At ten thousand gravities and with deceleration beginning at the halfway point, they would arrive at Arianrhod in a little over five and a half hours. The Black Demons had matched *America*'s acceleration, taking advantage of the boost to slip a bit farther out, positioning themselves between the carrier and Tango One.

By now, Gray thought, the Slan of Tango One were aware of the battlegroup's arrival. Enough time had passed by now to allow the light bearing news of the fleet's emergence to reach the alien ships.

There'd not been enough time for the light showing the enemy's response, however, to make the return trip. It was called *c-fog*, that peculiar fog of war caused by the snail's pace of light.

Gregory felt blind and helpless, knowing the enemy was watching them . . . and being unable to see exactly what they were about to do in response. . . .

Chapter Ten

Marine Perimeter
Tsiolkovsky Crater North Rim, Lunar Farside
0847 hours, EST

"Here they come!" Gunny Ames called. "On my command . . ."

Burnham watched from behind a low slab of a boulder as the hostiles deployed. The ground up here along the lip of the crater was a labyrinth of broken blocks of stone, offering plenty of cover. At her back, the cliff dropped away in a near-vertical descent a mile deep, and near the horizon was the uneven rise of Tsiolkovsky's central peak.

Her eyes, however, were on a pair of dust clouds far off on the northern horizon, fuzzy patches against the bright regolith, well separated and vanishingly minute. Her in-head data feed showed ranges of 51 and 55 kilometers, approaching at nearly 120 kilometers per hour.

Privates Duncan and Salvatore were crouched in the shadow of a nearby boulder, a slender 3-meter tube on a small tripod between them.

"Ready to fire, Lieutenant," Karen Salvatore said. "Uh . . . if you want to move, ma'am, now would be a real good time. CB fire, you know . . ."

Counterbattery fire. The enemy would home in on the incoming and backtrack on it, slamming the area with fire within seconds.

"That's okay, Marine," she replied. "I'll duck when you do."

She could almost hear the other's shrug, the rolling eyes, the unspoken mutter of *"Officers."* "Whatever you say, ma'am. . . ."

It didn't matter. Burnham wanted to see the firefight, to evaluate it with her own eyes rather than through the swarms of battlespace drones and robot cameras along the crater lip. She had a vested interest in this.

This wasn't Jenny Burnham's first time in combat. Three years earlier, as a newly minted second lieutenant, she'd been part of a Marine deployment to the embattled state of Gujarat, on the northwestern coast of the Indian subcontinent. Slowly submerging beneath the rising Arabian Sea for the past couple of centuries, Gujarat had revolted against Northern India, probably with help by anti-WC Islamists out of Paskistan. Her platoon had gotten into a running firefight with Muslims in Benap, a few kilometers from the border.

The White Covenant was a touchy subject for both Muslims and Hindus, and was seen by both as a government sanction against not only religion, but against national and cultural identities. When the Marines captured a pair of Muslim infiltrators in the seacoast village, the Confederation Military Command had ordered them to release the men and stand down. Four Marines had been killed in that fight by a Pakistani robotic drone; Burnham, her commanding officer, and the men and women in her platoon had been sworn to secrecy, on pain of imprisonment for up to ten years.

Burnham had protested the orders in writing to her superiors in Columbus. She'd been court-martialed, first by the Confeds, then, when the Hexagon brought pressure to bear, by the USNA Marines. She'd avoided a jail sentence but had damned near found herself bounced out of the Corps. Instead, she'd been fined three months' pay, and found herself assigned *here*, on the ass side of the moon, protecting a glorified electronic calculator.

Yeah, she had a score to settle with the Confederation. It was *personal*. Her beloved Corps had done its best to protect her, she thought, but the politicians in both Geneva and Columbus had a hell of a lot to answer for.

She was going to *enjoy* this.

"Multiple targets acquired," Ames's voice said in her mind. "Waiting on your order, Lieutenant."

"Kill the bastards," she said.

According to the on-line warbook, the Type 770 was an armored personnel transport nearly 20 meters long, each carrying up to a platoon's worth of men and equipment, and mounting two turrets topside armed with either high-energy lasers or with railguns. They were designed for work on airless worlds like this one, boosted along low, suborbital trajectories by fusion-fired plasma jets, though they also had four sets of track units for crawling on the ground. They had thick armor, especially forward, and sophisticated sensor and navigational suites.

And fifteen of them meant that Bravo Company was facing over six hundred troops—a full battalion's worth.

"Clear to six," Salvatore said, checking the area behind their weapon.

"Firing," Private Duncan announced. *"Move!"*

The next few seconds were a blur. Duncan and Salvatore triggered their weapon, a Mark V man-portable KK railgun known colloquially as a gauss rifle. It used a powerful magnetic field to accelerate a steel-jacketed lump of depleted uranium to almost 50,000 kps, a significant percentage of the speed of light. A tightly focused plasma jet out the back end reduced—but could not eliminate—the weapon's savage recoil. The tube jumped . . . but was snatched up immediately by Duncan, who grasped the carry handle over its breech and triggered his meta jets in the same, endlessly practiced instant.

Burnham fired a burst of her meta as well, soaring away

from the gun position in a low, regolith-skimming arc.

And then the sky went white.

Executive Office, USNA
Columbus, District of Columbia
United States of North America
0849 hours, EST

"Mr. President," the voice of Konstantin said in his mind, "the engagement has commenced."

"So I see."

He was receiving a direct image download from Konstantin, a montage of scenes from various robot cameras and drones along Tsiolkovsky's north rim, and from the top of the central peak as well. Several of the camera views turned to snowstorms of static at the same instant; the long-range view from the crater's central peak showed a dozen white flashes of light along the rim, as though someone had switched on a string of lights.

As the lights faded, Koenig switched back to a north-rim camera view. "What the hell?"

"Radiation analyses suggest that the Confederation forces are using AM counterbattery fire," Konstantin told him.

Antimatter, magnetically suspended within a shell fired either by railgun or small-caliber missile. When the warshot slammed into normal matter, the magnetic suspension failed, and the antimatter came into contact with its opposite, liberating a small nuke's worth of heat, light, and hard gamma radiation.

Koenig opened his channel to Whitney. "Marcus? The bastards are using AM on our Marines."

"That's against international law! Do you want me to send a formal protest to Geneva, sir?"

"Negative. But I want this transmission beamed real time to the Joint Chiefs, every department head and staff AI in the Hexagon, and to every news feed that will accept it. As of right now, we are at war."

Marine Perimeter
Tsiolkovsky Crater North Rim, Lunar Farside
0849 hours, EST

"You okay, LT?" Ames sounded worried.

"I'm fine," she replied. Swiftly, she checked through her suit systems. She was fine . . . though the shockwave had given her a nasty tumble across the rocks. "A little singed. What the hell hit us?"

"Antimatter warheads," was Ames's grim reply. "I think those bastards mean business."

"Let's show them we mean business too."

"Aye, aye, sir! Platoon! Stand ready for a second round!"

She checked the platoon feed, wondering how bad it was. Three names had gone black—Blakeslee, Matloff, and Wood—dead or their comm equipment had been fried.

But her sensor net was showing six of the Confed behemoths out there had been killed as well. That didn't necessarily mean that almost a third of the enemy troops were out of action as well, of course. Battlespace drones were showing a lot of movement out there . . . probably battlesuited troops who'd bailed out of crippled personnel carriers.

But it *was* a start.

"You ready to jump, Lieutenant?" Salvatore asked her. She and Duncan had set up their kinetic-kill semi-recoilless once again, and were targeting another dust cloud on the far northern horizon.

Modern ground combat resembled a kind of macabre dance, with small fireteams armed with heavy firepower firing at enemy targets many kilometers away, then moving—fast—to avoid the inevitable incoming storm of CBF. Antimatter. *Shit.* The only thing worse would have been pocket nukes . . . and Burnham didn't think the sons of bitches were *that* crazy.

"Ready," she said. "Fire when you've acquired your target."

"Fire in the hole!"

She jumped, and again the sky exploded around her in silent white light.

Executive Office, USNA
Columbus, District of Columbia
United States of North America
0850 hours, EST

Koenig continued to watch the battle as it unfolded, feeling mildly guilty that he was doing it from the safety of the Executive Tower, 380-some thousand kilometers away.

Not that he imagined himself *safe*, by any means. If Geneva was desperate enough to use AM warheads at Tsiolkovsky, there was a possibility that they could launch a general attack on the USNA. It was unlikely; reducing North America plus a fair percentage of Europe and Asia to rubble served *no* one's interests.

His advisors had already recommended that he leave the city as a precaution, but the Executive Office—though its viewall usually showed the view over the Freedom Concourse from eighty stories up—was actually buried well beneath the main building, nearly half a kilometer beneath the streets of Columbus. If he wasn't safe here, he wasn't safe, period . . . and maybe that would atone in some small part for watching men and women die while carrying out his orders a quarter of a million miles away.

So far, there was no sign that the Confederation was planning anything other than the base grab at Tsiolkovsky. The timing of the attack, however, was illuminating.

Koenig was tempted to wonder whether the fleet deployment to 36 Ophiuchi had been planned solely for the purpose of getting the USNA fleet out of the way. There were no capital warships available at all closer than Chiron, four and a half lights away, and only a handful of USNA fighter squadrons in-system. There were some USNA ships on High Guard, of course, but they were a good five hours away in the outer system.

He'd already given orders to the 516th Fighter Wing on Mars to get to Luna as quickly as possible. They were scrambling now, but Mars was currently twenty light minutes away and on the far side of the sun. It would be a couple of hours before they could reach Tsiolkovsky. He'd also ordered several reserve wings called up here on Earth, besides the ones out of Oceana, but it would be hours before they would be in the air.

The worst of it all, though, was the gnawing possibility of some kind of double-cross—the idea that Geneva had planned an outright attack on the carrier battlegroup almost twenty light years from Earth. He wanted to warn Steiger . . . but how? While Koenig could watch events on the moon unfold with only a bit more than a second's time-lag delay, there was no way to learn what was happening at 36 Ophiuchus in less than twenty-five hours, the minimum time for a passage at maximum Alcubierre warp.

Well . . . no. That wasn't entirely true, was it? A robotic HVK-724 high-velocity scout-courier could do considerably better, with a top Alcubierre speed of something like 360 light years in a day . . . or just over fifteen lights per hour. The problem was that HVK-724s required a lot of prep time and there weren't many of them in the USNA inventory. Worse, it would be a five-hour flight, minimum, to get one out to the outer solar system, where there would be a flat-enough metric to allow it to transition to FTL.

But it would be worth it to send a robot out to 36 Oph with an encrypted warning to let Admiral Steiger know what was going down back home.

Koenig checked his inner clock. According to the plan, the battlegroup would have emerged at 36 Oph A about an hour ago. By now, they would be well along on the acceleration in to Arianrhod.

Koenig opened a channel to the USNA naval base at Mars. They ought to have an HVK-724. How long would it take to get one ready to boost?

And could it get to 36 Ophiuchi in time to make any difference at all?

Lieutenant Donald Gregory
VFA-96, Black Demons
36 Ophiuchi A System
0851 hours, TFT

They'd reach 0.97 *c* and, operating according to standard ops procedures, cut their drives in unison. The combined fleet—along with the fighters flying CAP—hurtled starward through the misshapen sky.

"CAP One, CIC." Static blasted over and through the terse words from *America*'s Combat Information Center.

"Go ahead, CIC," Mackey's voice answered.

"Orders from CO-Big. You are out of position. Adjust your vector to return to Delta-one-five starboard, immediately."

"CIC, Demons, wait one."

Shit. They'd been caught. *CO-Big* was fighter slang for "Commanding Officer Battlegroup," in this case, Delattre himself, or someone on his staff.

"I don't know, Commander," Gregory said over the squadron's tactical channel. "I think we're getting some bent-space interference, here."

Both the fleet and the accompanying fighter CAP had been accelerating at ten thousand gravities for the past fifty minutes, and were now traveling at a hairbreadth less than the speed of light. Relativity—the bizarre distortions of space and time predicted by Einstein five centuries before—had taken hold some minutes ago. From the point of view of each ship in the squadron, the entire sky seemed to be crowding forward into a hazy mass of stars encircling the bow, and with a vast, empty blackness everywhere else.

Since fighters and fleet were both accelerating at the same rate, relativistic distortions to the communications links between them were minimal still, but local space was also severely distorted by each fighter's drive singularity, which put a dimple into spacetime just ahead of each Starhawk large enough to swallow the entire ship. The static of laser comm links through distorted space made voice communications increasingly difficult.

America's orders had been clear enough so far, but Gregory's suggestion, intended lightly, wasn't completely out of the blue. It wouldn't be the first time a commanding officer had claimed communications difficulties in order to ignore orders he felt were unwise, or worse.

There was a long hesitation, and then Mackey said, "By the book, ladies and gentlemen. Adjust acceleration by minus two hundred Gs to let *America* close with us."

Gregory started to say something, then thought better of it.

After all, there wasn't much they could do about it, one way or the other.

TC/USNA CVS America
In transit
36 Ophiuchi A System
0852 hours, TFT

Gray was fuming, helplessly furious. Someone on Admiral Delattre's staff had spotted Mackey's squadron pulling ahead and to port—obviously with the intent of screening the carrier from Tango One. The order had come from Delattre himself. *Get those fighters back in formation, close abeam of the ship!*

The order was emblematic of a basic difference in space combat tactics as interpreted by the Confederation and by the more daring fleet commanders of some of the Confederation's member states. *The book* said in no uncertain terms: keep your force together and intact, with each fleet element positioned to give support to all other elements. That included the tactical fighter squadrons flying CAP, as well as the various support vessels in the fleet, the destroyers, gunships, and light cruisers.

Official tactics, both within the Confederation at large and within the USNA Star Navy, tended to abide by this rule, and for an excellent reason. In the vast and empty depths of planetary space, with ships moving on various vectors at high speeds and under brutal accelerations, it was far too easy for a fleet to become scattered. Once scattered, individual ships could easily be attacked by small groups of fighters or by hunter-killer packs of light capital ships, and their defenses overwhelmed.

But some commanders were more relaxed than others in exactly how they read the book. Koenig had been one such; he'd been notorious, in fact, for bending rules and regs.

People under his command held that the only reason he'd not been court-martialed during his tenure as CO-CBG was because his tactics had been so successful. And Gray had tried to emulate him.

Both men were long-time students of history, including the history of naval warfare going back to long before humans had taken their wars into space. Some six hundred years earlier, during the Age of Sail, naval military doctrine had decreed that ships should adhere to the so-called Fighting Instructions, and with a similar reasoning. Ships had been expected to proceed in strict line-ahead formation to present massed broadsides to the enemy, and to avoid being surrounded. Admiral Horatio Nelson had ended the age of the Fighting Instructions when he'd broken the rules—and the Franco-Spanish line at Trafalgar.

While Gray didn't consider himself to be a Nelson, he did wonder why modern tacticians seemingly remained blind to the one absolute of military planning: *tactics must change with evolving technology*.

History was filled with examples—disasters, blunders, and pigheaded shortsightedness of epic decisiveness. During the American Civil War, troops had continued to maneuver and advance in solid blocks of infantry, despite rifled muskets and massed artillery. In World War I, commanding officers had continued to order mass frontal attacks against machineguns and entrenched troop positions. In World War II, naval air power had ended the reign of seagoing armored battleships.

In the modern age, technology continued to advance with breathtaking speed and complexity, ever moving, ever unfolding into new and more intricate forms. Twenty years ago, the singularity drive on a capital ship like *America* could give her an acceleration of around five thousand gravities, which meant it took over an hour and a half to boost up to near-c. Improvements in the way the singularity-induced warping of space was projected and shaped around the ship meant they could manage ten thousand gravities today, and reach 99.7 percent c in about fifty minutes. Reducing the time required to get from the emergence point to the inner regions of the target star system had changed both the strategic and tactical pictures. Battles had become more fluid and more far-ranging, with higher ship speeds, and enemy vessels such as the dozen or so ships of Tango One had become more dangerous to a fleet's deployment.

But that thinking, evidently, hadn't percolated up to Geneva's military high command yet . . . or been embraced by senior officers like Delattre and his staff.

Gray glanced up at the main screen wrapped around the forward half of the bridge. Fifty minutes after they'd begun accelerating, the fighters and the larger ships they were protecting had reached 0.997 c. Operating under linked navigational programs, the flickering drive singularities on all vessels, both the capital ships and the fighters on CAP, now switched off.

For some minutes, now, the universe outside had been transformed into strangeness.

Starbow.

They called it the Pohl Effect, after a pre-spaceflight writer who'd first described it. Physicists later had proven why the starbow could *not* exist . . . and were still arguing over why it appeared anyway in defiance of astrophysical law. A mathematical assessment of the shifting wavelengths of dopplered starlight showed that the colors visible inside each fighter's cockpit shouldn't change much, if at all.

The geometries of relativistic flight dictated that the entire sky be compressed forward by the physics of chromatic aberration—that was well understood. Also understood was the fact that wavelengths coming from stars up ahead would blue-shift far up the spectrum, while those coming from astern would red-shift into the far infrared. The light they were now seeing from the star ahead was 36 Ophiuchi A's deep infrared radiation, normally invisible to human eyes, blue-shifted now to visibility.

But as the ships inched ever closer to the unattainable goal of c itself, the starlight seemed to smear and stretch, and as the individual light sources were further compressed into a near-solid ring of hazy light 60 degrees forward, the distortion seemed to act like a prism, with the ring becoming a gloriously colored band, deep violet at the inner edge around the black disk of emptiness directly ahead, deep red at the outer edge, fuzzing off into invisibility, where it trailed into the emptiness to either side and astern.

According to the physicists, the starbow shouldn't be . . . but it *was*, ethereal, eerily beautiful, and mysterious.

America's AI pinged him through his in-head link. A targeting square against the starbow ahead and to port flashed red, indicating a change to Tango One's status. Relativistic distortions made it impossible for the human eye to track movement against velocity-smeared starlight, but the fighter's AI was watching the mathematics of incoming radiation rather than the light-generated image of the distant Slan warships.

Gray checked the elapsed time on both clocks—objective and subjective, scowling. *Time does fly*, he thought, *when you're having fun.*

It also flies when you're traveling at close to the speed of light.

He needed the in-head link with the ship's AI to untangle the relativistic effects, and to figure out what exactly was happening. The faster a ship traveled, the slower time ran, an effect called time dilation well-known from Einstein's relativity equations. The first fifty minutes of acceleration—fifty minutes objective, as measured for an at-rest observer—had for Gregory felt like a bit more than thirty-seven minutes, with his time running slower and slower the faster he was moving. Now, cruising at 0.997 c, time passed at a rate of thirteen to one. That meant that a full minute for the outside universe passed for *America* and her crew in only 4.6 seconds. It was like everything in the rest of the universe was moving thirteen times faster than it ought to, and in combat that was a deadly handicap.

"Give me an estimate on their course," he told the AI. "What are they up to?"

In his head, a new window opened, showing a three-dimensional schematic of the battlegroup's course—a bundle of green lines growing through emptiness. Ahead, a blue cone showed all the possible paths for Tango One. The cone would narrow as more data was received and processed, but right now it looked like a time to intercept of nearly thirty minutes.

Tango One was suddenly—*magically*—in two places at once.

And the nearer of the two was less than 30 million kilometers away. . . .

Lieutenant Donald Gregory
VFA-96, Black Demons
36 Ophiuchi A System
0852 hours, TFT

From Gregory's vantage point, Tango One appeared to have popped into existence only a hundred light seconds away, moving at very nearly the speed of light. He felt a terrible sinking feeling in his gut; the enemy spacecraft shouldn't be that close yet—shouldn't even be moving, not when they had only just seen the light from the Earth fleet moments before.

And yet . . . they were *here*. . . .

"Enemy spacecraft!" Mackey shouted over the tactical link. "Break port! Break! *Break*!"

With a thought, Gregory rolled his fighter left, his fighter responding to his mental command over the neural link. Twelve targets, spreading out . . . and the image he was seeing in his mind, he had to remind himself, was a minute and a half old.

Worse, far worse, a hundred seconds in objective time was only a hair more than seven seconds at this velocity.

And everything was happening at once. . . .

Chapter Eleven

TC/USNA CVS America
In transit
36 Ophiuchi A System
0853 hours, TFT

"Bring all weapons on-line," Gray ordered. "Secure all pressure bulkheads."

How . . . *how*? There was no way the enemy ships could have made the transit from the point at which they'd been lurking off to one side of the Confederation fleet's line of flight to here, where they could actually attack . . . not unless they were able to engage in *tactical* faster-than-light travel. The fact that *America*'s sensors were now showing Tango One to be in two places at once argued that this was, in fact, exactly what was happening.

Using Alcubierre Drive to travel faster than light between star systems was what was known as strategic FTL. *Tactical* FTL, also known as microjumps, was something else entirely. Human technology couldn't do it, and if the Slan had it, it meant trouble. Both faster-than-light Alcubierre Drive and the singularity drive used for intra-system travel and maneuvering worked by using projected gravitational fields, carefully shaped to avoid tidal effects, to sharply bend space.

Alcubierre Drive, however, bent local space so sharply that the ship to all intents and purposes dropped out of the universe altogether, into a spacetime bubble of what was glibly called metaspace. The effect was unpredictable, however, when used too close to major natural gravitational effects—the gravity field of a sun, for instance. That was why—depending upon the mass of the local star—incoming starships switched off their Alcubierre Drives and emerged within the target system at some tens of AUs out from the star.

But there was a far more basic reason that ships didn't zip at faster-than-light speeds from, say, Earth to Mars in an instant. When a ship was wrapped up in its Alcubierre bubble, *it was impossible to see outside* . . . and precise navigation became a nightmare. Ship AIs could predict the locations of planets and moons across distances of a light second or more with a high degree of accuracy, but if the time delay inherent in the speed of light was too great, predicting the positions of star ships, fighters, and orbital facilities or bases with the requisite accuracy became all but impossible. If the navigational and control systems on those Tango One ships had been off by even a few nanoseconds, they might have emerged within the Confederation fleet—a disaster for *both* sides—or they might have emerged too far from the fleet to do anything at all except play a game of catch-up with the advantage of surprise lost.

And yet, somehow, Tango One had moved within minutes of the light from the Confederation fleet's emergence reaching them, apparently dropping into their version of Alcubierre Drive and jumping to within two light minutes of the fleet in an instant. It could be chance . . . but in the middle of so much emptiness, Gray didn't believe in chance. The only alternative was that the Slan had a significant technological advantage over Humankind, one that might well mean that the Confederation could not beat them.

"Weapons!" Gray called.

"Weapons, aye." *America*'s weapons officer was Commander Laurie Taggart, a tough, no-nonsense AAC woman from Chicago. The Ancient Alien Creationists believed that

Humans had been genetically uplifted by aliens hundreds of thousands of years ago, and Gray sometimes wondered if the AACs in the Navy were afraid they were fighting their creators. Taggart, at least, had never let her beliefs interfere with her duty.

"Primaries on the largest Tango One warship," he said, "as soon as it's in seventy percent range."

"Aye, aye, Captain."

At near-c velocities, targeting an enemy warship could be tricky. The target would have moved in the time it took light to crawl back and forth between the two vessels, and even the best AI could not predict a target's course if the target was making periodic course changes to avoid incoming fire. Seventy percent meant that Taggart was to take a shot whenever her weapons system AIs predicted a seventy percent chance of scoring a hit.

America began to swing to face the enemy. Her primary weapons were her spinal mounted railguns, twin linear magnetic accelerators running for much of the vessel's length that could slam one-ton projectiles into an enemy ship with the kinetic energy equivalent of a hundred-megaton warhead. The carrier had not yet completed her turn when the enemy ships *blurred* . . . and then they were past the perimeter defense destroyers and within the Confederation fleet. The German destroyer *Mölder* flared into a tiny nova of searing light, her bow and stern tumbling off in opposite directions. An instant later, the *Worden*, a USNA heavy cruiser, took a hit that vaporized her aft-drive modules and left her a shattered hulk, leaking atmosphere and water in glittering clouds of ice crystals.

The Confederation fleet was being cut to pieces before it could even begin to respond to the threat.

"I want an analysis of those weapons," Gray said, addressing *America*'s primary AI. "What are they hitting us with?"

"We are detecting 511 kilo-electron volt radiation," the AI whispered in Gray's mind, "which is characteristic of positronium annihilation."

"My God . . ."

Positronium was a so-called "exotic atom," a negatively

charged electron in a bound quantum state with its antimatter opposite, a positron. Normally, the balance of the two as they orbited each other was unstable, decaying and bringing about a matter-antimatter release of gamma rays after a very brief interval of time—either 125 picoseconds or 142 nanoseconds, depending on the relative spin states of the two particles. By beaming positronium with particle velocities extremely close to the speed of light, however, it was possible to extend that short life span through relativistic time dilation.

That was the theory, at any rate, but human technology had not been able to turn theory into a working weapon. The Slan, evidently, had done just that. An energy fingerprint of 511 keV for the gamma quanta released identified the Slan weapon as para-positronium, the antiparallel spin variety with a lifetime of 125 picoseconds.

The European Union star carrier *Klemens von Metternich* appeared to stagger under a terrific impact, her 500-meter-broad shield cap shredding away in a vast, silvery burst of freezing water.

"Electrical potential cascading across the *Grant*'s hull suggests a different weapon," *America*'s AI continued, "likely an electron beam of some sort."

Electron beams were a more conventional technology, well understood and in use both by human warships and man-portable weapons. Shielding against them required negatively charged hull fields, but there were ways to smash through a ship's repulsive shielding, with a particle beam accelerated to high-enough velocities.

The fleet was up against one hell of a technological wall. . . .

Lieutenant Donald Gregory
VFA-96, Black Demons
36 Ophiuchi A System
0854 hours, TFT

Since the fleet was now in the coast phase of its flight path, with all singularity drives switched off, all of the fleet's ships appeared to be hanging motionless within the black vault of a weirdly distorted universe. The wreckage of the stricken vessels, the *Mölder,* the *Worden,* and the *von Metternich*, continued to pace the fleet, their velocities still matching that of the other ships. A fourth vessel—the USNA gunship *Ulysses S. Grant*—was hit by an invisible weapon that seemed to claw at her hull, shredding it. Gregory's instrumentation showed a surge of electrical potential searing across the stricken ship's hull, arcing into hard vacuum.

"Close and fire, Demons!" Mackey yelled. "Get in close!"

The Tango One alien vessels were incredibly maneuverable. Gregory rolled onto a new vector that put one enemy warship directly ahead . . . then watched it blur and vanish from his screens just as he fired his particle weapon. The beam missed, and in response a fusion beam slashed across his bow. He jinked hard right, changing course and acceleration constantly and randomly. Closer . . . he had to get *closer* if he was going to have a chance of hitting one of those things. . . .

His naked eyes would have been useless, of course, in the weirdly twisted skies of relativistic velocities, but his fighter's AI could tease data from the distortion and present it through his in-head links. He could see details of the alien hulls, now, within an open window in his mind, as warbook data scrolled up the side of the display. The largest ships—two of them—were Ballistas, according to the warbook—awkward, boxy-looking affairs with ugly, blotched paint schemes that looked like random slashes of green, red, and black. No two Ballistas were exactly the same, Gregory noticed; the designs of their hulls looked as random as their paint jobs. Each was around 300 meters long, all angles and sharp edges. The other ten ships had been designated as Sabers, leaner, squatter versions of the Ballistas painted black and red, each a third the length of their more massive consorts. Confederation Military Intelligence equated the Sabers with human destroyers, the Ballista with cruisers.

Stiletto fighters, like finned knife blades, spilled from several of the Slan warships, spreading out through nearby space. Fusion beams seared into the Confederation fleet, blasting comm channels with harsh static. The *Vladivostok* and the *Bhatkal* both were hit, the smaller *Bhatkal* vanishing in a silent flash of dazzling light, the bigger *Vlad* crumpling as the miniature black holes housed within her quantum power plant drifted free and devoured the Russian cruiser from within.

Gregory selected two of his Fer-de-lance missiles, targeting one of the Ballistas now just 20,000 kilometers ahead, and thoughtclicked the launch command. The missiles streaked away from his fighter and he spun the craft through 80 degrees, seeking another target. Silent explosions flared and blossomed within the distorted sky. As he twisted and turned, the starbow shifted with his movements, always centered on the direction the fleet was moving and stretching across some 60 degrees of view, but showing local distortions as his Starhawk changed vector.

Demon Five, Lieutenant Tammi Anderson's ship, vanished in a direct hit by a positron beam, a moth winking out in the light of a laser torch. Lieutenant Randy Gibb's fighter vanished an instant later in a fusion beam from an alien Stiletto. The European Union heavy cruiser *Cassard* was hit, her forward shield cap ripped apart, the remaining wreckage spinning end for end as it wheeled through space.

Neither of Gregory's missiles got close to its target. A fusion beam wiped them out of the sky.

Damn it, the Confederation fleet was *losing*.

TC/USNA CVS America
In transit
36 Ophiuchi A System
0855 hours, TFT

"Fire!"

At Gray's command, *America*'s twin kinetic-kill launchers hurled a pair of warheads at the nearest of the oncoming Ballistas, but the clumsy-looking Slan craft blurred and shifted to one side, easily avoiding the KK missiles. The technological wall they faced might well be insurmountable.

So far, most of the alien clients of the Sh'daar possessed technologies within a century or two of Earth's. This almost certainly was due to the Sh'daar penchant for limiting the technologies of their subject races, especially in the GRIN arena—but those technologies in turn fed others, including gravitics, ship drives and power plants, and beam weapons. The maneuverability of the Slan warships, coupled with the power of their weapons, meant that fighting them was like pitting ancient fabric-and-wood biplanes with piston-prop engines against modern fighters with gravitic drives and high-energy lasers.

The human fleet didn't stand a chance.

Lieutenant Donald Gregory
VFA-96, Black Demons
36 Ophiuchi A System
0855 hours, TFT

"Cover my ass!" Lieutenant Nathan Esperanza called over the squadron tactical channel. "I'm gonna take this to knife-fighting range!"

"Copy that, Nate," Gregory called back. "I'm on your six!"

Gregory dropped onto Esperanza's tail about 80 kilometers behind him, the two Starhawks arrowing toward a haphazard 200-meter collection of flat surfaces and sharp angles painted red, green, and black. A Stiletto peeled away from an enemy formation and closed on Esperanza from the flank; Gregory ordered his AI to program a cluster of Krait missiles for a cascade release, then triggered the launch.

In close space combat, you *had* to fight through the senses and the reactions of your AI. Everything in the sky right now—capital ships, fighters, Krait missiles, expanding clouds of white-hot plasma—was traveling in more or less the same direction at close to the speed of light, so Relativistic Temporal Differentials didn't figure into things . . . not yet. Within the unaccelerated universe outside of battlespace, time was proceeding some thirteen times slower than it was for Gregory and the others in the battlegroup, which meant that more enemy ships might be arriving in very short order.

But even ignoring RTDs, the relative velocities among attackers and defenders were so high that merely human reaction times were far too slow to manage events. The artificial intelligences on board the human ships, however, perceived, recorded, and reasoned many thousands of times faster than organic systems, even than electronically enhanced organic systems, and that fact alone made such combat possible.

Of course, the enemy must have AIs as well—or an alien equivalent. Slan technology was not at all well understood. The way the hostiles were maneuvering, snapping back and forth far too quickly for human perceptions to record or react to them, they *must* have some pretty good computer tech over there, either as independent AIs or as cybernetic blends of organic and machine intelligence.

On the other hand, Gregory thought, the Slan AIs couldn't be that far ahead of human systems. The Sh'daar control of the technologies developed by their client systems meant that they couldn't have much of an edge there.

And that meant that they *could* be beaten.

The question was how?

A chain of nuclear blasts strobed in a nearly straight line across the sky 20,000 kilometers distant, one VG-10 Krait after the next detonating in open space. The cascade maneuver had been designed to penetrate tough enemy defenses. The lead Krait would detonate well short of the target, and the expanding plasma fireball provided cover for the next Krait in line, which would fly through the expanding gas cloud to detonate closer to the target . . . followed by the next . . . and the next. . . .

The last two Krait missiles either struck the Stiletto or came quite close to it; the Slan fighter vanished in the double fireball, emerging as a spray of half-molten debris.

"Kill!" Gregory shouted, exultant. "Scratch one Stiletto!"

"Thanks, Nungie!" Esperanza called. "Arming Krait cascade and a Fer-de-Lance . . . target lock . . . *Fox One!*"

Esperanza released a cluster of Kraits followed by the bigger Fer-de-Lance . . . but the Kraits were swept from the sky by a fusion beam from the clumsy-looking target. The Fer-de-Lance, with a more powerful onboard AI, survived a few seconds longer, jinking and weaving back and forth as it bore in on its target . . . and then an electron beam fried its circuits and reduced it to a lump of dead metal and plastic. Esperanza's Starhawk rolled left and accelerated, falling out of its path toward the Slan warship . . . and then a fusion beam from the target caught the fighter and vaporized it in a searing flash of light.

Shit . . .

Gregory programmed a flight of Kraits to take independent and divergent paths to the target, then broke off, the sky tumbling wildly about him. Maybe with a dozen missiles all coming in from different directions at once, he would have a chance in hell of getting at least one twenty-megaton blast on-target. His Stiletto kill of a moment ago might have happened only because the pilot was focusing too hard on Esperanza's Starhawk, and not enough on what was going on in other parts of the sky.

Something struck his fighter, a savage shock, and then he was tumbling helplessly through strangeness. For several horrifying seconds, Gregory lost all input from his AI. That meant that his corrected visual systems were down, and he was looking at the sky as it really was . . . everywhere a black and impenetrable emptiness, with a tightly smudged glow of colored light squeezed into a 60-degree cone forward. The Starhawk's AI took incoming light and used mathematics to reverse-engineer the panorama, showing what the surrounding sky would look like without the relativistic distortion, and drew in such finicky details as the locations of both friendly and enemy ships, exploding missiles, and energy beams that otherwise would be invisible to the human eye.

He also couldn't tell how badly damaged his ship was.

Life support appeared to still be functioning, along with emergency power and the basic visual feeds from scanners on the fighter's outer hull, but he was tumbling, clearly, and his primary power plant and singularity drive both were down. If he couldn't fix them, he would continue drifting at a hair beneath the speed of light, unable to decelerate and re-enter the nonaccelerated universe. Commo was down, so he couldn't call for help.

A few terrifying seconds later, though, the AI came back on-line, initiating a damage-control reset, and the cosmos around him became again understandable. His singularity power plant came back on-line, and an instant later his drive indicators winked green, showing them powered down but ready for operation. His communications feeds came back as well, and he no longer felt quite so lonely.

He was drifting through the center of the Slan squadron, apparently unseen or at least unrecognized. His Starhawk was still tumbling, so possibly it was giving a good imitation of a derelict hulk or a lifeless piece of debris. One massive green, black, and red craft was closing with him at a few hundred kilometers per hour, would pass him by at a range of only a few kilometers.

Gregory realized that chance had presented him with an invaluable opportunity. The question was how best to make use of it.

TC/USNA CVS America
In transit
36 Ophiuchi A System
0856 hours, TFT

Two Ballistas and ten Sabers were penetrating the human fleet, fusion and positron beams stabbing and snapping in a savage storm of destruction.

"The railguns aren't doing shit," Gray said. "Damn it, they're mopping us up!"

As if to underscore that realization, something hit the

America, something huge and massively powerful, slamming Gray and his bridge crew to one side in their protectively enclosed seats. For a moment he couldn't move; his command chair had folded itself around him, absorbing excess energy, muffling the shock before releasing him. A shrill roar sounded in Gray's ears, and the air grew suddenly frigid. Alarms sounded: *pressure loss, bridge tower . . .*

Twisting in his seat, Gray looked back over his shoulder at the pressure-sealed doors leading to the flag bridge, and found himself staring into black emptiness.

The flag bridge was . . . *gone.* . . .

Lieutenant Donald Gregory
VFA-96, Black Demons
36 Ophiuchi System
0856 hours, TFT

"My God, look at *America*!" Kemper's voice howled over the communications net.

"She's been hit!" Mason added.

"Cut the babble, Demons!" Mackey called. "Keep focused on the hostiles!"

America was too distant to be seen with the naked eye, of course, but Gregory's AI showed him a long-range image when he asked for it. The star carrier *America*—a long, dark gray umbrella shape was in a slow tumble, out of control. He couldn't see any damage at first, but a telltale wisp of fog behind and beneath the sheltering reach of the forward end cap suggested that atmosphere was venting into space, and his AI's analyses of the carrier's status brought up a dozen red, blinking flags—communications network down, hull protective shielding down, power systems off-line, singularity drive off-line, weapons down, atmosphere breach in the bridge tower . . .

Things were freaking *bad.* . . .

The Slan warship ahead changed course slightly, obviously vectoring toward the stricken carrier. It would still pass damned close to Gregory's fighter, however, close enough for him to slam a full load of warheads up that thing's ass. The resultant detonations would kill him, he knew . . . but he stood an excellent chance of killing the Slan warship as well.

Or was there another way?

He consulted with his AI, his thoughts and the electronic responses of his fighter's computer network flashing back and forth so quickly that there were no words, no reasoning, just *awareness*, and at speeds far greater than mere organics could ever attain. His AI warned that the maneuver Gregory had just suggested was extremely dangerous . . . and had a high probability of ending with the Starhawk's destruction in a collapsing singularity.

But the AI had also detected a power build-up in the Slan craft as it readied its weapons to fire into the helpless star carrier behind them. It was less than a thousand kilometers distant, now . . . definitely knife-fighting range.

Gregory thoughtclicked an override, then gave a quick series of commands.

And his fighter's power plant and singularity drive switched on. . . .

TC/USNA CVS America
In transit
36 Ophiuchi A System
0856 hours, TFT

As the air pressure on the bridge dropped, Gray's shipboard utilities reacted automatically, sealing themselves off. A black nanofilm flowed from his cuffs to cover his hands, as close-fitting as paint, while his collar expanded, puffed out, then ballooned up and over his face, enclosing his head completely in a transparent shell that rapidly hardened into diamond-hard transparency. Designed for emergency use only, the suit had a small environmental unit positioned at the small of his back that would provide him with about fifteen minutes' worth of air, and power enough to keep him from freezing for the next hour or so.

He released himself from his chair and pushed up into the center of the bridge compartment, floating free. Slowly, the port bulkhead swung up and connected with his feet; the ship was in a slow and ponderous tumble, creating a very low-G illusion of gravity. The other bridge personnel appeared uninjured, their own utilities transitioning from normal uniform to air-tight space suits within the space of a few seconds. *"Damage control!"* he thought. *"How bad is it?"*

Data flooded into his mind.

"America has been hit by a positron beam," the ship's AI told him. "Most of the blast was deflected by our magnetic shielding, but the bridge tower has suffered a hull breach and major internal damage. Drives and weapon systems knocked off-line. Life support at fifty percent. Magnetic shielding at ten percent. Casualties unknown, but light. Ship is initiating repairs."

As he listened to the ship's AI, he read the damage reports coming in from each of the ship's departments, a litany of off-line systems and relatively minor damage. *America,* in fact, had only been grazed by the Slan positron beam. The only serious damage had been to the bridge tower, which extended from the ship's spine just forward of the rotating hab modules and docking bays, and just aft of the shield cap. Light casualties, Gray realized, might well mean only the officers and crew who'd been on the flag bridge a moment ago—Admiral Steiger and his staff, Admiral Delattre and *his* staff. . . .

And with a sharp, inner Jolt, Gray realized that with their deaths, he, as Steiger's flag captain, was now in command not only of the stricken *America,* but of the entire battlegroup as well.

Not that there was a damned thing he could do about that right now. With ship communications down, he couldn't talk to the other ships of the fleet, couldn't coordinate the defense, couldn't even receive the tactical feeds that would tell him what the hell was going on outside.

In fact, they'd come hellishly close to losing the ship's bridge as well as the flag bridge. The power surge through the bridge tower's electrical nexi and control systems had been the reason for most power systems being knocked off-line. *America*, however, possessed a sophisticated self-repair ability, the logical outgrowth of current nanotechnology in ship systems and structure. When he looked aft toward the flag bridge again, he could see a dense webwork of crisscrossing threads already stretching across the ragged tear where the bridge pressure doors had been, and as he watched, each thread doubled, then redoubled every second or so. The webwork grew thicker and thicker until, within a couple of minutes, the breach had been sealed, and air was pumping once again onto the bridge.

The bridge crew kept their emergency suits on, however, and a couple of ensigns moved from person to person, sailing across the middle of the compartment to reach each station, handing out larger backpack units that would provide air, power, and water for up to twelve hours.

The question was whether they *had* twelve hours. *America* was helpless, a kilometer-long target slowly tumbling through space, and outside, unseen, the Slan warships would be closing in. . . .

Chapter Twelve

12 November 2424

Lieutenant Donald Gregory
VFA-96, Black Demons
36 Ophiuchi A System
0856 hours, TFT

Gregory accelerated his fighter, closing with the oncoming Slan warship—one of the two Ballistas. What he was about to try had never been done, as far as he knew.

At least, if it *had* been done, the pilot had not lived to tell about it in debriefing.

He would only have an instant to wait. At his current velocity toward 36 Ophiuchi A, several seconds would pass literally in the blink of an eye. His AI, working at superhuman speed, was now controlling everything.

The singularity drive used by human ships projected a severely distorted sphere of spacetime ahead of the craft, essentially collapsing it into a micro-black hole powerful enough to gravitationally attract the ship at tens of thousands of Gs. The projection flickered, turning on and off thousands of times per second, always staying just ahead of the ship, which began falling—literally in free fall—toward the ever-receding microsingularity. A finessing of the fields collapsing the sphere of space distorted it to avoid the nastiness of tidal effects, and it was possible to project them closer or further from the ship's prow in order to fine-tune the acceleration.

Drive engineers referred to it as "bootstrapping," and since a ship—or its crew—did not feel *gravitational* acceleration, it had opened up, first, the solar system, and then access to the stars by allowing ships to boost to the near-light velocities required for Alcubierre FTL in minutes rather than a year or more.

The technology was not without some serious dangers, though. An engineering failure could drop a ship into a black hole of its own making, too fast a whip-turn around the singularity could generate centrifugal force enough to pulp a fighter pilot . . . and "dustballs," clouds of dust, hydrogen gas, and micron-sized debris collected by the singularities during the course of a long boost could end up hurtling off into space at near-c . . . where they might well pose a random navigational hazard millennia in the future and light years away.

And the plan Gregory had just proposed to his AI was juggling all three of those threats.

The Slan Ballista reacted to his sudden power-up and acceleration; Gregory's AI warned of weapon systems building up power, but his fighter had already leaped across the intervening distance, the green, black, and red hull of the alien ship expanding to form a massive cliff blurring across his sensor field.

His Starhawk's singularity projector switched on, and the fighter swung sharply as though turning on a hinge. The singularity field sank into alien hull metal, and there was a jolt, a hard one that slammed Gregory forward against the embrace of his seat . . .

. . . and then he was hurtling into emptiness once more, his fighter now spinning slowly end for end.

Behind him, the flank of the Slan Ballista seemed to unzip, spilling debris and gas in a plume of freezing vapor. His flickering drive singularity had buzz sawed through the Slan armor, ripping through hull metal and shredding internal structure. In that same eye's-blink instant, Gregory's

AI had triggered the fighter's beam weapons; with the alien vessel's hull shields and magnetic defenses down, the Starhawk's particle beams had burned deep into the massive vessel's core, causing savage and unrelenting destruction.

To get close enough to the Slan warship, he'd had to act like an inert lump of debris—harmlessly adrift through battlespace. Once his drive had engaged, the Slan defenses would react to him as they did to any incoming missile, but his AI had been able to time things so tightly that the enemy had been unable to respond until it was too late.

Now, though, he needed to bring his fighter back under full control. A pair of Sabers were vectoring in, looking for blood. Gregory punched his singularity drive to put some distance between him and incoming retribution. Fusion beams snapped across intervening space, but he was already accelerating, jinking back and forth randomly to make it tough for Slan fire control computers to predict his course.

He continued to monitor the damaged Slan vessel, however. There was a chance, if its weapons were still on-line, that it could lash out at him as he hurtled into the darkness.

The alien craft clearly had other problems, however. While the Starhawk's singularity projector had been flickering on and off several thousand times per second, the *last* projected black hole had been released intact inside the target's hull. Traveling with the same velocity as the passing Starhawk, it was eating its way now through the ship's structure, devouring everything it encountered.

After a few seconds, the Slan Ballista began to crumple. . . .

TC/USNA CVS America
In transit
36 Ophiuchi A System
0857 hours, TFT

"Ship systems are coming back on-line," *America*'s AI whispered in Gray's mind. "Fifty seconds until full power is restored."

Fifty seconds was an eternity in combat, but *America's* magnetic shields were coming back up, and plasma jets were already firing to correct her gentle tumble. In a circular pit in the forward part of the bridge deck, a combat tank repeated the display from the ship's Combat Information Center. One of the CAP fighters had just made a very close passage of a Slan Ballista, apparently disemboweling the far larger alien vessel with its singularity drive.

"Get me the ID on that pilot," Gray told the AI. Data appeared within his in-head. Lieutenant Donald Gregory, a colonial from Osiris. That boy was going to get a medal out of this . . . *if* he survived. If *any* of them survived.

"CIC, Bridge," he said over an open tactical channel. "Pass the word to focus everything we can bring to bear on that one remaining Ballista. Fighters too."

"Aye, aye, Captain," Commander Margery Holmes, the CIC boss, replied. "The fighters are already vectoring for the Tango One Ballista. They just might beat us to it."

Indeed, according to the combat tank, the seven surviving Starhawks of the Black Demons were swarming toward the remaining Ballista, releasing clouds of nuclear-tipped missiles. Mackey had obviously already had the same idea—kill that remaining Ballista and Tango One might be crippled, forcing the rest to break off.

Might. It was a long shot, but, at the moment, it was all the hard-pressed human fleet had.

Lieutenant Donald Gregory
VFA-96, Black Demons
36 Ophiuchi System
0858 hours, TFT

"Ferdie, set for launch. Fox one!" Gregory called. A Fer-de-lance dropped from his fighter's belly, the drive ignited, and the black sliver streaked toward the remaining Ballista, now 100,000 kilometers distant. "That's my last nuke!"

Chains of detonations were showing now ahead, working their way toward the Slan warship. Expanding clouds of plasma served both to make targeting the remaining incoming missiles all but impossible, but also tended to disperse fusion beams or positron bursts. The Black Demons were on a steep learning curve, adapting their tactics from moment to moment to counter each new Slan defense.

The use of large numbers of nuclear warheads appeared to be having an effect. Three of the Sabers had been destroyed already, their defenses overwhelmed . . . and now the surviving Ballista was twisting and jinking in a desperate attempt to escape the incoming missiles.

The missiles—Fer-de-lance and Lanceheads, mostly, but with a few of the big space-to-surface Boomslangs and Taipans as well—streaked through the expanding fireballs of a dozen VG-10 Kraits. Several were knocked out by the Ballista's antimissile defenses . . . but then a VG-44c Fer-de-lance slashed through the plasma cloud and exploded within a few meters of the Ballista's hull. A quarter of the enemy ship's bulk was vaporized in an instant; the rest began dissolving as warhead after warhead slammed home and detonated, until nothing was left of the massive alien warship but a cloud of white-hot gas.

"Kill!" Mackey yelled over the tactical channel. "Scratch another Ballista, two for two!"

Two larger missiles, the so-called planet-busting Taipan, and the slightly smaller Boomslang, flashed through the plasma cloud and began to circle.

"Kemper! Del Rey!" Mackey called to the pilots who'd fired those missiles. "Get your warheads under control. See if you can go after some of those Sabers!"

"On it, Mack!" Kemper replied.

"Black Demons, this is CIC," a voice replied from the ship. "The rest of Tango One appears to be withdrawing. Do not, repeat, do *not* pursue."

"Copy that, CIC. We'll be good. . . ."

In the distance, Kemper's Boomslang detonated, filling emptiness with light. Gregory couldn't tell if the shot had taken out any of the surviving Tango One warships or not.

There were five Sabers left in the sky, half of the original complement of ten, and they were definitely on the run now, accompanied by a school of the much smaller Stilettos. A moment later, the alien Sabers blurred . . . and were gone. The Stilettos continued accelerating, dwindling into the distance.

"Woo-hoo!" Kemper keened. *"Run,* you bastards!"

A couple of other fighter pilots joined in, but Gregory kept silent. The stark nightmare of the situation was that the twelve alien vessels of Tango One—the equivalent of ten Confederation destroyers and two light cruisers—had destroyed six capital ships and damaged four more, including the star carrier *America,* all in the space of a handful of seconds. Half of the Black Demons were gone as well. The alien beam weapons had been incredibly powerful, more powerful than anything the human ships could match.

And the fleet was still falling toward the inner system of 36 Ophiuchi A at near-c, with far more Slan warships—and larger ones—waiting for them there.

Worst of all, the enemy had demonstrated a disturbing capability: making tactical microjumps in apparent defiance of the gravitational curve of local, intra-system space.

Ever since the first encounter with a Sh'daar client species—the Turusch, at the disastrous Battle of Beta Pictorus more than fifty years ago—humans had been at a serious disadvantage. The Sh'daar philosophy that limited certain technological developments within the space they controlled still meant that most of their clients possessed military technologies some decades in advance of human capabilities. The divide was informally known as the miltech wall.

At a guess, however, Slan technologies might be centuries ahead of Earth. Comparing technologies between technic species too often was a matter of apples and oranges, since differences between cultures, philosophies, and languages made an understanding of alien science and engineering all but impossible. But the ability to pull off an in-system FTL transit was *huge.*

The miltech wall might simply be too high this time.

TC/USNA CVS America
In transit
36 Ophiuchi A System
0859 hours, TFT

"The enemy is in full retreat, Captain," Commander Holmes said. "They have cleared the battlespace at FTL speeds."

"Very well," Gray replied. "Keep an eye on them."

"Full power is restored to the ship," the AI told him.

"Helm, correct course to put us back on attack vector."

Though *America* had continued to travel at near-*c* toward Arianrhod even when she'd been disabled, she'd acquired some lateral drift during the attack. If that went uncorrected, she would be off-target when she arrived at her destination.

"Correcting course to attack vector, aye, sir."

"Comm. Open a channel to all ships."

"Channel open, aye, sir."

"This is Captain Gray, on board *America*," he said. "Admiral Steiger and Admiral Delattre are KIA. As flag captain of this squadron, I am formally assuming command. All vessels are to adjust their vectors to maintain an attack approach on the target."

Acknowledgements began coming in, from the USNA ships first, but then from several of the Confederation vessels.

"Captain, Comm," the communications officer said. "I have a private call for you, tight channel, from the *Napoleon*."

Here it comes, Gray thought. "Very well. Put it through."

"Captain Gray," a new voice said in his mind. "This is Captain Lavallée. As Admiral Delattre's flag captain, I remind you that *I* am in command of the fleet."

"With respect, sir," Gray replied, "Admiral Delattre transferred his flag to this vessel two days ago. The *America* is the flagship of this fleet, and I *am* hereby taking command."

"I regret, sir, that you see things that way. . . ."

It was the supreme nightmare of joint fleet operations,

a breakdown in the normal chain of command that determined who was in charge.

"Look, Captain," Gray said. "The worst thing we can do is get into an argument in the middle of an assault. I suggest—"

"No suggestions, Captain Gray. *I* am in command. The fleet will execute a near-*c* fly-by of the objective, then reorient for an immediate return to Sol."

Gray bit off an angry reply. It would be better if he knew exactly where he stood.

"Is he right?" he asked the ship's AI. "Does the chain of command go from Delattre to him?"

"That is unclear," the AI replied, "and beyond my provenance. The question will need to be settled by the Confederation courts."

"The Hague is twenty light years away. What does the Act of Military First Right have to say about it?"

"Nothing about this particular situation, Captain. The Act, as passed by the Confederation Senate, allows the Confederation Government to assume command of USNA fleet assets such as CBG-40, but the battlegroup was under the direct command of Admiral Delattre, who designated *America* as the flagship for the entire fleet. There is precedent for Lavallée to assume overall command, but there is precedent for *America* to remain the fleet flagship, with you in command. In addition, your rank of captain was confirmed August 7, 2419. Justin Lavallée was confirmed captain on November 15, 2419. You have seniority, Captain, by over three months."

The dilemma was a serious one. If Gray forced the issue, Captain Lavallée might pull the Confederation ships out of the attack, and that exchange just now with twelve Slan warships proved that going up against them with less than the full weight of the fleet was a very bad idea.

But there was more and worse. Lavallée had just announced his intent to pull a near-*c* fly-by. If Gray gave in, if he conceded the command to Lavallée, the entire fleet would flash past Arianrhod at 0.997 *c* . . . and *America* would be unable to recover the fighters she'd launched over an hour before.

"Captain Lavallée," Gray continued, "we need to work together on this. We must continue with the op plan as it was written. If we don't, we're going to have trouble recovering our fighters."

"The fighters are expendable, Captain Gray," Lavallée replied. "Our fleet is not. With the demonstrated abilities of the Slan ships, slowing for close combat at the planet would be suicide."

"Nothing has changed, Captain," Gray said. "We knew the Slan had a lead over us in miltech after Arianrhod fell."

"In case you missed it, Captain Gray, the Slan have tactical FTL. We cannot fight against that."

Unfortunately, the European Union captain might have a point.

Gray pulled up a navigational 3-D graphic in the bridge tank, showing Arianrhod in orbit about 36 Ophiuchi A, and the projected path of the fleet, a ruler-straight green thread skimming close past the planet and curling around it in a tight loop. Red stars marked the Slan ships identified so far. There were still only fifteen enemy warships in orbit about the planet, but scattered elsewhere through the system were four other outlying groups totaling twenty-two vessels, including the survivors of Tango One. When the fleet reached Arianrhod, those twenty-two outlying ships might shift in toward the planet, and the Confederation fleet would find itself up against all thirty-seven Slan capital warships. As Lavallée had just pointed out, the Slan ability to move tactically within the star system at FTL speeds gave them a tremendous—possibly an overwhelmingly decisive—advantage.

"Captain," Gray continued after a moment, "we can beat them if we concentrate our force. Tango One was only in contact with a fraction of the entire fleet. Once we decelerate into near-Arianrhod space, we'll be able to—"

"This conversation," Lavallée said, "serves no useful purpose, sir. The fleet will pass through the objective area at near-*c*. The USNA contingent can do as it likes. Transmission ends."

Lavallée's dismissal took one worry off of Gray's docket, at least—the horrific possibility that Confederation ships might actually open fire on *America* or other ships of the USNA contingent in an attempt to force them to comply with orders. But it also meant that CBG-40 would be on its own if Gray decided to follow the original op plan in order to pick up the fighters. CBG-40 was down to twenty-two ships, now, with the *Grant* and the *Worden* both destroyed. Several other vessels, *America* included, had been badly mauled and were still under repair.

Just how badly, Gray thought, did he want to recover those fighters?

The question was scarcely worth considering. *We are not abandoning those people*, he thought.

"We may have no alternative."

The unexpected voice in his head made Gray start. He checked his in-head, and saw his neural link to *America*'s AI was open; he'd not been aware that he'd left the connection in place after questioning it about the Confederation's Act of Military First Right.

"Damn it," Gray said. "We do *not* leave people behind."

"But thirteen capital ships—two of them supply and repair vessels—may not be able to eliminate Slan defenses in-system."

"Then we'll have to hope that the fighter storm buys us an advantage." *Fighter storm* was the slang term for the large number of fighters sent on a preliminary long-range strike against an enemy-held world.

"Indeed. And that raises another issue. Remember that there are a total of twenty strike fighter squadrons en route to Arianrhod, Captain, five of ours, but fifteen more launched from the four Confederation carriers an hour ago. The squadrons off the *Klemens von Metternich*, of course, no longer have a ship on which to recover. *America* does not have the hangar deck space to take all of them back on board. There will also be streakers."

Twenty squadrons—240 fighters. The fighters off the other remaining Confederation carriers—*Kali*, *Bolivar*, and *Illustrious*—should be able to trap on board their mother ships, though catching up to them and trapping at near-*c* always posed a really hairy challenge. The big problem, though, as *America*'s AI had reminded him, was streakers— fighters damaged in combat and hurtling off into deep space at near-light speeds, unable to decelerate or maneuver. Even relatively slight damage to a strike fighter might make it impossible to trap in a carrier's docking bay.

That was what SAR tugs—search and rescue vessels sent out to grapple with damaged fighters and haul them back to the carrier—were for. But recovering a damaged fighter at relativistic velocities was awkward and dangerous. Far better to dispatch and retrieve the SAR tugs at planetary speeds—no more than a few thousand kilometers per second.

And the number of open hangar bay slots for recovered fighters was also an issue. Of course, there might not be enough survivors from the fighter storm to raise a problem. There *would* be losses in the coming strike pass, of course, but *America* simply didn't have room for more than perhaps 100 fighters. Unless 140 or more were destroyed in the coming battle, *some* of those fighters would be unrecoverable.

Gray had been in fighter shoot-outs with high casualty rates—two thirds or more. Fighters were considered expendable; the idea was to send them whipping in past an objective at high velocities and ahead of the arrival of the main fleet. A fighter swarm could do incalculable damage to an enemy fleet or orbital defenses, allowing the heavies, arriving hours later, to simply mop up.

In Gray's experience, it was rarely that easy. Usually, the best the fighters could do was blunt the opposition's defenses enough that the heavies had a fighting chance when they got there, especially if the fleet was outnumbered or up against a better, more advanced technology. He knew. He'd been there.

And he knew from personal experience the terror of being left behind in a hostile system, light years from home.

"We'll find a way," he told the AI. "We *have* to."

He checked the passage of time, subjective and objective. At the fleet's current velocity, time was passing for them almost thirteen times faster than normal. It was now 0927; in a little more than three hours objective, it would be time to begin deceleration—if the battlegroup was going to do so. At this velocity, that worked out to less than fifteen minutes subjective.

The pressure to make a decision definitely was on.

It would have helped, he thought, if *America* could have waited until the strike wave of fighters hit Arianrhod before making that decision, but the hard physics of the situation made it otherwise. As he reviewed the opplan timetable, the numbers shifting and flickering through his connection with *America*'s AI, he noted that the fighters were due to pass Arianrhod at 1319 hours; if she was to enter Arianrhod battlespace at planetary speeds, *America* and her escorts would have to begin deceleration at 1239, almost an hour earlier.

"*America*," he thought, addressing the ship's primary AI again. "I need full amplification. *And* a full command-group brainstorm."

And new data began flooding into his mind.

Lieutenant Donald Gregory
VFA-96, Black Demons
36 Ophiuchi System
0935 hours, TFT

"Great job, Gregory," Mackey said over the tactical net. "Where'd you come up with that trick?"

"Not sure, Boss," Gregory replied. "I was just in the right place, is all. . . ."

"Patch your mission record back to CIC," Mackey told him. "They need to know about this."

"Jamming my nose into Slan hull armor and making like a can opener?" Kemper said. "Fuck *that*."

"We'll call it the Nungie maneuver," Del Rey added. "You have to be crazy as a damned Nungie to try it!"

"Considering that he just saved our asses," Jodi Vaughn said, "*and* the entire fleet, maybe you idiots should just lay off."

"I want *all* of you people to record this," Mackey said, "and have it ready for implementation. We're not going to have time to trap and rearm."

Gregory looked at his opplan timeline and saw what their squadron leader meant. While hours remained, objective, before deceleration, only fourteen minutes subjective remained to deceleration. The squadron would not have time to return to *America*'s hangar bays, rearm with new expendables—missiles and high-velocity kinetic-kill rounds—and launch again before the carrier began decelerating. Technically, *America* could cease deceleration halfway down the velocity slope in order to launch the CAP fighters again, but fourteen minutes wasn't enough time for the squadron to get all the way back to the carrier and then recover on board. In any case, the CBG needed to stick to the timetable. Ceasing deceleration for a fighter launch meant reaching the mission objective with excess velocity.

The six surviving fighters of VFA-96 were on their way in toward a hot battlespace zone with damned few nukes or KK rounds left.

And that meant that they were going to need every weapon and tactic available to them out here just to survive.

Chapter Thirteen

TC/USNA CVS America
In transit
36 Ophiuchi A System
1224 hours, TFT

The brainstorming passed like a dream, with images crowding in upon one another in rapid-fire sequence. The thoughts of fourteen men and women merged within the virtual reality of *America*'s AI, accelerated to transhuman levels as data cascaded through their electronically linked brains. The AI was running through thousands of overlapping scenarios, sequences designed to show the various alternative outcomes of different actions . . . if CBG-40 decelerated and faced the Slan at Arianrhod alone, if CBG-40 stayed with the main Confederation fleet and passed Arianrhod at near-*c*, if CBG-40 was joined by some Confederation ships but not others, if the Slan reacted by massing all of their ships at Arianrhod, if the outlying Slan ships stayed where they were . . .

Simulations even modeled what might happen if the Confederation fleet opened fire on CBG-40 . . . *not* one of the better scenario outcomes.

One outcome emerged from the virtual sequences with uncomfortable regularity, however. If the Slan fleet at Arianrhod was not engaged, directly and forcefully, those warships might very well seek to eliminate the source of the Confederation strike against 36 Ophiuchi.

If Arianrhod was just twenty-five hours from Earth, the converse also was true. The strike *had* to cripple the Slan fleet here, or risk a counterstrike against Earth itself. Hurt them enough, and maybe they wouldn't attack Sol and Humankind's homeworld.

Maybe . . .

Weighing in to the decision were the opinions and rationalizations of the members of *America*'s command staff. Command was not a democratic process, and the decision, ultimately, was Gray's alone . . . but he wanted to hear what the others thought. At the beginning of the mental staff meeting, nine of the other fifteen had voted to bypass Arianrhod at near-*c*. The fighters, they argued, would be able to accelerate after the fleet and would, eventually, be able to match speeds and trap.

Streakers unable to do so, and fighters off the *von Metternich* with no place to trap, all would be lost. But then, combat resulted in combat losses. There was no way to avoid that, and it might be better to lose a few dozen fighters than to lose much of the USNA battlegroup.

As the scenario run-through had continued, though, more and more of the command staff personnel had changed their minds. The balance now was solidly in favor of battling it out with the Slan, eleven to four.

Commander Laurie Taggart, *America*'s weapons officer, was one of the four, and the most outspoken of them. "I still say the Slan have demonstrated that they're too advanced for us to face them in a stand-up fight," she said. The flow of imagery through the simulation focused for a moment on what might happen if the USNA ships engaged the main body of the Slan fleet directly. The incoming fighter waves were swept from the sky . . . and when the main fleet arrived an hour later, ship after ship was smashed by antiproton and heavy fusion beams. *America* took a dozen hits, the carrier crumpling under the onslaught in a matter of seconds.

"Captain," Connie Fletcher said on a private channel. "Have you seen this?"

"What is it?"

"A feed from our CAP a few minutes ago. One of the pilots appears to have discovered a new weapon."

Gray looked at the imagery and other data passed on by the fighters from the battle a short while before. One of the pilots—Lieutenant Gregory—had sliced open a Slan Ballista with his own drive singularity.

Gutsy. And near-suicidal . . . but Gregory's attack appeared to have been the turning point in the skirmish, sending the remaining Slan warships back toward Arianrhod.

"I'm not sure our people will be able to use this," he told Fletcher on the side channel. "But we may be able to adapt this somehow."

"That's what I was thinking. I've already passed it to the Weapons Section to see what they make of it."

"Good. Keep me posted."

Another voice entered Gray's mind. "Deceleration in fifteen minutes objective, Captain," the ship AI reported. "That's a minute nine subjective. You wanted to be alerted."

"Thank you," Gray said. He interrupted the data flow, entering the simulation stream. "We are out of time, people," he told the others. "I'm giving the order to decelerate."

The command staff officers all acknowledged and dropped from the linkup, all agreeing without argument, even the holdouts. Although his was the absolute say-so in decisions like this one, Gray preferred to have his department heads on his side, committed to the course of action he'd chosen. Eleven for fifteen wasn't a bad ratio, and he knew that Taggart and the others would support him even if they didn't agree with his reasoning.

Gray swam up out of the deep, in-head session, blinking at the sudden glare of light on *America*'s bridge. "All hands," he said, using the ship's intercom. "This is the captain. CBG-40 will begin deceleration in thirty seconds, subjective. The Confederation ships have decided . . . to proceed without us, so it will be up to us to hit the Slan fleet as hard as we can, as decisively as we can, in order to make them think twice about launching a retaliatory strike against the Sol System.

"*Everything* is now riding on the USNA contingent. We are outnumbered, but the fighter wave will be arriving at Arianrhod soon, and we can be confident that they will be softening up the enemy defenses.

"I know that every member of this battlegroup will do your duty. Thank you."

And subjective seconds later, at precisely 1239 hours, fiercely focused singularities winked on astern of each of the USNA ships, and the *America* battlegroup began to slow.

Lieutenant Ronald Dorshner
VFA-112, Death Eagles
36 Ophiuchi System
1318 hours, TFT

"Coming up on the objective," Lieutenant Commander Meise, the squadron CO, announced. "Keep it tight. Weapons and attitude control to your AIs."

Lieutenant Dorshner checked to make certain that his Velociraptor was now solely under the control of his AI. VFA-112 was one of the strike squadrons off the *America*. From his perspective, just 30 minutes had passed since he'd accelerated clear of the carrier. In the non-accelerated universe outside, 349 minutes and 40 astronomical units had slipped past. He was still moving at near-light velocity, and the sky around him was sharply compressed into the familiar colored bands of light ahead.

With everything in the electronic hands of the fighter AI, there wasn't much left for Dorshner to do but sit and wait. Humans had their place in space fighter combat at slower speeds, carrying out maneuvers that required human creativity.

At over 99 percent of the speed of light, human reflexes simply weren't fast enough to provide useful input.

His weapons triggered, missiles and sandcasters first. The

missiles had to be released well before the closest point of passage, since they shared the fighter's velocity, and needed to be put on a vector that would swing them into the targets at that speed. At near-*c*, a few hundred kilos—the mass of the missiles themselves—carried enough kinetic energy to overwhelm the detonations of their nuclear warheads.

The salvo included his entire warload of AMSOs, twelve AS-78 anti-missile-shield-ordnance-containing warheads of tightly packed, sand-grain-sized spherules of matter-compressed lead. When the warheads detonated an instant later, clouds of sand hurtled across emptiness toward the Slan targets, again at close to the speed of light. Where the enemy's anti-missile defenses might wipe incoming missiles out of the sky, it was virtually impossible to do the same to hurtling clouds of dispersing sand. At the speed of light, even something with the mass of a BB carried tremendous explosive power.

An instant after his missiles and sandcaster rounds were away, Dorshner's beam weapons fired—lasers, particle-cannon bursts, and fusion beams—and the weapons continued to fire as the fighter swept past the target zone, the fighter pivoting on its axis to keep the beams on target.

And then he was past. He gave a thoughtclicked order, and his fighter began decelerating, braking at fifty thousand gravities.

He still couldn't see the Slan targets or the planet, now light seconds behind him, didn't know how much damage, if any, he and the other members of the fighter swarm had caused.

But they were about to find out.

Slan warship
Low Orbit, 36 Ophiuchi AIII
1319 hours, TFT

She sat in pitch darkness, her skin suit's light off to conserve the small power cells.

The Slan, Lieutenant Megan Connor had decided, must "see" by sonar, sending out pulses of sound and forming an image of their surroundings by listening to the returning echoes. She remembered that certain sea mammals back on Earth—dolphins and the now extinct whales—had used sonar to image their murky undersea universe. The fatty masses in the heads of dolphins that focused the sound waves, she recalled, were called melons. The mobile cones above the Slans' bodies, she was pretty sure, must be their sonar-imaging melons. The large, somewhat translucent flaps to either side of the upper body might be external ears, focusing returning sound waves.

The information did her no good at the moment, but she was determined now to make her escape. If she could somehow get away, somehow return to a human ship, what she'd seen and heard here might be of use.

The ship's artificial gravity dragged at her. Her suit could compensate, somewhat, when she was walking, but when she was just lying on her back she felt *heavy*—twice, nearly, her usual sixty-five kilos. For hours—her internal clock had logged seventeen since her capture—she'd been here, locked inside the small and lightless cabin to which her captors had led her earlier, after her interview with Old Captain Two-Heads, as she thought of the creature, and after the terrifying nightmare in the alien lab. She shuddered again at the memory, though they'd only hurt her once—by inserting a heavy-gauge needle into her arm right through her skin suit.

The suit had sealed off the resulting leak almost immediately, but the stab had left her terrified. The worst part had been the *not knowing*, as six aliens had surrounded her in the darkness, manipulating arms and legs, touching her, scanning her with unidentifiable devices, seeming to peer at her and *into* her with those blunt, featureless organs on the ends of those writhing necks. . . .

She'd tried to talk to them, by voice, by radio, by flashing her suit light . . . but she couldn't even tell if the beings were aware of her attempts.

And then, anticlimactically, they'd brought her to the cell

and locked her in. For the hours since, all she'd been able to do was sit in the darkness, listening . . . and wondering if the Slan were going to try to feed her, take care of her environmental needs . . . or if the interrogation was to resume.

Now, though, *something* was happening.

She could hear some sort of excitement outside the locked cabin door—rapid movement through the passageways outside, and the rattling clicks and buzzes that she'd begin to think must be Slan speech. It was difficult in the extreme to attribute anything like human emotions to beings so alien, but she had the impression that they were excited.

And then, out of nowhere, something struck the ship's hull with a terrific *bang*, and she was thrown from the low pad that served her as a bed in her cell. A thin, shrill whistle told her that the atmosphere was shrieking out into vacuum. Her captors' ship had been damaged . . . possibly critically.

She switched on her suit's light, and immediately saw four shafts of condensing vapor in the wet, hot air. Looking more closely, she was able to see tiny holes, each the size of a small pea, in bulkhead and deck, and she felt a cold prickle of dread moving up her spine. AMSO rounds—tiny spherules of compressed lead moving at extremely high velocities. One had missed her by less than 2 meters.

But that also meant that the Slan fleet was being attacked. Her heart beat faster as she stood up and made her way to the door.

She had a virtual tool in a hip pouch, overlooked by the Slan, who apparently hadn't recognized it for what it was. All fighter pilots carried one, a programmable utility multipurpose tool that could melt through tungsten steel, punch holes or seal them, glue together broken pieces . . . or unlock doors. She'd not used it earlier, reasoning that if it did get her out of her cell, there still had been no way to get off the Slan warship. Better to stay put for the time being, perhaps with the possibility of learning more about her captors.

Now, though, with the ship under attack and clearly damaged, there might be some way for her to take advantage of the situation . . . and the alternative was to wait here in the dark until the ship was either destroyed or its automatic repair systems kicked in, closing this window of opportunity.

If she could find her way, somehow, back to her damaged fighter . . .

The virtual tool was the size of her thumb, flat, and metallic green. When she held it in the palm of her hand, in contact with the maze of gold, red, and silver threads marking her glove's contact area, it linked with her in-head systems and announced that it was ready to work . . . and what job did she want done?

"Open the door," she thought, pressing the tool's business end against the seal of her cabin door, a low, broad oval shape a meter and a half high and perhaps three wide, a silhouette in keeping with the low-riding bodily structure of the Slan. There was nothing like a doorknob or activation switch, but the tool was smart enough to trace the electronic circuitry, find locks, override power supplies, even melt through mechanical tumblers or locking bolts, if necessary. Programmed by her in-head circuitry, the tool emitted a thin stream of nano agents that flowed along the seal, looking for a viable approach.

"Please stand clear," the tool told her, and she took a step back. The door gave a faint, high-pitched click, then dropped on hidden rails into the deck.

Pocketing the tool, she stepped out into the passageway.

The passageway outside was no higher than the door, and she had to stoop to move. There was no light, of course, but her suit light illuminated her way. She relied on her in-head navigational system, which now projected a small map in a mental window. She didn't want to go back to the control center where Old Captain Two-Heads had buzzed and clicked at her, and she especially didn't want to return to what she'd thought was likely a lab. Her arm still hurt from that needle, and for hours since then, Connor had been shaking with the dread that they would take her back there and try to remove her suit.

Ah. By cutting through *this* way, she should avoid both lab and control room, and just might be able to go straight to the hangar bay where they'd brought her fighter on board. The fighter was an inert hulk, but there might be one trick left in it, if she could get on board.

Abruptly, there was a wet, squelching sound ahead, and one of the Slan emerged from a side passageway, directly in front of her.

The sound, she realized, was very faint now. Her suit showed her that the atmosphere was rapidly thinning— down to half a standard atmosphere now, and still falling. Didn't these monsters have automatically sealing hulls, in case of a hull breach?

The Slan crossed the passageway in front of her . . . and collided with the bulkhead. For a moment, it lashed about with its tentacles, feeling along the wet bulkheads, its sonar organs questing in all directions, its side flaps extended wide open . . . and Connor realized that the Slan was the equivalent of *blind*.

They relied on their atmosphere to transmit sonar pulses, and as the air thinned toward hard vacuum, they were going deaf. She stepped aside, letting the bulky creature blunder past her and down the corridor in the direction from which she'd just come.

With hardening resolve, she began hurrying ahead, following the map displayed for her in her mind.

As she moved, though, she wondered how a being that imaged its surroundings with sound could possibly see the stars. . . .

TC/USNA CVS America
In transit
Approaching Arianrhod
1409 hours, TFT

The sky surrounding the USNA battlegroup had slowly expanded back to its original, undistorted form, and the two suns of 36 Ophiuchi and the tiny crescent of Arianrhod were clearly visible to unaided eyes and scanners.

They were beginning to pick up signs of the battle that had swept through the region over the past hour. At 1319 hours, the fighters launched that morning had reached Arianrhod, their AIs firing at targets within range as they passed. After one pass, they would have slowed to planetary speeds and begun engaging targets of opportunity.

At 1407 hours, the rest of the Confederation fleet, still travelling at 0.997 c, had passed through the same volume of space. Gray didn't know if they had engaged the enemy or not. By now, though, they were twenty-two light minutes ahead, still receding at near-c.

Assuming, of course, that they'd survived the passage, and assuming that Delattre hadn't changed his mind at the last moment and decelerated. There were no signs of the Confederation ships, however, so presumably they were farther up ahead, moving unreachably fast.

Myriad colored shapes—squares, triangles, circles—drifted against the backdrop of suns and planet, marking targets—red for Slan, green for human, yellow for unidentified, while squares were vessels under acceleration, triangles were drifting free, circles were dead. Blocks of text scrolled through the projection, giving vector information, mass, and status.

It took Gray several moments to sort out what he was seeing, even with the ship AI's help. Local battlespace was filled with red triangles and circles; the fighter swarm had managed to hit the Slan, and hit them *hard*. But there were still plenty of red squares, and the vector data displayed by each showed that they were closing on the incoming human warships.

"A lot of those Slan ships are leaking atmosphere," Commander Laurie Taggart observed. "Looks like they're drifting free, out of commission."

"So I see," Gray replied. "A lot of them . . . a lot of them don't look too badly hit. But they appear to be out of commission."

As they drew closer, and *America*'s scanners began showing close-ups of the drifting, brightly colored hulks, he saw the telltale damage from AMSO rounds—hull sections scoured away as if sandblasted, atmosphere leaking from hundreds of minute punctures and freezing as it hit vacuum, random and isolated patches of damage scattered across large areas of armor.

Twenty years before, Gray had acquired the nickname "Sandy" for his innovative use of AMSO rounds, throwing sand at Sh'daar warships at close to the speed of light and letting physics do the rest. The technique was a standard maneuver now, though it was only effective if the launching ships were moving at near-c when they released the sand clouds, imparting their velocity to the individual grains of matter-compressed lead.

But the fighter swarm had used it to good effect here as they'd swept past the enemy ships. The fighters had come through and pulverized them, and Gray allowed the tiniest bit of relief to seep through into his consciousness.

They had a chance, a small one. . . .

"Enemy coming into range, Captain."

"Commence firing."

America and her consorts began slamming round after round into the approaching Slan ships. Again, the enemy's point defenses proved superb as they wiped missiles and kinetic-kill rounds from the sky, but some of those rounds were getting through. An alien Ballista staggered as rounds shredded the forward portion of its hull; a pair of Sabers vanished in a nuclear fireball as a salvo of shipkillers from the *Henderson* detonated between them.

But the incoming fire from the Slan warships was devastatingly accurate. The destroyer *Bradley* and the heavy cruiser *Alvarez* both took direct hits that left them broken and helpless, and a second destroyer, the *Cumberland*, was crippled. *America* staggered as three rounds slammed into and through her forward shield cap. Ice vapor sprayed into space, mingled with fragments of hull metal.

In-head, Gray scanned the lengthening list of damage reports from within the ship, then shifted his full concentration back to the battle. The shield cap's interior was sectioned off by pie-wedge barriers that prevented all the ship's water stores from venting into space. The automatic damage-control systems were staying ahead of the smaller-scale problems so far, though the damage inflicted earlier on the carrier was not yet fully repaired. *America* was hurt, but still in the fight.

They were moving fast enough that the crescent of Arianrhod visibly swelled second by second until it swept past the carrier to port, filling that half of the sky as *America* pounded at Slan targets in all directions. *America* was still decelerating, dropping into a long, shallow curve around to the planet's day-lit side, but was still traveling at twenty-five kilometers per second, considerably faster than Arianrhod's escape velocity. The undamaged Slan vessels matched course and speed effortlessly, merging with the USNA battlegroup and closing to point-blank range.

The six surviving CAP fighters of VFA-96, however, had matched the battlegroup's deceleration, and were still moving in formation, positioning themselves to intercept Slan warships threatening the carrier. They were out of expendable munitions, according to the feed from their tactical net, but could still firefight with beam weapons and lasers. They were also attempting to use the new tactic, one evolved as a desperation measure by Lieutenant Gregory . . . getting in close enough to use their drive singularities as knife-fight weapons.

As he watched, one fighter slipped in close to a looming Slan Ballista by mimicking a tumbling scrap of wreckage, then straightened suddenly, its singularity flickering to life. . . .

But the Slan were learning as well. The fighter was struck point-blank by an anti-proton beam and vaporized before it was closer than 20 kilometers from its target.

"CAG?" Gray said over the CIC link. "Pass the word to the Demons. No more knife-fighting. I don't want them playing kamikaze out there."

"Right, Captain," Captain Fletcher replied. "I concur. Interesting improvised weapon, though."

"We'll have the Engineering Department take a look at it," he replied. "*After* the battle . . ."

Assuming, he thought with grim determination, *we survive it. . . .*

Lieutenant Donald Gregory
VFA-96, Black Demons
Arianrhod Space
1410 hours, TFT

Gregory guided his Starhawk toward the Slan ship . . . a different design from anything he'd seen so far. It was big, nearly 300 meters long—bigger than a Ballista, bigger even than a Trebuchet, and it was in close orbit around Arianrhod. It appeared to have been damaged earlier, probably during the fighter swarm's close passage. Vapor froze as it emerged from the dozens of tiny holes that riddled the massive hull, and one entire side had been ripped open, exposing interior struts, beams, and bulkheads. The color scheme, Gregory thought, once had been black and green, in broad, jagged stripes, but much of the ship's outer surface had been sandblasted down to bare armor. The ship's unique size alone suggested that it might be something special in the Slan fleet—a command ship, perhaps.

Whatever it might be, the Slan ship didn't appear to have noticed him as he drifted toward it, angling to pass over the quarter of the vessel that had already been ripped open by multiple AMSO rounds. He was still getting power readings from the ship; weapons and drive were on-line. "Demons, Demon Nine!" he called, identifying himself. "Got a big target, here, not in the warbook. Designating it as Tango-two-four. Taking a shot . . ."

His Starhawk's primary beam weapon was a "pee-beep," a StellarDyne Blue Lightning PBP-2 particle beam projector firing high-energy protons accelerated by a fierce projected magnetic field. He waited until he had a clear shot into the damaged enemy warship's interior, then triggered multiple rapid-fire bursts. White light flared within the ship's interior as the proton bolts hit home.

And then he was past, accelerating and jinking as the enemy's defenses opened up, seeking him. . . .

His AI pointed out the anomaly.

"Hey . . . Skipper?" he called.

"What is it, Nungie?"

"I've got a radio signal coming from the Slan I just toasted. Tight beam, highly directional."

"Are they surrendering?"

"No, sir. It's a distress call, Code Red-Alpha. Shit, sir, it's one of *ours*!"

"I've got the signal," Mackey replied. "IDs as VFA-140."

"What the fuck, sir? They're not on the fleet roster!" He was wondering if the Slan were sending a spoof, a fake message.

"No, but they're listed as planetary defense out of Caer Arianrhod. Sounds like the Slans might have a POW."

"Black Demons, CIC," another voice said over the tactical channel. "We've been monitoring your chatter. Break off your attack on Tango-two-four, and stand by to offer close assault support."

"Copy that, CIC," Mackey said. "What's going down?"

"We think there's one or more human prisoners on that Slan ship," CIC replied. "So we're sending in the Marines."

Chapter Fourteen

Slan warship
Low Orbit, 36 Ophiuchi AIII
1427 hours, TFT

Megan Connor crouched inside the ruin of her captured fighter, still in darkness, still weighed down by twice Earth-normal gravity, wondering how long it would be before *they* came for her.

There were two distinct values for "they"—humans and Slan. She was praying for humans . . . but knew how slim that chance actually was.

Her fighter's main systems were down, singularity generator dead, weapons off-line, life support gone, AI fried. All that was working was the crash kit, a pod containing emergency supplies against the possibility of a crash on a hostile world. There was a battery, a nanomedic kit better than what was built into her suit; recharge nano for her suit's air, food, and water cyclers; and an emergency radio transmitter smart enough to locate nearby friendlies and ping them with a tight-beam data burst.

There *had* to be human ships out there. If the Slan vessel had been hit, the attackers must be human, right? But she had to assume that the Slan would pick up any radio message beamed from the bowels of their ship . . . and nearby human ships might be too distant, now, or moving too swiftly to receive her SOS. Or the Slan warship's structure or defensive fields might block any radio signal, or . . . or . . . or . . .

All she could do was stay here, crouching in the darkness, waiting for someone—human or Slan—to show up.

If it was Slan, she didn't have many options. When she'd reached her fighter, she had at least been able to get at the emergency survival pod behind the seat. Now she had a weapon—a Solbeam Mk. VII hand laser. She'd not been able to get at it when they'd come for her before to drag her out of the wreckage. She held it now, though, feeling its heft in the darkness. It was *something*, at least, and comforting in her gloved hand . . . but the weapon had an output of only half a megajoule, with ten expendable battery caps for ten shots. That was plenty for dealing with most predators on a planetary surface, but if the target had any armor at all the thing was little better than a toy.

A *comforting* toy, to be sure, but a toy nonetheless . . .

Her suit's environmental readout was worrying. The surrounding air pressure, she noticed, had ceased its fall toward hard vacuum, and now was slowly rising once more. That meant either that the Slan were overpressurizing a still-leaking interior, or that their repair systems had sealed the leaks. Either way, the pressure now was at eight tenths of an atmosphere, and rising. At some point, the Slan would again be able to "see" their surroundings, would no longer be effectively blind.

A big part of the question lay in how sensitive Slan hearing was. That one she'd encountered in the passageway a few moments ago had been blind in half an atmosphere. Their sonar sense had evolved in an environment with about five Earth standard atmospheres; sound traveled faster, farther, and more clearly at higher pressures. What was their threshold? Humans could certainly still hear sounds at half an atmosphere or less, and it wasn't until you got pretty close to hard vacuum that all sound vanished. Perhaps Slan evolution had settled for a "good enough" lower threshold of two or three atmospheres. She wished she knew. It would be nice to know how long she had before they came looking for her.

Megan Connor only recently had become a USNA citizen. She'd been born and raised on Atlantica, one of the larger sea-steads, a free-floating city slowly circling the North Atlantic outside of the territorial waters of any land-based nation. Her mother had been a North American while her father had been from Ireland, and she'd received from them both a strong appreciation for freedom coupled with an almost libertarian mistrust of big government. When the Confederation had stepped in and taken over all of the Atlantic seasteads, claiming sovereignty over the Earth's dying oceans, Connor's family had fled west, moving first to New New York, then to the nation's capital at Columbus. They'd applied for citizenship and been refused; relations between North America and the rest of the Confederation—especially Pan-Europe—had been deteriorating for some time, and there was talk of deporting Ewan Connor back to Great Britain.

Megan had stopped the deportation order by volunteering to join the USNA military. By doing so, she'd been granted citizenship—and with that she could formally request citizenship for her parents and younger brother as well. She'd gone through the training downloads at Oceana, and a year ago she'd been posted to VFA-140; she'd not expected her first deployment to be to the ass end of creation, though. The Confederation's Dylan Research Station at Arianrhod was small, cramped, and had nothing like the amenities of larger and more civilized colonies. The handful of military personnel at the base had been fully integrated into Caer Arianrhod's general population. Most of the personnel stationed there had been Pan-Europeans, too, and that had put her at the center of a lot of unwanted attention . . . especially after she'd gotten into a knock-down, drag-out with Corrado Passeretti and nearly gotten herself arrested. She'd forgotten about the Confederation's damned White Covenant laws—no public discussions of religion, and *no* attempts at proselytizing. She'd made the mistake of asking the planetary environmentalist how he reconciled his Catholic dogma with his Randomist beliefs concerning the evolution of life, she'd been ordered to keep her libertarian filth to herself, and things had gone downhill from there.

The civilians at the base had called her "Rebel" after that, and the nickname had stuck. Her seven months at Arianrhod had rapidly devolved into nightmare. The other members of her squadron had been okay, since they all were USNA Navy; hell, most of them hated the Confederation almost as much as she did, but with Dylan Base integrated into the larger facility it had been all but impossible to avoid the locals.

She wondered if the base was still there, if any of the people who'd been stationed there with her for the past half year were still alive.

Bad, bad thoughts to be having while waiting in the darkness for the monsters to come . . .

She spent some time considering opening her helmet . . . but the atmosphere, she guessed, would take some time to kill her. The carbon dioxide might put her to sleep, but the effects might be countered by the high levels of oxygen.

She didn't know the chemistry well enough to predict what would happen, and she feared lying in the darkness, strangling on poison that might take long minutes to kill her. The laser . . . yeah, she could use it, a single, quick bolt through her brain . . .

She wasn't quite that desperate however, she found, not when there was even the slimmest of chances that Confederation forces were engaging the Slan ship. The emergency pod was transmitting. They might be coming.

No, she could hold on a little longer. . . .

Marine Assault One-one
Slan warship
Low Orbit, 36 Ophiuchi AIII
1510 hours, TFT

Marine Gunnery Sergeant Andrew Clegg watched the objective expand in his in-head, a ship larger than a USNA cruiser, its side torn and gashed by high-velocity AMSO rounds. He was encapsulated within an Apache Tear, a sleek, black teardrop of nanomatrix fired moments ago from the belly of the Marine transport *Inchon*, one of some 650 identical teardrops in the first wave—the bulk of 1st Battalion, 3rd Regiment, 1st Marine Division. MAPP-2 personal assault pods were designed to get a large number of Marines across distances of up to a few hundred kilometers in a hurry, to get them there and put them down, with their equipment, as quickly as possible, and with a minimum of casualties. The light-drinking qualities of the pod's nanomatrix made them all but invisible, even at close range, and the dedicated AIs residing within the shape-shifting hulls could fly the pods through a sharp and random series of maneuvers to throw off enemy point defense weapons.

Even so, this assault had been expensive already. The Slan had seen them coming and opened up with antiproton beams, slashing wildly at the sky. The battalion was down to fewer than four hundred by the time they gravdecelled in for the docking.

Exactly how the Slan had "seen" them was still unknown. Data provided by the Agletsch suggested that the species used sonar to perceive their surroundings. Judging from the electromagnetic fields surrounding their ships, they used magnetism, radar, and lidar to see in a vacuum, with the return signals converted to audio displays by their sensor suites, but how these were perceived by the beings was a mystery. Getting inside an alien mind, knowing how they thought or how they saw the universe around them was still all but impossible.

No matter. If the Marines could see them, the Marines could kill them. Clegg's black teardrop slipped past a tangle of torn and half-melted structural supports well inside the target vessel's hull and slammed into a bulkhead. The leading surface of nanomatrix switched its programming, becoming a nanodisassembler surface that melted through the unyielding polycarbolaminate bulkhead in seconds, then opening into the ship once it hit gas instead of solid.

His pod gave him the specifics of the atmosphere inside the alien ship: nitrogen 41%, oxygen 28%, ammonia 6.3%, carbon dioxide 5.6% . . . a hot, wet, rather nastily poisonous soup with an overall pressure just a bit higher than that at sea level on Earth. Didn't matter; he was wearing assault armor, a bulky suit as ink-black as the Apache Tear's hull. He dropped through the opening into the alien ship, twisting as he felt the tug of internal gravity and landing heavily on his feet.

The ship's interior was lightless, hot, and wet, the supersaturated air steaming in the cone of light from his helmet. His suit told him the gravity here was about twice Earth's—1.94 Gs. Non-spin generated, too, which meant the Slan had a pretty advanced technology, compared to Earth's. Human ships still needed to rotate hab modules around a central axis in order to mimic gravity enough to keep the crews healthy.

Turning, he glimpsed movement in the darkness, shadows jittering on wet, black walls. His armor's light showed something big and flat and rubbery-looking, a squashed bell-shape with a couple of weaving tentacles up top bearing massive, fleshy spindles. He triggered his Mk. 17 laser, sending an invisible ten-megajoule bolt into the target. The thing came apart in a messily wet explosion of liquid and partially burned flesh.

More movement ahead . . . but this resolved itself into another armored Marine. The tactical net in Clegg's head identified the Marine as PFC Carol Owens. "With me, Owens," he snapped.

"Right, Gunny," she replied. "Which way?"

He gestured past her, farther up the lightless passageway. "Signal's coming from *that* way."

On his in-head, Clegg saw the green blips representing others of the assault group winking on as they entered the alien ship. Tactical data feeds from all of the Marines began building up a picture, a map, of their surroundings.

The passageways were wide and low, only about a meter and a half from deck to overhead, and Clegg and Owens both had to stoop forward to navigate the lightless path. Their suit lights gleamed off black, dripping-wet walls that looked unpleasantly organic. Clegg tried hard not to think about intestines. . . .

The mission of the USNA Marines—originally the United States Marine Corps—had changed a great deal over the past six and a half centuries. They'd started as shipboard soldiers and sharpshooters, firing down onto the decks of enemy ships from the rigging, then added amphibious landings to their repertoire, storming ashore on enemy-held coastlines to secure beachheads for the troops to follow. For a long time, they'd served as a kind of elite but generalist special forces, and more than one U.S. president or Congress had tried to eliminate them as redundant.

As Humankind began its diaspora to the stars, it had taken its wars with it . . . and the Marines had followed. They still served in the ancient roles of shipboard police, of landing forces, of elite special operations personnel, but in addition they'd gone back to their earliest roots, serving as close-assault troops tasked with boarding enemy ships, usually for purposes of intelligence gathering, but also for the purpose of rescuing POWs. The Marines off the *Inchon* had been tasked with both objectives. Emergency radio transmissions from inside the disabled Slan ship proved that there were human captives on board . . . or at least a captured Stardragon fighter. But the fact that the ship was a larger, different design than other Slan vessels encountered so far suggested that it was some sort of command vessel. That was logical, too, if they'd taken a human captive aboard. Presumably, the Slan were as curious about humans as the humans were about them. It was tough fighting a foe whose very natures—both biological and psychological—were largely unknown.

"S-2, Assault," a voice said over the tactical net. "Good job! We're into the system."

S-2 was Lieutenant Commander Villanova, the intelligence officer on board the *Inchon*. A number of the Marines were cross-trained in xenointelligence work, with special

AIs riding in nanoinfiltration pods that melted into bulk-heads, tracked electronic circuits, and followed them into the local equivalent of a computer network. Those AIs would go to work attempting to crack both the alien language and their computer operating systems. The data would at the very least reveal how the Slan ships worked, possibly reveal their weaknesses.

And at best, it might permit the USNA fleet to communicate directly with the beings.

In any case, half of Clegg's mission was now complete, since the AI insertions were autonomous and would complete their tasks automatically. The other half was to rescue any human POWs on board.

Clegg didn't think about the second, unspoken part of those orders. If he couldn't rescue the human captives, he was to make sure the Slan couldn't take them back to their homeworld, or learn anything more from them.

He tried to think of killing any Slan prisoners as doing them a very large favor. . . .

Slan protector Vigilant
Low Orbit, 36 Ophiuchi AIII
1524 hours, TFT

The enemy, the sixty-times-sixty times 3600-times damned *Nah-voh-grah-nu-greh Trafhyedrefschladreh*, had breached the ship at dozens of points, were inside the *Vigilant*, apparently converging toward the central docking bay. Clear Chiming Bell listened to the three-dimensional spacial representation of the enemy forces, occasionally giving orders to its scattered shipboard forces, trying to throw up a screen around the advancing monsters.

It didn't help that its soldiers were still very nearly deaf. The ship's internal pressure was coming back up, but slowly, *slowly*, like partial sunrise back home. *Vigilant*'s crew had put on emergency respirators, but were still groping about in soundless low pressure.

The ship's internal sensors, however, were feeding data from passageways and compartments throughout the ship to the main computers, and those in turn created a sonic picture of the ship within Clear Chiming's mind. The Slan had evolved from communal subsurface animals living in tunnel mazes on the night side of a tidally locked world, emerging from the greater to the lesser night to hunt food animals and drag them back to the burrows. Their physiology and, more, their psychology revolved around the concept of myriad underground passageways. Even if sonar wasn't working, individual Slan were comfortable in close, enclosed spaces. The ship's command staff could relay instructions by radio, guiding the soldiers into position.

Like numerous other communal species across the galaxy, the Slan were organized in a kind of caste system—brute workers and soldiers, administrators and breeders, scouts, designers, and engineers. Clear Chiming Bell was *cht'!k'k't'!cht'k'k*, administrative caste of the third level, trained from hatching to oversee the activities of an entire sub-hive. It was used to seeing the larger sound-picture, and to giving orders to workers and soldiers as though those other hive-members were natural extensions of its own body.

The central docking bay. Why would they be interested in *that*?

Of course. The alien fighter. And when Clear Chiming Bell focused his instrumentation on that compartment, he picked up the repetitive pulse of radio chirps—an emergency beacon.

Obviously, that captured fighter was of tremendous importance to the aliens. . . .

Slan warship
Low Orbit, 36 Ophiuchi AIII
1535 hours, TFT

Cautiously, Megan Connor raised her head above the lip of the gaping hole in her fighter's dead hull. The Slan had seemed unaware of her skin suit's light earlier, so she flashed it briefly into the encircling darkness . . .

. . . and saw weirdly shifting shadows, low, humped masses moving in the darkness.

Slan. Dozens of them pouring into the cavernous compartment. They were wearing a kind of mesh armor draped over their squat forms, and were carrying glittering, metallic devices that might have been weapons. Connor ducked back into the shelter of her dead fighter.

She held the Solbeam hand laser, contemplating once again the need to kill herself before *they* reached her. And she recognized something . . . odd.

She'd come damned close to using the thing on herself a couple of times in the past hours, but each time she'd decided to *wait*, just a little. She'd made it this far, she was still okay . . . and the human brain, she was learning, simply could not cling to a fever's pitch of despair and terror for very long. Oh, the terror was still there, as was the feeling of hopelessness, but the monofilament's edge to those searing emotions had worn down a bit, had lessened enough that she was able to hold on a few *more* minutes . . . and a few more . . . and a few more after that.

The Slan in the hangar compartment seemed . . . agitated. Just maybe, the Marines were on their way in.

"This is Lieutenant Connor, VHF-140!" she called, using her squadron's tactical frequency. Her suit radio would not have penetrated the Slan vessel's hull, but if help was close, she might be able to make contact. "Lieutenant Connor, VHF-140! Does anybody read me?"

"This is Captain Charles Whittier, USNA Marines," a voice came back, static-blasted and vanishingly faint. She heard the voice continue for a moment after that, but the words were too distorted to make them out.

But it was the Marines, *here*!

She chanced another look over the edge of her lifeless Stardragon. The Slan appeared to be gathering in front of one bulkhead, 30 meters away. More were arriving moment by moment, coming in from each of the other bulkheads.

She did a quick count; there were at least thirty of them in the huge room already, probably more, though it was tough to tell in the glare of her light and the jerk and shift of the moving shadows.

"Captain Whittier!" she called. "This is Connor! Do you read me?"

"I read you," the voice replied. "Your signal is weak."

"Listen, if you're trying to reach me . . . there're about thirty Slan in the compartment with me. They're gathering behind a bulkhead like they're waiting for you to come through."

"Copy that. Are any of them with you?"

"They . . . I don't think they can see me." She went on to tell the Marine what she'd guessed about the Slan having difficulty seeing their surroundings in a low-pressure environment.

"The pressure's up to one point five, now," Whittier said. His voice sounded a little clearer, a little nearer. "How high does it have to be for them to see us?"

"I don't know. I imagine it will be pretty soon, though."

"Okay. We'll ride with it. Get down under cover."

"But I can—"

"Don't argue, Lieutenant! Get down!"

And the bulkhead beyond the waiting Slan exploded.

Marine Assault One-one
Slan warship
Low Orbit, 36 Ophiuchi AIII
1537 hours, TFT

Gunnery Sergeant Clegg ducked as the flare of light washed across the crouched Marines. His helmet sensors screened the worst of the glare, but nano-D breachers were powerful stuff. The nanodisassemblers released a great deal of energy in the form of searing heat and light as they took apart the molecules of the target—in this case a low, curving bulkhead between the Marines and the presumed location of the POW.

"Fireteam Alpha . . . *go!*" Captain Whittier shouted, and Clegg and three other Marines swept forward, moving through the still smoking breach in the wall.

After they'd entered the ship, Clegg and Owens had almost immediately begun gathering up other Marines as they'd moved deeper into the alien vessel, reaching platoon strength in minutes. Whittier was First Company's CO, and he'd shown up with fragments of three different platoons. Colonel Birney, the regimental CO, was holding the beachhead LZ with about fifty Marines; other Marines were moving through the ship, converging on the emergency beacon from the captured fighter.

Sergeant Patterson had slapped the nano-D charge against the bulkhead, and the Marines had moved back until the disassemblers did their work. Now they were going through.

Slan were waiting for them on the other side. *Lots* of them.

To his left and right, Marines began to die.

Slan warship
Low Orbit, 36 Ophiuchi AIII
1537 hours, TFT

As soon as the flash subsided, Connor lifted her head above the rim of the crater gaping in her fighter's hull. Marines in jet-black armor were coming through . . . directly into a maelstrom of enemy fire.

She wasn't certain, but it appeared that the Slan could see after all. They acted like it, targeting individual Marines and catching them in multiple beams—electron beams, she thought, because each shot snapped and glared like blue-white lightning, arcing among the Marines and bleeding off into deck and bulkhead and overhead. Three Marines went down in the first salvo, their armor savaged, peeled open and smoking. The Marines returned fire as they advanced, using lasers and man-portable plasma weapons. The Slan armor absorbed and deflected a lot of that energy, but couldn't block all of it. Slan troops were dying as well.

She didn't think the Marines were going to be able to get through that wall of Slan armor, however.

She saw only one possible way out.

Marine Assault One-one
Slan warship
Low Orbit, 36 Ophiuchi AIII
1537 hours, TFT

Sergeant Patterson slumped as what looked like a bolt of lightning punched through his helmet, blasting half of it into white-hot vapor and a grisly splash of red mist. Clegg pushed forward, pushed past the falling body, firing point-blank into the wall of alien Slan.

Modern combat rarely was fought at such tight, close quarters, and with so little cover. The scene was more reminiscent of a massed bayonet charge out of World War I, of hand-to-hand fighting in the trenches—brutal, inelegant, vicious, and bloody.

The Marines wavered. Not enough of them could come through the opening in the bulkhead at once to hold against the surge of aliens on the other side. Clegg took a step back, firing from his hip, not bothering to aim because the Slan were so thickly massed in front of him.

And then, suddenly, it was the Slan who were wavering.

Clegg wasn't sure at first what was happening. Those weaving, cone-shaped appendages, each wrapped in something like chainmail mesh, were twisting around to look behind them, to the rear. Clegg followed their alien gaze . . .

The woman was running directly at the Slan line, coming at them from behind. She wore a utility skin suit, black and tightly fitting and offering almost no armor protection at all, and a bubble helmet, and some sort of flight unit patch on her right shoulder. She was firing a small hand laser into the Slan, catching them in a withering crossfire with the Marines.

In point of fact, she wasn't doing a hell of a lot of damage. The Slan mesh armor was absorbing most of the energy pulses from her weapon, but the aliens appeared to be so startled by her headlong rush that they were scattering.

"C'mon, Marines!" Clegg yelled. "Take 'em down!"

"Ooh-rah!" several Marines chorused in the ancient Corps battle cry. Lance Corporal Sullivan fired a man-portable plasma weapon that seared through four Slan in a star-hot blaze of destruction. The alien bodies, he saw, *burned* in the high oxygen content, filling the chamber with greasy black smoke. Even the obviously dead aliens were twitching in horrible imitation of life as the fires consumed them.

Clegg saw an opening and forced his way through, scrambling over the tops of several dead or disabled Slan. The local gravity—almost two Gs—dragged at Clegg, but his armor employed powered biofeedback that amplified his movements and kept him upright.

He broke through just as the woman's hand laser failed, and she threw it aside.

Reaching out, he grabbed her arm and spun her about. "This way, ma'am," he said. Her rank tags said she was an officer, a lieutenant, and not even the confusion and noise of combat could derail basic military courtesy.

"Thank you, Gunnery Sergeant," she replied. The smoke was thick enough that she'd started drifting off in the wrong direction, but Clegg let his suit electronics guide the two of them back toward the main body of Marines. A Slan rippled in from the right, blocking the way, but Clegg opened up with his weapon and burned the ungainly, domed shape down.

"We got her!" he yelled at the others. "Start falling back by fireteam!"

"But we got 'em on the *run*, Gunny!" one young private screamed, his voice shaking.

"Move out, Jordan!" Clegg ordered. *"Now!"*

Marines helped other Marines, those who were disabled or hurt, and others dragged along the mangled, burnt-out forms of those killed in the sharp, short firefight.

The Marines would leave *no* one behind.

The Slan continued to retreat, fading into darkness and smoke.

And the Marines retreated back through the twisting tunnels toward the LZ.

"How . . . are we getting out?" the lieutenant wanted to know.

"Landing pod," Clegg replied. He grinned at her. "It'll be cozy, ma'am. But we'll fit!"

They reached one of the Apache Tear assault pods, visible only as a gaping, molten-looking hole in the bulkhead where the pod had eaten through from outside. "In you go," he said, guiding her. "It'll adjust to fit."

An assault pod normally *just* fit a single Marine, but the nanomatrix hull sensed the extra passenger and adapted to fit. The two of them nestled down within the pod's embrace, and Clegg gave the debarkation order.

The front of the pod sealed itself shut, and gravity vanished as the black teardrop hurled itself away from the Slan vessel. Imagery flooded Clegg's in-head—a slowly turning view of the receding side of the Slan vessel—and then they were dropping through open space once again.

"Thank you," the lieutenant said. "Th—*thank* you . . ."

And then she was sobbing, her helmet awkwardly pressed against his shoulder.

"No problem, ma'am," Clegg said gently. "It's what the Marines do."

But forty-three Marines had died to rescue this one fighter pilot.

He hoped the bill was worth it.

Chapter Fifteen

TC/USNA CVS America
Low Orbit, 36 Ophiuchi AIII
1555 hours, TFT

The Battle of Arianrhod, so far as Captain Gray could tell, appeared to be burning itself out. Most of the Slan warships near the planet were withdrawing. There were other Slan ships farther out—a number of them in the outer reaches of the star system like Tango One—but they so far were holding position, not moving toward Arianrhod and the battered USNA flotilla.

A respite, then. Good. Maybe the Slan had been hurt as badly as had the human fleet. Gray ordered *America* and her escorts to enter close orbit, with a thin and ragged screen of destroyers and frigates thrown farther out, at the million-kilometer line. *America* had been badly hurt in the battle, and needed repairs, and several other ships—the cruisers *North Carolina* and *California*, and the destroyer *Cumberland*, especially—had been savaged by the deadly Slan fire and were in no shape to undergo heavy acceleration.

Gray was under no illusions about the outcome of the battle. It wasn't a victory . . . not yet, not until the Slan had left the system and no longer posed a threat to the human ships. Given the disparity in technologies, though, Gray was more than willing to accept a draw and a moment's rest.

His first orders were to commence repairs on the damaged warships—especially on *America,* which had lost much of her forward shield cap. They would need a local water source to top off the ship's reservoirs before they could do much maneuvering.

He took the time to dispatch a high-speed courier back to Sol, reporting on the recent events at 36 Ophiuchi—both the sudden and unexpected cessation of fighting, and the defection of the other Confederation forces. Delattre's ships were decelerating now, and Gray was sure they would rejoin the fleet within the next few hours. What would happen after *that* was anyone's guess. As they dropped into orbit, scanners on board *America* had detected a courier drone leaving the Confederation fleet, no doubt with a request for new orders from Geneva.

But Gray decided he could face that particular set of problems later, when it was immediate enough to bite him.

Of more pressing urgency was the Slan.

Reports from the intelligence officer on board the USNAS *Inchon* had confirmed both that the Marine assault team had rescued a captured human pilot, and that they'd successfully infiltrated the enemy's electronics network with an AI hack virus. It was distinctly possible that the Slan had broken off the fight as soon as they'd realized that their computer net had been compromised. The ship attacked, the largest in the Slan fleet, might be their command and control vessel. If so, the other ships might be unwilling to follow orders from an HQ ship that now was controlled by the humans . . . or even to receive communications from that vessel, which might carry an electronic contagion.

Gray remembered that the ancient Sh'daar, at the Battle of the Six Suns in the Omega Centauri T$_{-0.876gy}$ dwarf galaxy twenty years ago, had also suddenly and unexpectedly broken off from a major battle, a battle that they'd been well on the way to winning. The Sh'daar and their assets appeared to have a habit of breaking off when there was even a chance of losing. An important bit of xenopsychology, that. Humans were more likely to go in, all weapons blazing, no matter what the odds.

And sometimes, *sometimes*, that strategy worked.

"Captain Gray?" The call was from *America*'s communications officer, Commander Pamela Wilson. "We have an encoded message, single burst transmission, coming through from *Inchon*. It's flagged urgent."

"Decrypt and patch it through, please."

"Aye, sir."

A new window opened in his head, and Gray found himself looking at the lined face of LCDR Raymond Villanova, the Marine ship's S-2. "Captain Gray, sir, there's been an important new development. I think the Slan want to talk. . . ."

Gray listened carefully to the rest of the message, as Villanova told him about Chesty$_2$'s discovery.

"Chesty sub-two" was the name of one of the artificial personalities residing within *Inchon*'s AI—specifically the subset of artificially intelligent software running the ship's intelligence department, and which had been copied and inserted into the Slan vessel during the Marine boarding action. Named for Lieutenant General Lewis "Chesty" Puller, with five Navy crosses the most decorated Marine in history, *this* Chesty had spent the last thirty minutes infiltrating the alien network, mapping it, and looking for a door.

And it was just possible that Chesty$_2$ had found it.

Almost nothing was known about Slan technology, and that included whatever it was they used for computers. Hacking into a human-built computer was tough enough, what with passwords and high-level encryption, plus security software running in the background designed to spot and block unauthorized attempts to break in. When you didn't know anything about the target operating system, or what it was running on, or even the language of the beings that had built the thing, the task became all but impossible.

Human-built AIs attempting to penetrate networks used by any of the Sh'daar client races, however, had an important advantage. Human contact with the Agletsch had early on

revealed a number of languages—most of them artificial—
that had been designed to help the diverse Sh'daar client species communicate with one another. If nothing else, each
had to communicate with their Sh'daar masters, no matter
what form of physical communication they happened to use.
The Sh'daar themselves, at least originally, were not a single
species, as it turned out, but a kind of federation of many
races, with many different forms of communication.

How *could* you run a galactic empire without a common
language? There were, Gray knew, races that communicated
by changing patterns of color on their integuments, by naturally generated radio, by moving tendrils or other external
organs to convey data in a form of semaphore, even by shifting patterns within internally generated electrical fields.

Spoken language—generating sounds that carried
meaning—was perhaps the most common form of personal
communication, but even here there was an astonishing
variety. The Turusch spoke with two separate voices, each
carrying meaning and which, when heterodyned together,
produced a third layer of information. The Agletsch themselves spoke by belching air from their upper stomachs
through the mouths located in their abdomens, and supple-
mented the sounds with curious weavings of their four eye-
stalks that carried emotion.

The spidery Agletsch, however, widely traveled traders
of interstellar information about tens of thousands of worlds
and intelligent galactic species, had devised a number of artificial languages—trade pidgins—that allowed the Sh'daar
to communicate with the weird zoo of beings that comprised
their empire. These pidgins were actually electronic in
nature, allowing sophisticated translators worn by the various species to talk to one another, and to speak with native
languages stored in the translation database.

But for such a thing to work, the computer networks involved had to be able to communicate with one another. That
implied a certain amount of standardization—an ability to
match clock speeds and to handle data packets and peer-
to-peer communications with some degree of commonality.

Earth's intelligence services still had no idea how such a thing might be accomplished, but evidently it *had* been done once, at least, probably a billion years or so ago within the Sh'daar home galaxy. The Agletsch and their pidgins hadn't been around then, of course—the Spiders, almost certainly, were native to *this* galaxy and *this* time—but they had evidently taken Sh'daar translation protocols and implemented them for modern Sh'daar client species, from the Turusch and H'rulka to humans and the Slan.

And as a result, intelligence software like Chesty$_2$ had something to work on. In particular, they could find language files and compare them with known files, a kind of electronic Rosetta Stone that allowed an unknown alien language to be cracked.

Initial data sent back from the *Inchon* suggested that the Slan did communicate by sound—specifically through modulations of rapid-fire clicks and chirps, many of them in the ultrasonic range, above the threshold of human hearing. Now, according to Villanova, Chesty$_2$ had found language files including the primary Agletsch trade pidgin, the language used by the Sh'daar to speak with many of their clients. The Slan computers included a language file based on such sounds.

What was more, the *Inchon* had just received a message in the Agletsch pidgin requesting direct communications . . . "Hive Master to Hive Master," as the oddly worded text put it.

The Slan, apparently, wanted to talk.

Gray considered this carefully. Direct communications with an enemy could have dire consequences. They could use that channel to insert a virus into the USNA networks, just as the Marines had done with the Slan HQ ship. With an advanced-enough technology, they might even be able to take over *America*'s systems to an extent that would result in serious damage or destruction for the human vessel.

On the other hand, *America* had quite good network security.

And if there was even a small chance of ending the conflict with the Slan . . .

"Open a channel to the *Inchon*," Gray told Wilson.

It was time to open negotiations with the Slan, before more fighting destroyed what was left of the human fleet.

Executive Office, USNA
Columbus, District of Columbia
United States of North America
1614 hours, EST

"Our ships are on the way in, Mr. President," Admiral Armitage told him. "*Pittsburgh* will be over Tsiolkovsky in another two minutes. The others should arrive within an hour."

"Thank you, Gene," Koenig replied. "Keep your feed open and let me watch over your shoulder."

"Of course, Mr. President."

Military personnel never liked it when their superiors watched through their command links—*especially* when that superior was the commander in chief. Koenig made a habit of not micromanaging his officers, however, so he thought he could probably get away with it this time. Eugene Armitage had been head of his Joint Chiefs of Staff for two years, now, and this was the first time Koenig had used his high-G pull as president to intrude on one of his subordinates.

He'd been following the battle on the moon for eight hours, now, linked in through the Marine tactical net. Not a lot had been happening for most of that time. Lieutenant Burnham's handful of Marines, deployed along the northern rim of Tsiolkovsky Crater sixty-some kilometers from the underground base housing the Konstantin super-AI, had stopped the advance of fifteen heavy gunrafts carrying approximately six hundred Confederation troops. Several gunrafts had been destroyed, killing an unknown number of the enemy; at the same time, enemy vehicles had pounded the crater rim with antimatter warheads, killing twenty-two Marines.

The ninety-eight Marines of Bravo Company, 3rd Battalion 2/3 still on their feet had dug in and were holding the high ground.

In a second in-head window, Koenig maintained a link with the Hexagon office of Admiral Armitage. Hours ago, he'd received confirmation that USNA fleet elements were on the way—four High Guard ships normally stationed in the outer solar system, and a light cruiser, the USNAS *Pittsburgh*, from Mars. Their presence over Tsiolkovsky ought to end the standoff there, though Koenig was forced to admit that the Confederation forces, in particular the Pan-Europeans, were acting irrationally, had been acting irrationally for several years now. They'd successfully grabbed the mid-ocean seastead habitats, and for years now had been pushing hard to take control of the USNA Periphery states. Almost anything, he thought, was possible at this point, especially with enough ships in-system to back up their claims. As with the USNA warships, the bulk of Geneva's fleet was out-system, but there were still at least thirty ships at Mars, on High Guard duty, or at Quito Synchorbital that might yet weigh in if things got really nasty.

He wondered why Geneva hadn't ordered the in-system ships to Tsiolkovsky . . . but decided that the Confederation leaders wanted to maintain something like plausible deniability. They were willing to sneak in and try to grab the base before USNA forces could respond, then argue the matter after they were already in control . . . but getting into a knock-down fleet action meant open civil war and no way to maintain the polite fiction of negotiations. Too, they wouldn't want to start tossing nukes around above Tsiolkovsky. After all, they wanted an intact and cooperative Konstantin . . . not a radioactive crater. That may have been the main reason they'd stopped bombarding the Marines with antimatter warheads, in fact. A stray round passing over the crater's north rim could travel far indeed in the moon's one-sixth gravity—far enough, perhaps, to strike Konstantin's mountain and wreck his subselenian base.

How far would Konstantin cooperate with Geneva if Confederation forces managed to capture it? Koenig wasn't sure. The super-AI didn't seem to think of itself as North American, but as a free agent in the service of Humankind.

Why this should be so when humans were pulling asshole stunts like fighting over it was beyond Koenig. Someday, he might get up the nerve to ask Konstantin . . . assuming he still had private access to it after this afternoon.

He shifted channels again, looking now through a camera mounted on Lieutenant Burnham's helmet. Sunlight glared off harsh white smoothly rounded slopes. He said nothing; lieutenants tended not to function at peak efficiency if they knew their commander-in-chief was looking on.

Something was happening. . . .

Marine Perimeter
Tsiolkovsky Crater North Rim
Lunar Farside
1615 hours, EST

"Koblesky! Hernandez!" Burnham shouted. "We've got motion at Number Twelve-Fifteen!"

The Marines had put out some hundreds of robot drones across the north face of the crater-rim slope. Some were stationary sentries, white pillars capped by particle gun turrets and sensor arrays monitoring the lunar panorama to the north. Others were crawlers, moving on spidery, jointed legs, or fliers kept aloft in the light gravity by electrostatic repulsion with the surface. Linked in with the Tsiolkovsky Net, the robotic swarm sent back constant updates on enemy positions and movements, on weapons, and on those communications that could be tapped. These last were, of course, encrypted, but the Marines had a code-cracking resource right next door that could turn the most opaque communications code transparent. Konstantin had been relaying updates to the Marines on intercepted radio and laser com chatter almost as quickly as it got the raw signals. There'd been nothing of great value so far, but it still gave the Tsi-olkovsky defenders a decided edge.

And meanwhile, the robots had been carrying out their own war across the blasted lunar regolith. The Confederation troops had loosed their own robotic army, and now devices the size of a man's hand were ambushing one another with lasers, with EMP discharges, and with self-guided bullets releasing clouds of submicroscopic nanodisassemblers.

Motion at one of the sentry positions probably meant the machine's optics had picked up the approach of another robot. If so, Marine robots would be dispatched to deal with it. Burnham linked in with the signal feed, however, looking through the robot sentry's electronic eye.

No . . . *not* another robot. Humans—a dozen soldiers in heavy Confederation armor. Like the Marines, the enemy's armor had photoreactive nanomatrix surfaces, and it was almost impossible to make out the forms as they slipped from boulder to boulder, from shadow to shadow, working their way up the slope below the left side of the Marine positions.

Koblesky and Hernandez were on that part of the perimeter with a man-portable CPG. They were linked into the tactical net and should have seen the enemy themselves, but Burnham's warning would also alert other Marines close by, let them know the Confederation troops were up to something.

Lightning flared, silent in hard vacuum, a focused beam of electrons striking regolith and boulders in an intense burst of energy hot enough to turn the silica in the ever-present dust to glass. The armor of the lead Confederation trooper turned black as its reactive nano died, then came apart in hurtling gobbets of molten metal, ceramic, and plastic.

The close-up view in her in-head window winked off as the enemy fired a directed EMP weapon, taking out the sentry robot. Without the remote imaging, she couldn't see a damned thing except the flashes of energy bolts striking among the boulders a kilometer or more down-slope. No matter. The enemy troops were precisely plotted now on her tactical map, and more distant sensors were now locked onto them. She did a quick trigonometric calculation with her in-head, then ordered Duncan and Salvatore to lay down some KK fire on that area. Burnham reviewed the positions of her own people, trying to decide whether to shift any of them to meet this new threat. The problem, of course, was that the threat might be a diversion, a feint designed to get her to shift to the west and weaken the east side of her perimeter.

"Task Force Burnham, this is Captain Raleigh, USNAS *Pittsburgh*. I understand you people need some help."

Burnham looked up involuntarily but, of course, the blackness overhead was empty except for the sun. She felt a sharp, almost savage thrill. Naval support! It was what they'd been praying for all day.

"This is Burnham. I copy you, *Pittsburgh*. Where the hell are you?"

"L-2. But I can see you just fine on your tactical."

Located 67,000 kilometers above the moon's equator above the center of the lunar farside, the gravitationally stable L-2 synchronous point was a convenient place to park the farside communications net station and some logistics depots . . . and apparently a USNA light cruiser as well.

And, just maybe, Koenig was protecting the comm net array as well. If the Confeds were crazy enough to try to snatch Konstantin from USNA forces, they might be willing to try for other American assets up here as well. The three big colonies on the lunar near side—Asimov, Heinlein, and Clarke—technically belonged to the United States of North America, not the Confederation.

But Geneva seemed to be having some trouble lately reading the legal fine print.

"Excuse me," a new voice said. "Captain Raleigh? This is President Koenig. I've been monitoring Lieutenant Burnham's combat zone feeds."

"Sir, yes, *sir!*"

"Think you can take out the remaining Confederation vehicles without hurting our Marines?"

"Sir, the Marine positions are clearly marked. Yes, we can do it."

"Do so. Destroy the remaining vehicles, then hold your fire. I want to give these people a chance to surrender."

"Aye, aye, Mr. President."

"Carry on, then."

"How long were you riding me?" Burnham shouted. Her face burned then, as she saw, too late, the double meaning. Riding could mean linking into a remote camera and communications net.

Or it could mean something quite different.

She heard Koenig chuckle. "Just a few minutes, Lieutenant. I would have asked first, but I didn't want you . . . distracted."

"No sir. I mean, yes sir. It's okay, sir."

"You've been doing a superb job," Koenig told her. "Semper fi."

And he was gone. Inside her helmet, Burnham shook her head. She knew that the president had been a Navy admiral—the hero of Arcturus and Texaghu Resch and the Six Suns of T$_{-0.876gy}$.

She was a little in awe of him.

But she could indulge in the sappy reveries of teenage hero worship later. Right now, the Confederation troops were surging up the slope. There were still six Type 770s out there, hull down and well camouflaged, and an instant later one of them slammed an antimatter round into the ridge 200 meters to Burnham's right and a little downslope. Harsh light seared the landscape around her, and her helmet optics blacked out to preserve her vision. When she could again see, the slope in front of her was alive with movement—the shift and crawl of active nanomatrix camouflage revealed only by minor imperfections in the visual effect as the armor bent light around the soldier inside.

Burnham tried to calculate how long it would take for kinetic-kill rounds to fall from 67,000 kilometers, and realized that the speed depended on how hard the crowbars were boosted from the cruiser's railguns.

Crowbars. She smiled at the ancient word, a reference to a straight, heavy length of steel used as a tool centuries ago. In the earliest years of the Space Age, kinetic-kill projectiles had been suggested as a deadly orbit-to-ground weapon precise enough to hit individual vehicles, powerful enough to punch through the armor of underground bunkers. A simple bar of metal, the weapon was as dumb as a crowbar . . . but if you could aim it precisely and accelerate it at tens of thousands of kilometers per hour or faster, it didn't *have* to be smart. Whatever it hit was dead.

She didn't have enough information to calculate the drop time. She considered calling Raleigh and asking for an ETA . . . and then the slope below blossomed in a line of incandescent white flowers, hot as the surface of the sun, expanding, unfurling, reaching into the blackness of the sky. There was no sound, of course, but seconds later she felt the shudder ripple beneath her boots as the shock wave passed.

Six Type 770s, six explosions.

She opened a comm channel to one of the command frequencies on which Konstantin had been eavesdropping. "Attention, Confederation soldiers," she said. "Your vehicles are destroyed, and it's a *very* long walk back to Giordano Bruno. I suggest that you consider disabling your weapons and coming up the slope slowly, with your hands up."

She spoke English, but the enemy's translator software would give them her message in their own language. There was no answer at first. There was a serious danger here, Burnham knew. The destruction of their vehicles might encourage the enemy troops to fight all the harder, knowing they had no other alternatives beyond surrender, taking the Tsiolkovsky base, or dying in the pitiless, harsh glare of the lunar sun.

And then there was the unpleasant possibility that the Confederation had naval forces on the way as well. Losing their Type 770s wouldn't matter much if they knew they had a ride home no matter what. *Pittsburgh*'s KK strike might simply up the ante . . . and call down a rain of Confed KK or antimatter rounds on the Marine positions in return.

"Hold your fire, American," a voice—a woman's voice—said at long last. "We surrender. We're coming up."

"Excellent!" Koenig's voice said. "A very good job indeed."

Ad Astra Confederation Government Complex
Geneva, European Union
2240 hours, local time

Ilse Roettgen scowled at the data scrolling through her in-head display. The battle on the moon, evidently, was over, with nearly two hundred Confederation troops killed and over four hundred captured by a mere hundred American Marines.

It was not to be tolerated.

And now the American president wanted to talk with her. She dismissed the winking in-head flag with a thought-click. Let him wait. Let him sweat. In another few hours, it wouldn't matter. . . .

She opened her eyes, returning to the diplomatic reception in the stadium-sized central oval of the Plaza of Light. The immense and iconic statue by Popolopoulis, *Ascent of Man*, towered overhead, one muscular arm stretched out to the heavens. Several thousand people were gathered in the plaza this evening, a glittering swarm of the Confederation elite, mingling, seeing, and being seen. The weather was perfect, the sky ablaze with stars—the fingernail crescent of the moon having set hours before. Attire ran the gamut from traditional-formal to nude, with many of the guests—especially the women—tastefully ablaze in liquid light.

The reception was for Chidambaram, the new ambassador-delegate from North India. He and his entourage were gathered at the foot of the giant statue, talking at the moment with Carol Spelman, the American ambassador.

The problem with the Americans, Roettgen decided, was their inconstancy. They whined and scrabbled for their precious independence like puppies in a box . . . but give them a measure of freedom and self-determination and they cried for Mother's comforting presence.

Chidambaram and Spelman had just been joined, Roettgen saw, by a pair of those horrible spider-bug things . . . what were they called? Agletsch. That was it. She didn't like them, didn't like most aliens, but she did recognize political necessity when she saw it. For 287 years, the *Pax Confeoderata* had spoken for all of Humankind in a hostile and bewildering galaxy. The Americans—the old United States, at any rate—had helped create the Pax in the aftermath of the Second Sino-Western War and the cataclysmic Wormwood Fall.

And for 287 years, the Americans had bitched and complained about being part of a one-world government. A true planetary government? No . . . they wanted their *freedom*. July 1st and July 4th and Cinco de Mayo . . . fireworks and Bill of Rights and free speech and self-determination.

But they also wanted strength and order and, above all else, *security*.

And what they could never grasp was the fact that freedom and security were mutually contradictory. You couldn't have them both, not completely. The best you could hope for was a half-assed balance between the two.

Their latest election had demonstrated an alarming drift in the USNA population toward secession and full autonomy. Koenig appeared to be a moderate, politically, but he'd been calling for greater independence, greater self-determination, for all of the states of the Pax.

And his speeches had sent shudders through the framework of the entire Confederation.

It was time to end this farce, before American dissent tore the Confederation apart. Earth, the Terran Confederation, needed to be united now as never before, strong and with one voice in the face of a hostile galaxy.

Seizing Konstantin was to have been the first step in the grand plan worked out by her military staff, and it had failed, but that was of little real importance. The capture of

Tsiolkovsky base was to have been as much a diversion as anything else . . . and if it had gone as planned, it would have given Geneva some leverage in the coming negotiations.

But right now, Roettgen thought, Atlantica gave the Pax all the leverage it was going to need. . . .

Chapter Sixteen

Washington, former District of Columbia
USNA Periphery
0710 hours, TFT

Shay Ashton looked up from the controls of the logger and planned her next move. Once, this had been one of the deeper and softer-bottomed of the swamps filling what once had been the downtown area of the old United States capital. Most of the water had been drained—the seacrete dams grown across the lower Potomac had enabled the pumping project to move ahead and reclaim land that, until recently, had been under half a meter or more of water. The logger was a titanic machine—each of its six wheels stood 6 meters high—had been brought in to begin removing the thick groves of mangrove trees filling what once had been open streets, traffic circles, and plazas.

Until a few years ago, the broad, central mall in the heart of the old city had been a swampy estuary under a meter of water at high tide, surrounded by the crumbling, clifflike ruins of ancient edifices and monuments shrouded in forests of kudzu. The city had been abandoned late in the twenty-first century. Sea levels had been steadily rising . . . and the First Sino-Western War has so thoroughly wrecked the U.S.

economy that massive preservation efforts—sea walls and drainage pumps the size of skyscrapers—had been abandoned. Most of Florida had been gone by 2080, and *still* the seas kept rising. Eventually, the government in its new inland capital had decided to write off the wreckage of the coastal cities. Rebuilding them would have cost in the hundreds of trillions, and the nation, still recovering from the financial stress of the war, then wracked by the Blood Death plague of the next couple of decades, simply couldn't afford it.

The Periphery was abandoned . . . at least officially.

And yet there *were* still people living there among the partially submerged buildings of Manhattan and D.C. and Boston—refugees with nowhere else to go, diehards who'd refused to leave, lawless gangs coming in from outside. Local government, at best, had been reduced to shifting alliances among warlords. At worst, there *was* no government, and tight-knit families had struggled for survival against anarchy in rooftop communes above the encroaching sea.

And for the most part, they were ignored by the government. For the most part too, the residents of the Periphery wanted it that way . . . no taxes, no Big Brother, no surveillance, no intrusive government regulations, hell, the whole thing was a libertarian's dream. True, no police protection; no high-tech computers or communications; few modern toys; no food distribution; no health care . . . but the inhabitants of the Periphery had been getting along just fine for more than three centuries, thank you very much. Life here could be hard, but most Prims—or "primitives"—preferred that to giving up their freedom in a squeaky-clean world changing too fast for healthy sanity.

But change was coming in any case.

Shay Ryan had escaped the Washington Swamp over twenty years before, joining the USNA Navy and becoming a fighter pilot. She'd done well, too, winning a Navy Cross for her part in the Sh'daar War . . . but a few years later she'd resigned. Navy Cross or not, the prejudice inherent in the naval service had just been too much. Periphery dwellers had, over the centuries, developed their own culture and their own way of life, and this often put them at odds with people from the USNA proper. For most of her squadron mates, it seemed, she would *always* be "monogie" or "Prim" or "swamp rat."

So she'd gotten out. She'd gone back to old D.C., married a swampy named Fred Ashton, and even taken his last name for her own—one of those cultural disconnects with USNA social norms that singled her out as something strange or dirty—a monogie, someone who believed in monogamous marriage.

Ten years later, Fred had been killed in a skirmish with marauders from the Virginia side of the swamp. Shay had led a number of her neighbors on a raid into Northern Virginia, wiped out the bandits, then somehow struggled on.

She'd been something of a celebrity with her neighbors, most of whom had never left the area. She also still had her military implants—nanotechnically grown circuitry inside her brain and various other parts of her body that allowed her to interface with a wide range of machines and computers. Various software packages and classified files had been deleted when she resigned, of course, but the hardware was hers. When Columbus had offered help in reclaiming the Washington Swamp, she'd volunteered, and her hardware had allowed her to link with and run heavy equipment like the Bunyan-425 logger.

Hell, it was just like her old Starhawk fighter. Just smaller. And slower. And unable to fly . . .

She was pulling a mangrove up by its tangled roots when Jeb Carstairs called to her over the logger's radio. "Hey, Shay! What the hell is that?"

"What's what?" She turned in her seat. The machine's high bubble canopy gave her a complete, 360-degree view. She saw it. *"Shit!"*

It was a troop flier, a big one, and not a USNA model. She recognized it, of course, even though she no longer packed a warbook recognition series in her in-head. Three times the size of the old Columbia Stadium, blunt nosed and massive, the UTT-92 Jotun troop transport was the size of a large cruiser, drifting in over the city from the southeast on silent electrogravitic impellers. Advancing slowly, it blotted out the early-morning sun, its shadow rippling across ground and water and the towering logger like the relentlessly incoming tide.

Stunned, Shay stared at the apparition for what seemed like minutes, though in fact it was only a few seconds. The markings on the slate-gray flanks identified the flier as Confederation, though Jotuns, she thought, were only used by the Europeans. It could carry a couple of thousand troops, and was heavily armed with turret-mounted lasers and particle cannons.

It appeared to be swinging around in order to touch down on the open expanse of the mall.

Ever since her husband's death, Shay had kept a laser carbine with her when she was working. She pulled it from its holster now, switched on the energy pack, and opened the logger's canopy.

Captain's Office
TC/USNA CVS America
Low Orbit, 36 Ophiuchi AIII
0813 hours, TFT

"We have a channel?" Gray asked.

"Affirmative," the voice of *America*'s AI replied. "Certain aspects of the virtual environment may be difficult to interpret, however."

"That's okay," Gray replied, bracing himself. "What is that old poem? 'To see ourselves as others see us'?"

"'To a Louse, On Seeing One on a Lady's Bonnet at Church,'" the AI replied immediately. "By Robert Burns, 1768."

"'To a Louse'?" Gray repeated, curious. "That's some kind of parasite, isn't it?"

Data flowed through his awareness. There were three thousand and some species of lice—wingless insects of the order Phthiraptera, only three of which ever infested humans. Images accompanied the data, of crawling, short-legged ectoparasites as alien-looking as anything Gray had met among the stars.

The human-feeding varieties—head, body, and pubic lice—were rarely encountered nowadays, thanks to full-body mediscans and sanitizer fields; they were still a nuisance in some of the Peripheries. Yeah, he remembered hearing about them, now, from his years growing up in Old Manhattan. He'd almost forgotten. In Burns's day, though, they must have been fairly common.

He scanned through the poem, written in an ancient Scots' dialect that at times was almost impenetrable. He shifted to the translation to get a better sense of the thing. The subject of the poem, evidently, was a tiny louse seen by Burns crawling on the Sunday bonnet of a young and well-bred woman in church. At first, the poet scolded the minute creature for daring to set foot on "Such a fine lady."

The final stanza was the one most often quoted. Translated, it read:

And would some power the gift to give us
To see ourselves as others see us!
It would from many a blunder free us,
And foolish notion:
What airs in dress and gait would leave us,
And even devotion!

A louse, it seemed, cared nothing for the difference between an aristocratic lady and a beggar. Both were sources of food, nothing more. To see Humankind through a louse's eyes might show certain human pretenses for what they were.

Gray chuckled at that. He'd never downloaded Burns before, but thought he might need to read more of the man, now. The man knew *people*.

And right now, Gray was going to get to see himself as the Slan saw him, a deliberate exchange of imagery with the other side. He was hoping this might give him some insight into the aliens, help him understand them better.

More important, for this exchange of data, both the Slan computers and America's AIs would have access to at least portions of one another's databases. Communicating with a previously unknown alien species was not simply a matter of hooking up a translation program and substituting your words for theirs. How you saw the universe was at least as important as the language used in describing it.

"Are you ready, Captain?" the AI asked.

"Go for it," he replied. "Open the link."

The subdued lighting of Gray's office winked out, replaced by blackness. Then, slowly, a picture began to build up, layer by layer, painted in pinpoints of sharp neon-blue light. The effect was . . . startling.

He was seeing, not the alien Slan, but himself. The idea was that, for both of them, seeing an alien through alien perceptions might be overwhelming, the data unintelligible. So you started simply, with what you knew: *yourself*.

He did not recognize himself, transformed, as he was, through the computer link with the Slan headquarters ship. The image in front of him was human-shaped, but lacked all detail and texture. He could see his nose—rounded and smooth—but the eyes were featureless swellings sunken within depressions in a blank face, the hair a vague, out-of-focus blur. There was no color save for the electric blue of the imaging. The entire body was frustratingly out of focus.

When he stared harder, trying to bring the picture into sharper resolution, he found his point of view actually descending into the shape. He could focus first on his shipboard utilities, then on his skin, then on the layers of muscle beneath his skin, then on his internal organs and the bright, hard tracings of his skeleton. He recognized the rapid pulsing of his heart immediately, behind his ribs . . . but what the hell was *that*?

It took him a queasy moment to recognize his own stomach, with a partially digested breakfast inside, reduced to semisolid sludge.

By concentrating in a different way, he found he could increase the level of detail. He could also get a strong three-dimensional sense, created, he guessed, by changing the positions of the paired Slan sonar organs. When he looked more closely this way, his implants showed up as bright threads woven over and through his brain, down his arms, and in the palms of his hands.

And there was more. Even when he focused on the outer layers—clothing or skin—he was aware of surging movement along narrow channels visible through the blue translucence, just underneath the skin and, in some cases, muscle. The sounds made by blood surging through veins and arteries, he decided, were adding an additional level of detail.

The Slan, by this point, Gray decided, must be fairly confused. The alien commander was receiving computer-generated images of itself as humans would see it, completely opaque. It occurred to him that the Slan might constantly be aware of other individuals as multilayered, as sum totals of skin together with everything inside.

It might also be difficult for the aliens, he thought, not to understand a species that didn't have this three-dimensional understanding of another being as somehow lacking something. Seeing them as crippled, or even blind.

It took him a while to see it, but he did notice that the Slan were not *completely* blind to optical wavelengths. One of the levels of information he was receiving was a kind of dull, fuzz glow superimposed on the audio image. The scant data available on Slan physiology mentioned a primitive light-sensing organ on the central hump.

Gray wondered what they used it for, why it had evolved at all. They certainly got a great deal of information through sonar alone.

He allowed himself to pull back and examine their virtual surroundings. The two of them, human and Slan, were in a tube of some sort, smooth, with ripples on the walls that gave it a distinctly organic feel. With Slan sonar vision, he could peer a little way into the wall, seeing fuzzy layers and, beneath that, the bright traceries of deeply embedded electronics, the more massive pipes of the plumbing.

The effect was amazing in its scope and depth, especially in that the Slan and human were not really facing each other physically inside the tunnel. The computers—both on board *America* and on the Slan ship—were working together closely enough to reproduce a detailed virtual reality between them, one that would allow human and Slan to see each other as if they were only a few meters apart.

"Okay," Gray told the AI. "I've seen enough, and it's giving me a headache. Let's switch back . . . whenever my opposite number is ready."

"It's been ready, Captain."

Gray's vision blurred, and then he was back in his own body, looking at the alien through human eyes.

In the aftermath of the alien vision, this was almost a relief. The Slan stood a meter and a half tall, but was almost twice that in diameter, most of its mass a large, wet mantle. He couldn't tell if the thing moved on legs or tentacles, or simply slid along the deck like a slug. The perimeter of the thing, sweeping along the deck, was a roil of writhing tentacles, most of them slender and thin, like spaghetti, but six were somewhat longer, and three of them, evenly spaced around the body, were each 2 meters long and powerfully muscled. A translucent flap opened to either side of the upper body, creating broad, membranous cups when open. Ears?

The thing looked a little like a terrestrial jellyfish, but far more substantial and massive. The skin—more like a rubbery hide—was a dark slate-gray, and the movements of the peripheral tentacles suggested tremendous strength.

"Okay, let me see it through its way of seeing things," Gray told the AI.

The being in front of him blurred, then shifted into the other way of seeing, a painting in harsh blue light. Letting his gaze move into the creature, Gray saw closely packed internal organs, but there was no way of telling what was what. Five muscular lumps each the size of a human head were spaced in a ring around the body's central core, and these were pulsing in a way analogous to a human heart . . . but more slowly, and in succession.

He didn't see any legs beneath the fleshy skirt. The Slan glided about on a single large, muscular "foot," like a terrestrial gastropod.

Presumably, the Slan was now looking at Gray through its own sonar sense. It, at least, Gray thought, had already had the chance to see a human that way . . . the prisoner rescued yesterday from their headquarters ship.

Lieutenant Megan Connor was on board *America*, now, and was still being debriefed on her experiences. Her initial descriptions of the strangeness of the Slan had been the factor that had led Gray to suggest this visual swap in the first place, a means of literally stepping into each other's shoes.

Okay, the Slan didn't wear shoes, or anything else, for that matter. But the metaphor still worked.

The AI referred to the being as it, apparently a direct translation of how they thought of themselves. *America*'s xenobiology department believed that the Slan were either hermaphroditic or, as with terrestrial ants and bees, that only a few members of the species could reproduce, that most individuals were of the neuter caste.

"!kt'kt'!'kt'cht'!k," sounded in Gray's mind, a rapid rattle of clicks and pops and clucking sounds. The Slan was speaking.

"I thought we had the translation program working," Gray said, annoyed. "What's with that noise?"

"Some concepts," the AI reminded him, "simply cannot be translated. That might have been a greeting, or an exclamation. Or both."

Great, Gray thought. Then he gave an inward shrug. How many expressions in English were little more than polite noise? Or depended on cultural or even biological context to make sense? *On the other hand* made sense only if you knew what a hand was . . . and knew that a person had only two of them.

"I am Captain Gray," he said in his mind. The AI would pick up his unvoiced thoughts and translate them for the Slan. "I hope we can arrive at a mutual understanding."

"Affirmation," a voice replied in his mind. "Too many have crossed into light, a terrible waste of resources."

"I agree. What is your name? How should we call you?"

"This one is Clear Chiming Bell, of the third caste of holding the mellifluous harmonies."

Gray wasn't sure if what he'd just heard was a military rank or a job description. Perhaps it was both. "And why did your forces attack us here in this star system?"

There was a long hesitation. "We are not sure what you mean by 'star system.'"

"The world we are orbiting now. We call it Arianrhod. It has been one of our colonies for one hundred forty-two of our years."

There was another delay. "What's the problem?" Gray asked the AI on the private channel. The ship's AI was closely monitoring both the virtual environment and the exchange of communications.

"The Slan is consulting its computer databases," the AI replied. "It is having difficulty with some physical concepts, apparently, such as 'year' and 'planet.'"

But how was that even possible? The Slan were space farers. They had starships, very *good* starships, with better drive systems than humans. How the hell could you leave your world if you didn't know what a world was?

"Are you getting good information from them?" Gray asked. Each time the Slan looked into its own computer database, *America*'s AI could look with it, look over its metaphorical shoulder, and uncover more data.

"I am. We are downloading data on Slan biology, on their relationship with the Sh'daar, and much else."

"And they're getting the same sort of stuff on us?"

"Almost certainly."

Good. Certain information in *America*'s memory would be carefully blocked from Slan probes, and the Slan computers no doubt employed similar blocks. But just a few moments of computer exchanges like this could tell both species a great deal about each other, information that normal, non-enhanced communication might never reveal.

"Are you having any trouble matching with their system?"

The AI hesitated. "No major difficulties. Their computer system is similar to our old DNA computers. Their biology does not employ DNA, however. They appear to use TNA instead—threose nucleic acid."

Gray nodded understanding. On Earth, enzymes and DNA had first been used in the very early twenty-first century to create a molecular computer more than 100,000 times faster than the best personal computers at the time. TNA was an organic polymer like DNA or RNA, but with a different chemical backbone. Though it had never been known to evolve naturally on Earth, when humans began encountering extrasolar life, they found that DNA was only one way among many of encoding genetic information. TNA, among others, ran the genetics of several extrasolar ecologies as an analogue of terrestrial DNA.

Evidently, the Slan had discovered molecular computing with their own version of organic chemistry. The interesting point from Gray's perspective was that they were *still* using molecular computing. On Earth, molecular computing had been a short-lived sideshow in the development of ever faster computers, a system rapidly superseded by even faster and more powerful quantum computers.

It was an interesting difference between human technology and the Slan, but there was nothing yet that Gray could use to his advantage.

"We were told," the translated Slan voice said after a moment, "that humans are *k'!k't!'cht'!k'!kt'!!!k*. Our AIs see no evidence that this is true, however."

"I beg your pardon?"

"The term *k'!k't!'cht'!k'!kt'!!!k* does not appear to translate into Agletsch Trade Pidgin," *America*'s AI said.

"Interesting. Who was telling them about us? The Sh'daar?"

"Presumably so."

"That term you just used did not translate," Gray said.

"The terms 'beg' and 'pardon' did not translate," the Slan replied.

"What were you told about us?"

"This one regrets the . . . translation difficulty," Clear Chiming Bell said after another moment. "This is . . . important. Do humans . . . it is difficult to say, difficult to make it make sense . . . pollute . . . contaminate . . . interfere with the sonic background environment in . . . in immoral ways?"

"I don't quite understand," Gray said. "What does that mean?"

He could almost feel the Slan struggling with alien concepts. "Making a clear understanding of one's surroundings . . . opaque. As if robbing the air. With sonic emissions?"

Gray struggled to suppress an outburst of laughter. On the face of it, the Slan appeared to be asking if humans *farted* . . . if they created noise contamination that interfered with the sonic "view."

But he didn't reply immediately because he had the feeling that the Slan meant something else, something much more serous than random gas emissions from the lower digestive tract.

"I'm sorry," Gray replied carefully. "I still can't make out what you're saying. Can you give me examples?"

"There are among us," Clear Chiming Bell said, "those who deliberately emit vibrations . . . sound energy in such a way as to . . . obscure our sonar picture of our surroundings. They violate the . . . guiding spirit of the Tunnels. Of the Community. They are . . . unsane. They are *k'!k't!'cht'!k'!kt'!!!k*. They are sent into the light."

Gray considered this. Okay . . . maybe he *could* see something in what the lumpish alien was saying. Tunnels . . . community. He glanced at a sidebar window running within his in-head, looking at the information *America*'s AI was garnering from the Slan THA computers during the conversation. The data coming back on their evolutionary biology suggested that they lived underground . . . possibly in hives, again like ants or bees. They didn't seem to possess the so-called hive mind usually attributed to such species, but if you packed a large number of individuals into narrow tunnels like the virtual one he was standing in now, there would be some pretty strong social rules governing how you acted, what you did, and how you did it.

They are sent into the light. Among some human religions, going to the light could be understood as a metaphor for death, and perhaps that was why the phrase had translated easily. So, among the Slan, some individuals so interfered with how the community saw their surroundings that they were killed, or, as another interpretation might have it, they were exiled from the community.

For the Slan sonic equivalent of passing gas?

Or for being different in a society that demanded uniformity, that enforced a harsh compliance to social custom or regulations.

But . . . was human society all that different? Gray smiled in a grim, humorless way. The major background culture claimed to be open and accepting, and yet for them the outsiders, the inhabitants of the Periphery, were . . . different. Immorally so in the way they clung to old traditions of monogamy and marriage.

Unsane.

Maybe in this one regard, human and Slan weren't that different from one another after all.

"The translation program is now substituting the word *sin* for the Slan term *k'!k't!'cht'!k'!kt'!!!k*," the AI whispered.

Sin was a loaded term, of course, one that carried a lot of unwanted religious baggage in English, but it felt right. What was sinful for a human follower of one religion or another would have nothing to do with what the Slan thought of as sinful, but they might see it in much the same way.

Lieutenant Connor had mentioned something pertinent in her report. When the atmospheric pressure dropped inside the Slan headquarters ship, the Slan had not been able to "see." Connor had said that individual Slan had seemed panicky, as well as completely disoriented.

Well, that made sense, didn't it? Render a large group of humans temporarily deaf, and they would have some initial trouble communicating, but they would figure things out and use sign language or gesture. But *blind* them, and they would be all but helpless. Vision was naturally the primary sense for humans, but for the Slan it was hearing.

For humans, deception often meant making things look different from what they truly were . . . a human donning a disguise, for instance. For Slan, deception might involve using sound to make a room, a tunnel, an individual seem different.

"I think," Gray told the being, "that I'm beginning to understand."

"An exchange, then," the Slan said. "Answer for this one a question."

"If I can."

"I observe within this simulation that you, Captain Gray, though human, do not possess your species' form of *!k'ch't't*. Are you, in fact, blind?"

"What the hell?" Gray said.

"Wait one moment," the AI told him. "I am examining their biology files." Seconds dragged past. "The translation program is substituting the term *sonar projectors* for the Slan term *'!k'ch't't.'*"

"Humans don't *have* sonar projectors," he replied.

"I am examining the records they made during their interrogation of Lieutenant Connor." There was another uncomfortable pause. "It is possible, Captain, that the Slan believe that female breasts are sonar projectors."

And, this time, Gray burst out laughing.

Chapter Seventeen

Conference Room
TC/USNA CVS America
Low Orbit, 36 Ophiuchi AIII
1115 hours, TFT

The virtuinteractive unfolded in their minds like a movie, one in which the men and women linked into the system experienced as if they were actually present within the scene. From their perspective, they seemed to be floating above a world. Swirls of cloud showed the presence of atmosphere, but the data assembled so far was painting the image of a world very unlike Earth.

The images were computer-generated, but were closely based on the data storage of the Slan headquarters ship. The Slan didn't have visual records, of course. Their equivalent was stored as sonic maps, and *America*'s AI was still learning how to translate that data into visual imagery.

From what Gray was seeing on his in-head, the AI was doing a pretty good job.

He'd called a meeting for all department heads on board all of the USNA ships, a total of more than two hundred men and women, plus a number of AIs. Planetary data appeared within side windows in their in-heads, confirming the alienness of the place.

Planetary Data Download
Thadek'ha*

STAR: Unknown

SPECTRAL TYPE: K2 V

MASS: 0.70 Sol; **RADIUS:** 0.69 Sol; **LUMINOSITY:** 0.28 Sol

TEMPERATURE: ~5,800o K; **AGE:** ~5.1 Gyr

PLANET: Planet unknown

NAME: Thadek'ha, roughly "Community" in Agletsch Trade Pidgin

COORDINATES: Unknown

TYPE: Terrestrial/rocky superEarth; oxidizing atmosphere

MEAN ORBITAL RADIUS: 0.47 AU; Orbital period: 140d 15h 20m 52s

ROTATIONAL PERIOD: 140D 15h 20m 52s, tidally locked with parent star

MASS: 6.78 Earth; **EQUATORIAL DIAMETER:** ~23960 km = 1.8 Earth

MEAN PLANETARY DENSITY: 5.60 g/cc = 1.01 Earth

SURFACE GRAVITY: 1.92 G

HYDROSPHERE PERCENTAGE: 12.4%; **CLOUD COVER:** Unknown; **ALBEDO** (day side): ~0.20

SURFACE TEMPERATURE RANGE: ~30°C to ~80°C

SURFACE ATMOSPHERIC PRESSURE: ~5.15 atmospheres

PERCENTAGE COMPOSITION: N_2 54.5; O_2 27.8; CO_2 5.3; NH_4 4.11; H_2S 2.9; SO_3 2.8; CH3 2.2; Ar 0.3; others <500 ppm

AGE: 5.1 billion years

BIOLOGY: C, N, H, S_8, O, Se, H_2O, CS_2; mobile, subsurface heterotrophs in symbiotic relationship with nonmotile chemosynthetic autotrophs and subsurface lithovores

DOMINANT SPECIES: "Slan"*

*Terms transliterated from Agletsch Trade Pidgin. "Slan" derives from the Agletschi *Slan'k'thred'n*, meaning, approximately, "Dwellers in Night."

A lot of the data was still guesswork, but *America*'s AI was confident that most of it was fairly solid. There were no guesses, of course, as to where in the sky Thadek'ha might be located, or how distant it might be. That would be information very carefully guarded indeed by the Slan, who would fear warlike aliens like humans showing up in the skies of their world with mass drivers and orbit-to-surface nukes.

The point of view for the linked-in personnel descended toward the planet, angling toward the so-called twilight zone between the day and night sides. Thadek'ha, a massive world nearly twice the diameter of Earth and with nearly twice the surface gravity, had long ago become tidally locked with its orange-star primary. Why this should be was not yet understood; the star and its planetary system were half a billion years older than Sol and its retinue of planets, but Thadek'ha was far enough from its somewhat smaller-than-Sol primary that tidal locking was not likely, as it was for worlds so close to their primary that they circled it in a matter of a few days.

If Gray had learned one thing about the cosmos, however,

in twenty-some years of star-faring, it was that the universe always came up with surprises, exceptions, and truly *alien* ways of doing things.

Normally a world gravitationally locked to its primary had a day side baking under an eternal noonday heat, while the night-side temperatures plunged far below zero. If the world had a fairly thick atmosphere, however, temperatures tended to be averaged out over the entire planet. Venus, in Earth's solar system, was a good example. Thadek'ha, though nowhere nearly as hellish as Venus, was still unpleasantly hot from the human perspective; even the native Slan, apparently, avoided the day-lit side, where temperatures were too high even for them.

Their corporate point of view descended over the world's twilight zone, revealing deep blue vegetation—much of it something like moss, a springy, exuberantly spreading ground cover. Chains of small seas linked by winding rivers steamed beneath an orange sun balanced on one horizon. Presumably, libration—the tendency of a tide-locked world to nod back and forth, like Earth's moon—caused the sun to rise, set, and rise again in the same spot over the course of weeks or months. At the moment, the sun was bisected by gently rounded mountain peaks on the horizon. White fliers—not birds, not insects, but something of both, with long, curling ribbons for tails—rose in teeming swarms from the shores of a large lake.

The panorama was spectacularly beautiful—blue vegetation, green water reflecting a green-tinted sky, and orange clouds. It was hard to keep in mind that had the humans actually been present over that pastoral scene, they would have died in seconds in the hot, poisonous atmosphere.

And the point of view continued to descend, moving now through the blanket of blue moss, through dirt and rock, and emerging in the darkness of a low and smooth-walled tunnel. The tunnel was filled with movement.

America's AI gave the scene light enough for the humans to see by. The Slan filling that tunnel were so closely packed together that each pressed against its neighbors, fringe tentacles touching, even caressing the bodies of those ahead and behind. They traveled single file, with each tunnel strictly one-way. Gray could not tell what the purpose for all of the activity was, but he was forcibly reminded of human red blood cells surging through a narrow capillary. Perhaps what he was seeing was analogous—individual Slan carrying out some sort of metabolic function for the hive as a whole. The activity appeared to be automatic—mindlessly robotic.

"The scene represented here," the AI informed them, "represents life on the Slan homeworld thirty million years ago, before the Slan evolved intelligence."

"Before!" Villanova, the intel officer on the *Inchon*, exclaimed.

"These might be termed proto-Slan," the AI continued. "They appear to operate on a purely instinctive level, like termites."

The point of view drew back, pulling out of the tunnel and again surveying the planet's surface from the air. The surface was different, now. Black bubbles with an iridescent sheen, hundreds of them, rose in tight clusters and in geometric patterns from the blue moss. The sun was lower now, hidden behind the mountains, the sky ablaze with orange and green light.

"This simulates a more recent time," the AI said. "We're not sure how recent, but certainly within the last few thousand years. At an unspecified time within the past thirty million years, the Slan evolved intelligence, developed an advanced culture, and spread out across the surface of their world."

America's AI went on to describe a civilization shaped primarily by the biology of Thadek'ha's inhabitants. Blind to color, they didn't share human notions of beauty, and were unaware of the blue of the moss, the orange of the sun or, indeed, of the sun at all through their sonar sense. Their optical organ, positioned high on the central dome of their body and eternally looking up, likely had evolved to warn the proto-Slan if they wandered out of a tunnel and onto open ground. If the sun was too high in the sky, apparently, the hive-burrowers would swiftly die, fried by solar radiation.

"Our single biggest question," *America*'s AI said, "was how the Slan could ever discover astronomy. Those living within their world's twilight zone might be aware of their sun, but they would never know the stars. According to references within their database, however, they became aware of the stars when they learned of something they refer to as The Mystery."

The simulation grew darker, the viewpoint moving farther around into the dark side of the planet. Stars appeared.

"Any way we can get an ID on that cluster?" Gray asked.

At the zenith, stars were tumbled together in a blaze of light, hundreds of them, with tangled wisps of gas and dust glowing softly against the night. Behind the cluster, a nebula glowed in raw hues of red and white.

"We are looking," Commander Blakeslee, *America*'s navigator, said. "No matches yet with any of the astrogational files in the data banks."

That was no surprise. There were tens of thousands of open star clusters scattered across the galaxy, most of them far beyond the tiny region known to humans. More, even a small change in the angle of view would dramatically change any cluster's appearance.

The nebula, Gray thought, might be more easily identified; though again, which way you looked at it markedly affected its shape. If the ship's Astrogation Department could identify that cluster, though, it might lead to the discovery of the Slan homeworld.

And that could be an extremely effective bargaining chip in any future negotiations with them.

"Slan vision, while poor by human standards, and lacking color, is still sensitive enough to see this cluster and the associated nebula in its night sky, probably as a bright, out-of-focus blob. Observation would have shown it crossing the sky with their planet's orbit of its sun. It would be visible, of course, for half of the planet's 140-day year. From what we've been able to glean from their records so far, that cluster, The Mystery, is what led them first to develop means of translating electromagnetic radiation—including visible light—into sound, which they could then see when it was displayed on their instruments. It made it possible for them to discover space, the wider universe beyond their world, and then to navigate it. By any standards, a remarkable scientific, intellectual, and technological feat."

Another change of scene . . . and the point of view had pulled back to orbit, where a fleet of starships fell through sunlight and into shadow—Ballistas, huge and ponderous, with their distinctive green, black, and red color schemes, together with numerous, smaller red and black Sabers and a swarm of blue and black Stilettos.

Gray looked hard at those ships. Something wasn't adding up.

"Why," he asked after a moment, "are their ships color coded?"

There was silence from the watchers. Not even the AI responded for a long moment.

"Interesting point," Commander Taggart said. "If the Slan are blind . . ."

"Exactly. They're not even *aware* of color. The color slashes and patterns on those ships look random, no two alike, but the overall color is consistent among each type. Green, red, and black for the Ballistas, red and black for Sabers, blue and black for their fighters. How, if they're color blind?"

"It seems likely," *America*'s AI said, "that they had help in reaching space. This may be evidence that they have help in the building of their military spacecraft."

And that made two Sh'daar client races known to have been given help in escaping their homeworlds. The H'rulka, living, communal balloons evolved in the upper atmosphere of a gas giant similar to Jupiter, were thought to have received help from outside—obvious when you considered that their homeworld had no solid surface, no way to develop fire, mining, smelting, fossil fuels, nuclear power, or any of the other developments necessary for a technic civilization. The H'rulka, in their few direct communications with humans, had revealed precious little about the species they referred to as Starborn.

This, Gray thought, might be a second line of evidence pointing to the ancient Starborn. The Department of Extraterrestrial Relations, back on Earth, had declared that making contact with the Starborn was a Class A-1 priority. It was quite possible that the species, about which nothing was known, was none other than the Sh'daar themselves, or yet another *va Sh'daar*, a Sh'daar client species.

And yet . . .

Twenty years before, in a dwarf galaxy 800 million years in the past and tens of thousands of light years distant, Humankind had learned that the original Sh'daar were, in fact, a collection of species, a kind of interstellar federation or association occupying the galaxy now known as Omega Centauri $T_{-0.876gy}$. Those species had undergone what humans knew as the Technological Singularity and their federation had collapsed. Most of the original species, referred to now as the ur-Sh'daar, had vanished—exactly where or how was not understood. The ones left behind had become the modern Sh'daar, and they had carried with them a monstrous dread of the literally transformational power of advanced technology.

And the Sh'daar remnant had set out to make certain that a technological rapture of that sort could never again occur. GRIN technologies—Genetics, Robotics, Information Systems, and Nanotechnology—were targeted as the driving forces behind the Singularity. Block those, and the Singularity would not take place.

The war with the Sh'daar was essentially one of self-determination, with Humankind determined to continue developing all available technologies, with the Sh'daar equally determined to suppress those technologies that they considered to be threats.

But if the Sh'daar mistrusted technology that much, if they wanted to limit it, why would they assist younger, less advanced cultures in developing it? Why would they put atechnic species like the H'rulka onto the path of spaceflight at all . . . or help the Slan discover that they lived in a much vaster universe than they knew, and help them navigate the empty vacuum to other worlds? There was, Gray thought, a lot more to it than met the eye.

It was a seemingly insoluble mystery, but if there was a solution, that solution might be vital for Humankind's long-term survival.

"Have we uncovered any other information that might point to the Starborn?" Gray asked.

"No," *America*'s AI replied. "Nothing, at any rate, that we've been able to recognize."

"Continue your explorations of the Slan databases, then," Gray said. " 'Know your enemy . . .' "

" '. . . and yourself, and you will win a hundred battles without a single loss,' " the AI said, completing the ancient truth. The aphorism was drawn from Sun Tzu's *Art of War*. Gray wondered if the AI was trying to give him a not-so-subtle reminder that it was equally important to know *yourself* in order to win.

Right now, the intent of the fifty-two surviving Confederation ships under the command of Justin Lavallée was as unknown to Gray as the identity of the mysterious Starborn.

And he didn't like being so deeply in the dark.

Executive Office, USNA
Columbus, District of Columbia
United States of North America
1235 hours, EST

The conference in Koenig's office had been going on for almost half an hour, now. Present were Koenig's chief of staff, the secretary of state, and the Executive Office chief counsel.

"I hope you realize, Mr. President," Pamela Sharpe said, "that by escalating this situation, we may well be looking at open war with the rest of the Confederation."

Sharpe was the USNA secretary of state, which meant that it was her job to advise the president on matters relating to foreign policy . . . including war.

"I'm *quite* aware of that, Pamela," Koenig replied. "But they're the ones attacking us, okay? We *do* have a right to defend ourselves."

"But . . . naval forces?" she said. "A small assault team on the back side of the moon is one thing, but—"

"They have troops on the ground in our Periphery. We need naval support to block them."

"*Missouri* and *Amazon* are approaching Washington now," Admiral Gene Armitage told Koenig.

"And *Pittsburgh*?"

"Still at L-2, sir, keeping an eye on Bruno Base. The Marines are redeploying there."

Koenig considered this. Bruno Base was probably of minor importance, especially since Lieutenant Burnham's platoon had pulled the Confederation's fangs lunarside. They might be able to bring the '*Burgh* to Earth . . . or possibly to SupraQuito in case the Confederation was planning a grab there as well. SupraQuito was technically a Confederation synchorbital facility . . . but it was staffed primarily by USNA naval personnel and civilians.

No. One problem at a time . . .

Missouri and *Amazon* were Mississippi-class High Guard sentinel ships, designed to patrol the outer solar system in search of planetoids that might one day threaten Earth . . . and ships seeking to change the orbit of planetoids to turn them into weapons.

Wormwood had been the first such attack, an asteroid nudged into a collision course with Earth by a rogue Chinese Hegemony ship. Despite efforts to turn the incoming body aside, a part of the rock had fallen into the Atlantic, smashing the coastlines of Europe and the Americas.

There'd been a second Atlantic tsunami in 2405, generated by a Turusch one-kilogram high-velocity impactor streaking in past the sun and exploding in the atmosphere. The shock had been as savage as if the incoming mass had been a small asteroid, and something on the order of 50 million people had died. The disaster had underscored the need to stop asteroids on intercept orbits, whether those orbits had been set by chance or by design.

High Guard sentinels did not possess Alcubierre Drives, so they could not travel between the stars. They did pack the armament of a naval destroyer, however, and their gravitic singularity drives gave them a fair degree of maneuverability. Koenig hoped they could take on the Confederation forces now moving into several of the coastal Peripheries—Washington, D.C., Manhattan, Baltimore, and Boston. There were reports of Confederation spacecraft in low orbit, and of troops coming ashore from immense Jotun transports.

That datum itself was of interest. Intelligence suggested that the Jotuns had come from the floating seasteader city of Atlantica, currently riding the Gulf Stream north 100 kilometers off the coast of Virginia. It was possible that the Confederation had moved in and taken over the seasteads eighteen months earlier expressly to use them as staging points for an invasion of the USNA Peripheries.

"Do we have any Marines in a position where they could board those seasteads?" Koenig asked.

"Marines and SEALS Team Twelve, Mr. President. At Oceana."

Koenig nodded, thoughtful. SEALS—the acronym stood for the elements within which those elite naval commandos operated: sea, air, land, and space. They were among the best close-combat forces available to the USNA—highly trained, superbly motivated, and possessing exceptional cybernetic and nanomedical enhancements.

If they were stationed at Oceana, though, they might be vulnerable. Oceana had started as a naval air station in tidewater Virginia, a base slowly submerged by rising sea levels late in the twenty-first century. It now was an oceanic complex, built partly on the sea floor and partly on massive pylons above the surface, providing support for American combat naval air and space units. It was less than 150 kilometers from Atlantica's current position, however, and the

Confederation would be well aware that it was there. If the enemy decided to escalate, Oceana would be an early target.

"Good," Koenig said. "I want the SEALS off of Oceana and on their way to Atlantica as soon as possible. The Marines . . . let's hold them for the Periphery . . . especially New York and D.C."

"I would recommend one battalion of Marines be reserved for follow-on at Atlantica, sir," Armitage told him. "As follow-on after the SEALS get on board . . . and as reinforcements in case the place is more heavily defended than we think."

"Do it. Can you provide air cover out of Oceana?"

"We have three aerospace squadrons there now, Mr. President. They can be over Atlantica in minutes."

"Okay. Send one to cover our forces at D.C., one on CAP to protect Oceana, and one to hit Atlantica." He thought for a moment. "What are we missing?"

"If I might suggest, sir . . . the *political* side of things."

Koenig gave a grim smile. He'd dropped back into admiral mode, giving orders about military deployment and strategy, and not addressing the fact that war is, ultimately, the pursuit of politics by other means.

"Ilse Roettgen isn't talking to me at the moment," he said. "We're going to need to get her attention."

"If beating those troop carriers out of Bruno Base doesn't get it, Mr. President, I don't know what will."

"Let's see if grabbing Atlantica back from the bastards will turn up the volume for her. Meanwhile . . . I want the Periphery protected."

"We're not on solid legal ground with that, Mr. President," the other man in the room pointed out. He was Thomas St. James, and he was the president's executive counsel. He was a true cyborg, with the top of his head artificially enlarged to create space for additional components, both organic tissue cloned from his own stem cells and silicon. A network of gold and silver wires appeared to be etched into his hairless scalp in rectilinear patterns, allowing him a constant interface with several very powerful AIs, experts in both international and extraplanetary law.

"What's the problem, Tom?" Koenig asked.

"Great Britain versus Falklands, 2233. Russian Federation versus Ukraine, 2280. Manhattan versus New New York, 2301. Confederation versus Belgium, 2342. The United States of North America formally abandoned those territories now called the Periphery."

"Well, yeah . . . but we still own those territories, even if we don't control them."

"Not exactly. After the Blood Death, the Second Chinese War, and the Nanotech Economic Collapse, the government simply could not afford to provide basic services like police or medical help, much less reclaim or rebuild flooded cities. Article 31 of the Confederation Constitution, dating from 2133, declares that Geneva has both the right and the responsibility to assume full government control of territories abandoned by local government or which have otherwise slipped into anarchy."

Trying to talk with St. James was like in-heading a law text download, a bit of self-torture guaranteed to give you a headache. "Is that the pretext they used for taking over the Atlantic seasteads?"

"No, sir. That was carried out under the Confederation Oceanic Crisis Management Act of 2412."

"And Tsiolkovsky?"

"The databases have not yet been updated, but they have publically declared Konstantin to be a world heritage treasure serving all Humankind. I expect that they will defend their actions today by appealing to the World Heritage Act."

"The bastards *attacked* us," Armitage growled. "On the Lunar farside, and now along our East Coast! We can't just . . . just surrender to their damned lawyers!"

"We're not going to surrender, Gene," Koenig said.

"If we fight, it will give the Confederation the pretext they need for declaring us in rebellion. It means civil war, Mr. President, and a nasty one."

"*All* civil wars are nasty," Koenig replied. "But the worst part about this one is the timing. If the Sh'daar are making a new move . . ."

"Geneva's pulling this shit now on purpose, Mr. President," Armitage said. "They want us to fold right away so we're not divided and fighting each other when the Sh'daar get here."

"Possibly," Koenig replied. He moved his hand over a contact plate on his desk, calling up a virtual display screen that floated in the air between them. The imagery was from a robotic security drone in D.C., peering from a mangrove tree at the ponderous mass of a Confederation Jotun. Armored troops were pouring down the lowered ramps and splashing through the shallow water still covering the National Mall. In the distance, the ancient gray dome of the old Capitol Building rose from a mass of trees and clinging kudzu.

"This is not going to stand," Koenig said. "I want those people taken down, Gene. *Now*."

"Mr. President," St. James said. "I really must advise—"

"I've *heard* your advice, damn it. We stop them. We stop them before the Sh'daar get here. And we'll worry about the legality of it all later."

He switched off the robot-eye view. "You gentlemen are dismissed."

Chapter Eighteen

Washington, former District of Columbia
USNA Periphery
1440 hours, TFT

Shay Ashton took careful aim at the lead armored figure struggling up the muddy flats below her position, perched on the slope of a hill still called the Georgetown Heights. The targeting data fed from her laser carbine appeared in her in-head, showing the magnified image of the Confederation soldier with a bright red targeting reticule superimposed on his chest. Battlespace sensors were relaying data about the target's radio and laser-com linkages and data crossloading; he or she was an officer, and a fairly high-ranking one at that, if the amount of radio traffic was any indication.

She thoughtclicked the trigger . . .

A puff of vapor high on the soldier's chest marked a direct hit. The figure staggered . . . but the armor, its surface almost perfectly reflecting the colors and shapes of the surrounding swamp, was already healing itself. Ashton's carbine, more than powerful enough to deal with Virginian cross-river raiders, simply didn't have the oomph to penetrate modern combat armor.

She ducked back behind the cover of a low concrete wall,

then began crawling to her left. Seconds later, the patch of wall where she'd been hiding shattered in smoke and hurtling fragments of stone.

Before long, they were going to run out of places to hide.

Picking away at the invaders this way was all but useless. *Sometimes* you got lucky, but it didn't happen often. She'd racked up eight kills so far in as many hours, and probably hurt another dozen in the running firefight through the old Washington ruins. You had to hit the enemy's armor *just* right; the joint between helmet and chest plastron, just below the ear, was a good aim point. Another was the visor strip on the helmet. Hit that right, and you might overload the circuitry and blind the soldier, at least temporarily.

But if your aim wasn't perfect, the chances were good that the armor would just shrug the bolt off.

Shay's people had no armor, and had already died by the hundreds.

"We've got the popper set up!" a voice called over her in-head. "We're gonna try for the Jotun!"

Ashton shifted her attention to the nearest of five Jotun transports, just a kilometer away, hovering over the swampy ground of what once, centuries before, had been called the Ellipse. Local folklore still called it that, though no one remembered what it was, or why part of the mangrove swamp had been given a name drawn from geometry.

"Okay," she replied. "Make it count!"

"Popper" referred to a K-40 antiarmor warhead fired from a tripod-mounted launcher. The things were a century out of date and probably wouldn't make it past a Jotun's point defense lasers, but they had to try.

Where they'd dug the antique up in the first place Ashton couldn't even begin to guess.

The weapon fired, a streak of light snapping from the hillside to Ashton's right. She saw the missile, a tiny point of light weaving and jinking as it closed on the immense transport . . . but then it flared and vanished, still 300 meters from its target. Turrets on the Jotun's dorsal surface pivoted, seeking the location of the launcher.

"Get the hell out of there!" she yelled, and then a portion of the Georgetown hillside vanished in a cascade of flame and hurtling debris.

She didn't have an in-head tactical display, but the lack of response over her com told her she'd just lost a couple more members of her dwindling army.

More explosions erupted among the crumbling ruins further up the heights. The defenders had no way to more than scratch the invaders; the Jotun, now, was drifting ponderously toward the hill, climbing out of the swamp, brushing aside trees and the occasional stone tower with contemptuous ease.

It was time, Ashton thought, recalling the military slang she'd learned twenty years earlier, to "get the hell out of Dodge."

"All units," she said over the tactical channel. "We're not doing any good here. Pull back . . . pull back. . . ."

"Boss, these are our *homes* here!" someone cried.

"Yeah, and they're going to be our fucking tombs if we hang around much longer! Fall back! That's an order!"

Ashton wasn't sure who had put her in command. It had just . . . happened. She had the in-head hardware, of course, to set up a tactical net, and that was a big part of it. More, she had combat experience—something more than fighting off Periphery raiders from across the Potomac Estuary.

But it was not a job she'd looked for. She'd *had* it with the military two decades ago, when she'd resigned from the USNA Navy and returned to the D.C. swamp.

They'd made good progress over the past few years, draining parts of that swamp and putting up the Potomac levees, but there sure as hell wasn't anything here worth fighting for. *Dying* for . . .

For God's sake, let the bastards have it.

The Jotun was a lot closer, now. Its turrets shifted this way and that, picking out tiny running figures ahead of it and burning them down. It would reach her position in another minute or two.

She felt a cold stab of fear. If she got up and ran now, the gunners in that transport would see her and burn her down as well. If she stayed where she was, those columns of armored soldiers advancing up the slope would reach her and kill her or worse. If she found a place to hide—inside a wreckage-covered basement or hole, perhaps—they would pick her up sooner or later with their sonic mikes or heat sensors and the result would be the same.

She'd waited too fucking long. . . .

Best, then, to go out fighting. She shifted her position so she could see the troops in the Jotun's shadow, and again took aim. Her in-head showed a target lock and she thought-clicked the trigger. . . .

The landscape was blotted out by a white flare of light, and a violent shock picked her up and flung her backward. Blinking, trying to clear her head, she saw the Jotun's dorsal surface slashed open, saw flames erupting from its exposed interior.

"What the fuck?" she asked aloud.

Then a pair of Starhawks shrieked overhead, cleaving the sky on white-slash vapor trails ripped from tortured air. Two more Starhawks followed, and Ashton's mouth dropped open at the sight of the spacecraft—fighter craft that she once had piloted herself. For a moment, she was stunned, uncomprehending, but then the reality began to assert itself, and she realized that reinforcements had arrived over ancient Washington at last.

"Hit 'em!" she screamed. Not thinking, she picked herself up and stood, staring, gaping . . . then waving her carbine. *"Get the bastards!"*

And the defenders of Washington began to advance once more.

Captain's Quarters
TC/USNA CVS America
Low Orbit, 36 Ophiuchi AIII
2315 hours, TFT

Gray had just removed his uniform and tossed it in the disposal when a chime in his in-head announced a visitor. He opened a window to the door's security link. It was *America*'s weapons officer, Commander Laurie Taggart.

He opened the door through the link; taboos against social nudity had long since evaporated, especially in the Navy, where men and women had to live and work together in quarters that could verge on the claustrophobic. "Hello, Commander," he said. "What can I do for you?"

"I was wondering . . . um . . ."

She was staring. "Sorry, Commander. Do you want me to get dressed?"

"No, sir. It's not that. There's something . . . *personal* that's been bothering me. I wondered if we could talk."

Interesting. Most personal problems on board ship were handled by one of the chaplain psychs . . . or by Commander Sara Gutierrez, *America*'s executive officer. Traditionally, a ship's XO was responsible for handling a ship's internal issues, including any personnel problems, leaving the skipper free to focus on mission, strategy and tactics. Gray tried to be accessible to his crew, however, and wasn't going to order her to leave. He did, however, go to the uniform dispenser and order a new utilities pack. He slapped the wad against his chest, and let the nanoweave flow across his body, growing a fresh uniform in seconds. Social nudity was fine, but there was a certain propriety demanded by his station if not by society. He ordered a couple of chairs to grow out of the deck, the white carpeting blurring and flowing to become soft black leather, and gestured to one. "Have a seat."

"Thank you. I know I should probably see Chaplain Carruthers about this, sir . . . but you were *there*."

"I was where?"

"At the Sh'daar galaxy. Eight hundred million years ago."

"Ah."

"You . . . you know that I'm Church of AAC."

Gray nodded. Though personnel could keep their religious affiliations, if any, secret, many chose to have it recorded in their files. Gray had seen Taggart's file data months before while reviewing the histories of the officers on board *America*.

"My church believes that aliens created *Homo sapiens* something like half a million years ago. And those of us in the Navy . . . well, everyone in the congregation kind of looks to us for . . . for confirmation."

"And you're all wondering if the Sh'daar are God."

"Well . . . we wouldn't put it quite that bluntly, sir, but, well, yes."

"Why the Sh'daar?"

"Sir?"

"There are thousands of technic species scattered across the galaxy, Commander. We know that much from the Agletsch *Encyclopedia Galactica*. Some of them have been around for a half million years, easy. The Dhravin, for instance."

"But what if it *is* the Sh'daar?"

"Would that make a difference, Commander?"

"Well . . . yes, sir. It would. Of *course*." She shook her head, shoulder-length red hair tossing impatiently. "If the Sh'daar are renewing their war against us, it puts us in the position of waging war against our creators."

"A *defensive* war, Commander. They attacked us, remember."

"Yes, sir."

Gray thought for a moment, then said, "AI . . . cease recording." An acknowledgement winked on in his in-head. Normally, everything senior officers in the fleet said and did was recorded and stored, but he didn't think there was a need here.

And he didn't want Taggart to jeopardize her career.

"Okay, Commander. We're now off the record. And you can drop the 'sir' stuff. I'm Trev. Or Sandy."

"Thank you . . . Trev.

"Why does it matter if the Sh'daar *are* our creators?"

"Well, they must have had a reason. . . ."

"Maybe. Or maybe they just needed some convenient slaves to do their dirty work."

Gray was thoroughly acquainted with the Ancient Alien Creationist myth. Lots of people in the Manhattan Periphery had believed those stories when he was growing up. The idea had been floating around at least since the twentieth century—that aliens had come to Earth half a million years or so ago and tinkered with the human genome. The most popular story took off on ancient Sumerian myth, with legends that beings called Anunnaki had tried to colonize the Earth, and created humans as slaves. Other stories, however, emphasized that the visiting aliens had been benevolent, uplifting Humankind for more noble reasons.

In this, Gray was a dogmatic agnostic. There *were* archeological mysteries that centuries of human investigation had not yet explained. Baalbek: a platform in Lebanon that included thousand-ton blocks of stone in its makeup. Yonaguni, Dvaraka, and others: monolithic structures discovered on the sea bottom off Japan and India and submerged for thousands of years. Pumapunku: the incredibly massive, intricate and apparently machine-tooled stone architecture of a temple group in the Andes Mountains apparently scattered by something as powerful as a nuclear blast. There were plenty of other sites around the Earth, enigmatic, ancient, and sadly uncommunicative about who had built them, and how.

Gray was willing to believe that Earth might once have had visitors from Somewhere Else, though he was suspicious of claims that early humans were incapable of building large and complex structures, that places like Giza or Teotihuacan *must* have been built with alien technology.

But had aliens created humanity? The jury was still out on that one.

"My church doesn't accept the Anunnaki hypothesis," Taggart said. "For us, the extraterrestrial gods elevated humans from the apes because they wanted companionship."

"I see. And then they left us on our own?"

She frowned. "Captain, I'm not trying to convert you."

"I know. If you were, it would be a clear violation of the White Covenant, and we would not be able to have this conversation."

She smiled. "The Covenant is Confederation Law. Are we still bound by that?"

Gray frowned. "You know? I'm honestly not sure. I think we'll need to have the lawyers sort that one out once we get back to Earth." He thought a moment more. "I'd have to say, though, that we're officially still part of the Confederation, even if Lavallée did take off and abandon us. At least until we're told otherwise."

Justin Lavallée's desertion was a sore point throughout the USNA flotilla. The Confederation ships had burned past Arianrhod at near-c, abandoned their own fighters, and kept on going, accelerating for the far side of the system. Some hours ago, word had come through that the Confederation ships had dropped into Alcubierre Drive. Likely, they would head into emptiness for a few light years, re-emerge and re-orient themselves, then head for Earth. That would put them back in Earth orbit in another two days . . . maybe three.

And God knew what they would tell Geneva about Gray's unwillingness to surrender command of the USNA contingent.

We'll worry about that later, he thought.

"Okay, so the damned Covenant's still in force. But I *need* to talk about this, Trev. Suppose the Sh'daar *are* the creators? Suppose we're rebelling against the gods?"

Gray sighed. The fleet faced so many more pressing problems right now . . . not the least of which was establishing some sort of working long-term truce with the Slan. Things looked good so far, but the Slan were so *different* in the way they thought, in how they saw the universe. In any given exchange, it was incredibly difficult to understand them, and harder still to be sure that they understood you.

"The Sh'daar are not God, Laurie," Gray told her. "If they were, I think they would have found a way to tell us. Something a little more persuasive than sending their client races to attack us."

"But we know that eight hundred million years ago," she said, "the Sh'daar were raptured. . . ."

That again. Certain Christian sects on Earth, Gray knew,

were convinced that one day the faithful would be snatched up into heaven, leaving the unsaved to face God's wrath. They called it the *Rapture*, an odd twist to Christian eschatology first developed in the 18th and 19th centuries. Most Christian sects held that the Rapture—a term never mentioned in the Bible—simply referred to the final judgment at the end of time. But a few held that believers would be "caught up in the clouds" prior to the end, with nonbelievers left behind to face terrible suffering, the "Great Tribulation," as their world came apart. Gray, curious about the terminology, had downloaded several essays on the topic.

Records *America* had accessed within Omega Centauri $T_{-0.876gy}$ had shown the physical forms of hundreds of mutually alien species belonging to the ur-Sh'daar federation simply . . . *vanishing* from their worlds. Human researchers hadn't yet figured out the mechanism for that disappearing act, and couldn't even agree on what they were seeing, but all agreed that the records showed the moment of the ur-Sh'daar Technological Singularity, when their levels of technology reached a point where the outward form and nature of those beings had somehow changed beyond all recognition or understanding.

It had been inevitable, Gray knew, that some of those fundamentalist religious sects would take that transformation as evidence of an alien rapture.

"We don't know what happened to the ur-Sh'daar," he told her. "All we know is that a number of them were left behind at the moment of Singularity, the ancestors of the modern Sh'daar, and that they were terrified by what happened."

"Yes . . ."

"So terrified they've been trying to block advanced technological progress in every species they meet." Gray hesitated. The White Covenant expressly prohibited attempts by one person to change the religious beliefs of another . . . but he very much wanted Taggart to understand. "Can I ask you something? Something that might violate the Covenant?"

"Of course."

"First off, the AAC believes that what happened to the ur-

Sh'daar was a kind of Rapture, right? God's chosen snatched away and never seen again. Well, the Sh'daar were the ones left behind. That tells me they aren't God and they weren't His chosen."

"I see where you're going. . . ."

"Maybe you don't. Because my question is . . . if what you mean by 'God' is the creator of the universe, someone who cares about his, her, or its creation, why were so many of the ur-Sh'daar left behind? Think about the emotional scarring inflicted on an entire interstellar civilization, scarring that's driving them to conquer and to wage war on other species almost a billion years later. Does that sound like a loving God?"

"We're not supposed to question—"

"*Bullshit!* If we're not supposed to question, why do we have minds? Logic? Reason? What happened in Omega Centauri a billion years ago was a tragedy, not an act of love, and certainly not an act of creation!"

She didn't reply. She sat in the chair, staring at her knees.

"If aliens came to Earth thousands of years ago," Gray went on, relentless, "if they changed the human genome to create us . . . it was an act of technology, not of love or caring.

"And as far as we can make out, the Sh'daar used time travel through an artificially constructed gateway into their future to enter our galaxy . . . we're still not sure when, but it probably was well over a hundred thousand years ago. They set up a base somewhere in this time and began conquering or absorbing every species they encountered, until they finally got to us fifty-some years ago.

"If they *were* our creators, what the hell took them so long? What, did they make us, then go away, only to come back in the twenty-fourth century? Damn it, Laurie, *it doesn't make sense.*"

"But we know that the creators work in mysterious ways. . . ."

"They give us brains to figure out the universe, to develop science and discover how things work and to use logic and reason to make deductions about who and what we are . . .

and then slap us down for believing what we've learned? Right. . . ."

"That's not the way it is!" She was almost in tears.

"Laurie . . . your personnel files say you have a base IQ of one thirty-two, enhanced to one sixty. You have a Logic Quotientof one twenty, and a Reasoning Aptitude Score of point nine five. You've got a *brain*! Okay? *Use* it!"

After a time, Gray widened his chair and she sat next to him, his arm around her shoulders.

"What . . . do you believe, Trev?" she asked him after a long while.

"I'm not sure," he replied. "I grew up in the Manhat Ruins, and didn't have the time or the inclination to worry much about God. Then my wife developed some health problems, and I took her to the nearest facility that could treat her, on the other side of the Line."

"'Wife'?" She repeated the word as though it had a faintly unpleasant taste.

"Periphery culture. I was a monogie. One partner, in a relationship called marriage."

"I've heard of it. Some folks in Chicago practice that too." She shook her head. "But why?"

"Life in lots of the Periphery areas can still be pretty touch and go. Small family units have good survival value."

"And some people just like exotic relationships."

He looked away. The topic still hurt a bit. "Well, in any case, the treatment . . . *changed* her. She didn't . . . didn't feel anything for me any longer, and she went off on her own. Joined a line marriage somewhere Upstate." He shrugged. "I guess I had a hard time seeing God or God's love in any of that."

"That's the *traditional* view of God," she told him. "The AAC teaches that extraterrestrial gods made Humankind, but still watch us from beyond the Veil . . . and that they'll return someday. . . ."

"An all-powerful spirit who *could* banish evil, sickness, loss, and suffering but chooses not to—or high-tech aliens who use magical technology to snatch their own into the clouds . . . they're both just versions of the man behind the curtain, you know? And both scenarios cause a lot more trouble intellectually than they're worth. They rob us of free will, and promise us that we can't possibly make it on our own, individually or as a species. I think that if there's something or someone out there that we can call God, it's going to make more sense than anything we've been shown so far."

"I wonder about that," Taggart said. "Who was it who said the universe is stranger than we imagine, but it's stranger than we can imagine?" Her gaze went distant for a moment. "Ah. Haldane."

Gray nodded. He was accessing the historical data from *America*'s AI as well. "J. B. S. Haldane," he agreed, scanning through the available data. " 'Now my own suspicion is that the universe is not only queerer than we suppose, but queerer than we *can* suppose.' " The quote had gone through a lot of variations and mutations since 1927, with riffs on the same theme from Sir Arthur Stanley Eddington and others.

The data on Eddington included a number of quotes as well, and one in particular caught Gray's attention. "We have found a strange footprint on the shores of the unknown. We have devised profound theories, one after another, to account for its origins. At last, we have succeeded in reconstructing the creature that made the footprint. And it is our own." The quote was from Eddington's *Space, Time, and Gravitation*, first published in 1920.

Reaching through her link with the AI, he pointed the paragraph out to Taggart. "You wanted to know what I believe, Laurie?" he asked her. "What about the possibility that our technology will advance to the point where someday, to all intents and purposes, *we* are God? We don't need aliens to fill the role. Just time."

She smiled at him. "People have been burned at the stake for ideas like that."

"Well . . . if you see a crowd with torches and pitchforks on the way to my quarters, let me know."

They enjoyed a companionable silence for a long time.

Gray caressed her shoulder. He found himself . . . wanting her.

Generally, he kept such impulses under a tight and unyielding control. While the social conventions of both the USNA and of the Confederation as a whole viewed sex between consenting adults as natural, healthy, and something to be celebrated, people in positions of authority—such as the captain of a Navy ship—still had to be careful of *anything* hinting at favoritism or an abuse of power.

And even more to the point, as he'd just reminded her, Gray himself had grown up as a monogie prim. *One* partner . . . or at least only one at a time.

Gray had not been celibate in the twenty-some years since Angela had left him. He'd had other partners, a few cautious sexual liaisons, but always discreetly, tentatively, and with a certain degree of guilt. . . .

"They say the captain of a ship is God," she told him after a time, "at least of his own little world."

Gray closed his eyes. "Not really," he said. "Too many constraints and too much bureaucracy. Maybe we're just godlike aliens."

He opened his eyes, and her uniform was gone.

He drew her close, using his link to lengthen and widen the chair beneath them.

And a long time later, he realized that he didn't feel guilty at all.

Chapter Nineteen

14 November 2424

TC/USNA CVS America
Low Orbit, 36 Ophiuchi AIII
0925 hours, TFT

Once again, Gray stood within a virtual world, an imaginal space generated by two mutually alien sets of computer networks, human and Slan. The AI and *America*'s Xenosophontology Department together had learned an enormous amount during the past twenty-four hours, piecing together aspects of Slan biology and psychology to get a better idea of how they saw the universe around them.

The tunnel walls, for instance, now to Gray's eyes glowed with a kind of multilayered luminosity of oily rainbow color that represented, very roughly, the effects perceived by the Slan when they scanned their underground surroundings with sonar. Tunnel walls black and featureless to human eyes—or ears—to Slan sound organs glowed rich with layered information and reflected subtle harmonics that evidently were pleasing to their aesthetic sense.

"Thank you for meeting with me again, Clear Chiming Bell," Gray said.

"These exchanges are mutually beneficial," the Slan replied, its voice sounding in Gray's mind. "We should continue, whether we end the fighting or ultimately decide to end this conflict."

"It is our hope to end it."

"A possibility, one among many. Our navigators have been . . . surprised to learn of what you term cosmology. Further explorations of this cosmos might better wait until we better understand this thing you call space."

For the Slan, the aching gulf between one world and another, between one star system and another, simply didn't exist. How could it, when there was no atmosphere to transmit sound? Thadek'ha was a vast series of enormous rooms or caverns, the surface of Thadek'ha was simply a cavern without a clear ceiling or walls, and Arianrhod was merely another cavern located someplace else that could only be reached by entering a ship and manipulating the controls. For them, the entire universe as just a collection of such places, and terms like *planet*, *star*, and *galaxy* had no meaning for them.

"We can help," Gray pointed out. "Evidently, the Sh'daar chose not to tell the Slan much about the universe. They used you. Like a tool."

"Tools," the Slan commander said, "are intended for use."

"But when the tool is intelligent," Gray replied, "shouldn't it have a say in how it is used? Ignorance distorts our understanding of our surroundings. It robs us of our ability to make informed decisions. It *enslaves* us."

"In conclave," the being told him, "we have determined that withholding information about one's surroundings is equivalent to deliberately distorting that information. It is . . . immoral."

Gray played back a single word of the Slan's speech, isolated and recorded by *America*'s AI. *"K'!k't!'cht'!k'!kt'!!!k."*

"Exactly," Clear Chiming Bell replied. "This information has been . . . disturbing. Deeply so."

"Have you found the devices we told you about yet?" Gray asked. "The Sh'daar Seeds?"

It was clearer than ever that the near-blind Slan had had substantial help leaving their world. The records *America*'s

AI had been able to access didn't give many clues to who or what had provided that help. One distinct possibility, however, was the implanting of Sh'daar Seeds.

Sh'daar Seeds had been discovered twenty years before during the engagements with Turusch and H'rulka forces at Arcturus and Eta Boötis. They were tiny devices—a millimeter or less in diameter—planted within the tissues of individuals of various of the Sh'daar client species. Their function and their mechanism were not yet well understood, but it was clear that each Seed wired itself into the nervous system of its host, allowing it to record that host's experiences, and to transmit that data elsewhere to any Sh'daar receiver within a set range—a few million kilometers at most.

At Omega Centauri T$_{-0.876\text{gy}}$, far away and in the remote past, the Koenig Expeditionary Force had discovered that the Sh'daar were not, in fact, a distinct race, but a kind of cooperative gestalt of many mutually alien species—the Baondyeddi, the Adjugredudhra, the Groth Hoj, the F'heen-F'haav Symbiosis, the Sjhlurrr, and many, many others. Known collectively now as the ur-Sh'daar, all of those species had gone through a Technological Singularity . . . but all of those species had also included individuals who'd rejected much of the high technology that had brought the Singularity about. Called "Refusers," they'd gone on to become the Sh'daar known to Humankind today, who, through conquest or through coercion, forced myriad species to reject certain technologies. They seemed to keep tabs on their client races through the Seeds, which monitored technological developments and reported back to the Sh'daar Masters at frequent intervals.

There was another possibility, however, one arising from speculation about current Sh'daar technology. What if the Sh'daar Seeds did more than simply spy on the Sh'daar clients? What if they could offer advice . . . make suggestions . . . or give orders? What if the Sh'daar group mind could actually reside within billions of individuals scattered across a large portion of the galaxy?

Sh'daar Seeds did not exist in every member of every

client race, but they did appear to have been planted within each race's leaders—those that had distinct leaders, at any rate. For some, like the Turusch, they served as a kind of guiding overmind. For others, like the Agletsch, they appeared to be nothing more than listening devices.

But what if every being carrying a Sh'daar implant was a potential robot, a kind of zombie slave carrying out orders from distant masters? That a Sh'daar gestalt mind existed was beyond dispute. But what if that group mind extended much, much farther than anyone had yet suspected?

Gray doubted that the Sh'daar reach was that long. Transmission of seed data did not appear to be possible over more than very short planetary distances, and sending data across interstellar gulfs might only work by storing it within seeded individuals on board starships.

But Gray was uncomfortably aware that every detail of this in-head conversation might be being recorded by a tiny computer buried within Clear Chiming Bell's mantle.

"We have," the Slan replied after a long moment. Had it been trying to decide whether or not to tell him? "Mine rests . . . here."

In the simulation, a brilliant blue star winked on just above and behind the Slan's light-sensitive organ, between the bases of the two writhing sound organs. "It was implanted when I took command of *Vigilant*."

Of course it would have been. Leaders included *military* leaders, and the Sh'daar would be particularly interested in the activities of ship commanders exploring or attacking enemy-held star systems.

"We," Gray said, "have not accepted the Sh'daar implants."

"That *is* why this war is being fought," Clear Chiming Bell replied. "To force your compliance with Sh'daar reason."

"And why should we comply?" Gray asked in what he hoped sounded like a reasonable tone. "We perceive the universe differently than do they. We have the right to determine our own future."

There was another long pause. "The term 'right' does not translate."

Would a species living as a part of a vast hive ever develop the concept of individual rights? What about the rights of a species to self-determination?

And how could he explain the idea to a being that could not even imagine the possibility? "Rights are the . . . expectations of beings derived from their own natures, and recognized by others of that species. "You have a right to eat. To ingest nutrients?" Gray thought about last night, and smiled. "Or the right to engage in reproductive activity. . . ."

"The ingestion of nutrients is a biological function, and a basic requirement of life," the Slan said. "I do not see how that could be subject to the recognition of others. As for reproduction, that is a biological function of certain castes within Slan society. Again, how would this be subject to the recognition or approval of others?"

"For my species," Gray replied, "there are what we think of as . . . as unalienable rights, rights granted by nature." He hesitated, wondering if he should get into the difference between *un*alienable and *in*alienable rights . . . and decided against it. If many humans didn't know the difference between the two, he wasn't about to try to explain it to a Slan.

"But . . . a right to reproduce? Surely that would apply only to those chosen by the community as breeders."

Gray decided to sidestep that one. "A right to be *free*. A right as a culture to determine our own path. A right to choose to develop our own culture and technology."

"Your words are being translated by the network," Clear Chiming Bell said, "but I am having trouble grasping the sense."

"We may be too different, you and I, for perfect understanding," Gray replied. "But . . . if the Slan have the right to experience their surroundings without deliberate distortion by others, without . . ." and he played again that snippet of sound drawn from a recording, *"k'!k't!'cht'!k'!kt'!!!k"*— the fringe of tentacles around the Slan's base twitched in apparent reaction—"then my species," Gray continued, "can decide for itself its own future, without interference by the Sh'daar, without interference from *you*."

"The seeds," Clear Chiming Bell said, "speak to us. It is they that guide us to . . . new places in our ships."

Confirmation. AI probings of the Slan vessel's TNA computer systems had shown that they possessed the technology to capture incoming electromagnetic radiation and translate it into sound pictures; they *could* see the stars . . . or hear them, rather. They'd first become aware of EM radiation thanks to The Mystery . . . and to the perceived heat and light of their own sun, but it was a hell of a long way from those clues to the ability to navigate among the stars.

They *had* to have had help . . . and evidently that help had been provided by the Sh'daar.

"The Sh'daar were your guides, bringing you out among the stars," Gray suggested. "Is that true?"

"The Voices led us," Clear Chiming Bell agreed.

"But the Voices didn't give you the whole truth, did they?"

"We are learning . . . a very great deal from your computer systems," the Slan captain agreed. "Such vast, such *aching* distances between these bodies you call stars and planets. The seeds never told us. . . ."

Gray played the recording once again. *"K'!k't!'cht'!k'!kt'!!!k."*

The translated voice Gray was hearing over the network link carried no emotional inflection, of course, but he imagined that he could hear something like anguish behind them.

Or perhaps it was only a longing, a wistfulness.

"We were told only what we needed to know," Clear Chiming Bell said.

"So that the Sh'daar could use your species," Gray said. "For *their* purposes."

How much of a sense of personal individuality did the hive-dwelling Slan possess? Could they experience outrage at having their entire species drafted as a kind of military tool, as cannon fodder to fight Humankind . . . to die for an alien cause that they had never chosen?

"And in what manner," the Slan asked, "does your species wish to use us?"

" 'Use you'?"

"I suspect," Clear Chiming Bell said after a long hesitation, "that each species has its own version of the truth. Humans. Slan. The Sh'daar. What is true for you may be *k'!k't!'cht'!k'!kt'!!!k* for the Slan."

That simple statement seemed to demonstrate that the Slan were more rational in certain ways than were humans. The concept of situational ethics was difficult for most humans . . . and impossible for some.

"We always seek to exchange information," Gray said. "And we want the fighting between your kind and mine to cease. Beyond that . . . we believe that all species should be free to develop in their own way. We have no claim upon the Slan."

"If we agree to help you," Clear Chiming Bell said, the words coming slowly, "you will help us learn more of worlds and stars?"

"Absolutely."

"We must discuss this further, myself and my fellows. This current cessation of hostilities . . ."

"The truce."

"Yes, the truce. You agree that this state of affairs should continue?"

"Of course. We would rather talk to you as friends than fight you in battle."

"An interesting distinction. And one that I believe I do understand, one with which I agree."

And the virtual tunnel faded away in Gray's mind.

He wondered if the negotiations had just scored a breakthrough.

With the Slan, it was hard to tell.

Lieutenant Donald Gregory
VFA-96, Black Demons
Arianrhod Space
1020 hours, TFT

They were bringing in the European Union fighters.

Lieutenant Gregory banked left, bringing his Starhawk

into formation with an incoming flight of ten Franco-German KRG-60 Todtadler fighters originally off the *von Metternich*, Death Eagles roughly the equivalent of USNA Velociraptors in design and capability. There were seventeen of them, morphed into winged landing configurations, and they were on a direct vector for *America*.

"Keep in tight," Commander Mackey said over the squadron tac channel. "Let 'em know we care."

"Fuck, Commander," Kemper said. "I don't trust these puppies."

"Neither do I, Happy. That's why we keep it tight."

Rumors had been sweeping through *America*'s flight deck since the abdication of the fleet's non-USNA contingent. The possibility of all-out civil war had been an oft-discussed topic for months, now, but the scuttlebutt had really begun flying when Lavallée's squadron had refused to begin deceleration, sending them on a trajectory past Arianrhod and into deep space.

Now the Confederation fighters left behind were coming in. They'd been scattered all over the inner system, some of them badly damaged. SAR tugs were going after the streakers and junkers now; the ones that could still maneuver under their own power were being herded in by flights of fighters off the *America*.

Trust, Gregory thought, was in damned short supply at the moment, not only for the Confederation pilots, but for the Slan as well. If the aliens decided to attack *now*, there wasn't a lot the human forces could do to defend themselves.

America drifted in low orbit up ahead. Even from out here, she looked a mess. A third of her forward shield cap was gone, and there were savage scars along the spine structure aft. The hab mods were still rotating, providing artificial gravity, but a Slan beam had slashed through the bridge tower forward. Temporary scaffolding had been attached to the tower, partially enclosing it. Repair robots were swarming among the crossbeams and struts, restoring the carrier's nanomatrix hull.

Some of that damage was so severe that *America* was going to have to be sent home. At least her drives hadn't been damaged, and she should be able to accelerate enough to 'cube. The worrisome part, Gregory knew, was that the hull had been significantly weakened, and that the stresses of dropping into and out of metaspace might cause a catastrophic failure.

If the Slan were going to renew the battle, this would be the perfect time.

So far, though, the Slan ships had been keeping their distance. There'd been speculation within the squadron that they were awaiting reinforcements. After all, 70 Ophiuchi was a mere ten light years distant, and there was supposed to be a fair-sized Sh'daar client fleet there—Turusch and H'rulka fleet elements, plus Nungiirtok ground forces, and possibly Slan as well.

Two fighters of Gregory's squadron, Mackey and Benning, slipped in beneath *America*'s long spine, closely flanking the first of the Pan-European Todtadlers, following the fighter in along the landing approach path from just a little astern. If the Confederation pilot did try anything aggressive, the two Black Demons behind him would have him nailed in an instant.

That first fighter trapped in Bay Two without incident. Next, it was time for Gregory and his wingman, Lieutenant Vaughn to move in astern and to either side of the second Confederation fighter, escorting it in toward the rotating flight deck, timing their approach so that the opening slid into perfect alignment just as the Confederation fighter reached it. Vaughn and Gregory broke left and right, flashing past the hab modules and the open framework of the savaged shield cap. Throwing out drive singularities to the side, they whipped around in a tight turn and circled aft once more. They would escort each Confederation fighter in before docking with the carrier themselves.

"VFA Ninety-six, CIC," a voice said in Gregory's head. "New orders."

"Now what?" Lieutenant Pevensy asked.

"Probably more CAP," Gomez said. "We've been on freaking CAP since we got here."

"Anything's better than baby-sitting these damned Ewwws," Kemper said. The term was a bit of recently invented slang drawn from "EU," the Confederation's European Union. It was quite a versatile word, actually, one that could be expressed as an exclamation of disgust, or without the emphasis, could refer to a female sheep.

"Quiet down," Mackey said. "CIC, this is Ninety-six. Standing by for orders."

"We're launching a spybot," the voice of CIC replied. "We need to give it an escort to the Slan Onager."

Onager was the newly minted class name for the Slan headquarters ship. The word meant "mule," but was the name of another ancient projectile-throwing machine like ballista and trebuchet. The spooks on board *America* must have come up with a new spy-eye, and they wanted to send it in for a close look at the alien command vessel.

The squadron wheeled through space. What looked like another Starhawk dropped from one of the hab-module launch tubes, drifted toward them, and joined the formation. The fighter in fact was an HVK-724, a high-velocity scout-courier modified to look like a fighter. It was uncrewed, save for a powerful AI modified to serve both as pilot and as a so-called AI/Spy-I. The squadron would need to get it close enough to the Slan headquarters vessel that it could link in with the intelligence AIs already on board the alien vessel . . . and do so undetected.

"I thought the Slan were supposed to be cooperating with us," Gregory said as they accelerated toward the distant Onager. It was orbiting Arianrhod, but much farther out—nearly a million kilometers distant.

"It's always a good idea to know something about the other guy that they don't *know* you know," Mackey replied.

The bulky Slan Onager grew swiftly larger. Stiletto fighters spilled from the vessel's flanks, swarming, protective, but appeared to be simply . . . watching.

In another moment, the Starhawks had swept past, maintaining a straight-line vector deeper into space.

"Mission accomplished," the robot spy told them. "RTB."

Return to base.

Gregory wondered what the AI had learned in so brief a pass.

TC/USNA CVS America
Low Orbit, 36 Ophiuchi AIII
1035 hours, TFT

"Captain Gray," *America*'s AI whispered in his head. "We have learned something that may be of serious import."

"What is it?"

"A new data reserve in the Slan network picked up by the HVK-724 we just launched. We may now have a motive for the Sh'daar attack."

"Show me."

And *America* spread the information out visually within Gray's in-head.

"The Sh'daar appear to have become quite agitated in recent weeks," *America*'s AI explained. "New orders, lots of them, and reports of warships gathering at a staging area referred to as *Hu-vah-scha'n*."

In Gray's mind, sonar images from Slan records were stroked by human AIs until they coalesced into visual imagery. Gray saw ships—Turusch, H'rulka, and Slan—in orbit over a world of blue-green seas and orange land. The scene was dominated by large ships—the H'rulka giants were a kilometer or more across—but there were clouds of minnows drifting in the shadows of their larger consorts.

"We count forty-three capital warships," the AI went on, "including planetary bombardment vessels and fighter carriers. They appear to be readying for departure."

"Where?"

"Earth."

"You're sure of that?"

"Affirmative."

"Where is this 'Hoo-vuh' . . . whatever it's called? The staging area?"

More sonic images coalesced into an animated graphic—a star system, a double star—was shown surrounded by several planetary orbits, four around a type K0 sun, three around the slightly cooler K4. A scattering of targets was clustered around the second planet of the brighter sun. Gray recognized the image immediately. The star was 70 Ophiuchi, the second planet the world Osiris.

"So the attack here at Arianrhod *was* ordered by the Sh'daar," Gray said. "It's not a random strike by an out-of-control client race."

"Affirmative."

"And now they're getting set to attack Earth again."

"Affirmative."

"Why?"

"Interpretation of Slan communication records is difficult," the AI told him. "But we do have a visual recording that was transmitted as sonar data to the Slan *Onager* several weeks ago. We've been able to reconstitute the visual data. . . ."

A window opened within Gray's in-head perception. A ring of blurred night, swirling against a blue-white haze hanging in empty space. The blur, he realized, consisted of a number of bodies orbiting a common center of gravity, but moving so swiftly it was almost impossible to distinguish them.

He recognized the scene immediately from recent briefings, however—the Black Rosette, sixteen thousand light years from Earth. Six black holes, each the size of a small planet, whirling about one another at 26,000 kilometers per second, ripped and tore at the fabric of space within the plane they defined. The space between the black holes showed a stately procession of . . . other places. Other universes, perhaps, if theory was correct, revealed in blue light and a fierce haze of ultraviolet and X-ray radiation.

Three ships—the USNA research vessel *Endeavor* and two military escorts, *Herrera* and *Miller*, drifted across the artifact's face, silhouetted against that eerie glow. Something moved deep within the weirdly twisted space among the fast-rotating black holes . . . and then, suddenly, savagely, all three ships were torn apart.

"The Sh'daar used a word to describe something emerging from the Black Rosette," the AI said. "We have the translations in both Agletsch and in Slan, but it is difficult to translate concisely into English. We can, however, get a sense of the meaning."

"And what is that?" Gray asked. He stared into the depths of the Rosette, as if to somehow penetrate that swirling light show.

"The Agletsch word is *g'rev'netchjak*," the AI replied, "and refers to something so horrifying as to defy description. The Slan word is identical to the phrase we've now translated as 'sin,' meaning something that offends all rational sensibility, something that breaks all the rules."

"My God. What is it?"

"We don't yet know, Captain," the AI told him, "but whatever it is, the Sh'daar appear to be terrified of it.

"Intelligence conjectures that they are so afraid of whatever has emerged from the Rosette that they decided to attack Earth, to settle with us before they have to face this . . . this unnamable thing."

The image in Gray's mind faded out, and he wondered just what could so frighten a species as old and as powerful as the Sh'daar.

And that in itself was an extraordinarily disquieting thought.

Chapter Twenty

TC/USNA CVS America
36 Ophiuchi AIII
0925 hours, TFT

Sandy Gray leaned back in his chair at the ops planning table, listening to the reports being delivered by various of the ship's section and departmental heads. The command staffs of the various other ships of the squadron were virtually present, listening in over their in-heads. Since the news of an impending attack on Earth had come through hours before, there was a new sense of urgency in the staff deliberations.

Urgency and, just possibly, a note of fear.

Twenty ships of the USNA contingent's initial force of twenty-four had survived the battle, but four of those remaining were badly damaged—*America*, the heavy cruisers *North Carolina* and *California*, and the destroyer *Cumberland*. In addition, all of the ships were low on expendables—missiles of various types, and massive kinetic-kill rounds for the railguns. They would need to put the provisioning tender *Shenandoah* to work before they fought another major battle.

The repairs to *America* continued. The flag bridge had

been sealed off, and communications links had been grown through to the ship's bridge, allowing Gray to command both the ship and the entire squadron. The worst damage was to the vessel's forward shield cap, a disk-shaped reservoir 500 meters across and 150 deep that served both as radiation shielding at relativistic speeds and as holding tank for maneuvering reaction mass, about 27 billion liters of water when it was full. Both the Alcubierre and normal-space drives were on-line again, as were the ship's weapons systems. All that remained were some final structural repairs to the ship's spine, buttressing weakened areas enough that they would survive high-G maneuvering.

Unlike fighters, which were small enough to make use of grav singularities for precise maneuvering, a capital ship the size of the *America* needed to use more traditional means for turning, orienting, and station-keeping—specifically the thrust provided by plasma jets firing super-heated water drawn from the main reserve. Much of that water had bled off into space when the shield cap was shattered during yesterday's battle, however, and *America* wasn't going to be traveling much of anywhere until her water supplies were replenished.

Getting that water was the responsibility of Lieutenant Commander Richard Halverson, of the ship's Engineering Department.

"The Nav Department has identified a good water source for us," Halverson was telling the group. "Planet IV in this system is a small ice giant, about the size of Neptune back home. It has a ring system—almost-pure-water ice. We won't even have to shuttle it up out of a gravity well."

"Fred?" Gray asked. "Can we make it that far without thrusters?"

"If we boost when we're at the proper alignment," Commander Fred Jones, the ship's senior helm officer, told them, "we can do a straight-line approach at, say, fifty Gs. We won't need to rattle the cage at all."

The singularity drive allowed them to travel in free fall; even at a high-G boost, the ship would not feel the stresses of acceleration or deceleration. Maneuvering thrusters, however, subjected the entire ship to the forces of acceleration—"rattling the cage"—and Gray wanted to avoid that if at all possible. He was worried about the damage to *America*'s spine. Free fall was one thing. Subjecting the spine to the twists and shocks of lateral acceleration or centrifugal force was something else entirely.

"Very well," Gray replied. "You'll need to do some mighty precise work to line the ship up properly."

"We've already been running simulations through the primary AI, Captain. I think we're good to go."

"Outstanding. Now, the big question . . ."

"What the Slan are going to think when we move out-system," Commander Gutierrez suggested.

"Actually, Sara," Gray said slowly, "that shouldn't be a big problem. I've had a number of discussions *in virtuo* with Clear Chiming Bell. He seems to believe that further conflict would be pointless. My impression is that they're pulling out."

"What?" the CO of the destroyer *Atkinson* said, startled. "Are we sure of that?"

"As sure as we can be, Captain Lang. Remember, we're still having to feel our way through conversations with the Slan. The xenopsych people tell me that the Slan don't think in terms of absolute victory or defeat in conflict. For them, a battle is more of a shoving match—a sumo bout—and the side that gets shoved the hardest is expected to leave quietly."

"That's a hell of a way to fight a war," Captain Soltis of the *Washington* observed.

"Maybe by our standards," Gray said. "Commander Kline? What does X-Dep have to say about that?"

Lieutenant Commander Samantha Kline was the head of *America*'s Xenobiology Department. With *America* frequently coming into contact with nonhuman species—allies, enemies, and unknowns—it was vital to maintain a department that could study those alien sentient races, seeking to understand their biologies, their cultures, and, perhaps most important of all, their psychologies.

"We have a long way to go before we fully understand the Slan," Kline said. "But we do now know that the Slan evolved in quite a different environment than ours. They never possessed anything like nation-states, mutually alien cultures, or racial differences. In fact, they come damned close to possessing a true hive mentality."

"You mean it's like we're facing one huge, thinking being, instead of a whole race?" Captain Janet Lockhart, of the railgun cruiser *Turner* asked.

"Not quite. Termite mounds and beehives on Earth approach that concept—a hive can be thought of as a single organism—but that's because the individuals aren't sentient. For the Slan the distinction appears to be more psychological than anything else. Individuals within the community think for themselves . . . but those thoughts all are shaped by culture and social conditioning toward supporting the community. If you're a Slan, you don't do anything that harms the group; if you do, you're insane."

"Japanese culture on Earth has parallels to this," Captain Richard Imahara of the frigate *Ramsey* pointed out. "Traditionally, they have a stronger group ethic than do Westerners. It's all about the workplace, the school, the city, about pulling for the team because that's the socially proper thing to do, and *not* about the individual."

"To a certain extent, possibly," Kline said. "A lot of that is the effect of population crowding, especially since global sea levels started rising. But the Slan have that group ethic on steroids. You don't kill other group members, any more than you or I would cut off our own hand. When an individual *does* violate the communal ethic, for whatever reason, it's such a big deal that that individual is 'sent to the light.' As far as we've been able to determine, that means it's exiled to the day side of their homeworld, where it soon dies of radiation exposure.

"Apparently, warfare of a sort *did* appear after new Slan colonies branched off on the planet's surface, but it seems to have been a highly stylized affair, constrained by the needs of the overall community. Essentially, if two groups disagreed about something, they'd fight until one side or the other was proven to be stronger . . . and the weaker would give in. As the Captain said, a shoving match. *Never* all-out war."

"The Slan seem never to have developed the idea of total war," Gray added, "or of hanging on to the bitter end, of fighting to the last man. . . ."

"So . . . we won?" Gutierrez said. The XO sounded amazed. "We proved we were stronger, and we just *won*?"

"Keep in mind, Commander, that we don't know all the rules, yet," Gray told her. He'd already gone through Kline's initial report, and knew just how poorly humans understood the Slan, even yet. "We don't know what might trigger a change of mind . . . a willingness to start a *new* shoving match."

"Exactly," Kline said. "We don't yet understand their concept of war. They bombard civilian colonies from orbit—like Silverwheel—because they don't seem to understand the concept of civilian or noncombatant. And yet they seem incapable of totally destroying an enemy by wiping him out. I would imagine that they would be horrified by the very concept of genocide."

"So . . ." Taggart said, "are we still fighting them or not?"

"Good question," Kline said. "X-Dep has recommended maintaining a cautious approach. Don't turn your back, don't take *any* chances with them until we understand them better."

"Unfortunately," Gray added, "we're going to *have* to take a chance . . . several of them, in fact. It is my intention to take this squadron to 70 Ophiuchi and stage a high-velocity raid. A fly-by stage spoiler."

The statement triggered a storm of voices, both out loud around the conference table and over the virtual network. "But sir, we can't take on a fleet that big!" Captain Geary of the *Henderson* exclaimed.

"Sir! Estimates based on the Slan computer records say the Sh'daar have between fifty and sixty capital ships at

Osiris," Lieutenant Commander Villanova added. "We just don't have the ships to face off with that kind of force!"

"We can disrupt the enemy's plans," Gray said simply. "And that may be enough."

It would *have* to be enough.

The tactic called fly-by spoiling was a direct outgrowth of modern space-military operations. A fleet would emerge from Alcubierre metaspace, accelerate to near the speed of light, then hurtle past the target planet deep in-system, precisely as had Lavallée's fleet the day before. If the enemy force was in preparation for a deployment somewhere else, it might well be scattered and disorganized, taking on munitions, fuel, and supplies. The problem was the weakened state of the USNA squadron. Twenty ships were left, and 20 percent of those were so badly damaged they might not survive another fight . . . or even the maneuvers necessary to get them to 70 Ophiuchi. And judging by the image translations gleaned from the Slan ship, the Earth squadron would be heavily outnumbered when it got there.

"If I may say so, sir, that's damned . . . risky," Captain Garrison of the *Inchon* said. It sounded as though he'd almost said something else other than "risky."

Like "stupid" or "lame-brained" or perhaps "fucking idiotic." And Gray would have been forced to agree.

"Yes it is," he replied. "You and *Inchon* will be facing a different kind of danger, however."

"Sir?"

"*Inchon* won't add that much firepower to a near-*c* fly-by of Osiris, and we won't be hanging around long enough for us to deploy your Marines. You'll be better employed staying here, and encouraging the Slan to get the hell off Arianrhod."

"*Here.*" Again, Gray heard what might have been a bitten-off protest, but Garrison merely said, "Aye, aye, sir."

"We will also leave the most badly damaged ships here, and the *Shenandoah*, of course. With luck, the Slan will think we're leaving behind a major fraction of our fleet."

Gray would have liked to take Osiris back from the

Sh'daar. Their forces had been holding the place for fifteen years, now, and as a staging area it was perfect for future strikes against the Sol System and Earth.

Someday . . .

If there were humans still alive at Osiris, the brutal truth was that they'd survived this long, and they would survive a bit longer. Arianrhod, however, was a different matter. Silverwheel, the main research base on the surface, had been home to twenty thousand people, with hundreds more in orbit at Caer Gwydion. Their fate was unknown, though Lieutenant Connor had reported that the Slan had been firing into both indiscriminately several days before. The Marines off the *Inchon* could secure Silverwheel, and the ship's Marine fighters would be useful in finding other survivors scattered across the Caer Arianrhod Archipelago.

If the Slan let them.

"The main issues," Gray continued, "are getting *America* fit for transition again, and replenishing the squadron's expendables."

"America?" Gutierrez said. "Wouldn't we do better shifting your flag and leaving the old girl here?"

"No," Gray replied. "We're going to need fighter support at Osiris, and we're leaving the *Inchon* here. If Lavallée hadn't taken the other star carriers with him, it might be different."

"Bastards . . ." someone at the table muttered.

By now, it was clear that all of the Confederation ships under Lavallée's command had transited into Alcubierre Drive and, presumably, were on their way back to Earth. Apparently, they hadn't even engaged the Slan fleet as they'd whipped past Arianrhod. Most of their fighters launched earlier had managed to catch up with the *Illustrious*, the *Bolivar*, and the *Kali* by pegging a few more decimal places onto their percentage of c figures, but five hours and twenty minutes after they'd passed through the Slan fleet, the Confederation contingent had reached the 40-AU limit from 36 Ophiuchi A and winked out into metaspace.

The Pan-European fighters off the disabled *Klemens von*

Metternich had stayed behind, of course, along with about a dozen fighters from the other carriers that had gone streaker in the battle, falling helplessly away into the night. *America*'s SAR tugs were still working at rescuing as many of those fighters as possible and hauling them back to Arianrhod orbit.

"That's okay," Gray said. "They're headed back to Sol. If the Sh'daar *do* launch a strike at Earth, Lavallée's ships will be needed there."

Hours before, Gray had dispatched a message drone with a coded message intended for USNA Military Command on Mars, and for President Koenig. The message included details of the battle . . . and the all-important information that both Steiger and Delattre were dead, that the non-USNA contingent had broken off under Lavallée's command, and that Gray had assumed overall command of the American ships.

They would know the situation back on Earth within twenty-five hours.

And Gray expected to be on his way to 70 Ophiuchi well before that time.

"Maybe we should high-tail it back to Earth too," Gutierrez suggested.

"If we can manage to pull off a good spoiler, Commander," Gray replied, "they might not need to make a last-ditch stand in Earth's own backyard. The farther away we can stop them, the better, right?"

"Yes, sir. But if they're waiting for us . . . if the Slan tell them we're coming . . . we could lose the whole squadron."

"Then we'll just have to make sure they *don't* know we're coming."

Much later, far into the night watch, Gray lay in bed with Laurie Taggart, holding her close. The gentle pattern of her breathing told him she was asleep. Good. He'd needed some time to think. . . .

He'd switched the bulkheads of his quarters to show the view outside *America*'s hull, partly so that he could keep tabs on the repair efforts outside, but also for the sheer, icy, spectacular beauty of the scene. Though his quarters were in a rotating hab module, providing a steady half-G of spin gravity, the image had been stitched together by computer from various cameras mounted on the non-rotating portions of the hull.

Hours before, *America* had been judged fit to make the short boost to the fourth planet of the 36 Ophiuchi A system, a hazy blue-green sphere two astronomical units out, an ice giant named Goewin by the original research station colonists. Like the larger Saturn back in the Sol System, Goewin possessed a spectacular ring system, multiple bands of white-silver light composed of uncounted trillions of bits of water ice, ranging in size from grains of sand to a fair-sized house. Swarms of shepherd moons tugged and nudged the rings into distinct bands separated one from another by narrow grooves of emptiness. Gray couldn't see those grooves from here, though they'd been clear enough during the orbital approach to Goewin. *America* now orbited within the outer fringes of the outermost ring, and the ring system as a whole was visible only as a ruler-straight white line slashing through the center of the planet's disk.

Scattered across the sky were moons showing various phases, the hazy glow of multiple comets, the shrunken orange face of 36 Oph A. A few kilometers away, the massive provisioning ship *Shenandoah* had docked in the shadow of a moon too small to have a name. The moonlet's icy surface had been melted away, revealing the coal-black carbonaceous interior, and swarms of unmanned picker ships were busily ferrying raw material up to *Shenandoah*'s capacious storage bunkers in steady streams. The moon, a potato-shaped mass perhaps three kilometers long, had a CH-core beneath its icy crust, the letters standing for *carbon* and *high metal*. Carbonaceous chondrite bodies contained large amounts of organic compounds, as well as significant amounts of silicates, oxides, and sulfides, plus, in this case, over 5 percent water by mass. The metallic component was mostly nickel-iron, but there were traces of other elements as well.

And there were other mining targets within nearby space. Hours before, one of *Shenandoah*'s robot miners had been dispatched to rendezvous with a 1.5-kilometer asteroid half an AU sunward, together with the squadron's ore hauler, the aging T-AK cargo ship *Altair*. Though it was not widely known even yet, *all* of the metals accessible on and within Earth's crust had come from the rain of meteors and asteroids that had pummeled Earth's surface after the planet had formed and cooled. All of the nickel and iron, all of the cobalt, gold, platinum, manganese and *all* of the other metals that had been part of the original accretion of the planet had sunk down into the unreachable core during Earth's molten youth. The metals available to human industry, from the copper and bronze ages on, all had arrived much later. Human civilization had, in a sense, been mining the asteroids since the very beginning.

Mining asteroids *off* the Earth had been a large part of what had propelled humankind off its homeworld. In the mid twenty-first century, dwindling reserves of silver, copper, gold, lead and other common elements had been nearly exhausted. A single 1-kilometer type-M asteroid, however, contained over 12 trillion dollars' worth of industrial and precious metals; a 30-meter high-metal asteroid might hold 50 billion dollars' worth of platinum alone. Quite early on in the migration of Humankind into the Sol System, then, technologies for extracting and refining both metals and volatiles from barren rocks had become the principal drivers of space-born industry and colonization, as well as robotics, spacecraft propulsion, and space-based nanotechnics.

Those technologies were especially important for interstellar naval vessels now. The pure elements being separated and stored in *Shenandoah*'s bunkers would go into her nanufactories to create everything from air and food to missiles with fusion warheads, microcircuits for regrowing damaged electronics, raw materials for the repair robots now clustered around *America*'s shield cap, and even fresh uniforms for the crew. The robotic assembly lines on board *Shenandoah* were already cranking out new SG-101 and SG-112 fighters at the rate of one per three and a half hours.

The only question was how long the fleet could afford to wait before shutting down the repair and resupply operation and boosting out-system. At the current rate of nanufacture, the squadron's reserves would be completely replenished within fifty hours, but Gray wanted to be long gone by that time. The longer they delayed boosting for 70 Oph, the greater the chance that they would arrive there after the Sh'daar had already departed for Sol.

Laurie stirred in his arms, nestling closer. "Mmm. You still awake?"

"Watching the repair," he replied, absently stroking the hair at the back of her head. "Wondering when to boost for Osiris."

Wondering if they *should* boost for Osiris . . . or make for Earth instead. Geary, Villanova, and *America*'s Exec all had raised some good points.

In particular, he wondered about the Slan. Throughout the day, and as *America* and her consorts had shifted out-system to Goewin, more and more of the Slan ships had been pulling back from Arianrhod and accelerating off into deep space. Analyses of their outbound paths suggested that some were heading for 70 Ophiuchi, that others were on their way to other, unknown places deeper into the heart of the galaxy.

He had to assume that the Slan would communicate with the other Sh'daar clients at Osiris, telling them human forces were at 36 Oph, that they'd beaten the Slan there and forced the Slan to pull out. Inevitably, that would mean the Sh'daar themselves would know. What would their response be?

And that, more than anything, was what decided him, in that moment, on carrying out the spoiling raid at Osiris. They would go, and they would depart as soon as the basic repairs on *America* were complete. The Sh'daar were—they must be—as much in the dark about human intentions and capabilities and the way they saw the universe as humans were about the Slan or Turusch or the Sh'daar themselves.

"You've already given all the necessary orders, haven't you?" Laurie said.

"I suppose so."

"Then c'mere, Sandy Gray. Spend some time with *me*."

He snuggled closer, kissed her, letting his hand wander. But as he looked up at the bulkhead projections again, he saw the stream of picker ships flowing up from the crater already eaten into the shepherd moon's surface and vanishing into the gaping maw of *Shenandoah*'s receiving bay, Gray had a new idea.

Or, rather, a new iteration of an idea he'd had once before, twenty years earlier, when he'd acquired the nickname "Sandy" in the first place.

He kissed Laurie Taggart again, but as he did so he was linking through to the bridge, and issuing a string of new orders.

Only after those orders had been transmitted to the *Shenandoah* and the *Altair* would he be able to turn his full attention on the woman in his arms.

He just wished he knew what Clear Chiming Bell was thinking right now. . . .

Slan Protector Vigilant
Low Orbit, 36 Ophiuchi AIII
2330 hours, TFT

Clear Chiming Bell studied the aural representation of nearby space displayed above its console, and—not for the first time—wondered what the aliens were thinking.

Within Slan culture, *community* was everything, and what counted most in any conflict was that the community be protected. Part of what that meant was using the minimum of force necessary in an engagement . . . and that depended on the loser of the engagement accepting defeat when the victor showed the greater strength.

Simple enough . . . but for the system to work, both sides in an engagement had to be working by the same set of rules. And the more that Clear Chiming Bell learned about the humans, the more it was becoming convinced that they did not—*could* not—understand the rules of civilized behavior.

That prospect, the Slan leader thought, was the single most terrifying aspect of the human monsters. Clear Chiming Bell had become aware of this in the behavior of the prisoner they'd picked up in space after the battle for the planet. The strange being had been captured, had clearly been helpless . . . and yet somehow it had escaped from its quarters when the humans invaded the *Vigilant* when by all logic it *should* have stayed put. Apparently it had communicated somehow with the invading forces and joined them, managing to escape when they withdrew.

The fact that those forces had attacked at all, attempting to rescue the prisoner against overwhelming odds, was . . . unsettling, as was the audio of the prisoner attacking an entire *t'k'tch* of Slan soldiers from the rear with a low-powered weapon that appeared to fire bursts of tightly focused electromagnetic radiation. Soldiers scattered, startled by this unexpected assault, giving the main body of humans an opening to attack from the front.

The human should have stayed in its fighter . . . no, *should* have stayed in its quarters. Worse by far, the alien soldiers shouldn't have sacrificed so many of themselves to save one captured individual. Risking so many members of the community for one life? The action was inexplicable . . . and completely un-Slanlike.

But Clear Chiming Bell had a terrible feeling that he was seeing a measure of the humans' true strength, here, and it was a strength the Slan could not hope to match.

The Slan fleet commander was well aware that the humans had used the opportunity presented by breaching the *Vigilant*'s hull to implant devices that allowed them to penetrate the Slan computer network. Slan soldiers would have done precisely the same if they'd boarded a human warship. But the details of that desperate firefight within *Vigilant*'s docking bay were devastatingly incomprehensible.

It opened a channel to the ship's navigational officer. "Cool Tunnel Deeps," it said. "Program for transition to the main fleet."

"We work together," the officer replied, giving a formal reply. "What of the rest of our group?"

"We move together," the commander said. "We will abandon this place."

"Does such a decision align with the Community good?"

"It does," Clear Chiming Bell replied. "Until we better understand these humans, it most assuredly does."

Clear Chiming Bell found itself disturbed by the human view of the universe. Rather than thinking of *places*, like distinct tunnel complexes more or less side-by-side, they saw this place and that one as unbearably tiny and lonely motes lost in an immense vacuum, separated by unimaginably vast gulfs of emptiness.

The thought was terrifying, and bespoke a terrible, terrible loneliness.

The Slan commander yearned for the embrace of Community, the bigger, the busier, the better.

The Fleet Community would rejoin, and perhaps hold the emptiness at bay.

Chapter Twenty-One

TC/USNA CVS America
In transit, 36 Ophiuchi AIII
1130 hours, TFT

America accelerated outbound, racing for the 40-AU limit, where the gravitationally warped topography of space was flat enough to allow her transition over to Alcubierre Drive. Sixteen ships flew in formation with her, including the provisioning vessel *Shenandoah*, which now had a vital role to play at 70 Ophiuchi.

Gray studied the readouts for the system. Little was known about the strength or deportment of Sh'daar ships around Osiris. The translations of Slan audio data suggested fifty to sixty ships, as the intelligence officer on board *Inchon* had pointed out, but it was unknown how many of those might be warships, and how many were transports. Dating the information was problematical as well; the Slan means of determining date and time were still a mystery, and the Osiris imagery might well be out of date.

What Gray was counting on was the sheer difficulty in targeting incoming ships moving at near-*c*. Even for technologically advanced cultures like the Sh'daar and their clients, tracking incoming targets that were only scant seconds behind the light revealing their presence was a monumental task, requiring high-precision optical systems, tremendous computing power, and a great deal of luck. The easiest way to deal with an incoming fleet, actually, was to spread "O-mines," drifting obstacles, in the ships' paths—bits of debris, KK projectiles, even BB-sized pellets. With the ships moving at near-*c*, and the obstacles drifting into their paths at normal orbital speeds, the release of energy when they collided was astonishing. Clouds of sand worked particularly well . . . the origin of Gray's nickname, his handle.

The problem was that you had to know *exactly* where the target was going to be and make certain the obstacle was there at the same instant; even an exploded cargo ship full of sand rapidly dispersed when its cargo was sprayed across distances of more than a few tens of kilometers, and aiming the thing like a giant shotgun was more a matter of guesswork than precision. It was even tougher when the oncoming ships were jinking left-right, up-down, and giving the targeting networks electronic migraines.

The Slan had not demonstrated any particular proficiency in targeting high-velocity warships as they passed.

And Gray was counting on that to preserve his command during an Osiris fly-by.

But a great deal depended on just where the enemy forces were placed when the USNA ships arrived, and how many of them there were.

"Captain, this is Comm."

"Go ahead."

"Sir . . . a message drone just dropped out of metaspace twenty-three light minutes away, bearing one-one-five by zero-three-nine. The message is coded for us, sir. From the Joint Chiefs, *and* Mars."

"Let me see it." Something from the Joint Chiefs was essentially from President Koenig himself. And having it come from HQMILCOM Mars made it doubly serious.

"Message decoding, sir."

In Gray's mind, the message came up in print.

TO: Radm Jason Steiger, CO USNA CONTINGENT/CBG-40
FROM: JCS AND CO/USNAMILCOM, MARS
RE: Orders
DATE/TIME: 14 November 2424/2340h
PRIORITY MOST URGENT

1. Confederation military forces have initiated hostilities against USNA base Tsiolkovsky on Luna and against periphery areas of the continental USNA. Initial actions successful but further attacks expected momentarily. It must be assumed that a state of civil war now exists within the Terran Confederation, and specifically involving USNA military forces against Confederation forces, particularly those of Pan-Europe.

2. All USNA military vessels are hereby required and directed to return to Earth synchorbit at earliest opportunity.

3. Use utmost caution in dealing with non-USNA Confederation vessels in the task force. Non-USNA vessels should be considered hostile. Assume orders from Geneva direct Delattre to seize or destroy USNA vessels CBG-40.

4. Use best judgment in disentangling forces, and in breaking off in the face of enemy forces.

This is a mess, Jas. Watch your back.

SIGNED (1): Cutwaller, ADM, CO/USNAMILCOM, MARS
SIGNED (2): Armitage, ADM, JCS

MESSAGE ENDS

Damn. The message had been dispatched before news of Steiger's death had reached Earth. That personal message tagged on at the end made the dry recitation of orders unusually piquant. Eugene Armitage, the commander of the Joint Chiefs, Gray remembered, had been both a personal friend and a mentor of sorts to Jason Steiger.

Even with faster-than-light travel, interstellar military operations were dominated by one factor—the sheer, mind-numbing vastness of the empty space between star systems. Fleet commanders had an extraordinary degree of freedom—and responsibility to go with it—in their operations. Gone were the days when the president and command-staff level officers could micromanage a battle via satellite from halfway around the world.

But the communication lag between CBG-40 and Earth had just dropped a nasty piece of hot shrapnel into Gray's lap. He'd broken off from the rest of the Confederation fleet—or, to be fair, they'd broken away from *him*—so at least that wasn't an issue. But the battle group was now minutes away from transitioning to Alcubierre Drive for a twelve-hour jump to 70 Ophiuchi. A strict interpretation of these new orders would require him to abandon the Osiris fly-by and return immediately to Earth.

That was not quite as simple an issue as it seemed, however. To reset onto a Sol-bound flight path, they would have to decelerate, come about to align with the fourth-magnitude speck of light in the sky that was Sol, then accelerate back up to near-c in order to engage the Alcubierre Drive. Either that, or they would have to make the jump away from 36 Ophiuchi, re-emerge, acquire Sol, then accelerate again. Either way, they might lose another day.

And the message from Armitage had been sent before Earth knew about the looming threat of an attack from Osiris.

"Comm," Gray said.

"Comm here, sir."

"Is the update transmission loaded and ready to dispatch?"

"It is, sir."

"Send it now."

"Aye, aye."

Gray had recorded his intent to re-deploy to Osiris and attempt to cripple the Sh'daar forces being readied there for a strike against Earth. He'd not been requesting permission; his decision to launch the drone just before dropping into the unreachable darkness of metaspace under Alcubierre Drive had underscored that fact. By the time Earth learned of his intention, he would already be at Osiris engaging the enemy.

At least Earth would know where CBG-40 had gone, and would be able to reach him with subsequent drones at Osiris.

"Should I acknowledge receipt of that last communication, sir?"

Gray thought about this. He was tempted to say no. It would be easy enough to claim he'd deployed to 70 Oph before the order from Earth even reached him. Had the message drone emerged just a little farther away, the radio broadcast would not have reached the fleet before it had dropped into metaspace.

But . . . no. He might end up court-martialed for what in fact was direct disobedience of orders, but so far as Gray was concerned the greater threat to Earth was the gathering Sh'daar strike force, not political squabbles at home. He would play this one straight, and let the folks back on Earth know exactly where he was going and what he was doing.

Even if he was doing it before they could tell him not to.

Operating out here on the edge of damn-all, far from the oversight of command staffs and presidential advisors did absolute wonders for your sense of perspective.

"Acknowledge," he said. Moments later, the drone accelerated off into darkness.

And minutes after that, *America* and the other ships of CBG-40 flashed over into Alcubierre Drive.

Osiris lay twelve hours ahead.

Executive Office, USNA
Columbus, District of Columbia
United States of North America
1325 hours, EST

"Mr. President," the office AI whispered in his mind, "you *must* evacuate. The elevator is waiting for you."

"Yes, yes," Koenig said, irritably. "Just a moment . . ."

"The situation display is being repeated in the bunker, sir. You can continue your work there."

"I *know*, damn it. Just give me a minute."

His human aides and a couple of Secret Service agents were standing in his office, waiting for him, but he ignored them as he was ignoring the nagging voice of the AI secretary. A translucent display field hung suspended above his desk, showing planets and planetary orbits, and the arcing curves of incoming ships. So far, most of the incoming vessels were small stuff—destroyers, gunboats, the North Indian light cruiser *Godavari*—but five heavies had rounded the sun moments before and were clearly vectoring on Earth. Other ships—the carriers and other heavy capital ships—were expected soon. He was watching HQMILCOM deploying its meager assets to block the approach paths of the Confederation Fleet's main body.

Things were about to get very interesting.

"Mr. President," Marcus Whitney said, almost pleading. "We need to get to the basement *now*!"

"All *right*! All *right*!"

He switched off the display and rose from his seat. The Secret Service fell into step with him as he strode across the holographic carpet display, his aides scrambling to keep up in his wake. Through the outer offices and past the security station, the Executive Tower's main emergency elevator was located down the passageway, still within the security suite. More agents waited at the elevator, holding it for him.

The secure bunker was located almost 2 kilometers below the Freedom Concourse in the heart of downtown Columbus, at the bottom of a high-speed maglev descent through the center of the Executive Tower and into the facility known as the PRESCO, the presidential secure complex. Privately, the people working in the Executive Tower simply called it the Basement. It housed the offices of the Joint Chiefs and most of the Earthside USNA Military Command complex, as well as the Situation Room and secure communications facilities that linked the office of the President with both civilian and military USNA assets across the solar system.

The underground base had been hardened to withstand—it was believed—a one-hundred-megaton nuclear explosion at the surface.

"Welcome to the Basement, Mr. President," his first secretary, John Casey, said as the facility's armored outer doors slid aside and he walked in. "We have a possible hostile strike force ten million kilometers out."

"I know." He'd been tracking those five Pan-European ships for the past hour as they'd skimmed past the sun and dropped into an intercept course with Earth, traveling at ten percent *c*. A week ago, those five vessels had been reported at the Confederation military base at Circe, at Epsilon Indi some twelve light years from Sol. Geneva had called them back to Sol, evidently to take part in this attack.

They'd been planning this for a *long* time.

"Analyses of their flight path suggests a weapons strike somewhere in North America."

"I know. *Pittsburgh, Missouri* and *Amazon* are vectoring to cut them off," Koenig replied. "*Burke* and *Spruance* are still an hour away. What about the *Jones*?"

The frigate *John Paul Jones* was in space dock at Quito Synchorbital, undergoing a long-needed refit. Earlier that morning, her skipper—Don McCluskey—had reported that he might be able to get his ship clear of the dock and into action if he could take it slow. The aging frigate still had a gaping construction hole in her side, and was in no shape for high-G maneuvers.

"Captain McCluskey reports he's still trying to get past the grudge list."

"Tell him to boost with his painters dangling if he has to," Koenig growled. "But *get the hell out there*!"

"Yes, Mr. President."

Koenig walked to the workstation maintained for him and for the military chief of staff. Admiral Armitage stood up and stepped out of the circular cockpit. "Keeping the chair warm for you, Mr. President."

"Thanks, Gene." He looked up, scanning the floor-to-ceiling projection hanging in front of one wall, some fifty meters wide. Those Pan-European ships were a lot closer now. "How long before those hostiles launch?"

"Any second now, sir. Depends on how close they want to get."

The *Pittsburgh*, Koenig noted, was vectoring toward the lead enemy ship, which was perhaps half a million kilometers in advance of the others. According to the data tag hanging beside the enemy vessel's icon, she was the *Ognevoy*, a Russian strike cruiser. Her name reportedly meant "Curtain of Fire," and she'd been designed with planetary bombardment in mind.

The two High Guard sentinels, *Missouri* and *Amazon*, were vectoring toward the main body of incoming hostiles. Koenig winced. Those two were heavily outclassed, the equivalent of a pair of frigates facing the heavy cruisers *Montcalm* and *Brahmaputra*, the destroyer *Kondor*, and a second planetary bombardment ship, the *Estremadura*.

Against firepower like that, the sentinel ships didn't stand a chance.

Other ships were on the way in, but nothing else could arrive in time to block those five Confederation ships. There were reports of confused fighting elsewhere—on Mars, on Luna, even in Synchorbit; the civil war was spreading wildly, and out of control.

Pittsburgh launched on the *Ognevoy*, a volley of red pinpoints leaping from the icon marking the USNA ship toward the red bombardment vessel. The Russian ship's point defenses opened up, wiping most of the shipkillers out, but then the remaining missiles began detonating in rapid succession, the fireballs swelling in the *Ognevoy*'s path. The Russian passed through one of the expanding clouds.

"Hit," an AI said aloud. "Major damage to the *Ognevoy*. . . ."

Several people in the bunker cheered, but Armitage silenced them with a sharp "*As you were!* We're not out of this yet. . . ."

Montcalm and *Kondor* were exchanging fire now with the *Amazon*. A high-energy laser clawed at *Montcalm*'s forward shield, causing some damage, but two powerful electron beams snapped out from the Pan-European vessels and caught the *Amazon* amidships. There was a brief, bright flare of light, and then the forward half of the sentinel ship was drifting free, slowly tumbling, as a cloud of debris spread out from astern.

"Hit on the *Amazon*," the AI reported. "Telemetry indicates terminal damage. Crew fatalities estimated at one hundred percent."

Damn . . .

Nuclear warheads from the *Missouri* detonated alongside the *Kondor*, which disintegrated in a cloud of sparkling fragments. *Pittsburgh* was altering her course, now, to intercept the main body of Confederation vessels. Both the *Montcalm* and the *Brahmaputra* were concentrating their fire now on the *Missouri*, now, and in moments the remaining sentinel vessel was drifting powerless and helpless, her drive modules riddled at long range by beams from the more powerful Confederation cruisers. The *Pittsburgh* released a spread of VG-44c ship-killers, then opened up with her own spinal-mount particle weapon, damaging both enemy vessels, but not in time to save the *Missouri*. *Pittsburgh* took a railgun hit . . . and then another. The cruisers altered course slightly, closing on her. . . .

The *Estremadura*, the Spanish bombardment ship bringing up the rear of the Confederation squadron, loosed three warheads the size of Velociraptor fighters twenty seconds before taking a hit from one of the *'Burgh*'s Fer-de-lance killers. *Pittsburgh* saw the launch and altered course, trying for an intercept, but she was badly positioned, too far off the enemy missiles' track to get a shot.

"Three space-to-ground warheads inbound," the AI announced with maddening calm. "Analysis of their track suggests they are targeting the east-central reaches of North America between Chicago and the Washington Periphery."

That was an enormous area, a thousand kilometers across.

Chances were good, however, that at least one of those warheads was targeting Columbus, smack in the center of the target area . . . and possibly all three of them were, for insurance.

They want to decapitate us, Koenig thought. *Take out the government.* A couple of seconds later he realized that they were after *him*. The computer-generated graphics on the wall in front of him had the look and feel of a movie or a complex game. It was unpleasantly easy to forget how deadly that game was.

Pittsburgh fired, trying to hit the warheads, but she was too far. *Brahmaputra* and *Montcalm* concentrated their fire on the *Pittsburgh*, as *Estremadura* fired a second volley.

"Three more space-to-ground bombardment rounds fired," the AI said. "Probable impact in east-central North America."

Pittsburgh was breaking off, badly damaged. There was nothing in the sky now between Earth and those incoming rounds.

And then another green icon drifted into view, positioning itself in front of those incoming salvos. It was the *John Paul Jones*, just launched from spacedock at Quito Synchorbital, limping, but her weapons batteries coming on-line. She fired, and two of the warheads vanished.

Both *Montcalm* and *Brahmaputra* shifted their fire from the crippled *Pittsburgh* to the *Jones*. The *Jones* ignored the fire and continued concentrating on the incoming rounds. Koenig found himself clenching his fists so tightly that the nails bit flesh.

"Forty-five seconds to impact," the AI announced.

The *Jones* hit another warhead, one in the second salvo. The survivor in the first salvo was past the destroyer now, hurtling toward Earth at over 30,000 kilometers per second.

"Have those warheads been analyzed?" Koenig asked. "What are they throwing at us?"

"We're not getting radiation, Mr. President," Armitage told him, "so it's probably not nukes. Smart money's on nano-D warheads."

Nanotechnic disassemblers, packed into a warhead and used as a weapon, the one weapon that could eat through hundreds of meters of blast shielding as easily as through loose earth. *Not* good. . . .

"Nano-Ds are banned under the Geneva Protocols."

"Maybe Roettgen hasn't read them. Or else she's damned desperate."

The Geneva Protocols of 2150, drawn up in the aftermath of Wormwood Fall, formally banned the use of hyperde-structive weapons on Earth—including near-c impactors, asteroid impacts, thermonukes of over one megaton, and, once they became available on a city-wrecking scale, nano-disassemblers.

Of course, there was no international agreement as to just how to punish a rogue state that used such weapons. Nor did the Sh'daar or their client races care anything about human treaties. But the Geneva Protocols were at the very heart of the *Pax Confeoderata*. For Roettgen to go this far in her power grab was astonishing, given that other member-states of the Confederation, especially North India and several of the Pan-Europe states, would condemn her for doing so.

"Damned desperate" didn't seem to cover it by half.

"Give me a virtual channel to Roettgen," Koenig said. He linked into the bunker's communications suite in-head, and waited for the connection to complete.

A long moment passed. In an electronically intercon-nected world where anyone could talk directly to anyone in an instant or two, a delay of ten seconds seemed ridiculous.

"Madam Roettgen does not appear to be accepting your call," Whitney told him. "We're getting her avasec."

"Then I'll talk to that."

Avatar secretaries—avasecs—were digital sentients used by CEOs, government leaders, Net celebrities, and anyone else who needed a degree of insulation from the electronic chatter across the Net. Such personal AIs could be pro-grammed to emulate their owner to a degree that would fool most ordinary callers, could make decisions on the impor-tance of incoming messages, and report back to the owner when it was convenient. They were required to carry a tag identifying them as AIs and not humans, though there were ways around that detail. By leaving her identifying tag in place, Roettgen might be deliberately telling Koenig that she didn't wish to speak with him.

The channel opened, and Roettgen's face appeared in Koenig's mind, indistinguishable from the real person. "This is Madam Roettgen's personal AI secretary," the face said. "The president is not available at—"

"I know," Koenig said. "But you can give her a message for me."

"Recording."

"We are tracking incoming missiles that we believe are fitted with nano-D warheads aimed at one or more of our cities. This is in violation of the Geneva Protocols of 2150, and a serious violation of international law.

"I am willing to believe that some of your military subordinates have . . . ah . . . taken this step without your personal knowledge or approval."

It was a possibility, though Koenig doubted that this was the case. The Chinese Hegemony had distanced themselves from the Wormwood asteroid strike of 2132 by blaming it on a rogue ship commander, and Roettgen might well be hoping to do the same thing. The important thing at the moment was to give her an honorable way out, an excuse rather than trapping her.

"I very much hope that this is the case," Koenig continued, "for *your* sake, Madam President. I promise you that if those city-eaters hit, every detail of the attack will be documented and published across the Net. I doubt very much that the Confederation will survive that sort of—"

The image of President Roettgen changed in his head, the formal business attire replaced by casual clothing, the face becoming harder, sharper, more deeply lined. Even the President of the Confederation Senate wasn't above a bit of electronic vanity, it seemed.

"It's me, President Koenig. For *your* sake, surrender. Now."

"Call off your nano-dogs, Ilse," Koenig replied. "You're destroying the Confederation."

"No, Herr Koenig. It is *you* who are destroying the Pax!"

On the big screen, two more of the incoming warheads were wiped away. There was still a chance. . . .

"I don't see it that way, Madam President. And I certainly am not going to cave in to the threat of high-tech mass murder. Nano-D is expressly—"

"Nano-D?" She looked shocked. "We are not using nano-D. This is some kind of trick." Either she was being truthful or she was a damned good actress.

"We're tracking . . ." He looked up at the big screen again, checking. "We're tracking two warheads inbound from the *Estremadura*. Our best analysis suggests that they are non-nuclear. They're too large to be incendiary, chemical or biological warheads, and too slow to be relativistic kinetic-kill rounds. That would seem to leave nano-D, wouldn't it?"

Pittsburgh managed a precisely targeted long-ranged shot from behind, destroying one of the inbound rounds. Koenig didn't mention it to Roettgen. She would have battlespace sensors as good as those employed by the USNA.

"We have fighters from Washington and from Oceana trying to reach that warhead," Armitage said. "Intercept is going to be damned close. . . ."

"*Kill it,*" Koenig snapped.

"Yes, sir."

"Impact in ten seconds," the AI announced. "Target is now confirmed as Columbus, D.C."

"Damn it, Gene, the Columbus, D.C., metro area has a population of over three million people. . . ."

The warhead traveled those last 300,000 kilometers, more than half the distance from the Earth to the moon, in a few pounding heartbeats, seared into Earth's atmosphere, and plunged on a shaft of superheated ionization toward the geopolitical region known as Ohio. An incoming flight of Starhawks fired their particle beams in unison from 500 kilometers away. . . .

But too late . . . *too late*. The warhead, massing nearly fifty tons, detonated 100 meters above the surface and 300 meters south of the Freedom Concourse, firing a shotgun blast of microscopic dust particles at the ground and towering buildings below. Each dust mote was programmed to reduce anything it touched to its component elements. Water vapor in the air flashed into hydrogen and oxygen atoms; ferrocrete walls dissolved into iron, silica, oxygen, carbon, and other elements; people in the street disintegrated from the top down, evaporating into free carbon, hydrogen, oxygen, nitrogen, phosphorous, sodium, and dozens of others as bonds between atoms were broken and molecules dissolved.

And the dust kept moving, kept devouring as it ate into the buildings and the parklands and vegetation and walkways between them.

The energy in all of those molecular bonds amounted to a very great deal of heat, and in an instant, the fireball was growing, swelling, rising on a column of superheated air. Much of the nanodust was destroyed in the fireball, but far more reached the ground within the next second and continued eating its way into the surface. The destruction, now, was uneven. Partial buildings began to fall as winds kicked up by the heat shrieked with hurricane force. Sections of pavement caved in . . . skyscrapers crumbled, floor upon floor collapsing down onto lower floors in roiling clouds of dust. Horribly, many humans caught in the open were only partially disintegrated, randomly mutilated by the fast-spreading plague.

Most of those who didn't die immediately were immolated in the firestorm sweeping through the heart of the city.

Stunned, Koenig and the bunker staff watched the devastation by way of surveillance cameras and drones throughout the city above them. As the drones began succumbing to the nano attack in rapid succession, the view jumped back in jerky steps, revealing a yawning, still-spreading crater with a white-hot interior, collapsing rubble, a spreading ring of roiling dust. They could feel none of this in the bunker 2 kilometers down, but graphics on secondary monitors showed the destruction gnawing down through bedrock toward them.

On the surface directly overhead, the Executive Tower, half eaten away, began to fall. . . .

Chapter Twenty-Two

TC/USNA CVS America
Osiris space, 70 Ophiuchi AII
0715 hours, TFT

The *America* battle group had burst out of metaspace well beyond the 40-AU limit and immediately launched her fighters. After that, they began accelerating at high-G boost sunward, a journey of almost six light hours.

CBG-40 was deployed in three assault waves. Leading the way, all by herself, was the ancient cargo freighter *Altair*.

The *Altair* was listed as a fleet auxiliary vessel. She didn't have an Alcubierre drive, couldn't travel faster than light, and so made jumps across the light years nestled into a hollow along the much larger *Shenandoah*'s spine. Her grav drives could accelerate her at ten thousand gravities, allowing her to match the pace of the rest of the fleet.

She'd been designed and launched nearly a century and a half earlier and, despite numerous updates to her drives and computer network, was considered to be well past her expected life span. She'd been retained on the fleet lists because new ships were expensive and because after the Sh'daar Ultimatum of 2367, fleet appropriations had focused on conventional FTL warships—on battle cruisers, destroyers, and star carriers like *America*.

And mostly, of course, she'd been retained because she still *worked*. Provisioning vessels like *Shenandoah* would maneuver into a resource-rich zone—an asteroid belt, perhaps, or the fringes of a gas-giant ring system—and deploy robot miners to begin breaking down and returning raw materials to the ship. Resource freighters like *Altair* could be deployed to more remote areas, load up on water ice, carbon, iron, or other resources, and return them to *Shenandoah*'s capacious bunkers. The *Altair* had facilities on board for a small crew—six or eight people—but normally was deployed as a robot under the command of an AI. Even with near-*c* capabilities, mining operations tended to be long, drawn-out affairs that taxed human operators with their monotony.

Altair currently was carrying some fifteen hundred tons of asteroidal debris—the maximum load possible for a freighter of her class. Since the earliest years of the twenty-first century, it had been understood that most asteroids were loosely bound collections of smaller rocks and debris enclosed within a blanketing shroud of dust. *Fluffy* was the word often used to describe them, though even a small asteroid represented tens of billions of tons of fluff. *Altair* had rendezvoused with this particular mass half an astronomical unit from Goewin, using her on-board fleet of robot miners to pull a small fraction of the asteroid into pieces and loading them into her cargo bays. Most of her cargo consisted now of closely packed rubble, the spaces between each rock filled in with dust. She'd cast loose from *Shenandoah* moments after emergence from metaspace, swung to orient on Osiris, and kicked in her full, ten-thousand-G acceleration.

Altair was uncrewed, save for her on-board AI.

Next behind the *Altair* were four squadrons of fighters, launched from the star carrier *America* beginning immediately after emergence, formed into open strike formation, and boosted to near-*c*. This time, they didn't use their full acceleration; it was important to remain in formation astern of the *Altair*.

And finally came the capital ships—*America* and sixteen smaller vessels, escorted by *America*'s two remaining fighter squadrons. *Shenandoah* accompanied the formation, following in *America*'s gravitational wake. She was unarmed save for mining and sampling lasers, and possessed little in the way of armor. Gray had not wanted to leave her unescorted at the edge of the Osirian system, however, where her isolation would make her an easy target for any passing Sh'daar warships in the area . . . and where she would be five and a half light hours away from learning the outcome of the battle, or anything else happening in close to the local star. Nor was Gray willing to detail a destroyer—or even just a couple of fighters—to stay behind with her out there on the cold, dark fringes of the system. He needed every weapon he had for the attack on the Sh'daar forces.

Besides, her skipper, Captain Linda Alvarez, had volunteered to make the fly-by of Osiris with the rest of the force. She could at the very least draw off a little of the enemy's defensive fire from the warships, and just maybe there was something else she could contribute to the battle. Gray and *America*'s command group had worked out the details during the flight out from Arianrhod.

The *Shenandoah* might be able to contribute more to the fight than simply being a target.

Gray sat in the command chair, watching the big screen on the forward bulkhead, allowing his in-head to add details and downloaded data as it became available. The *c*-fog was slowly clearing as the squadron hurtled down the dark light-hours, getting closer and closer to the objective. At a range now of just thirty light minutes, they were seeing events transpiring around Osiris that had happened just half an hour before. There'd been no outlying squadrons, no pickets on the way in. The entire enemy fleet appeared to be concentrated in orbit around Osiris—and over the past few minutes they'd been spreading out in a cloud extending perhaps a half million kilometers from the planet. The tactical idea would be to keep their ships spread out so that one nuke couldn't destroy more than one vessel . . . and to give them more options for fire and maneuver when the human squadron passed through. There were, Gray noted, now that they were close enough to detect them on radar, a large number of inert objects—several tens of thousands of them—dispersing across the fleet's path. Those would be obstacle mines, O-mines, and were probably nothing but lumps of rock. A ship hitting one at near-c, however, would be vaporized.

The good news was that even tens of thousands of O-mines would be all but lost when scattered through many billions of cubic kilometers of space. The chance of any of the human ships hitting one were relatively low. They were a threat, but not strategically significant.

Thirty light minutes out . . . but at 0.997 c the subjective time on board the human ships would pass at a rate of thirteen to one—just two minutes and eighteen seconds.

Altair, he thought, was getting close to her flash point.

Lieutenant Donald Gregory
VFA-96, Black Demons
Osiris Space, 70 Ophiuchi AII
0715 hours, TFT

His unaided vision showed only the weirdly compressed starbow colors of relativistic flight, but his AI fed Gregory images teased from the distortion and made intelligible. He studied the unfolding display through his in-head, watching as his AI identified ship classes and assigned potential targets as they emerged from the c-fog. Fifty-seven enemy ships ID'd so far . . . three quarters of them *big* ones, Slan Ballistas and Trebuchets; Turusch Papa, Romeo, and Sierra-class cruisers. Perhaps a quarter were ship designs unknown to Gregory's warbook, and representing, therefore, new species with unknown technologies and capabilities.

Gregory stared at the image of the planet—at Osiris, his home.

Osiris—70 Ophiuchi AII—was one of the very few garden

worlds known to Humankind . . . a planet with a breathable atmosphere, a temperate climate, and an evolved biochemistry similar to Earth's, a place where humans could walk in the open without environmental suits or oxygen masks. Humans couldn't eat the native life—the local sugars were left-handed rather than right, a tiny difference in evolutions that meant they couldn't utilize Osirian nutrients—but numerous gene-tailored Earth species had adapted well since their introduction in 2214, and by now perhaps a quarter of the sprawling southern continent had been taken over by the imported ecology. The capital city, New Egypt, had had a population of more than 5 million; the colony as a whole had numbered around 12 million, with cities like Luxor, Sais, and Dendara scattered from the Aten Sea to Point Horus. There was even a native species that might be sentient—the Marine cuttlewyrm—though communicating with an atechnic species that apparently exchanged information by changing color patterns on its mantle posed some unique problems for the xenosoph people.

The world still harbored some enigmatic mysteries. Chief of these was the speed of evolution on the surface, the result, planetologists thought, of high radiation from the sunspot-tortured type K0 primary. The system was believed to be less than 2 billion years old, compared with 4.6 billion years for Earth, and yet surface vegetation and the exuberant marine surface flora had generated oxygen enough to make the atmosphere breathable for humans. When Earth had been 2 billion years old, the highest form of life in her zoosphere were single-celled algae and bacteria that hadn't yet even invented sex. The cuttlewyrms and their kin had not developed backbones as yet—they were similar to the squid and octopi of Earth's seas—but they did possess highly complex nervous systems, and their behavior suggested a keen if bizarrely alien intelligence.

Gregory's family had been xenobiologists studying the cuttlewyrms from a research colony at New Alexandria, up on the Naucratis Coast.

No one knew how many of those people were still alive

there, twenty years after the Sh'daar had moved in and taken over. New Egypt had been nuked, that much was known. It was possible that none of the human population had survived . . . including Gregory's family.

Twenty years was a long, long time.

The worst of it was that in a few moments, Gregory would be hurtling past the world he'd once called home, at a hairbreadth beneath the speed of light, with little to no chance whatsoever of learning whether there were humans still on the planet.

His family . . .

Donald Gregory remembered clearly the chaos at the Nuit Starport outside the capital, with oily smoke hanging in vast clouds that cast shadows across the city. Despite the posttraumatic memory therapy, he still had dreams . . . nightmares. . . .

He remembered the lines of refugee children, remembered screaming that he didn't want to go. He remembered clinging to his mother, and the pain in her eyes and in his father's voice. *"Don't worry, Donny. We'll be together again soon. I promise you."*

His mother had been crying . . . his last memory of her.

"So how's it feel to be going home, Nungie?" Kemper asked him over the tactical net. Gregory was so entangled in the memories of an eight-year-old boy that he didn't even feel the jab of that hated handle.

"Don't know, Happy," he replied. "I'm not going home, am I?"

"Might be a good thing," Kemper said. "After we *c*-gun that planet, there might not be much left of it!"

"Heads up, people," Mackey snapped. "Thirty seconds subjective! And the *Altair*'s gonna blow in—"

And on his corrected in-head display, the freighter *Altair* flared into a dazzling white star.

In fact, Kemper was being his usual asshole self, poking at him just to get an emotional rise out of him. *Altair*'s course had been precisely planned, and tweaked on the way in to make sure that Osiris was not in the line of fire.

Still, even the best-planned vectors could be affected by very minor and unforeseen elements of the local gravitational matrix, and the detonation of tons of chemical high explosive might well—would almost certainly—shift a few random bits of debris into unpredictable intercept paths with the planet.

A quarter of a million kilometers ahead of Gregory's fighter, the freighter *Altair* and her cargo had been transformed into a fast-spreading cloud of debris, over two thousand tons of matter ranging in size from multi-ton chunks of the disintegrated freighter down to dust- and sand-grain-sized specks, all of them traveling at 99.7 percent of the speed of light. At that velocity, even flecks of paint from *Altair*'s hull carried the kinetic punch of several kilograms of high explosive. The tactic was officially known as relativistic bombardment, and had been introduced by "Sandy" Gray two decades ago. Most people called it *c*-gunning, because it was like firing an immense shotgun at the enemy . . . but with the pellets moving at relativistic speeds.

And a large portion of the Sh'daar fleet was orbiting now in the path of that deadly cloud of projectiles.

Slan Protector Vigilant
Extended Orbit, 70 Ophiuchi AII
0716 hours, TFT

Clear Chiming Bell expanded its ear membranes around its body, the better to focus on the audio representation of *Vigilant*'s surroundings, a vast gulf of emptiness punctuated by pure tones representing ships, and anchored by a deep and richly textured rumble that was the planet half a million *t!!t* distant. The ship tones were overlaid by complex harmonics giving information on vector—direction and speed. Only moments before, a series of targets had appeared moving inbound at very nearly the speed of light itself. The Slan commander clicked out orders . . . and then the nearest of the approaching targets exploded, its pure tone replaced by a fluttering, fast-rising cacophony of harmonies and near-harmonies indicating small fragments hurtling toward the Sh'daar fleet.

Ships around the *Vigilant* began vaporizing as fragments plowed through them. *Vigilant* was hit, the deck lurching sharply as warning tones sounded. The ship's gravity flickered a few times, then died . . . and Clear Chiming Bell drifted helplessly into the center of the compartment.

Slan were not well-adapted for zero gravity. They could thrash the fringe of tentacles around their heavy mantle, but their bodies were too massive for that to give them much momentum in any direction. Clear Chiming Bell was helpless.

The humans. The humans they'd encountered at the other planetary system—it had to be them. Clear Chiming Bell had reported the Slan defeat to the Sh'daar net when they arrived at this gathering place, of course, and warned of the possibility that they would be coming here. Clear Chiming Bell had hoped this would not be the case, however. The humans were . . . *disturbing* in the intensity with which they waged war.

It had seen records gleaned from the human computer networks. These creatures were capable of . . . of atrocities on a planetary scale. They seemed to care little for community as Clear Chiming Bell understood the concept, and they seemed capable of fighting to the death, literally unable to know when to quit. That alien twist made them deadly to the Sh'daar Alliance. Communicating with the strange, blind creatures was definitely preferable to fighting them, but the Sh'daar Seed within the growing fleet here at the *Hu-vah-scha'n* staging area had ordered them to proceed with preparations for the attack on the human homeworld.

But the humans had just fired an unknown but powerful relativistic weapon at the Sh'daar fleet. Their warships would be close behind that first strike, seeking to follow up their advantage. Clear Chiming Bell was not sure that the Sh'daar ships could mount an effective defense.

The Slan commander could still speak to its subordinates,

even if it couldn't reach the controls. "Launch all fighters!" it chattered. "Quickly! Quickly!"

Acknowledgement came back from several stations, including the auxiliary command center. The ship was damaged, but still operational.

"Get the gravity working again!" it snapped. "And ready all ship weapons for close combat!"

To fight the humans, Clear Chiming Bell thought, it would be necessary to match their warlike demeanor . . . to fight them all-out, without quarter, until their homeworld and all of their colonies had been reduced to radioactive rubble. The Slan hated that thought; it was disgusting . . . *alien*, and yet Clear Chiming Bell could see no alternative.

The Sh'daar Alliance would have to destroy the humans to the last blind, living creature . . . or the Alliance itself might be destroyed.

Lieutenant Donald Gregory
VFA-96, Black Demons
Osiris Space, 70 Ophiuchi AII
0716 hours, TFT

On his in-head, time adjusted so that he could see what was happening, Gregory watched the scattering of bright flares across the volume occupied by the enemy fleet, as pieces of the *Altair* and chunks of rock slammed into and through fragile metal and ceramic at near-*c*. Each impact released unimaginable torrents of raw kinetic energy as intense heat, as light and hard radiation, as savage impact. He saw half a dozen flashes across the night side of Osiris as well, and inwardly flinched.

God willing, those missiles hadn't landed near cities occupied by humans. Six impactors out of tens of thousands wasn't a bad percentage, but the collateral damage down there might still be unacceptably high. Even if the cities had been spared direct impacts, they might well be doomed by the water strikes.

Twenty years earlier, a Turusch kinetic-kill impactor massing less than a kilogram had struck the Atlantic Ocean at relativistic speed. The tidal wave generated by that attack had scoured the Periphery of North America, and low-lying portions of Europe, South America, and Africa as well, killing tens of millions of people. Similar tidal waves were spreading out now from dozens of impacts in Osiris's north-hemisphere ocean. If anything was left of New Egypt or the other colony cities down there near the coast, the tsunamis might well wash them all into barren nonexistence.

Were there humans down there after twenty years?

Had the c-gun blast just killed any who might have survived?

The damned Sh'daar had owned Osiris for so long now that the chances were good there were no humans left to suffer the effects of friendly fire. There was no time to worry about it . . . or to think about lost parents and relatives.

"Ready with the sandcaster rounds!" Mackey ordered. "On my mark in three . . . two . . . one . . . *fire*!"

Twelve AS-78 AMSO missiles dropped from his Starhawk and accelerated. They wouldn't be able to get that far ahead of the hurtling flight of SG-92s, but they did slip into trajectories carrying them toward the densest concentrations of Sh'daar spacecraft. In rapid, ripple-fire sequence, the AMSO rounds detonated, sending clouds of matter-compressed lead spherules toward the enemy in expanding, cone-shaped clouds, if anything, more deadly and precise than the use of the *Altair* as a relativistic shotgun.

Seconds later, the rounds began exploding . . . many of them in apparently empty space between the fighters and the planet. O-mines, Gregory thought. Obstacle mines orbiting through battle space to block a relativistic fly-by like this one. The sand might clear a path through the artificial debris fields.

And then enemy spacecraft were being struck as well, a devastating volley of high-energy destruction sleeting through them at the speed of light. Explosions flashed and swelled and faded, like multitudes of lightning flashes seen in thick clouds from orbit, ghostly and utterly silent.

But Gregory had no time to more than glimpse the multiple flares of raw light. In seconds, his fighter plunged into the Osirian battlespace. Human reflexes and perceptions were far too slow to handle the flood of data pouring through his data links. His AI took charge of his weapons systems, delivering missiles and particle beams at targets selected moments before, all while jinking wildly to avoid enemy missiles, mines, and other fighters. In seconds, his entire warload of missiles had been expended. Explosions blossomed around him, most in the distance, a few terrifyingly near. A Black Demon fighter 12 kilometers off his starboard side vanished in white-hot fury as it struck a Sh'daar obstacle-mine overlooked by the sandcaster rounds. He checked the roster: Lieutenant Caryl Mason. She could not have felt what hit her.

Another Black Demon fighter flared and vanished. Jason Del Rey . . . his fighter hit by a Slan positron beam. Those beams were everywhere now, slashing, weaving an intricate and deadly web across the path of the incoming fighters.

Other fighters in other squadrons were dying now . . . striking O-mines or taking fire from the Sh'daar warfleet surrounding them. Sh'daar ships were dying as well. Gregory was all too aware that the survival of the *America* battlegroup depended on how much damage the fighters did to the enemy fleet now.

And yet the actual battle now was in the metaphorical hands of the AIs, machines with far faster reflexes than mere humans.

Two kilometers off his starboard side, Jodi Vaughn's fighter took a glancing hit from a positron beam, fragments of her Starhawk exploding into a cascade of white-hot stars . . . and then what was left of her fighter seemed to crumple in upon itself, collapsing, compressing . . . then disappearing, as the wreckage was devoured within the singularity powering her ship.

"Jodi!" he yelled, unable to silence the anguished scream.

Somehow the fears for family lost these twenty years paled at the death of someone loved here and now. Jodi . . .

She'd been friend and confidant, far more than playmate. And she was gone in a fraction of an eyeblink.

Something huge flashed across his port side, and then he was past, hurtling on into deep space. Lieutenant Andrew Bennings died on the way out.

The entire battle had lasted only for as long as it took a fighter traveling at close to the speed of light to plunge through the battlespace volume, a sphere roughly 1 million kilometers across . . . three and a third seconds.

The battle was over almost before Gregory could register the fact, and there'd been precious little he could have done to affect the outcome. His AI maintained control of the Starhawk . . . and a very good thing, too. He was numb, unable to move, unable to think.

A frequent argument heard both back at Fleet Command HQ and in the squadron recreation decks on board fleet star carriers held that crewed fighters were anachronisms, that a strike fighter could do its job purely under robotic control. Most human pilots, however, stubbornly held that there were mission elements that demanded a human brain—albeit one with cybernetic enhancement and AI links. As far as Gregory was concerned, robots were good—and vital for operations at near-c—but you still needed a human in the loop to make the decisions upon which human lives depended.

Except that, right now, Gregory wasn't entirely human. *Jodi* . . .

Quite often in modern combat, the human element simply wasn't in the equation. As feeling returned, shock and a numb emptiness replaced by anger and a searing hatred, Gregory was ready to flip end for end and re-engage the enemy. He wanted to kill them, burn them, punish them for what they'd done to Jodi . . . to Mason and Del Rey and Bennings and all the others . . . to his family . . . he wanted to kill them . . . *kill them.* . . .

In a standard planetary assault, the squadron's pilots would have spun their fighters about, decelerated, then boosted back into the battlespace around the planet, re-engaging the enemy and awaiting the arrival of the fleet. The squadron's orders this time, however, were to keep moving; they would rendezvous with *America* out near the 40-AU limit, assuming, of course, that the star carrier survived the next few moments.

America and the other capital ships of the fleet would be running the Sh'daar gauntlet in less than five minutes.

Gregory was left to sit within the embrace of his fighter, alone with some very dark thoughts.

TC/USNA CVS America
Osiris space, 70 Ophiuchi AII
0721 hours, TFT

At a whisper below the speed of light, *America*'s battle-group dropped into the fire-wracked volume of space surrounding Osiris. Captain Gray was hyperlinked with the ship's main AI, which allowed him to perceive events transpiring outside the ship at an accelerated rate. He would pay for the privilege later in migraines and insomnia that normal nanomeds couldn't touch. He'd worry about that later. Right now, he needed, somehow, to penetrate the *c*-fog and understand what was happening.

Out of fifty-seven Sh'daar vessels that had shown up on the initial scans of the area around the planet, twelve appeared to have been destroyed, and perhaps another nineteen were disabled, an excellent outcome for the first strike. Some of the disabled ships, however, would likely be back in action soon as their damage control protocols took effect . . . and there were still at least twenty-six Sh'daar capital ships untouched and awaiting the human battlegroup's arrival.

So the odds were down to seventeen to twenty-six. Those odds weren't good, but they weren't impossibly bad either. Sh'daar battle fleets, Gray knew, had trouble with efficient command control after being *c*-gunned, especially when they were mixed fleets. Spread out as they were, it might be possible to engage a few enemy ships at a time, overwhelming them with the massed firepower of the entire human fleet.

At least, that was the idea. *America*'s battlegroup flashed down through the last few tens of millions of kilometers and entered the contested battlespace, releasing clouds of AMSO rounds and long-range antiship missiles to blast out a clear path for themselves.

The railgun cruiser *Turner* engaged the enemy directly first, slamming high-velocity rounds into a lone H'rulka warship, a kilometer-wide sphere apparently already damaged by the fighter strike. *America* exchanged fire with a Turusch Romeo, then, a second later, with a Slan Ballista. The heavy cruiser *Washington* was struck by a barrage of KK projectiles and vanished in a searing blaze of starcore light. The accompanying fighters engaged Turusch Toads and Slan Stilettos.

Ships on both sides died, vaporizing in intense nova flares of light and hard radiation . . . or tumbling helplessly in clouds of shredding wreckage . . . or collapsing into the black holes of their own gravitic drives and power plants.

Gray's mind, accelerated through the ship's AI, watched, catalogued, analyzed, calculated. In modern fleet combat, often the best a fleet commander could do was set all of the pieces in motion, then just sit back and watch as the resulting battle played itself out across a handful of seconds. There simply was no time to react as the two fleets interpenetrated, no possibility of changing tactics or outmaneuvering the enemy. You lived or died, succeeded or failed based on your initial planning and the luck of the draw.

The enemy ships, Gray saw, were widely dispersed across the target battlespace, and the damaged ones were having trouble maneuvering to meet the human fleet's onslaught. Through his AI links to the rest of the battlegroup, he directed his ships to focus on the undamaged enemy ships. The objective for the operation, after all, was to cause enough damage to the entire Sh'daar fleet that they would not launch their own assault on the Sol System and Earth.

Damaged ships might be repaired and brought back on-line, but that would take time, and damaged ships would not be able to make the faster-than-light passage across sixteen light years to Earth.

The number of damaged Sh'daar ships was up to twenty-five, now, with six more destroyed. That left just fourteen untouched enemy vessels. The human battlegroup had suffered five losses so far—all of them destroyed. The odds had dropped to twelve to fourteen . . . and Gray made a command decision.

"Comm," he snapped.

"Comm here, sir."

"Make to all ships. Initiate deceleration and engage the enemy at non-rel velocities. Order the strike fighters to decelerate immediately and rejoin the fleet in battlespace."

"Aye-*aye*, sir!"

"We are still heavily outnumbered, Captain Gray," the AI pointed out with emotionless reserve. "Besides the fourteen undamaged warships, there are twenty-five damaged Sh'daar vessels. While the damaged ships are having difficulty maneuvering, most appear to have their weapons systems intact."

"I know," Gray replied. "But this is our chance to *end* this thing, once and for all! It's why we're here!"

"Understood. We have passed through the battlespace, and are now initiating deceleration. The other ships of the battlegroup have acknowledged the order, and are decelerating as well."

CBG-40 began the cumbersome evolution of reversing course.

Astern, the enemy slowly and clumsily maneuvered to meet them.

Chapter Twenty-Three

Slan Protector Vigilant
Extended Orbit, 70 Ophiuchi AII
0723 hours, TFT

Damage to the *Vigilant*, it turned out, was relatively slight. Clear Chiming Bell had at last made it to the deck by snapping its ear flaps shut, then slowly opening them, using puffs of expelled air to waft itself back to its control station. Shortly after that, the ship's artificial gravity was restored, and the weapons came back on-line.

Vigilant was again ready for combat.

The human fleet had devastated the assembled Sh'daar forces. There was still a chance to pull things together, however, *if* the Sh'daar Masters could pull some organization out of the chaos of multi-specific discordance.

The Sh'daar, as the Slan experienced them, existed as a kind of electronic network nestled within the linkages between minute computers implanted within billions of individuals of a number of mutually alien species. The net at the star the humans called 36 Ophiuchi had been relatively small, non-sentient, and limited in scope to observing and recording events. The net here at the staging area was larger and better realized, with hundreds of computer nodes in the various ships and on the surface of the planet.

The problem the Sh'daar faced, however—their single, sometimes overwhelming weakness—lay in that mutual alienness of their subject species. The Slan could understand the H'rulka fairly well—titanic gasbags evolved within the atmosphere of a gas giant world who communicated using natural radio. The Turusch, dual-brained beings that thought and spoke in harmonies that gave rise to nested meanings, were far more difficult to relate to. A third Sh'daar-dominated species, the Agletsch, had developed a kind of *lingua franca* allowing interspecies communication with a wide variety of Galactic cultures, but in fact that worked only with beings physiologically capable of working within a certain range of sounds locked into a claustrophobically narrow band of frequencies.

It was unlikely that even the Sh'daar themselves, whatever they really were, fully understood their subject races, that they understood them well enough to truly communicate with them. They nudged, they urged, they suggested . . . but they couldn't *lead*.

Nor could they explain. Clear Chiming Bell knew from its few times of direct linkings with the Sh'daar that something about the humans terrified them. Something had happened that had led to a truce, of sorts, with the humans . . . but then something else had happened, forcing the Sh'daar to, once again, attempt to destroy them.

The nature of the threat, however, appeared incommunicable. For a species that used sound both to communicate and to reveal its surroundings in precise detail, that failure of clarity was bewildering, a failure verging on . . . sin.

The Masters had shown the Slan the stars. They'd helped the Slan leave the world, the caverns of their birth, and cross the aching emptiness to other worlds. They'd shown the Slan worlds similar enough to their birthworld—like the humans' Arianrhod—that they'd become a truly Galactic species, potentially immortal, spreading across hundreds of Slan-friendly worlds.

Were they also capable of *k'!k't!'cht'!k'!kt'!!!k*?

Were they in fact withholding or distorting information in an immoral way?

Or were the Sh'daar literally incapable of communicating clear and precise meaning about the humans?

Either possibility was . . . disturbing.

The enemy vessels appeared to be decelerating. They would be returning to the death-blasted gulf around the planet to complete what they'd begun.

Clear Chiming Bell gave the orders for the Slan contingent to meet them.

Lieutenant Donald Gregory
VFA-96, Black Demons
Osiris Space, 70 Ophiuchi AII
0725 hours, TFT

The orders had just come through: they were re-uniting with the battlegroup, then returning together to Osiris! Gregory's deepest longing, a need that had been driving him, gnawing at him since the age of eight had just been handed to him by an arbitrary decision made out of the blue by the brass back on board the *America*, and the realization left him weak, almost paralyzed.

The fact that it had been handed to him hard on the heels of Jodi's death had plunged him into a swirling emotional black hole from which there seemed to be no escape whatsoever.

Home.

The word scarcely carried meaning for Gregory any longer.

Somehow, he'd managed to wall off the shock of Jodi's sudden death, but he still felt an all-embracing numbness that left him moving along on auto-pilot. As he'd continued hurtling out-system, away from the fire-blasted horrors of Osiris, he'd stopped thinking about home and family. Right now, he didn't want to think about *anything*. . . .

Gradually, as minute followed relativistically compressed

minute, the numbness receded, replaced by a fierce and unrelenting fury.

Was home something he could fight for if Jodi's death had
been the price?

And would it be home any longer? It would be, he realized with a sick twisting in his gut, a home that had been
occupied by enemy aliens for twenty years, a world where
home and loved ones might well have been incinerated two
aching decades before.

Despite this, he found that he welcomed the decision
by *America*'s command staff. Apparently the destruction
wrought by *Altair*'s sacrifice, by the high-velocity passage of
four fighter squadrons, and by the fly-by of the battlegroup
itself had, all together, hurt the enemy enough that Captain
Gray had decided to stay and fight.

"So, Nungie," Kemper said over the tactical channel.
"You get to go home after all, huh? Heh. I wouldn't count
on your relatives waiting at the spaceport for ya, though!"

"Leave him alone, Happy," Nichols snapped. "Stop riding
him."

Ted Nichols and Gregory hadn't been particularly close.
He was a quiet and somewhat reserved pilot from Ottawa
and a member of the Navy's aristocratic elite, and that alone
always had put up a barrier between him and the colonial
from Osiris.

But he *had* known that Gregory and Jodi were . . . involved.

"Fuck, I ain't riding the poor bastard, Teddy. The fact is,
colonials are as bad as Prims. They shouldn't be wearing
fighters in the first place!"

And that, Gregory thought, was the overwhelming weakness of the Confederation space-fighter arm, that twisted
sense of better-than-thou privilege, of *elitism* that separated
pilots into "us" and the have-not "thems." The sheer, fucking aristocratic arrogance of most of the pilots infuriated
Gregory, left him shaking inside . . . and, very slowly, it
helped him focus.

He wouldn't let them win, wouldn't let them put him

down or Prims like Jodi. He was as good as any of them, and by God he would prove it.

He was going *home*, and whether home and family were still there or not, he would help kick the aliens off Osiris and make the place his home once more.

"Eat my fucking wake, Kemper," he growled. "I'll see you at Osiris."

TC/USNA CVS America
Osiris space, 70 Ophiuchi AII
0729 hours, TFT

It would take almost fifty minutes for the *America* battle-group to kill its forward velocity, by which time it would have traveled almost 450 million kilometers . . . or three more AUs. Call it three more hours before they would be able to re-engage the enemy. The fighter squadrons, well out ahead of the fleet, nonetheless would be able to cancel their forward velocity in about five minutes and, boosting at fifty thousand gravities, would be able to make it back to the planet and match local vectors in something less than another eight minutes.

But the fighters would be low on expendables—missiles, AMSO rounds, and KK projectiles—having dumped as much in the way of munitions as possible during the brief moments of their Osirian fly-by. They would still be able to generate laser and particle beams, of course, so long as their quantum power plants were still functioning, but they would be at a serious disadvantage with an enemy that could mag-netically shield against incoming charged particles.

And so Gray had directed Connie Fletcher to bring the squadrons back on board America. There would be some tricky maneuvering involved; the fighters would have to pass *America* on the outbound leg of her flight path, turn around, accelerate to catch up, then dock while *America* killed her own acceleration in order to accommodate the trapping squadrons. They would lose some time, too, since the carrier could not be under acceleration while fighters were land-ing. There were just too many vector variables involved in an operation where a mistake of a tenth of a percent would still result in a difference in relative velocities of hundreds of kilometers per *second* and a staggering release of kinetic energy that would vaporize the fighter and cripple the star carrier. Safer by far to have *America* cut her acceleration for the time necessary to bring her chicks back on board.

The squadrons would re-arm, then launch again during the return flight.

And this time they would stay within the battlespace until the big boys joined them.

For Gray, the real agony lay in the big unknown. Would enough of the battle-damaged Sh'daar warships be able to repair themselves during those intervening three hours to put the human battlegroup at an impossible disadvantage when the fight was rejoined? There was no clear answer to that. The enemy had nanomatrix hull construction—or its alien equivalent—allowing them to repair damage in fairly short order. The Slan HQ ship had suffered serious pressure loss in the fight at Arianrhod, but had repaired the damage, at least to an extent, by the time the Marines boarded her.

The problem was that comparing technologies between mutually alien cultures was not a comparison of apples and oranges, which at least were both related as fruit. Human technology was different from Turusch technology which was different from Slan technology not only because the latter two were more advanced, but because the thinking, the ways of looking at the universe, and the histories of the steps leading to the present in each culture were dif-ferent as well. A being's language, sophontologists argued, helped shape how it perceived the universe and how its brain worked at a basic, quantum level. Mutually alien technolo-gies, it seemed, could be compared only in certain gross and relatively inefficient ways—by measuring the relative energy outputs of starship drive arrays, for example. The Slan could do that trick of accelerating at high-G inside the 40-AU limit of a star's gravitational matrix, a clear advantage over human vessels, but, if anything, their beam energy outputs in combat were a bit less than the human equivalents. They also seemed to have a different philosophy about warfare—for them, it was more of a test of strength and will between two able parties than it was one of enforcing one's political will over another—and that appeared to have a bearing on their technology as well.

No, not apples and oranges. Stars and sea cucumbers, maybe.

And that left Gray wondering how good the enemy force would be three hours hence, when battle was rejoined. Damn it, the human force needed an advantage, something to help tip the scales in their favor.

He had one hidden ace, in the *Shenandoah*, and the wrinkle he'd explored already with Linda Alvarez, her skipper.

And just maybe he had another one as well.

Emergency Presidential Command Post
Toronto, Ontario
United States of North America
1005 hours, EST

"My God, they made a job of it, didn't they?"

President Koenig sat before the monitor, watching the scenes being transmitted from a cloud of news-camera drones swarming over the former capital of the United States of North America. What had been the center of the city of Columbus was now pocked by a gigantic bowl-shaped crater nearly three kilometers across and almost half a kilometer deep. A ring around the crater reaching another five kilometers had been burned out by the fireball. There was no radioactivity as there would have been in a nuclear strike, but the damage nevertheless was appalling.

The Scioto River tumbled now over the smooth curve of the crater's northwestern edge, a waterfall vanishing into steam clouds deep inside the crater's depths. Other rivers on the east side of the city were vainly attempting to fill the hole as well. It would be a while before the crater's depths cooled enough that the infalling water no longer flashed into steam on the way down. When that happened, the crater would slowly become an almost perfectly circular lake.

Geneva's strategy, Koenig's advisors thought, had been to fire a succession of nano-D warheads into the crater, creating a cascade of destruction that would have eaten all the way down to the Executive Towers' deepest, most heavily armored basement and devoured it. Fortunately, only one warhead had struck, and the trillions of nano-disassemblers it had unleashed had run through their limited lifetime before they'd gotten beneath the half-kilometer mark.

In any case, the president, his cabinet, and much of the USNA Congress was no longer in the underground bunker. Shortly after the destruction of the city above, they'd been hustled onto a special maglev train that had zipped them silently away through an evacuation tunnel running deep and straight through the Earth's crust, traveling the 500 kilometers northeast to the city of Toronto in less than ten minutes. Still the capital of Ontario and the largest city of the Canadian provinces, Toronto's downtown York Civic Complex had office space enough to accommodate the USNA government, at least for the time being. It would be crowded—Koenig's own staff was packed into small offices three and four to a room, and his own office was smaller than Marcus Whitney's office back in D.C.

No matter. They would manage. By *God* they would manage!

Communications relays, throughout the USNA and in space, were being set up to allow Koenig and his people to communicate with the outside world—including with Geneva—without giving away their actual physical location.

There would be no repeat of Columbus. Koenig had vowed this.

That the damage to Columbus had been only a crater a half kilometer deep—well, thank the *Pittsburgh*, the *Amazon* and the *Missouri* for that blessing! Their last-ditch stand out in trans-lunar space had kept the rest of the warheads from reaching the ground, and had likely saved the USNA government from the Confederation's attempt at political decapitation.

Whitney knocked on his open door, and Koenig looked up. "Ah, Marcus. Do we have a channel open to Roettgen yet?"

"No, sir. Not a word out of them. Intelligence thinks that maybe she was caught by surprise, that a rogue element fired that nano-D. If so, they must be scrambling like demons to cover their asses now."

"We may be able to use that," Koenig said. "We can believe them if they claim it was a rogue admiral launching that attack." *Just like with the Chinese Hegemony almost three centuries ago*, he added, keeping the depressing thought to himself. *We give them a way to save face, to back away from their mistake . . . and maybe the human species survives for just a bit longer. At least until the* next *crisis.*

But damn it, just once it would be nice if a government could be held accountable for its actions.

"Yes, sir," Whitney said. "But there's other news."

"Eh? What?" Until the command center's communications network was fully up and working, Koenig couldn't have automatic data feeds coming through to his in-head. It was frustrating how *slow* information could travel.

"A message drone came through from CBG-Forty a few hours ago. The signal just now reached Synchorbit, and was relayed non-Net to General Mancuso."

And *that* gave a good indication of how screwed up communications could be, vital information coming in through private calls to his generals. The Hexagon had been damaged by the Confederation attack on Columbus, but not destroyed. Mancuso had most of his staff hidden away now down in the Hexagon's labyrinthine subsurface warrens.

"Tell me."

"Carrier Battlegroup Forty had a break with the rest of the task force at Thirty-six Ophiuchi. The Confederation elements are probably returning to the Sol System under the command of Captain Lavallée. Admiral Steiger is dead. So is Admiral Delattre. Captain Gray has taken command of the USNA ships and is en route to Seventy Ophiuchi."

"Seventy fucking Ophiuchi!" Koenig yelled, his voice ringing from the walls of the narrow room. "Why in God's name is he going *there*?"

"We don't have a lot of details, sir," Whitney said. He sounded nervous in the face of Koenig's fury. "But Gray reports that the Sh'daar appear to be massing at Osiris for a strike at Earth. He intends to launch a spoiling raid . . . maybe delay them, maybe make them think twice about even trying it."

Koenig sank back in his chair, relief warring with rage. Damn it, he needed Gray and his ships *here*, not sixteen light years away at 70 Oph.

And yet, if he'd managed to block a Sh'daar strike at Earth . . .

He sighed. Even with ultra high-velocity message drones, it was impossible to manage a battlegroup light years away. When he'd commanded CBG-18 twenty years before, Koenig had often made use of that simple fact—the commanding officer on the scene knew the situation better, and had more up-to-the-second information, than the people watching from Earth and Mars. And now Gray was doing the same thing.

Koenig had to assume that Gray knew the situation better than even the president, his commander in chief . . . and that he would be making the best decisions possible, as determined by his unique experience and viewpoint.

And Gray's call had probably been a good one. Earth's military, certainly, had been watching the situation at 70 Ophiuchi since the system had fallen twenty years ago. That Sh'daar bastion thrust deep into the sphere of Terran space had been a constant threat, a possible staging area for a new strike at Earth. The Confederation had frequently reviewed plans for a counterattack, but somehow those plans always had been shelved. Other crises—not least of which were the political divisions and sparring within the Confederation itself—had always intervened.

Koenig remembered all too well the earlier Sh'daar raids two decades earlier—a Turusch raid that had resulted in tidal waves buffeting Earth's Atlantic coastlines. And there'd been a later scouting expedition by a H'rulka vessel that *could* have turned out much more badly than it had.

Gray would remember those threats as well. He'd been there too, as had Koenig. But none of that helped Koenig here and now, with the Confederation suddenly at the USNA's throat.

What was that old saying? *It doesn't rain but it pours. . . .*

Of one thing he was sure. The USNA could not defeat both the Sh'daar *and* the Confederation, not alone. At best, Gray would delay the enemy at Osiris . . . and it would be up to Koenig to somehow make the Confederation see reason and unite once again.

Because Earth would have to stand united against the Sh'daar, or what had happened to Columbus would be *nothing.* The Sh'daar would return to the Sol System sooner or later, they would annihilate Mars and Luna and the Synchorbital, and they would turn the surface of Earth herself into a molten sea of glass.

Somehow, Koenig had to bring together a divided Earth . . . or Humankind might well face extinction.

Lieutenant Donald Gregory
VFA-96, Black Demons
Osiris Space, 70 Ophiuchi AII
1002 hours, TFT

"Thuh-ree . . . two . . . one . . . *launch!*"

Gravity vanished. Gregory's Starhawk, suspended over the open mouth of the launch bay, released its magnetic hold and fell toward the starscape sweeping past below. In free fall, pushed by a half G of spin-grav acceleration, he fell into the shadow aft of the curve of *America*'s huge shield cap. A nudge from his thrusters and he edged into formation with the rest of the squadron.

"*America* CIC, this is Blue One," Commander Mackey said. "Handing off from PriFly. All Demons clear of the ship and formed up."

"Copy, Blue One," a voice replied from *America*'s Combat Information Center. "Primary Flight Control confirms handoff to CIC. You are clear for maneuver."

"Thank you, *America*. Boosting at one thousand gees on my mark, in five . . . four . . . three . . . two . . . one . . . *punch it*!"

The five surviving fighters of VFA-96 accelerated, the bulk of the star carrier *America* swiftly dwindling astern. Two other tattered squadrons, VFA-112 and VFA-218, had already vanished into a star-clotted night ahead; another would be assembling behind the Demons and trailing in their wake. VFA-90, the Fire Hawks, and VFA-215, the Black Knights, both were flying CAP with the fleet.

So many empty slots, now.

Gregory had . . . taken care of the emotions surrounding Jodi's death just a few hours before. Minutes after docking with America, he'd paid a visit to Sick Bay and had a Corpsman there inject him with CRF nanoblockers.

CRF—Corticotrophin Releasing Factor—was a stress-related neurotransmitter that became sharply elevated in people who'd lost a close partner. It was especially significant in people who'd lost a spouse, but it could cause trouble as well for pilots with close friends killed in combat. The nanoblockers sealed off neuron receptor sites from CRFs and helped the pilot get past the potentially deadly depression that could follow. The treatment was temporary—sooner or later Gregory would have to deal with Jodi's death—but at least now he could function.

He'd not told the Corpsman that he'd lost his lover. The deaths of so many fellow members of his squadron at once—Benning, Mason, Del Rey . . . and, yes, Jodi Vaughn—would have been enough in itself to put his CRF levels through the overhead.

There was no time for the luxury of mourning the dead now, not with the final struggle about to unfold squarely in his face. His thoughts nudged his Starhawk into the vector designated by his op-order downloads, and he concentrated on the ship and the orders and the operation, and not on . . . anything else.

With the fleet traveling at a little less than half the speed of light, the surrounding sky didn't show the weird distortions of relativistic velocities. Osiris shone dead ahead as a brilliant white star with two tiny attendants—its moons Ptah and Amun.

Five fighters.

The *Shenandoah* possessed nanufactories that could turn asteroidal rock into new Starhawks and Velociraptors in less than a day. What could not be quickly replicated were new pilots . . . and all of *America*'s fighter squadrons had suffered serious losses during the past few days. After the fight at Arianrhod and, now, Osiris, the Black Demons were down to five—Gregory and Mackey, Kemper and Nichols, and the woman they'd rescued at Arianrhod, Connor.

Lieutenant Megan Connor had volunteered to go back on flight status. According to the scuttlebutt, she had been offered the chance to opt out of squadron operations entirely, to transfer to a desk. Apparently, she'd been through a pretty rough time while she'd been a prisoner of the Slan on board their flagship, and CAG had told her she could stand down. She'd refused.

Some of the other Starhawk pilots had been ragging her about being a dragon—she'd flown an SG-101 Stardragon with VFA-140 at Arianrhod—but she'd accepted the jibes with good humor and a few wisecracks about the flying antiques of VFA-96, giving as good as she received. Gregory liked her, and hoped he'd get the chance to know her better. He felt a strange kind of kinship with her; if he'd lost his home to the Sh'daar, well, then, so had she.

So she would be flying as a replacement pilot with the Demons. *America*'s fighter wing had been scrambling to come up with reserve pilots. The word was that even Captain Connie Fletcher, *America*'s CAG, had strapped on a Velociraptor and was flying with VFA-112.

With only five Black Demons left, CAG had decided to send them ahead of the battlegroup as part of the assault wave, instead of putting them—as was more usual for the older Starhawks—on CAP. It didn't much matter one way or the other. All six of *America*'s squadrons would be in the thick of it in just a few more minutes, now. Accelerations were being set so that the wave of strike fighters would enter battlespace just ten minutes ahead of the main fleet.

Ten minutes was an eternity in space combat . . . but the thinned-out Demons would go into the fray knowing some high-power help was barreling in right behind them.

Chapter Twenty-Four

16 November 2424

TC/USNA CVS America
Osiris space, 70 Ophiuchi AII
1058 hours, TFT

Gray watched the half-disk of Osiris swiftly growing larger. *America* was still decelerating, but would enter the Osirian battlespace traveling at better than 20,000 kilometers per second, far too fast to be captured gravitationally by the looming planet, but slow enough to target the enemy warships still clustered near the planet.

To target . . . and to be targeted as well. Slan positron beams were deadly. Switching the hull magnetic shielding of the battlegroup to "plus" would repel those particles . . . but attract the electron beams favored by the Turusch. Cycling between plus and minus would help—that was the defensive strategy when attacked by enemy vessels with both electron and proton weaponry—but antimatter positron beams did a *lot* more damage than ordinary positively charged proton beams.

But Gregory hoped they might have a partial answer to that. He opened the tactical channel. "Captain Alvarez?"

"Yes, Captain."

"You can release your toys, now."

"Aye, aye, sir!"

On the graphic imagery running ion his head, Gray could see the *Shenandoah*—huge, massive, nearly two thirds as long as *America* herself, running parallel to America's course, her bunker doors opening wide. Three T-AK freighters identical to the sacrificed *Altair* detached themselves from scooped-out hollows in the provisioning ship's flanks and began accelerating clear of her, becoming, in effect, enormous missiles guided by the AIs on board.

At the same time, a cloud of robots emerged from the big ship's bunkers and began dispersing ahead of the battle-group.

GKM-1100 mining robots were smaller than a Fer-de-lance shipkiller, each a complex assembly of gripper arms, tools, and nano-D applicators mounted atop a one-meter drive assembly. They weren't fast—each could boost with only a few hundred Gs of acceleration—but there were thousands of them spilling into hard vacuum and zeroing in on the enemy ships.

The enemy, of course, had no way of knowing exactly what they were. If they scanned for radioactives they would come up empty, but those motes could be kinetic-kill warheads, high explosive, mobile O-mines, singularity-triggered fusion warheads, or almost anything else. Thousands of robots closed on the nearest enemy ships, and those ships had to assume that they were the greater threat, and turn their weapons on them.

Slan positron beams slashed and stabbed, vaporizing hundreds of the robots.

The survivors kept coming, accelerating all-out now. Some slammed into enemy hulls at tens of thousands of kilometers per second, hard enough to blast gaping craters in hull metal. Others decelerated abruptly and, reverting to their primary programming, began taking the enemy ships apart literally molecule by molecule.

GKM-1100s were designed to reduce asteroids to their most basic elements—iron, carbon, hydrogen, oxygen, and so on, sequestering the free atoms and either storing them or sending them along in a stream back toward the *Shenandoah*. Normally, their programming blocked any attempt to disassemble a ship or orbital station, but Alvarez's programmers had killed that part of the instructions, installing instead a friend-foe interrogation routine that should keep them from eating friendly vessels.

Those robots that survived the barrage of Sh'daar particle beams and point-defense lasers slammed into hull metal, burrowed in and anchored themselves with nano-D claws, and began to feed. . . .

The three robot freighters entered the battlespace next, accelerating more quickly than the other ships of the fleet, jinking hard as they came, to make themselves difficult targets. Again, the Sh'daar defenses had to assume that they were a threat—they certainly did not appear in the equivalent of a Sh'daar warbook and so were completely unknown. The lead ship, *Alcyone*, was nudged by a detonating warhead and went into an uncontrolled tumble. The *Vega* and the *Deneb* were hit almost in the same instant, *Deneb* vaporizing under direct hits by multiple Slan positron beams, while *Vega* lost her drive complex, drifted out of control at 50,000 kps, then exploded in a dazzling starburst of molten fragments. *Alcyone* hit the Osirian atmosphere a few seconds later, traveling swiftly enough that a large part of its mass probably made it all the way down to the surface as it burned.

Gray watched the procession of robotic attacks. The battlegroup was entering Osirian space now, spreading out to avoid grouping targets, jinking to throw off enemy targeting routines. The robot miners had distracted the Sh'daar fleet, which had been forced to deal with thousands of individual threats, many of which now were attached to their hulls and chewing their way inside. The three freighters had pulled many of the enemy ships off station toward the planet, leaving them vulnerable as the battlegroup arrived.

"Comm, make to all ships," Gray said quietly. "Fire."

Following a meticulously detailed fire plan worked out in conjunction with the battlegroup's AIs, the human ships concentrated their fire on the larger Sh'daar vessels closest to the planet. A pair of Slan Ballistas and a Turusch Romeo-class cruiser flared nova-bright under that tightly focused fire: lasers and particle beams.

But the enemy defenses were already rallying, adapting to the attack and replying in kind. The railgun cruiser *Turner*, rotating to slam kinetic-kill projectiles into a massive Turusch warship of an unknown class, took three direct hits in as many seconds. Slan Stilletos were swarming close, overwhelming the huge cruiser's point defense system . . . and then the ship's midsection exploded, ripping in two.

The destroyer *Atkinson* was vaporized in a focused concentration of positron beams.

America's AI identified one of the targets with a winking red circle in Gray's mind. "The Slan Onager-class command vessel," the AI told him. "You wanted us to ID it in particular."

"Thank you. Transmit the canned message."

"Transmitting."

"And continue pressing the attack. It may take them a while to chew on that. . . ."

Slan Protector Vigilant
Low Orbit, 70 Ophiuchi AII
1104 hours, TFT

"A message from one of the human ships!"

"Let me hear." Clear Chiming Bell listened to the signal coming through its console. While *Vigilant*'s computer network had been purged of the alien spy software, the translation programs created during that brief exchange of communications existed still.

Clear Chiming Bell was startled to learn that the incoming message was in the Slan language. The humans had kept their translation sequences as well.

What was startling was not the fact that they knew how to convert to Slan speech, but that they were, in a cultural sense, approaching the Slan on their own figurative ground. To a Slan, it was a way of saying "I am part of your community," and that implied statement shocked Clear Chiming Bell to its core.

For a long moment, it listened to the clicks and chirps and cluckings of the message. When the message ended, it listened to them again.

The shock now was much, much worse. . . .

Lieutenant Donald Gregory
VFA-96, Black Demons
Osiris Space, 70 Ophiuchi AII
1105 hours, TFT

Gregory twisted his Starhawk around in a heart-stopping turn, whipping around the tight knot of collapsing space and onto a new vector. Because it was space itself that was bending around the projected drive singularity, and his fighter was simply following a straight line, he felt none of the fierce changes in acceleration such a turn might be expected to generate. To his point of view, the surrounding starscape suddenly shifted and spun, and then a Slan Trebuchet appeared directly ahead, a brilliant icon at a range of less than 10,000 kilometers. He bumped the acceleration up and flashed across that intervening distance in an instant.

Slowing sharply, he pivoted his fighter nose-on to the Slan giant and triggered his gravitic singularity. He felt the shock as the micro-black hole chewed through the alien hull . . . and then he released it, his Starhawk continuing to fall past the alien vessel as the singularity ripped the enemy open, gutting it, spilling internal debris into vacuum in a sudden gush of escaping atmosphere.

"This is Demon Four!" he called. "I nailed a Treb pretty good! Copy position and sic the dogs on it!"

"Copy, Demon Four," a voice replied. "On the way."

A number of GKM-1100 robot miners had been held in

reserve, but those were being released from the *Shenandoah* now, clouds of hungry machines descending on crippled Slan and Turusch vessels, seeking out gashes and holes in enemy hulls and vanishing inside.

Several alien ships were being devoured now from the inside.

Ahead, closer to the planet, an icon marking the Slan Onager was accelerating. Gray shifted vector to intercept.

Slan Protector Vigilant
Low Orbit, 70 Ophiuchi AII
1104 hours, TFT

Clear Chiming Bell played the human message a final time.

"These worlds (places) are parts of the human community.

You have attacked our community.

Now you will be sent to the light. . . ."

Where the aliens before had been bundles of contradictions, the concise phrasing of the incoming message suddenly made the humans seem . . . reasonable. Even sane.

Slan did not think in terms of *territory*. Instead, they recognized community, and the relationship between individual members of the hive. To capture an enemy's world was . . . all but meaningless. A world was just a place, and there were many, many places.

But the humans were speaking now as a Slan might speak, *thinking* like Slan, and the realization was unsettling. It was like attacking other Slan, a part of the Community, and that was . . . *sin*.

"All ships!" Clear Chiming Bell chirped and clicked to the rest of its fleet. "Retreat . . . now! Break off and retreat! Recall the fighters, take them back on board."

Long moments passed, as the Slan commander braced itself for the order it knew would come. The fighters were streaming back into the Slan vessels, now, as the capital ships continued to put distance between themselves and the contested world.

Within its mantle, the Sh'daar Seed spoke. "You break formation!"

"We will not fight with Community, self against self. The humans are Slan!"

"The Sh'daar Collective is Community. We are Slan. We are you."

Clear Chiming Bell considered this. It had heard the argument before, but right now it seemed weak. The Sh'daar "community" was scarcely worthy of the name, a haphazard collection of mutually alien cultures and worldviews loosely guided by virtual beings governing through their computer networks from a distance. The Sh'daar themselves were disembodied voices, without form, without tangible reality. Compared to the human message, the Sh'daar response felt like a distortion of Clear Chiming Bell's sonic surroundings.

Sin . . .

What, the Slan wondered, was "sin" to the humans? Or to the Sh'daar?

Where did the Slan Community's best interests lie?

Clear Chiming Bell was under the command of the Community Conclave, deep within the home tunnels of Thadek'ha. The Conclave had agreed to help the Sh'daar as payment for space travel . . . but they'd described the humans as lacking any sense of proper community—as *animals*.

That, clearly, had been a lie. The humans were terrifying in their understanding of warfare, but they *could* think like Slan. The Community Conclave needed to be informed of that fact.

Slan did not lie; to do so would be to distort reality. The Sh'daar, however, *had* lied, and in so doing had committed a type of *k'!k't!'cht'!k'!kt'!!!*, obscuring the truth and replacing it with illusion.

"Return to the battle!" the Sh'daar Seed commanded.

Clear Chiming Bell's ear flaps snapped shut, a gesture meaning both "no" and "I am not listening."

The silent reply was lost on the Seed.

"Return to the battle!"

"No," Clear Chiming Bell replied at last. "The humans are monsters, but I suspect the Slan have more in common with them than with you. We must discuss this in Conclave."

Shifting to nearly the speed of light, the Slan vessels began to make the transition into metaspace and disappear.

TC/USNA CVS America
Osiris space, 70 Ophiuchi AII
1110 hours, TFT

The Slan ships were blurring, then vanishing, pulling their disappearance trick into faster-than-light drive despite the nearness of the local star. Two Ballistas remained in sight for several minutes more, as Stiletto fighters streamed on board.

Then those ships, too, winked out, transitting to metaspace nearly instantaneously.

Six Turusch cruisers remained apparently intact, along with some dozens of damaged ships, both Slan and Turusch. The single H'rulka giant spotted earlier had been destroyed.

"Target the Turusch ships," Gray ordered, but even as the battlegroup began closing on them, they, too, began winking out.

Interesting, Gray thought. *They can make the transition inside the 40-AU limit too.*

Had that technological twist come courtesy of the Sh'daar, or a Sh'daar client species? From what they'd learned of Slan history during the download from the Onager, the Slan barely understood the concept of space travel, and probably didn't know how their own drives worked. That close-in transition trick must have come from the Sh'daar.

For the moment, the important thing was that the Slan seemed to have responded positively to the bit of propaganda Gray had beamed at their command ship. *America*'s xenoso-phontological team had worked long and hard with the AIs studying recordings of the various communications with the Slan commander, extrapolating the alien psychology from what could be gleaned of their physiology and homeworld.

What they'd come up with, Gray thought, had been a masterpiece, playing on the Slan devotion to community, and their horror at having their perspective on reality distorted. By subtly presenting their human opponents as members of a community that had been attacked by the Slan themselves, the message had raised the possibility that the Slan were attacking beings like themselves rather than animals that knew no better.

At the very least, it would have raised questions within the Slan community about why they were serving the Sh'daar as cannon fodder.

The nature of the Sh'daar—the modern remnant of the left-behinds of the Omega Centauri star cloud 876 million years before—still was not well understood. They appeared to be primarily a virtual civilization, electronic life forms existing and interacting within computer and communications networks. That in and of itself represented a paradox; the Sh'daar, the xenosoph people believed, had been that part of the original ur-Sh'daar civilization that had not undergone their version of the Technological Singularity. For almost a billion years, they'd been trying to suppress technology in other, younger species. And yet, during those hundreds of billions of years, they themselves had transitioned to something else: *virtual life*, and apparently a virtual life still desperate to keep other species from undergoing their own transitions.

There was so much humans didn't yet understand about the enemy. That lack of understanding could be fatal—fatal for all of Humankind. But maybe CBG-40 had managed to hold off the final day of reckoning by just a bit.

"Communications," Gray called.

"Communications, aye, sir."

"Prepare a message drone, and dispatch it to Earth." He let out a sigh, unaware that he'd been holding his breath. "Tell them we're on the way home."

Lieutenant Donald Gregory
VFA-96, Black Demons
Osiris Space, 70 Ophiuchi AII
1111 hours, TFT

The Slan Onager had slipped away into metaspace long before Gregory could approach it. His vector, however, was carrying him past Osiris.

Past his old home.

He decelerated hard, braking his Starhawk's velocity from tens of thousands of kilometers per second to five, allowing the planet's gravity to pull him around its bulk at an altitude of less than 200 kilometers. It was a heaven-sent opportunity. He *had* to take a close look or else he would always wonder.

The first leg of his fly-around brought him in over Osiris's night side, and the north-hemisphere ocean. His AI opened up all channels, listening for anything that might indicate human life. As he skimmed the planet's atmosphere, he began broadcasting a query, in effect an electronic questing asking "Is anybody there?"

There was no reply as he skimmed around into a dazzling orange sunrise. Osiris's cloud tops, marking the swirling vortices of enormous cyclonic storms, burst into full view beneath his keel.

Is anybody there?

A coastline appeared ahead and he accelerated slightly, slicing through the upper edges of atmosphere. Nuit Starport, the place from which he'd departed this world as an eight-year-old two decades earlier, was no longer there, the site marked now by an immense desert of glass, flashing and sparkling in the sunlight. New Egypt, the colonial capital, had been glassed over as well.

Is anybody there?

High-resolution imagery showed new construction along the shores of the Naucratis Coast. New Alexandria was still there, but the familiar domes were . . . gone. The squat, massive bunkers with slanted walls was characteristic, Gregory knew, of the Nungiirtok, the lumbering, 3-meter ground troops employed by the Sh'daar in their ongoing war against Humankind.

Is anybody there?

In answer, a trio of shipkiller missiles emerged from underground silos and climbed into the Osirian sky. The Nungiirtok were still down there.

Well, that stood to reason, didn't it? The Sh'daar retreat had been on the precipitous side. No time for an evacuation of their personnel on the surface.

His AI recorded everything in high definition and with 3-centimeter resolution. Gregory's thoughts nudged the fighter's control systems, and he accelerated harder, rising clear of the last thin tatters of the atmosphere and boosting into deep space once again. Osiris dwindled rapidly astern. By the time the missiles got clear of the atmosphere, their target was long gone.

"All squadrons, this is *America* Primary Flight Control," a voice called. "RTS, repeat, RTS."

RTS. Return to ship. They were being recalled.

There'd been no reply to his broadcasts as he'd swung past Osiris. He had to assume that everyone he'd known, everyone living there, was dead.

"*America*, Demon Four, on my way," he acknowledged. He hesitated, then added, "Fly-by of Osiris negative for human settlements."

"Hey, Nu . . . Gregory," Kemper's voice cut in. "It might not be that bad, y'know?"

"That's right," Connor added. "If they're out in the bush, no radios, no advanced technology . . ."

"Or there might be a camp somewhere," Nichols pointed out. "They could still be alive down there somewhere. . . ."

The others in the squadron must have been linked in with his fighter. He checked his comm settings, and saw that the squadron tactical link had been open during his passage over the planet.

"With the Shaddy fleet kicked out," Kemper told him, "it's a cinch we'll be sending in the Marines, right? Don't give up on us, man."

"Thanks," Gregory replied. "We'll see what the high-def scans show."

"Let's go home, people," Mackey said.

And the image of the star carrier *America* grew large in their in-heads.

Emergency Presidential Command Post
Toronto,
United States of North America
1125 hours, EST

"Damn it, where's our communications?" Koenig demanded. "The bastards could be plastering the entire country with nano-D right now, and we wouldn't know!"

"No reports of further attacks off-net, sir," Whitney reassured him. "We'd know if there were."

Koenig nodded. Normally, the office of the president of the USNA was at the center of a staggeringly rich, complex, and information-dense web of high-tech communications, connecting it to cities and military bases across the North American continent, to embassies and consulates around the globe, to SupraQuito and to bases on the moon and on Mars. At any given time, Koenig could access a Net as detailed and as intricate as the one employed by Geneva or, for that matter, by Konstantin up at Tsiolkovsky.

He felt utterly lost and isolated without that supra-global connectivity. Right now, a handful of ships and High Guard sentinels were fighting the Confederation in near-Earth space, and he had no idea how the fight was going. Hand-to-hand fighting had been reported on the ground in Washington, D.C., in Baltimore, and in the Manhat Ruins, as Geneva tried to assert its control over parts of the USNA Periphery. Americans had been dying in the mud just 500 kilometers from Toronto, and he didn't know the outcome there, either, or if the battle had even yet been resolved. On the far side of the moon, a Marine assault force had been dispatched to Giordano Bruno. Again, the battle might be over, it might still be raging, and the president of the USNA had no clue as to what was happening.

His only connection with the outside world, right now, was through the global Net, the non-government portion of the communications and computer web that served as a kind of electronic nervous system for Earth. He could look in on various cities through security drones or corporate offices. He could watch the major news nets, though most of them were focused right now on the enormous crater that was Columbus; for the most part, they were still hours out of date. Even the big one, TNN, the TerraNews Network, still didn't seem to realize that the Earth Confederation had just crumbled into the jerking, spasmodic collapse of full-scale civil war.

And he could link in through person-to-person in-heads. Whitney had set up a bank of aides in a nearby room who were doing nothing but contacting people they knew on the outside by private link, as the intelligence people sorted through the data and tried to make sense of it, to distill it down to something the president would find useful.

Koenig was amused even while he was feeling frustrated. They were using technology centuries out of date in order to try to put the USNA government back in control.

And if they managed to achieve that control . . . what, Koenig wondered, would he do with it? USNA fleet elements were sharply outnumbered. Without CBG-40 or other fleet elements stationed at other systems, the USNA defenses would soon lose any control of the high ground of space whatsoever.

And when that happened, there was little Koenig could do but surrender.

What the hell was happening with the fleet? Attempts to contact officers or crew on ships like the *Pittsburgh* so far had failed.

And then a possible answer hit him.

He put through a private call, opening a channel by commercial relays from Toronto to Synchorbit to L-2 above the lunar farside . . .

. . . and down to Tsiolkosky base, and the super-AI Konstantin.

"Ah, Mr. President," the AI's voice said after a long moment as the connections were established. "I've been trying to call you, but your normal communications channels appear to be down."

"Tell me about it," Koenig growled. "We're having to use the civilian networks."

"Which are adequate to the purpose. I have news for you."

"First, I want to know if we can use these civilian networks to link in to your Net. We're almost blind down here, since Columbus was wiped out."

"I saw the TNN feeds, yes," Konstantin replied. "Where are you now?"

"I would rather not say," Koenig said. "We're trying to keep this end of the conversation shifting between a few hundred sites across the country, to keep Geneva guessing. I'd rather not lose another city."

"Understood, though I am sure you realize that your problems in establishing a clear channel lie in your attempts to maintain anonymity."

"Yes, but right now I have a hundred people trying to use the phone service to see what's happening all over the world, and that's what's making us blind. I want to see through your network."

"I am establishing the connections now," Konstantin said. "There. You have direct access to my data feeds now."

Behind him, Koenig heard several people cheering. Wallscreens that had previously shown static were switching on, now. Koenig glanced at them. One showed ragged-looking men and women with a miscellany of weapons rushing past some sort of titanic air- or spacecraft, grounded in mud. The background looked like the D.C. swamp. Another showed Ilsa Roettgen's face as she spoke earnestly with a number of Confederation military officers. A third was being relayed from a battlespace drone. Koenig could see a large warship, a cruiser, he thought, moving through space. Mars lay in the distance, ruddy and small. The cruiser, black with scarlet trim on shield cap and drive pods, looked like an old Jianghu class, flanked by a trio of Sújué fighters—Chinese Hegemony.

"May I draw your attention to the cruiser, Mr. President?"

"I see it. What's it doing off Mars?" The Chinese had major space-military bases at Synchorbit, at Grimaldi on the moon, and at Mercury, but nothing anywhere close to Mars.

And then a thrill of realization clicked for Koenig.

"I noted that our forces were severely restricted in scope and number," Konstantin said, "our space-navy forces especially. After witnessing the attack on Columbus, I took the liberty of talking to some other military powers."

Koenig felt a cold chill. Taking liberties was not something AIs were able to do, generally. Millions of times faster than humans, they nevertheless operated within what programmers referred to as "limited purviews," meaning that they could follow orders . . . but not give them, and they were unable to make important decisions independent of the humans who'd created them.

"What military powers?" Koenig asked slowly.

"The Chinese Hegemony," Konstantin replied, "and the Islamic Theocracy."

Neither power was a member of the Confederation. Indeed, they'd been blocked from full membership consistently for centuries.

"I see," Koenig said. "And what do they want in return?"

"The Hegemony desires full membership within the Confederation, assuming, of course, that our faction wins the current power struggle. They have, as you are seeing on the screen in front of you, agreed to extend military help to the USNA, specifically to block incoming fleet elements under Geneva's command."

"Captain Lavallée."

"His flagship, the *Napoleon*, and a number of other Confederation warships entered the outskirts of the Sol System eight hours ago. He has received a promotion to rear admiral, and his command of the Pan-European battlegroup has been confirmed by Geneva."

"I see. And what do the Islamists want?"

"They are unwilling to provide military assistance until they receive a personal assurance from you to the effect that the White Covenant will be rescinded, again assuming our faction is victorious."

That rocked Koenig back a bit. The Chinese had been refused membership in the Terran Confederation because of Wormwood Fall, the small asteroid nudged out of orbit in 2132 by the Chinese vessel *Xiang Yang Hong*. Beijing had always claimed that the disaster had been caused by a rogue captain and, who knew? Their claim might well be accurate. The ship's skipper, they'd reported, had been enraged by the destruction of Fuzhou, his home city. That had been almost three centuries ago. Maybe it was time to incorporate the ancient Middle Kingdom into interstellar politics.

The Muslim demand would bear careful thinking about, however. The White Covenant had been enacted three and a half centuries ago, in 2074. That had been a chaotic and violent era of Earth's history, one of global warfare between the Islamic world and the West. While a billion Muslims had been willing to live in peace with other religions, hundreds of millions more, ground down by poverty and illiteracy and the tyranny of local states, had grown up in breeding grounds for the more obnoxious forms of Islamic fundamentalism, of the sort that rioted and burned buildings and even burned whole cities over some perceived insult, or at the urging of some crackpot imam. The wars of the twenty-first century had been horrific, and hundreds of millions had died.

At the end, Islamic worship was permitted on Earth *only* under the provisions of the White Covenant, which declared that a person's religious beliefs were his own, and that proselytizing—or using threats or warfare to force conversions—violated the basic rights of man. Those who disagreed had been forced to emigrate—to Mufrid, out at Eta Boötis, among other worlds.

Islam had acquiesced to the White Covenant only after being soundly defeated by the Western Alliance, and had never truly accepted its provisions. It was, after all, their duty under the holy Quran to bring *all* of Humankind under the banner of Allah, His Prophet, and the Sharia, the religious law and moral code of Islam.

Could Koenig, in good conscience, agree to such a thing? Assuming he could win, of course.

"I trust my decision meets with your approval, President Koenig," Konstantin said. "The situation seemed desperate, and required desperate measures."

"Let's hold on the Islamic Theocracy question," Koenig said. "But if the Chinese are willing to help us, hell, yeah, they can join our club. We should've let them in centuries ago."

"Had we done so, we might find ourselves facing them as enemies, rather than admitting them as allies," Konstantin said. "Ah . . . the first shots have been fired."

On the screen, nothing much appeared to be happening, though the fighters accelerated suddenly and left the protective shelter of their vast consort. Moments later, however, someone in the command center cheered.

"Direct hit on the *Napoleon*!" a man yelled. "Hits on the *Mastrale* and the *Köln*!"

"*Napoleon* is heavily damaged and breaking off," someone else called out. "Hot damn, the Hegies have 'em on the run!"

"Where did the Chinese come from?" Pamela Sharpe asked. "Why are they helping *us*?"

"Seems we've been doing a little back-room negotiating," Koenig said to the room. "Maybe Beijing wants us to forgive and forget Wormwood."

Back-room, as in the back side of the moon. Koenig still wasn't sure what he thought of Konstantin's sudden independence of thought, but at the moment he was willing to take any help he could get. He'd already noticed Konstantin's use of the term "our faction." Could AIs take sides in a human political struggle?

Evidently, this one could. And had.

And Koenig was very, very glad of the fact.

The civil war wasn't over by any means. But Konstantin had bought the USNA the precious time that it needed.

And maybe that would be enough.

Epilogue

TC/USNA CVS America
The Black Rosette,
Omega Centauri
16,000 light years from Earth
1420 hours, TFT

Admiral Trevor "Sandy" Gray stared into a vista of incomprehensible and complex wonder. Whatever it was that had emerged from the Black Rosette, whatever it was that had destroyed *Endeavor*, was incomparably beautiful.

Two months had passed since CBG-14's return from 70 Ophiuchi. There'd been two tumultuous, eventful weeks after their emergence at the 40-AU limit of the Sol System, followed by forty-four days of quiet and introspective seclusion within the tightly wrapped spacetime bubble of Alcubierre Drive, and that had brought them . . . here.

"It's incredible!" Laurie Taggart said.

They were standing side by side in one of *America*'s officer lounges, a quiet compartment with comfortable furniture, low lighting, and a gently curving, deck-to-overhead viewall almost 15 meters wide.

"It's all of that," Gray agreed. Words seemed such poor, such poverty-stricken things in the face of such beauty.

The two of them were comfortably nude after a swim in the rec-center pool. Others in the lounge, a handful of ship's officers, were dressed or not, from uniform to utilities to off-duty civvies to social nudity, depending on preference. Military regs had little to say about fashion statements during off-duty hours.

The ship—the entire battlegroup—was still on high alert, but after twenty-four hours of watching that . . . that *thing* out there, Gray had decided to leave the bridge in Commander Gutierrez's capable hands and take some much-needed downtime with his weapons officer.

You could not stay keyed to the highest possible emotional and mental pitch all the time. So far, there'd been no indication that the . . . call them the *Builders* . . . thing, or things, outside had deliberately destroyed the *Endeavor*, or, indeed, that there was any threat at all.

America and her battlegroup had arrived, were hanging motionless now in space, observing . . . and trying to decide what their next step should be.

The Builders had, so far, taken exactly zero notice of their presence.

"This might be what it takes to end the war back home," Taggart observed. "If that doesn't get Humankind to pull together, to come together as one united species, I don't know what will."

"Maybe. But they're still human, after all. Don't expect miracles."

When CBG-40 had arrived at Earth, it was to find the Confederation sundered, a civil war in progress. The USNA capital had been destroyed in what could only be described as an atrocity, a war crime on an unfathomable scale. Geneva so far had refused to admit that they'd given the order. The nano-D strike on the city had been the act of a renegade squadron commander, now dead in the fiery immolation of the *Montcalm* a few moments after the destruction of Columbus. USNA forces had beaten off invasion attempts at several points along the Periphery, and captured Bruno Base on the moon.

And elsewhere on Earth, the horror of Columbus had forced the Confederation loyalists back on the defensive. Russia and North India both had seceded from the Confederation and announced alliances with the USNA. But as if to balance the equation, Mexico and Honduras had seceded from the USNA. There was bitter fighting now along the Texas and California borders.

How it all would resolve no one could tell. Much depended on how the various colony worlds would choose.

Once that issue was resolved, perhaps a Marine assault force could be dispatched to Osiris. The fates of colonists lost twenty years ago, however, definitely took a backseat to events on Earth, here and now.

Somewhere in the chaos, President Koenig had found the time to summon Gray to the temporary capital beneath the city of Toronto, promote him to rear admiral, and confirm his command of CBG-40. That command was stripped down a bit, now. America's battlegroup now consisted of only *America*, one cruiser, the *Edmonton*, three destroyers, and the provisioning ship *Shenandoah*. And almost as soon as his command had been confirmed by the USNA Senate and the Hexagon, new orders had come through.

The battlegroup was being deployed to Omega Centauri, to observe and report on the "Thing" that had emerged from the Black Rosette four months before, and destroyed the RSV *Endeavor*.

Gray hadn't decided yet whether the deployment was intended as punishment, or simply as a means of getting him out of the way. While the Senate had been effusive in its praises of his actions at both Ophiuchis, 36 and 70, the Hexagon was somewhat less than enthusiastic. Gray *had* disobeyed a direct order to return to Earth after the fighting at Arianrhod.

"*I* understand," Koenig had told him after the promotion ceremony. The president had shrugged. "When you're out on the ass-end of nowhere, you have to do what you think is right at the time. But unless it's done by the book, the brass won't like it. You know that."

Gray did indeed.

And now he really *was* on the ass-end of nowhere, sixteen thousand light years from home, confronted by . . . *that*.

The visuals transmitted by the *Endeavor* during its last few seconds of existence hadn't shown much except for an intense light emerging from the Rosette. Presumably, whatever had come through from the other side had set up shop here in the heart of the Omega Centauri star cluster and begun disassembling stars.

Hundreds of thousands of stars had been taken apart, leaving vast, dark streaks through the glowing heart of the globular cluster. Black holes—other than those making up the fast-rotating Rosette—had been brought together. Stars had been merged with stars, creating a central beacon fifty times Sol's mass and illuminating the cluster's central core with searing blue light, an intense hazy glow fifty light days across.

And out from that central sun.

It was hard to avoid the thought that what they were seeing was an enormous, deliberate structure of some kind, an unimaginably vast construct of curving beams and platforms and spheres and connectors of pale blue mist. Close measurement of those shapes had revealed something disturbing. They were *bent*, twisted in eye-hurting ways that did not make sense by the rules and regs of ordinary geometry.

Somehow, that bizarre and alien construction involved not only normal space, but higher dimensions as well. It was anchored by stars and within the depths of the central sun, and extended outward into otherness, extending—impossibly—throughout the entire cluster, across perhaps two hundred light years. And yet . . . the light from anything farther out than a couple of light months would not have reached this spot where the battlegroup observed. By rights, they should be able to see only a fraction of a light year.

But not only space, but time as well had been warped in this place. Beams a hundred light years long reached into vastness and vanished into some space that was not space, some time that was not time.

The overall effect was indescribably lovely, in gentle hues of blue and violet, with deep and subtle ruby reds in places where structures vanished from the ken of normal spacetime.

It was beautiful and it was awe-inspiring.

It was also unintelligible to human reason and understanding.

What, exactly, was it?

"The alien gods," Taggart said, her voice small and far away.

"I'm not sure I can buy that," Gray replied. "I mean . . . beings so powerful they can do *that*. What the hell would they need with humans, anyway? They land on Earth, teach people to plant crops or build pyramids . . . why? Those beams are light years long, and they've reworked time so we can see it all. Beings like that . . . I'm not sure they would even notice the Earth."

"I don't know," Taggart said. "I don't know. I don't even know what I'm looking at." Tears glistened on her face. Was it happiness at seeing evidence of the gods she worshipped, Gray wondered? Or terror at this unimaginable expression of the ultimate Void, the Black Unknown?

For Gray, Laurie Taggart's ancient alien gods had often seemed . . . petty, somehow. Jehovah was a space alien, dropping nukes on Sodom and Gomorrah, or tinkering with human genetics. *Ridiculous.*

And yet . . .

Gray was thinking now of another mystery that had filtered down across the galaxy, footnotes from a thousand alien civilizations within the Sh'daar Collective.

"I wonder," he whispered.

"Wonder what?" Taggart asked.

"I wonder if these are the Starborn?"

The term would work until something better came along . . . until they learned more.

But for now, the glowing bridges, buttresses, and arcs of the Builders' stellarforming remained impenetrably enigmatic.

And humans could only watch . . .

And wonder.